OUT OF THE DARK

TDS 2

Out of the Dark

Editor: Jenn Lockwood | Jenn Lockwood Editing

Proofreader: Mary | On Pointe Digital Services

Cover Design: Danah Logan

Interior Formatting: Danah Logan

ISBN: 978-1-7360990-1-8 (ebook)

ISBN: 978-1-7360990-4-9 (paperback)

ISBN: 979-8-9851796-8-2 (paperback - discreet cover)

ISBN: 979-8-9851796-0-6 (hardback - discreet cover)

A NOTE FROM THE AUTHOR

Trust Lilly and Rhys.

Out of the Dark (OOTD) is the <u>second</u> book in **The Dark Series Trilogy.**

Each book in The Dark Series is unique to its main characters. They write the story; I'm just along for the ride. As they get older, their characters grow throughout the series, make mistakes that can have you either relate to, like, or dislike (possibly even hate) them. They are raw and flawed, but we love them anyway.

Lilly & Rhys's story is a dark, new adult, romantic suspense trilogy consisting of **In the Dark**, **Out of the Dark**, and **Of Light and Dark**. Everything will be explained throughout the series.

While the entire series is intended for **MATURE** (18+) readers, please be aware the trilogy is a **SLOW BURN**.

The books are labeled dark due to the themes that may be considered **TRIGGERS** for some. **Reader discretion is advised.**

(For a more detailed list of potential triggers and tropes in this book, scan the below QR code.)

For D.K., the real-life Denielle to my Lilly. We met by chance so many years ago and bonded over the most random statement. Since that day, you've been the person I turn to for anything and everything. I couldn't ask for a better partner in crime and lifelong best friend.

PLAYLIST

Scan the barcode below to listen to
The Dark Series Trilogy Playlist.

PROLOGUE

LILLY

It's dark. My head is pounding, and my eyes won't open. Why won't my eyes open? I swallow, and a metallic taste registers in my brain—blood. Why am I swaying? More awareness seeps in. I'm being carried. Arms are placed under my legs and back. It's him. I just know. The sound of my heartbeat is thrashing in my ears. I need to fight, but my body doesn't obey. My arms won't move. My eyes still won't open. My lungs constrict as a primal scream builds, but no sound comes out. Suddenly, my body connects with a flat surface, and a sharp pain shoots through my shoulder. A whimper escapes, but it's just the whisper of a sound compared to the cry echoing inside my head. I feel a prick in my upper arm, then...*blank*.

Agony. That's the only word that comes to mind when the fog clears. I hurt. Everywhere. What the—? Oh God, the accident. He was there. He took me. *Again*. Everything starts slowly coming back. My heartbeat instantly accelerates, but I force myself to lie still, keep my eyes closed, and take stock. I'm on a soft surface; the fabric under my fingertips feels smooth—a comforter or duvet? Not important—yet. I wiggle my fingers, followed by rotating one arm ever so slightly, then the other, and —stars explode behind my eyelids. Shit, that hurts. The sensation is excruciating yet numbing at the same time. Like someone held a hot blade against my skin for so long that my body shut off its pain receptors. Pressing my lips together, I keep from crying out. Next, come the legs. I'm able to bend my knees and slowly move them left to right. I'm not paralyzed; a crushing weight lifts off my chest. However, my entire body is sore, and something is definitely wrong with my shoulder.

I blink my eyes open. A small light next to me hurts, and it takes several minutes for my vision to adjust. I'm in a bedroom. It looks familiar, but not. I force myself to inhale and exhale through my nose to calm my rapid breathing.

I can't fight when I'm hyperventilating.

Slowly I turn my head to the side. When I can't get a decent overview, I slowly push myself up with my uninjured arm until I'm in a sitting position. The walls are the same shade of lavender that I remember, almost the same I have at home—this is beyond weird. All the furnishings are white and antique-looking; my gaze travels over a familiar chair. The. Chair. Out of the corner of my eye, I register a doorway to the left. Subconsciously, I know what I'm going to see next—who I will see next.

Closing my eyes, I inhale through my nose—three, two, one. Exhaling—three, two, one. I open my eyes.

The door is wide open, and I meet familiar hazel eyes. Eyes I thought were familiar when I first saw them. Now I understand why.

"You!"

"Hello, Lilly."

CHAPTER ONE

RHYS

FOUR DAYS. THAT'S HOW LONG SHE'S BEEN GONE. I CAN'T EVEN utter her name in my head. The first day was a complete shit show; everyone was yelling at everyone, though Dad directed his anger mostly at me. I can't even fault him for that. She's gone because of me.

At the end of day two, he sent me to my room because I wouldn't stop cursing out the cops and, later, the agents who turned our kitchen into their command center. The FBI replaced the local cops when they officially linked Lilly to the missing girls. But the motherfuckers can't find a trace of her. They're the fucking FBI and can't find her. Nothing. What use are they?

See, cursing a lot.

WES LEFT THIS MORNING; I guess he couldn't take being around me anymore either. I don't blame him. I'm either swearing, throwing shit, or vegetating; not to forget the few times I went across the hall and sobbed on her floor like a goddamn baby. My best friend has been with me since we found her car—or, as the federal morons call it, "the scene of the accident." She was kidnapped, for fuck's sake; she didn't just drive into a ditch and decide to take a spontaneous vacation without telling anyone.

She. Is. Gone.

It's almost six in the evening, and I'm sitting on the floor at the foot of my bed, legs bent, arms resting on my knees, replaying Tuesday once again in my head. I've done nothing else for the past seventy-two hours, but I can't stop either.

BY THE TIME Wes and I got to my car, Lilly's Jeep was already out of sight. She turned right, which could get her anywhere: the highway, Glen Meadow, and Fallsbrook. Both towns are just about four miles, depending on if you take Main Street or 52nd Street out of town, and then there are the back roads. The back roads! Somehow, I knew that she'd take one of them instead of the main roads. She'd want to be alone, and that included cars and people as well. I was about to reverse out of the parking spot when Denielle stopped me by slapping her hand on the hood of my Defender.

"Not now," I growled under my breath.

"Where are you going?" I heard her muffled voice as she walked to the passenger side.

Wes lowered the window so I could respond, "I'm going to find my girlfriend."

What kind of question was that?

"Do you think that's smart?" Her voice was so full of disdain; it still makes my skin crawl.

"What are you trying to say?" I snapped back at her, driven by my guilt in all of this.

She inhaled deeply before saying more calmly, "You lied to her. You just stood there when your psycho ex humiliated her in front of half the school. She feels betrayed. Do you really think she wants you to find her right now?"

Denielle got her point across; I royally fucked up. I knew she was right. But there was no question; I had to go after Lilly. The thought of losing her over this threatened to suffocate me, and deep down, something was telling me that I would if I didn't at least try to find her. Though, I didn't realize how literal it'd be.

"I have to go," was all I replied.

She leveled me with a hard look and nodded. "Okay." With that, Den opened the back door, got in, and settled in the middle of the backseat. Slapping her palm on my headrest, she commanded, "Let's go."

Who put her in charge all of a sudden?

I glanced at Wes, and then Den through the rearview mirror, before finally pulling out of my spot. As I put the car in drive, I looked over to the school's main entrance, a direction I purpose-fully avoided until this point. As expected, a large group of students lingered on the steps leading up to the two sets of double doors, openly following the show. I even saw a few teachers who attempted to guide everyone back inside but were completely ignored. And to no one's surprise, Kat stood front and center, arms crossed, and eyes fixed on me.

How could I've ever been with someone like her?

My gaze turned into tunnel vision, and a red haze forming in front of my eyes briefly replaced the panic about finding Lilly. The urge to get out of my car, walk over, and throttle my psychotic ex was overpowering my senses.

"Rhys!"

Denielle's barked tone snapped me out of the stare-down with Kat, and my focus immediately was back on what was important. Finding Lilly.

THERE ARE three back roads between the surrounding towns. One is not paved and can barely be called a road. I doubted she'd take that one. So, we had a fifty-fifty chance. I took the wrong one. I chose the wrong fucking road.

Did I already mention that I'm dropping a lot of F-bombs lately?

My error cost us twenty-five minutes, and when we finally drove down the other road, I immediately saw the flashing lights. My hands tightened around the steering wheel to the point that the stretched skin over my knuckles started to burn. Denielle leaned forward between the seats with her hands covering her mouth, eyes wide. Next to me, Wes expelled a string of curse words while gripping the door with one hand and the side of his seat with the other. I pushed the pedal to the floorboard until we came to a screeching halt behind another car. I was out the door before Wes could unbuckle his seatbelt. Sprinting around the other vehicle, I passed an older couple standing in the middle of the road. There, halfway in the field, was Lilly's Jeep. It was flipped upside down, and I could see the deflated airbags. My knees threatened to buckle at the sight.

No, no, no.

I frantically started to look around, hoping to find some trace of her, but deep down, I already knew. The doors to the ambulance were wide open—the back empty—and the pit in my stomach deepened even further. Cruisers were half blocking the road on either side of the scene. Without thinking, I started forward and came face to face with one of the cops. The top of his head didn't even reach my nose, but he outweighed me by probably a hundred pounds—not muscle.

"Where do you think you're going, buddy?" he asked me in a nasal tone.

Buddy?

The blood was rushing in my ears, and I could barely make out my voice when I responded through gritted teeth, "This is my girlfriend's car. I need to get to her!"

The man's entire demeanor changed from *I'm-a-cop-what-do-you-think-you're-doing-here* to something I couldn't decipher. He peered at his partner, who was slowly walking over. I noticed faintly that Wes and Denielle had taken position on either side of me.

"Um, son, what's your name?"

What the fuck?

I was about to tear past them when Denielle touched my forearm ever so slightly. I glanced to the side, and she mirrored the cop's expression.

"What?" My gaze jumped back and forth between them.

The second cop cleared his throat. "Son, there is no one in the car. It was empty when we got here."

With that, my legs gave out, and I crumbled to the ground, head in my hands. "No, no, no, noooooooo!" My scream echoed in my head long after my voice gave out.

I remember that Wes and Denielle dragged me back to the Defender, and Den sat in the backseat with me, holding my shaking hands, silently crying until my mother arrived. Her blood-curdling scream will be etched into my brain until the day I die. After that, everything was a blur until Dad came home later that night.

I CAN'T SHAKE the feeling that it's my fault. If I had just told Lilly about Kat. But my brain-to-mouth connection was completely severed when my ex cornered her, and my gorgeous girl retaliated in the form of a right hook. I didn't see the attack coming, but I wasn't surprised either. When Lilly gets pushed too far, her instincts take over. Years of training have drilled that into my brain as well. The corner of my mouth lifts, recalling Kat's stunned face. No one had ever dared lift a hand against her, not even when she slapped Rebecca Corbin in junior year for accidentally spilling water on her. But the whole time, I was rooted to the spot. I willed my body to move, take a stance, but it wouldn't obey. And then she was gone.

Lilly. I make myself think her name, and it reverberates in my mind. My insides constrict, and I wrap my arms around my midsection, bending forward, swaying back and forth. If I could hold her one more time and tell her how sorry I am, how much I love her. Tears are running down my face again, and I don't care to wipe them away.

IT'S how I still sit when my phone begins to vibrate on my desk. I ignore it as I have for the past four days. People stopped calling. This is the first time in—fuck, I have no clue. Lilly was reported missing on Wednesday, but for all I know, the official version is that she took off after the showdown in school. I haven't bothered asking, and my friends learned pretty quickly not to mention anything related to Lilly around me.

The vibration starts back up. I ignore it again and then a third time. What. The. Fuck? I push myself up on the bed with one hand and reach my desk right when it stops ringing. My screen is lit and shows three missed calls from "UNKNOWN". Bile rises in my throat. It starts ringing once more, and I squeeze my eyes shut. Maybe it's all a dream? The sound of the vibration on the wooden top of my desk is like a jackhammer in my ears. I know who will be on the other end, but I can't bring myself to move. The caller hangs up, or my voicemail takes over, I'm not sure. I. Can't. Fucking. Move. Again. When I think this is it, the screen lights up once more, and this time, my body obeys. I dive for my phone. My hands shake so badly that it slips out of my grasp twice before I can get a hold of it. After drawing in one last breath, I swipe across the screen and hold it to my ear. My voice won't cooperate.

"Rhys?"

That voice. A sob escapes my hoarse throat.

"Are you there?" Her tone is low as if she is trying not to startle me. I thought I'd never hear that voice again.

"Yes." It's barely a whisper.

"Hey." This one word settles over me like a soothing blanket, and I hear the smile in Lilly's voice.

"Cal, I'm so sor—" But I can't finish the sentence. My throat constricts, and I swallow several times.

"It's ok. I don't have much time."

That snaps me out of it. "Where are you? Did he hurt you?" The hand that is not holding the phone balls into a fist.

"I'm fine. That's why I'm calling. I...I just wanted to let you know that I'm safe. I'm fine."

She's safe?

"What do you mean? Is he threatening you? Where are you? The house was taken over by the FBI; they will find you."

"No, they won't. They can't trace the call." She exhales, resigned. "I...I had to hear your voice. And tell you that I'm okay. I'll explain everything to you when I see you."

Explain? See? Wha—?

"What are you talking about? Babe, where are you? See me when?" I'm shouting now, and I don't doubt that my father will burst through that door in the next few seconds.

"I have to go," she rushes out. "I'll call again. Please tell them to stop looking for me. They won't find me."

Is she fucking brainwashed?

"Please don't hang up," I go from shouting to begging.

"I have to go." There is a pause as if she wants to say something else, but then all she says is, "I'll see you soon."

"Calla?"

Nothing. She hung up.

LEGS GIVING OUT, I sink to the floor, and my dad chooses that moment to throw the door to my bedroom open. I'm in front of my desk, staring up at him taking over the doorframe. His eyes are wide, and he's surveying the room as if I have Lilly stashed in the closet. And is that—yup, he's holding his forty-five in one hand.

"What happened?"

I stare.

"RHYS!"

My mom's smaller frame is mostly hidden behind my father, and I see more feet in the hallway.

"TALK!" my father roars.

My mom pushes past him. "Tristen, STOP!"

She squats beside me and takes my free hand. The other one still holds my phone in a death grip. "Honey?"

"She's fine," is all I rasp out.

My mom's hands fly to her mouth, followed by her wrapping herself around me and starting to sob. I can't hold back any longer and join her. I don't care that my father and several agents are hovering in my room; it's just mom and me. Mourning Lilly.

CHAPTER TWO

LILLY

HIS TONE IS ALL CASUAL. "HELLO, LILLY."

I stare. No matter how hard I try, no coherent sentence will form. How did I miss this?

"You."

Right, I already said that.

My breathing has slowed down. I should've known.

The corners of his mouth quirk up, and he shrugs lightly. "Me."

His nonchalant attitude sparks something deep in my core, and instead of being terrified, like someone kidnapped—for the second time—would be, I bare my teeth at him. "You're psycho." It also helps that the gut feeling that I'm in no physical danger is even stronger now that we are face to face.

He shifts, crosses his arms over his chest, and leans against the doorframe. His posture emanates confidence, not predator. "I've been called that before—and worse."

What the ever-loving—

There is a familiarity between us that I can't shake, something beyond my kidnapping past with him, something beyond our first in-person interaction ten years later.

"Nate." My voice holds a warning note.

NATE HAMLIN. Tall, blond, hazel eyes, and a genuine smile. That's who's standing across from me. I talked to him—even shook his hand. And I...I had no clue. He played me, another person that purposefully manipulated me. I steel my jaw.

"We should probably talk." Nate straightens from the doorframe.

His words bring me back to the present, and I focus on my captor.

No shit.

I keep quiet but tip my chin up. I'm snubbing my kidnapper; I'm not sure if that's brave or utterly stupid.

"May I come in?"

Is he serious? I scowl. "You kidnapped me; please come in." I wave him inside with my uninjured arm in an exaggerated arm gesture—unable to refrain myself from mocking the man in front of me. Maybe I did lose my mind after all? Or the car accident caused some weird fear-diminishing brain injury?

Nate slowly moves into the room and sits down in the bergère chair I remember from my first *stay* with him.

He rests his arms on his legs and looks me straight in the eyes. "I probably deserve that attitude."

You think?

"Why don't you tell me what I'm doing here? Why me?" The number one question that's been on my mind since I found out who I am—or more accurately, who I'm not.

"That requires a longer answer." He looks almost apologetic.

I frown. "I'm going out on a limb that I'm not leaving anytime soon?"

Where does this sass come from? Denielle is the sassy one, not me. But no matter what, he seems amused by it, not angry.

Nate smirks. "You remind me of Audrey."

Audrey. It's the same name he mentioned ten years ago in my memory. Though, back then, he was all emotion, less collected.

Do I want to know? But I ask before I can think about it further. "Who is Audrey?"

He replies without hesitation. "My sister."

Uh, what?

He looks at a spot on the wall above my head, and we sit in silence. I wait.

"Audrey died twelve years ago. She was six." His voice is pained.

Six? Is this why he's been kidnapping all these little girls?

"I'm...sorry?" My response is more a question.

He continues as if I hadn't spoken. "She died in a car accident together with my mother."

Shit, this time, no words will form. What are you supposed to say to your kidnapper who just spilled his family drama? I just sit there. But instead of saying more, he gets up and walks out, closing the door in the process. I don't hear a click or anything that would suggest I'm locked in, but I know I am. I don't bother checking.

I HAVE no clue how long I've been in this room. It seems like days, but it's probably just a few hours at most. Eventually, I can't sit still anymore, and I ease off the bed. A sharp pain shoots through my shoulder, and I wince. Not moving for so long, I forgot about the injury. It's not dislocated—been there, done that. But something is wrong with it. I cradle my arm to my chest. A few years ago, Rhys and I sparred; Rhys attacked, I didn't pay attention, and hit the ground the wrong way. Tristen was not happy with him. The memory brings the first smile to my face since waking up. Rhys. My chest constricts. I was furious with him when I left school, but now...all I want is to wrap my arms around him and let him hold me. What is he doing? Are they looking for me? He's probably out of his mind. Moisture starts building up in my eyes, and I swallow several times over the lump in my throat before I'm able to focus on my surroundings again. I refuse to show weakness.

Slowly, I start moving around. I'm pretty sure it's a different room from my first time with Nate.

God, I sound like I'm talking about a past vacation.

I recognize the white chair and matching dresser, but the bed is different. It's white but doesn't have the same antique style as the rest of the furniture, or a canopy. Also, this one is queen size versus the one back then was for a child, maybe a twin? I have no clue—smaller. The walls are the same pale lavender, but no mirror. I'm standing by the foot of the bed, across the spot Nate occupied not too long ago, when something registers. There is another door to the left and a window to the right on either wall. The old room had neither.

Why didn't I notice that before? Oh, right, because I was focused on the guy who kidnapped me. *Twice.* Looking back and forth between both, I'm rooted in my spot, not sure which one to check out first. What if they are just props and not real? I wouldn't put it past someone who takes little girls.

Three deep breaths later, I'm able to make my feet move toward the door. The doorknob turns without issue, and I'm facing—oh, wow. One of the most stunning bathrooms I've ever seen, a perfect blend between old and new, appears in front of me like an oasis in the desert. I could fall to my knees and kiss the floor because I don't realize how badly I have to pee until I see it. Everything is black and white. The room is rectangular, with the door on the narrow side and a white clawfoot tub with black feet across on the other. There are white subway tiles to the ceiling, the black grout creating a steep contrast, and the floor has an almost ornate pattern of black-and-white mosaic tiles. A square, white sink sits on top of a black table to the left. The toilet is located between the sink and the bathtub. On the other wall are two black metal towel racks with fluffy white towels draped over them. And are those—the initials L.A.H. jump out at me. What. The. Fuck? I ignore the disturbing discovery for now, because nature calls. Closing the door behind me, I triple-check the lock before I take care of the most pressing issue. When I wash my hands, I come face to face with someone in the mirror I barely recognize. My hair is plastered to the side of my head, caked with dried blood. There is an inch-long gash on my forehead that has been cleaned and stitched up, but the rest of me is still covered in grime. Dirt covers my hair, and looking down on myself for the first time since waking up, I can see it's not just in my hair. My clothes are filthy, and I have a sudden urge to clean myself thoroughly.

I mean, who wouldn't want to take a shower in this situation? It's the most normal thing in the world to find out you were kidnapped after you drove your car into a ditch, and instead of trying to escape, you'd rather take a shower. Makes sense, right? I cover my face with my hands.

Maybe I'm the crazy one, after all?

Screw it. I turn on the shower and watch the steam rise. After confirming once more that the door is indeed locked, I peel off my clothes, taking it easy on my shoulder, and step under the hot spray. The temperature borders on the edge of burning, but instead of turning down the temperature, I let the scorching water wash away all the emotions crashing over me like waves breaking against the edge of a cliff, trying to overtake my mind and body but unable to grab hold. I shut my brain off, refusing to deal with any of it. If I let it in, I lose control.

A seemingly endless amount of time later, I'm sitting on the edge of the tub, wrapped in one of the large L.A.H. towels—nope, no...still not acknowledging the letters. Looking down at my exposed arms and legs, all four limbs are bright red from the heat of the water.

I debate my next move; I don't want to put my old clothes back on, but I have nothing else. Ten years ago, Nate had clothes for me. I take the gamble and ease open the door. Making sure he is not camped out in my room, I step out of the steam-filled bathroom.

My room? Good Lord, what's wrong with me?

With the towel securely fastened and no Nate in sight, I walk over to the dresser and open the top drawers. Bingo! Beyond creepy, but bingo nonetheless. There, neatly folded, are a bunch of dark-colored tank tops and long sleeve shirts. One drawer down, I find a large selection of sweats and leggings, everything close to my size. I grab a tank top, a loose black long-sleeve shirt, and a pair of gray sweats and move back to the bathroom to get dressed.

In the little basket under the sink-table is a brush, and I gingerly disentangle my wet and knotted hair, careful not to come near the stitches. Maybe I should've covered them somehow before the shower. The last thing I need is an infected head wound.

Sitting on the bed a little later, I feel like the shower not only washed away the dirt, but also my last bit of strength. I'm exhausted to the point of barely keeping my eyes open. I push the grime-stained pillows to the floor and lean back onto the remaining ones.

MY EYES SLOWLY EASE OPEN. The room is dark, and there is a blanket draped over the lower part of my body. Nate was in here. My stomach rolls, and I swallow several times. Yesterday's adrenaline rush is officially gone, and the severity of the situation sinks in. I'm kidnapped. Again. I rub my trembling hands over my face, and pulling them back, I realize the room is not fully dark. In my exhaustion, I forgot about the window. It's covered in white drapes, but given the amount of actual light coming in, they must be heavy blackout curtains. Slowly sitting up, I slide one foot off the bed and then the other, taking stock again. My shoulder still hurts, but the pain is not as sharp as yesterday; it's manageable. On the nightstand, I find a bottle of Advil and a glass of water. Greedily, I drink the water, but I leave the pills. Not that he couldn't have put something in the water, but taking the pills is pushing my comfort level.

My heart beats double time but curiosity wins out, and I close the distance to the window. Easing one panel back, I don't know what I'm expecting, but definitely not...this. The sun is still low, but the rolling hills covered in grapevines are already bathed in sunlight. The scene is surreal.

Who is Nate Hamlin?

AS IF ON CUE, there is a knock, and before I can say something, the door swings inward. Nate is dressed similar to me in gray sweats, and the long-sleeve black shirt emphasizes his broad shoulders. Well, this is a bit awkward.

In addition to the whole kidnapping thing, of course.

We stare at each other. Refusing to talk first, I raise my eyebrows, and his mouth quirks up.

"Good morning, Lilly."

I mimic his casual tone, "Good morning, Nate." Aaaand the sass is back in full force—no more shaking hands.

His eyes crinkle. "Would you like some breakfast? It's time we talk. This conversation is long overdue."

He's offering answers; my pulse instantly speeds up. I jerk my head in a quick nod, unable to hide my eagerness.

"A few ground rules, though."

This was too good to be true.

I tilt my head to the side, waiting.

"I don't want to treat you like a prisoner."

I snort, but he holds out a hand to stop me from commenting. "It will all make sense soon enough, but you need to understand that there is no way for you to leave. You are free to walk around, but the property is locked down."

What the hell is that supposed to mean?

He steps back, gesturing for me to walk past him out of my

prison cell. Okay, cell is an exaggeration given the luxury it holds, but still.

In the hallway, he passes me, and I follow him through seemingly endless white corridors with espresso-stained wooden floors, lined with large windows facing more of the sunny hills. We go down a set of narrow stairs that leads into a massive kitchen, and I can't help taking it all in with wide eyes. Everything is pristine and looks like how you imagine a hotel's kitchen, but it's also...homey. The appliances are all state of the art; the white cabinets have dark-centered cup pulls and give the room a country-like feel. Who needs a kitchen like this?

He sees my awed expression and explains, "This used to be a vineyard that allowed for guests to stay."

Gesturing for me to sit at the long oak table, which can easily hold twenty people, he gets to work on breakfast. I scan the kitchen, and my eyes fall on an enormous knife block with more knives than I can count. Glancing back at Nate, he is watching me with raised eyebrows. "You can't leave, even if you overpower me."

But instead of feeling intimidated, I shrug sheepishly. "A girl has to try."

Shaking his head, he turns back to the fridge and mumbles something along the lines of "So much like your sister."

"What did you just say?"

But he ignores me.

"Nate!"

Nothing. Ugh.

CHAPTER THREE

LILLY

NATE PREPARES A FEAST; THERE IS NO OTHER WORD FOR IT. Pancakes, eggs, bacon, muffins—reheated, not fresh, but still— and toast with the largest selection of jams I have ever seen outside of a hotel buffet. I wonder if they are still housing guests? It seems like way too much food for one—currently, two people—living here. Living here? I mentally slap myself.

"I never expected a kidnapping victim to be treated like this," I quip, gesturing to the amount of food displayed in front of me.

"You are not a victim, Lilly." His tone is calm, but his shoulders are rigid.

"What else would you call my current situation?" Why doesn't he scare me? Despite my training, I'm pretty sure he could easily take me down.

Nate frowns. "I guess you're right." No other comment.

We eat quietly until I can't hold back anymore. "What do you want with me?"

Slowly, he lowers his piece of toast and leans back. He rubs his palms on his sweats under the table. Is he...nervous?

"I've thought all night about how to explain everything to you. I think it makes sense to start with my...story and then come to your part in it."

I wait for him to continue.

Wiping one hand over his mouth, he looks out the window and takes a deep breath. "My birth name is Nate Hamlin, but in public, I go by Altman."

Altman? He can't be serious.

"As in *Altman* Hotels?" I interrupt, my voice shrill. I was kidnapped by one of the wealthiest people in the world.

Well, fuck me.

"The one and the same." Facing me, he almost looks apologetic. "My father's name was Hamlin, but when I took over the business, I started using my mother's maiden name."

"Was?" *His father is dead, also?*

"He died a year after my mother and sister."

I'm not sure what to say. Is that what made him crazy? I know better than to ask.

"My parents' names were Payton Altman and Brooks Hamlin. My mother was the heiress of the hotel empire. My father was a patent attorney," he explains. "They met while my father was an intern in the Altman legal department. My sister was Audrey Hamlin, but I already told you that. Audrey was born when I was fourteen; she would've been eighteen now."

That makes him, what? Thirty-two?

Guess I was off with my late-twenties estimate.

The pain recalling his sister is written all over his features. Nate is staring out the window, and when he doesn't say anything, I prod carefully, "What happened?"

Why do I sympathize with this man? I tell myself that I'm just curious, like when you see an accident. You shouldn't watch, but you do it anyway to see if you can figure out who's at fault.

His gaze snaps back to me as if he completely forgot I was in the room. "Sorry," he mumbles. "I was told my mother found out that my father had an affair a few years prior. She was leaving him. She picked Audrey up from school and was on her way home to pack their belongings when she ran a stop sign. They collided with a truck and died on impact."

"That's...terrible." It truly is, but what does that have to do with me?

His lips press together for a brief moment. "I was away at school. I left early that year to take summer classes. My father was in a drunken stupor and, apparently, forgot he had another child. I got a call from our family attorney..." He trails off again.

"I'm...sorry." I sound like a broken record.

"I found out what happened when I came home for the funeral. The press ambushed me the minute I stepped out of the terminal at LAX. People at the wake kept giving me *the look*. These *your-father-was-the-reason-you-lost-your-mother-and-little-sister* pity side glances."

Now we're getting somewhere. Nate blames his father for his sister's death.

"I refused to speak to my father during the time I was there. I went back to school the day after they were buried, but I lost focus. I couldn't concentrate, school lost its appeal, and I stopped going to my classes. My therapists later said that I partially blamed myself, because I had promised Audrey to come home the weekend before to take her to the zoo. But I stayed at school to prepare for the fall semester."

Yup, definitely blames himself, too.

"About a month into it, my roommate forced me to go out with him and our usual group of friends. But someone brought a couple of guys I'd never met before. Somehow the conversation became about who I was: the *heir* to the Altman Empire. My mom's death had made national news, given the fact who she was. One of the new guys started making comments about how convenient it was for me that my mother *and* sister were dead. Another chimed in that it was her dumb fault, and she should've never been behind the wheel—should've used a driver as all the 'rich bitches' do." He makes air quotes around the two words.

Whoa—

"I lost it." Recalling the story, his voice sounded robotic, but this last sentence is spoken in a low growl. The change in his demeanor sends a chill down my spine.

"What did you do?" I whisper. Scenarios run through my head—one worse than the other.

Nate continues in the same detached tone. "I was told that I tackled him and started beating on him—his head, to be precise. Two of my friends had to pull me off. I don't remember any of it. I blacked out."

My eyes bulge as his words sink in. "What...uh, what happened to the guy?"

Did he kill him?

"I put him into a coma."

Ho-ly shit.

One has to evoke some serious strength to do that with bare hands. I should be scared, but oddly enough, I am still not afraid for my safety. We sit, and I focus on the remnants of my breakfast in front of me. I'm no longer hungry. As captivating and disturbing as this story is, I'm getting more and more confused.

"So, uh—what does that have to do with me?" I ask carefully.

Nate's hazel eyes, which have been vacantly staring at the wall behind me, now glower at me. "I'm getting to that," he barks.

"Okay," is my meek response.

Maybe I'm a little scared.

He wipes his hands over his face. "Fuck, I'm sorry. I haven't told anyone the whole story in years."

"It's fine." My voice is still a whisper, definitely no backtalk this time.

"Just, uh... Let me get it all out. You'll understand." His eyes have gentled, and it's evident that his reaction was less geared toward me than caused by the tragedy he is reminded of.

I nod.

"Given who my family is, I had the best defense in court. My attorney was able to negotiate a plea deal that landed me in a medical facility instead of jail. While I was...away, my father took his life."

I press my lips together.

"After my discharge, I returned home—my parents' home in LA," Nate clarifies. "I wasn't going back to school. Not only did I have to figure out my mother's estate, but I also had to sort out my father's affairs. It took weeks to get a handle on things. And then, I found a stack of letters and pictures in his desk at the house."

My heart starts hammering in my chest. This is leading up to the big question.

"The letters were addressed to my father. The pictures were of a little girl, ranging from baby age to about five years old. I didn't have to read the letters to see the resemblance."

Nate fixes his eyes on me, and I hold my breath. Rubbing my hands against the cotton of my sweatpants, I fight the urge to tell him to stop.

"The return address was an Emily Sumner."

This. Is. It. Bile starts to rise in my throat, and I swallow hard. My hands are trembling as I reach for my mug, having to do something to not look at Nate.

He waits for me to collect myself. I drink half of my almost cold tea before I dare look in the hazel eyes that were so familiar from the first day, but yet, I would've never made the connection.

"Emily and your father..." I rasp. There is too much saliva in my mouth. I keep swallowing, but it's not helping.

Nate nods.

"Can I go back to my room?" There is more, his face tells me as much, but the urge to run is too overpowering.

"Do you remember the way?" He's sending me alone. I'm not sure what this means, but I also don't care.

"I think so." I stand up and bolt out of the kitchen the way we came. I don't look back; I don't look around. The thought of trying to escape doesn't cross my mind. I need to be alone.

I WAKE up on top of the comforter in the room Nate has given me—my room, as I've started calling it. (Prison cell didn't seem or feel right no matter what the circumstance.) The sun is high in the sky, and I must've fallen asleep for several hours. I replay Nate's story in my head, and immediately, my pulse is speeding up. This is the third—no, fourth—no, I don't know what number—revelation in the last three months that has made my life a *fucking* lie. And on top of that, I start cursing like Denielle.

I was kidnapped as a child. My memory was erased. My parents are not my real parents. My brother is not my brother, but now my boyfriend. My biological parents are also not my parents—well, half of them anyway. And lastly, I do have a brother—half-brother, but nonetheless a brother—who kidnapped me. *Twice.*

With that last thought, I scramble off the bed and through the door to my left. I make it by a matter of an inch before the remnants of my breakfast make a reappearance. This time, there is no Rhys or Denielle to comfort me, to hold my hair, or to help me clean up. I'm alone in the fancy, black-and-white bathroom attached to my lavender-colored non-prison-cell overlooking a beautiful vineyard I cannot leave. Pulling away from the white porcelain bowl, I lose my last bit of composure, and the tears start flowing. Everything I've bottled up since I left Denielle's house Monday raises to the surface, and the first sob breaks free, followed by full-on body tremors. I wrap my arms around my middle and rock back and forth, crying anything but silently. I miss Rhys, and I no longer care that he kept Katherine's malicious games from me. All I want is to be held in his arms and hear his voice telling me that everything will be okay. But he's not here. No one is here. I'm alone, trapped in God knows where.

. . .

I EMERGE a few hours later from my room. After my breakdown, I took another shower and again rinsed all the emotions away. Being numb is the only way to keep my sanity—at least to an extent.

The sun is about to set, and I haven't seen Nate since I left the kitchen this morning. Unsure what to do, I wait in my room until the hunger wins out. For some reason, I am not surprised that my door is unlocked. Yes, he said there is no way for me to leave the property, but I know that his partial confession this morning has changed everything already. I'm no longer confined to my room.

I start my exploration with the kitchen. I find a leftover muffin wrapped up on the counter and instantly devour it. My initial hunger sated, I glance around, and my gaze lingers on the knife block. A voice in my head tells me to grab at least one knife, a small one that I can hide in the pocket of my sweatpants, but if it were that easy to escape, Nate wouldn't let me roam free—sister or not. Interlacing my hands on top of my head, I close my eyes.

Sister. God, I still am in denial.

I start moving through the kitchen, my fingers grazing the black-and-gray marble countertop as I walk. Besides the stairwell I've now taken three times, there is a door next to it. It's set back, and from the angle of the table, I didn't notice it earlier.

Should I? Oh, what the hell.

I ease the door open and find another hallway similar to the one upstairs—white walls and espresso-colored floors. This one holds artwork on the side that doesn't contain floor-to-ceiling windows. Slowly inching down the corridor, I take in the paintings. I don't know much about art, but the pictures in combination with the heavy wooden frames make them appear priceless. Knowing that he is an Altman, they probably are.

There are several closed doors between the paintings, but I

don't dare try to open any of them. My curiosity only goes so far. An archway opens up into a massive...um, what is this? A living room? A sitting room? Based on my estimate, its vaulted, coffered ceiling is far above the second story I know this house has—maybe even a third? Brown and beige leather couches and armchairs are arranged in various groupings, creating multiple seating areas. One of the most gigantic fireplaces, reaching all the way to the top of the wall facing the vineyard, is framed by more floor-to-ceiling windows. The small fire burning in it looks minuscule compared to the size of that thing.

I stand in front of the fireplace, still trying to gauge the magnitude of it when Nate steps up beside me.

How the hell does he do that?

"How are you feeling?" He sounds genuine.

Out of the corner of my eye, I see him staring at the flames as well.

"I'm not sure." Truth. Similar to the day Rhys told me everything, too many emotions assault me. Three months ago, I focused on the rage and anger to stay in control; now, there is so much to process. A voice in my head tells me I haven't heard the half of it yet. Taking a shower has helped me calm down, numb myself, but I can't run to the nearest bathroom whenever I'm getting overwhelmed.

Though I'd probably be clean at all times with how the revelations keep coming.

The silence elongates, and I attempt to take stock in my head. There is rage. My hands automatically ball into fists when I think about my parents—birth parents, adopted parents, whoever they are. They all lied to me about something. Did Henry have any idea I'm not his daughter? Did my biological father, Brooks, not want me? There's disappointment in Emily, who cheated on her husband—the man I believed to be my father for the last three months. Relief, for having some answers. Fear of not seeing Rhys again. Confusion about Nate because, despite seeming completely sane whenever we talk, he is mentally ill. He kidnapped four other children, for Christ's sake. And for what reason? I still don't know the answer to that.

As if sensing my thoughts, he asks, "Do you feel up to talking some more?"

Do I?

He sounds hesitant. But instead of answering his question, I counter, "How do you always know when to show up? Do you have a tracker on me?" I'm mostly joking, but still, I hold my breath, waiting for his answer.

He huffs out a laugh. "No."

I finally sneak a peek at his profile, and I see him smirk at my suggestion.

How can he seem so...normal?

I shrug. "So? How do you do it?"

Nate turns to face me. After a pause, he points to an upper corner of the room then to another on the opposite wall. "That's how."

I follow his finger and scan the areas he indicated. Squinting, I notice a small black dot on the white wall. Cameras? If one doesn't search for it, it appears merely like a dirt stain. Then it sinks in, and my jaw drops. With a knot in my stomach, I whirl around to my half-brother. "Are there cameras in my room? In the bathroom?" I'm mortified.

He has the decency to look somewhat guilty. "In your room, yes. In your bathroom, no."

Oh, thank goodness.

"However, your bathroom has a microphone for safety reasons."

"Safety reasons?" I shriek, aghast.

"I would never spy on you like that with a camera, but my computer is analyzing the sounds and alerts me if it identifies anything that could be considered a threat."

Oh, so puking my guts out and crying is not considered dangerous by his computer?

Immediately knowing where my thoughts went, he says, "It

did alert me earlier, but after checking the recording, I figured that was not something you would've wanted me to witness."

He is right on that account, which deflates my outrage—a little. However, I can't refrain from demanding, "I want the camera in my room gone. And the mic." Standing there with my hands on my hips, glaring up at my kidnapper-slash-half-brother, must make for an entertaining sight. The ridiculousness of the situation is not lost on me.

Nate's shoulders slump slightly. "I can't do that."

I'm about to protest, but he holds up a hand. "I will switch both to monitoring only."

What does that even mean?

My frown triggers him to elaborate. "The computer will analyze the threat level and send an alert. But I won't be able to view the footage or listen to the recording without your permission."

"How do I know that you're telling the truth?"

"You don't. However, my security network is very...proficient. I can put a personal password on every camera on the property. To prove to you that you can trust me, you can put the password for your cameras and mics in yourself. Only you and the system can access them."

I have no idea if he's pulling all that out of his ass, but what else am I supposed to do?

CHAPTER FOUR

LILLY

I'M STANDING IN NASA'S COMMAND CENTER. AT LEAST THAT'S what it looks like.

I had followed Nate from the sitting room, as he called it, through an arch into the connecting foyer. A vast double staircase leads to the floor above. It comes together in a gallery overlooking the entryway, as well as the various seating areas in front of the massive fireplace on the other side. A set of wrought-iron double doors—the exit, if I were able to leave—takes over half of the wall opposite the arch and is dead center between both sets of stairs. Despite the pristine white walls everywhere—except for my room—the dark wooden floors give this place a feel of...home.

God, I need my head examined.

Upstairs, Nate stopped in front of a regular-looking door... until I noticed a large panel set into the wall. I stared wide-eyed as he unlocked the room with his retina scan. His. Freaking. Eye. Oh, and a fingerprint. Don't let me forget the fingerprint. When I thought it couldn't get worse, the panel slid up, and—was that a mic? Yup, it was a mic. He said a random string of words, and something inside the door clicked. I gawked at him incredulously.

When he saw my expression, he deadpanned, "I'm not always alone on the property."

Of course you're not. How silly of me.

Now, my brain is trying to comprehend what I'm looking at. There are six, at my guess, 50-inch flat-screen TVs mounted on the wall to the right, all of them off. An antique-looking desk that reminds me of the one from the *National Treasure* movie sits in the middle of the room, in complete contrast to the tech surrounding it. There are more monitors centered on the desk with two keyboards in front of them and two laptops at either end.

I turn in a circle and realize there are no windows. Based on what I've seen from the rest of the house, he must've had them removed. Pictures cover the wall opposite the screens, arranged in no particular order or pattern as it seems. Without waiting for Nate's permission, I step closer. My gaze immediately finds several pictures of a young Nate—probably eighteen or so—with a little girl, which I assume to be Audrey. They have the same light hair color and facial features—the same as me. The realization hits me like a punch in the gut, and I can't stop myself from gasping. It's as evident as the fact that I look nothing like the McGuires—like Rhys. *Don't think of him right now.* My chest constricts, and I start moving along the wall, trying to focus on the photographs instead. I discover about a dozen more of Audrey, ranging from infancy to around five or six years old. In some pictures, she is with a gorgeous woman in her thirties. The woman has flawless, almost ivory skin. Her hair is a shade between red and hazelnut, which, if not natural, would make a person look washed out. On her, however, it has a striking effect. In one of the pictures, she is wearing a red ball gown, which highlights her pale skin, rubicund hair, and slender figure even more. She looks like royalty. This must be Payton Altman.

"My mother."

Despite his voice being low, I jump at his words. I was so absorbed in my half family, he might as well have shouted in my ear. My hand flies over my heart, and I try to get my breathing under control again.

"She was beautiful," I whisper. I can't bring myself to speak at a regular volume.

"Yes, she was." Nate is in his own head and stares toward a section of pictures in the bottom corner of the wall. I follow his gaze and find the only picture containing four individuals. In the background is a Christmas tree; Audrey is on Payton's lap in a tight embrace. Nate sits next to his mother and sister with one arm slung around his mother's shoulders. All three radiate happiness. On the other side of Payton is a blond man with angular features. He is squatting, face angled toward Audrey, but his expression is blank. There is no emotion, a complete contrast to the rest of the photograph, which shouts holiday joy. His skin is sun-kissed, but not too tan, and his light-blond hair is shaggy and curled at the ends. Is this...?

"Yes."

Did I ask that out loud?

"You look a lot like him," I tell Nate. I'm not sure what else to say. What is the appropriate reaction here?

"So do you." He's just stating a fact, but the black hole inside of me rips open further.

Who am I? Where do I belong?

"It was our last Christmas together as a family," he murmurs.

I'm about to move away from the picture when something unexpected happens. A sharp pain punctures my brain like an ice pick, and I crumble to the floor, holding my head. Squeezing my eyes shut, I see a multitude of colors as if fireworks were set off behind my eyelids. My stomach rolls, and I curl into myself. I don't remember if I cried out loud or not, but the next thing I see is Nate hovering over me with wide eyes.

"Are you okay?" Panic laces his question. He sits on his haunches, waiting for me to straighten up. His hand hovers slightly above my shoulder, as if he wants to help me up but is scared to make that connection.

One of my hands is still at my head, and I have to force myself to lower it to my lap.

"I'm fine, just a memory," I say without thinking.

Crap! That's probably not something I should share with him. The line between kidnapper and brother is blurring, and that puts me on edge. Questions my sanity.

"What do you mean?" Confusion replaces the panic in Nate's voice.

When I don't reply, he initiates the first physical contact since the handshake a few weeks ago. Consciously or unconsciously, I don't know, but what I immediately notice...I don't flinch away.

This is not good.

Nate leads me to a couch set against the third wall, where the floor-to-ceiling windows should have been. It is mostly hidden behind the massive desk, which explains why I didn't notice it until now. As soon as we reach it, he lets go of my wrist, and I slump down into the plush leather cushion.

"Explain, please." His command is gentle but a command nonetheless. The hair on my neck stands up.

I pull my legs underneath me, and my gaze briefly flickers to his face before settling on my hands resting in my lap. I have the sudden urge to tell him everything. Why? I'm not sure. Maybe because I want to share it with someone else. Perhaps because he is my half-brother. Or perhaps I'm simply on the verge of an emotional breakdown.

"That's how it all started," I whisper and wait for Nate to react, but he just studies me with narrowed eyes.

I continue, "That's how I found out that I am not who I thought I am. I started having migraines. Combined with memories of my past. Of you." This time, I lock eyes with him, and for the first time, Nate is unnerved.

We sit in silence, and he is opening and closing his mouth

several times. It seems that he doesn't know how to respond. I assume he isn't aware of what my parents did to me, that I couldn't remember—still can't. Do I want him to?

Ah, screw it.

"After you dropped me off at the hospital and threatened Emily, they erased my memory. I was so messed up that they thought I wouldn't be able to have a normal life. And because they were scared of you, they sent me away."

There, I put it all out there—no sugar coating.

Nate stares at me, lips pressed in a thin line. Then, with blinding speed, he jumps off the couch and is in reach of the desk within two steps. He grabs one of the laptops and hurls it across the room against the picture wall. Half the pictures shatter to the floor from the force, and the computer joins the chaos in multiple pieces. His entire posture is rigid. His hands grip the back of his neck, and his chest is heaving up and down. For the first time, I'm scared. His outburst is so abrupt and makes me wish I'd phrased it differently.

I need to stop poking the lion.

I don't move. I barely breathe. I want to hide in my room, but I don't think I would make it out of here—if the door would even open with the gazillion security measures it takes to get in. Finally, after several minutes, Nate turns toward me, and what I see shocks me to the core. His eyes shine with unshed tears, and his expression is pure anguish.

"I'm so sorry," he rasps out.

It's my turn to open and close my mouth. Nothing. I can't come up with a single word. He's insane. He kidnapped me. He took the other girls. That means he's crazy. *Right?* But what I see is remorse in its rawest form. What am I supposed to do with that?

"Why?" is all I come up with. Why did you kidnap me? Why didn't you just come to me? Why did you threaten Emily? And why the other girls? All those questions are packed into this one word, and he understands. He slumps back down beside me and puts his head in his hands, elbows supported on his thighs.

"I snapped." Nate's voice is hoarse. He talks toward the floor. "Twelve years ago, something broke inside of me. Then the bar incident happened. I found out about you and had a second chance at a family. I was just discharged and still on, like, five different meds. Meds that were supposed to help with my rage and guilt. But they also muddled my rational thinking. I had to have you. My sister. No matter what the cost."

Okay, sadly, I can see that.

"But why the other girls?" I probably shouldn't push the issue, but he seems to be willing to give me some answers right now. He's quiet for so long that I think he's going to ignore the question.

"I don't know." His reply is barely audible.

Well, that confirms that he's crazy.

I'm not sure what to say. I can understand that, after losing his family, he was...lost? But still, no sane person kidnaps little children for a few weeks to feel less lonely. Before I can prod further, it's Nate's turn to ask questions again.

"So...you remembered the hospital? That's why you came back?"

I stare at the blank monitors on the wall as if they show a rerun of what happened the last few months. The three weeks I thought I'd lost my mind. The night Rhys confronted me. How I ended up in the school parking lot after fleeing the house. The discharge papers and how I decided to go to California. I'm exhausted. I'm tired of the secrets in my life. I don't want to constantly be on guard. It's like something falls into place, and I pivot on the couch, facing my half-brother. He must've sensed the shift in me, because he mirrors my posture, and his entire focus is on me.

"No more secrets." My voice is firm, confident. It's not an act; I'm done with the secrets. Keeping what happened in the last three months to myself won't do any good in this situation. But in return, I want answers from him.

Nate's knitted eyebrows indicate that he doesn't understand the meaning of my words, so I elaborate.

"I'll tell you everything. Everything I remember and figured out about what happened to me. In return, I want answers as well. No more secrets. You say we're family; then we need to deal with this like one." Yep, a cheap shot and slightly manipulative, but it's also the truth. At this point, he is the only blood family I have left, crazy or not. I *need* to know where I come from.

Understanding dawns in his eyes, and he holds out his hand. I stare at it for a moment, hesitant to take it. But my need for answers wins out, and I place my palm in his. It's a brief contact. He squeezes my hand with a quick shake up and down, and it's settled.

I TELL NATE EVERYTHING. From my first migraine to the reason why I left school this week. I've been talking for so long my mouth is parched, and I'm emotionally drained. The clock on the wall shows one a.m., and I realize we've been in here for hours. Nate hasn't spoken once. Every so often, his facial expression changes to something I interpret as surprise, but he never comments.

At some point, he resumes his previous position with his elbows on his thighs, staring down at the floor, though his stiff posture is a dead giveaway of him listening.

When I finally finish, I take a deep breath. Nate doesn't react; his focus remains downward. The first words out of his mouth are, "I caused you a lot of pain."

It's a simple statement, and he doesn't expect a response. He doesn't want me to make him feel less guilty; he knows what he has done. Which, in return, makes me question my earlier assessment of his sanity.

"I guess it's my turn." Our eyes lock for the first time. He is just as exhausted as I am.

I want my answers, but my ability to focus is dwindling fast. "Let's postpone your turn for tomorrow."

"Yeah, that's probably better." The relief in his eyes is palpable.

I still have one request, though, that I didn't dare ask until now. "Nate?"

"Yes?" He tilts his head to the side, wary.

"I want to talk to Rhys." I'm not asking him; I will make this call somehow, but I'd rather have his support. Nate faces forward again but peers at me sideways, and I brace myself to utilize my last bit of energy for a fight.

"Okay."

"Okay?" I ask in disbelief.

He sighs heavily. "Yes, okay. From everything I just heard from you, I am smart enough to know that 'no' is not an option. You are as smart and as stubborn as the rest of your family."

I suck in a breath. My family? Is he referring to him and Audrey? Or Rhys? Or even Emily?

"But I'm asking you for more time. I want you to hear me out before you make the call."

The condition.

Rhys is probably going crazy, and so are Heather and Tristen, I'm sure. I don't even want to think about Natty. Closing my eyes, I nod in concession. Arguing will do no good, as much as I hate waiting, or making them wait. It's the only option I have until I get my bearings of this place.

CHAPTER FIVE

LILLY

IT'S MID-MORNING WHEN I STUMBLE INTO THE KITCHEN. I still don't have access to a clock, so I go by the sun's trajectory when I finally make my way downstairs.

I woke up earlier to the room flooded with light. In my exhaustion, I forgot to close the drapes last night. Groaning, I flipped over and dragged one of the pillows over my head. It was definitely too early to get up, but I also didn't feel like moving and closing the blinds. The pillow did the trick, and I managed to fall back asleep for a while longer.

After waking up for the second time, I lay in bed, replaying the events of the previous day. This seems to have become a regular occurrence. Something came to the forefront, and my hands flew to my mouth to stifle the gasp that tried to escape me. I didn't want the mic to alert Nate; we didn't change the password yet. Still covering my mouth, I squeezed my eyes shut and remembered last night's *migraine*. With everything that happened, I had pushed it to the back of my mind and completely forgotten about it. Nate was probably too distracted as well to ask what my most recent memory had revealed. But now—in the light of the new day—it was all back. What did this mean? A knot formed in my belly, and I knew I had to tell him. But first, I wanted to hear more of his side before I revealed my trump.

NATE IS SITTING at the massive kitchen table with a mug in front of him, staring out the window. He doesn't react when I drop down across from him in the same chair as yesterday.

"Hi," comes out as a croak, and I clear my throat. I wipe my all-of-a-sudden damp hands against the black yoga pants I pulled out of the drawer today.

His eyes flick to me. "Good morning. Did you sleep okay?" He sounds genuine, like a big brother. I swallow the lump in my throat—*my brother*. My heart starts beating double time. My emotions are contradicting each other again, and I'm more confused than ever. And I thought being in love with your adoptive brother was complicated. Try to enjoy spending time with your half-brother who kidnapped you. I want to bang my head against the tabletop.

Maybe I have Stockholm Syndrome?

"Uh, yes. Thank you. You?"

"I didn't sleep much."

He stares at a spot behind me, seeming distracted, and I raise my eyebrows. His gaze swivels back to me. He blinks once, twice, then his focus is entirely on me. "Sorry. I was working most of the night."

Working?

"You work?" I ask, baffled, before I can stop myself. Why wouldn't he work? Even rich people work.

Nate chuckles. "Yes, the hotels don't run themselves."

"Oh."

He pushes back from the table. "I had to make sure we're not getting interrupted today, so I was working ahead. How about you eat something and then I'll show you the property? I believe it's my turn to give some answers?"

He phrases it like a question. Does he expect me not to want answers anymore? I fight the urge to roll my eyes. At the precise moment that I'm about to say that I'm ready now, my stomach growls, and I resign myself to nourishment before answers. After all, I haven't eaten much in, what, forty-eight hours? Seventy-two?

"How long have I been here?"

Nate stops his retreat and turns back to me.

"It's Friday. You slept for close to twenty-four hours after the accident." His tone is calm and matter-of-fact, but I see...*something* flash across his face. It's gone as quickly as it appeared. I wonder if he recalls the day I *didn't* wake up.

He turns and leaves the kitchen. I make myself a cup of tea and throw a slice of toast in the toaster oven. After grabbing a banana from the fruit basket, I rifle through the pantry—which could hold our entire kitchen at home—until I find a jar of peanut butter. Sitting back down at the massive table with my PB&B sandwich, I think about Nate's response. Friday. That means I've been gone for three days. Shit. My sense of time is all off. Heather is probably beside herself. I don't even want to think about Rhys. Or Natty. I'd lose my mind. I have to make this call.

THE CLOCK on the stove shows 11:39 when Nate saunters back in. He has my boots in one hand and a long, black, fleece jacket in the other.

"You really planned this out, huh? Buying me all these clothes and whatnot?" I gesture at his arm and then at the clothes I'm wearing, fully aware of how snide I sound.

Mimicking my smart-ass demeanor. "This is Margot's jacket, for when she comes here with me."

Who the—

I narrow my eyes at him, and he gives me a smug smile. "My fiancée. We come up here every few months, and she keeps clothes in one of the rooms. Your jacket got ruined in the accident and would be too warm anyway."

Fiancée? But he's crazy. How can he have a fiancée?

"Fiancée?" I'm too stunned to ask in a full sentence.

Nate doesn't answer and throws the jacket at me instead. I snatch it out of the air, and I hold it out, eyeing it like it's going to explode. Peeking at the label in the collar, I recognize the brand from Denielle. This thing costs more than all my jackets combined. Before I can say anything else, Nate is back out of the room, and I have to scramble with my boots to follow him. With Margot's fancy jacket in hand, I find him waiting in the foyer, leaning against the rail of one of the staircases.

"Ready?"

As ready as I'll ever be.

I nod and follow him out of the massive wrought-iron door, coming to a halt. I'm standing in a ginormous circular driveway. In the center is a Mediterranean-inspired fountain—currently turned off. Behind it is the beginning of a long, winding driveway lined with trees on either side and leading God knows where. I still have no clue where I am. I walk toward the fountain and then spin in a circle. *Holy—* The estate is even grander than I assumed. The outside is the same color scheme as the inside. The walls are a blinding white, as if freshly painted, with dark-brown window trims and shutters creating a dramatic contrast. The roof has a similar shade and stands out against the bright-blue sky. To the left, I can see the beginning of a four- or maybe five-car garage; that part of the building is at an angle, so there could be even more.

A warm breeze caresses my face, and I briefly close my eyes. "Where are we?" I can't hide the awe in my question.

"Northern California. Not far from Santa Rosa, actually."

I'm back where it all started. My eyes pop open. What did I

expect? Somehow, I'd thought that he moved somewhere else after what happened ten years ago.

Nate starts walking to the right with his hands clasped behind his back. The narrow cobblestone path seems to go the entire length of that side of the building. When I catch up, he doesn't look my way but keeps a slow and steady pace.

"This estate belonged to my grandfather. He purchased it not long before he passed away, and I don't think either my mother or father knew about it. If they did, they seem not to have cared for it. I came across the title when my mother's attorney handed me the paperwork for the Altman 'Empire'." Nate makes air quotes around empire before he sticks his hands in the pockets of his hoodie instead of interlacing them again. I take in today's attire. Instead of sweats, he's wearing faded jeans that have probably seen better times and a dark-gray hoodie of no apparent brand. Not something I would expect from a billionaire, but so far, everything I've learned about Nate Altman-Hamlin contradicts itself.

He continues, which pulls me out of my fashion observation. "The first time I came here was a few weeks after my discharge. I couldn't stay in LA, deal with all the people. So, I moved up here. My grandfather had already restored the majority of the property, and I finished the rest over the years. Added my touch to it."

You mean your spyware.

"I don't know what his intention for the property was, but I decided to keep it. I started growing grapes again about eight years ago but opted against the winery part of it. When the time comes, the grapes go to another vineyard ten miles from here. I have staff that takes care of the property when I'm not in residence. When I'm here, I prefer my privacy. I don't stay long enough these days to require them to be around. I actually prefer to do things myself. I don't know...it helps me relax."

I listen, fascinated. Nate sounds so normal. We reach the edge of the house, and the path branches off in several directions. One follows along the side of the house, one seems to lead toward a small park, complete with stone benches, and the last disappears between the grapevines on the nearest hill. Everything is perfectly landscaped, not one blade of grass longer than the other. We follow along with the house until we reach the backside of the property, and I realize that it's a massive U-shape, which also explains the angle of the garage. Centered between the two arms of the U is a rectangular pool flush with the obscenely perfect manicured green.

"This place is huge."

"It has twelve guest bedrooms, each with a bathroom, not including my rooms, the library, and several sitting rooms. As I said, I have no idea what he intended for it. Most of the rooms are empty; I have no plans to open the property up for guests again."

"Is this where you brought..." *The girls?* I can't stop myself but, at the same time, can't finish the sentence. However, Nate is fully aware of what I'm asking. Hands still in his pockets, his chin dips to his chest, and his shoulders slump forward. His gaze flickers to me before he lowers it to the ground.

"Yes." His tone is eerily quiet, and I can't make out if his crazy side is making an appearance or if he feels...guilty?

"How did you know where to find me this week? Or the day at the gym?" I'm not ready to pursue the other topic. Mentioning the gym, I realize something else. "Wait...one of the pictures—you were in it."

"I have a guy," Nate murmurs.

A guy?

He continues before I can voice my confusion. "My security. He worked for my grandfather, and I kept him on the payroll when I took over." His admission that he had someone spy on me makes my blood boil. My entire body goes rigid.

"You paid some creep to spy on me? What the fuck is wrong with you? Did he know your plans for me? You're sick." Every word makes the bile in my throat rise further, and I basically spit the last sentence at him. I'm beyond caring if I make him angry. However, I'm not prepared for his next action. I'm ready to tear past him when Nate places a hand on my forearm and stops me in my tracks. Instead of getting mad for disrespecting and verbally attacking him, he looks at me with understanding.

"George is the best at what he does. He started as a P.I. for my grandfather, investigating people that tried to sabotage the business. Over time, he's become my head of security. I needed help when I was discharged from the hospital, with the press, with the business...with life. In the beginning, he only worked for me when I had a specific, uh... need. Over time, he became more. Yes, he is paid for his *discretion*. Yes, he was following you. No, he wasn't aware of me planning to bring you back with me. He stayed back to deal with the consequences of my decision. George knows *everything* I do or have done." Nate emphasizes the last part, and I grasp the meaning.

Oh God, the girls.

I feel sick, but Nate tightens the hold on my arm and keeps talking. "George knows you're my sister. He's known for a long time that I have a half-sister." After a pause, he adds, "He's the one who returns them."

"Why would he let you do it in the first place?" My voice is shrill, bordering on hysterics. Not for me, but for the little girls.

"He doesn't; he travels a lot. But when he finds out—and since he checks in on me regularly, he always finds out—he steps in. I've never harmed any of them, but he also doesn't just let me...continue. If he could be with me 24/7, he would, but his job requires him to be away a lot. Don't ask me why he hasn't handed me over yet. That's something you have to take up with him."

Nate lets go of me and turns away. I can't make out his face, but I see his stiff posture and notice he has his arms wrapped around his midsection. His next words are a raspy whisper. "He is the *only one* I trust to help me make things right. He—" his voice cracks. "He takes care of me."

This grown man in front of me sounds and looks utterly broken. I try to wrap my head around it. When I think he won't say anything else, he turns back to me. "We said no more secrets; that's why I am telling you this. I want you to be the one other person in my life I can trust—with everything. Help me make things right."

My eyes widen at his admission.

"I was doing business in Virginia, and Hank, my business partner, was with me most of the time. There was no way for me to check on you on my own, and I wanted to learn as much about you as possible. I asked George for his help. I couldn't understand how you all of a sudden showed up in California. Why now? Where were you for the past ten years? You had disappeared without a trace, and I'm good at finding things—"

Things. Nate focuses on something in the distance. His tone screams sincerity to me. In these short few days, I've seen enough of Nate Hamlin's different *personalities* to know his intention was solely to find out as much as he could about me while staying away. It warms me as much as it causes the hair on my arms to stand up.

I focus on something else from his last statement. "Didn't you say your friend's name is Todd?" I remember clearly that he called the Asian guy at the gym Todd.

"Hank Todd, yes."

Oh.

"Why did you have to scare me?" The force behind my voice is gone.

"I didn't see another way to separate you from your friends." He is still looking past me, and the fire ignites again.

"You seem to be a brilliant guy, genius-level smart. Even you should realize that what you did was wrong. You manipulated me. You scared me. YOU TOOK ME AWAY FROM MY FAMILY!" My voice rises with every word until I am screaming at him at the top of my lungs.

"THEY. ARE. NOT. YOUR. FAMILY!" he roars back, his nostrils flared, eyes blazing.

There is the monster.

Any other person seeing this six-foot-three guy would be terrified. He emanates rage. But I am not.

We're facing off in the middle of the lawn behind the estate, surrounded by a breathtaking landscape, both breathing heavy, eyes locked and unable to move. I have no idea how long the standoff lasts before Nate shoves his hands through his hair and does a one-eighty, turning away from me. Stalking off, he doesn't take his hands away from his head until he reaches a set of iron patio furniture on the terrace spanning the entire building's backside. He slumps down in one of the chairs and supports his elbows on his legs, his head still cradled in his hands.

Unsure what to do, I watch Nate for several minutes. When he doesn't move, I slowly walk toward him and lower myself in the chair opposite him.

"Nate?" I prod. There is a possibility my action will backfire on me.

He inhales deeply before lifting his gaze. Raw anguish fills his eyes, and I suck in a breath.

Who is this man?

"I know there is something wrong with me; I'm not...normal. I probably should've never been released from the hospital." He sighs, resigned. "Most of the time, I don't remember what I did until it is too late—until George steps in. But the voice in my head tells me that this is the only way to not feel lonely for a little while..." He lets the sentence trail off.

"The voice?"

Please don't tell me you hear voices.

He must've seen my bulging eyes, because he huffs out a laugh. "Uh, not the way you're thinking. I meant it in a figure-of-speech kind of way. I don't hear actual voices."

"Oh, thank God." A giggled sigh escapes me, and we both smirk at each other until reality sets back in.

"How do you intend this to go?" I gesture back and forth between us. One breath, two, three.

"I have no fucking clue. I haven't thought that far ahead," he admits.

"Let's keep talking?" The suggestion is out of my mouth before I can second-guess it.

"You still want to?" He sounds hopeful—like a little boy—and I don't have the heart to make a sarcastic remark.

I wait for doubt to set in, but it doesn't come, so I shrug. "I do." And not just because I am stuck here; I want to get to know my half-brother. My chest constricts, unsure how or when that changed.

His head is slightly tilted as if to assess if I'm sincere.

"So...uh, you're engaged?" I have to start somewhere that doesn't revolve around our history, and it's not the time to push the call.

His gaze flickers to the side before it returns to me. "Margot, yes." He has a ghost of a smile on his face.

"Tell me about her," I push further.

"We met about three and a half years ago at a birthday party for Julian's girlfriend, Celeste—now fiancée. Julian has been my best friend forever, and I used to hang out at their house all the time—it was my time to be me. No past, no Altman Hotels, just me. Anyway, Margot was there with a guy who knew Celeste, and it was obvious she was miserable." Nate chuckles at the memory, and I marvel how natural it, all of a sudden, feels to listen to him talk about his life. He has a best friend and a fiancée.

"The guy started flirting with a waitress, and Margot was about to leave when I intercepted her. She was stunningly beautiful, and I knew who she was. Margot comes from family money, and initially, I was mostly attracted to her because of who she was. She wouldn't be with me for my money; she has enough of her own. I didn't have to worry about a secret agenda. And if I'm honest, she made me feel somewhat normal for the first time in years. This was right after—well..."

"Just keep going." I know what he means; I memorized the timeline, but I can't focus on that. This is a topic for another time. And the time will come sooner than I'd probably like.

"We started going out, and I realized there is more to her. She can be vain and eccentric, don't get me wrong; she has never worked a day in her life, and she has quirks everyone rolls their eyes at, but she also has a generous heart. She is involved with several non-profit organizations and, despite her wealth, tries to give back in her own way." I want to ask him why she doesn't make him feel less lonely, but I don't dare.

"When did you decide that she's the one?"

My question gives me another chuckle. "Margot made that decision for me. More or less."

My eyebrows narrow.

"I don't believe in a soulmate; that there is *the one*. Margot and I work well together."

"I don't know about that." My thoughts immediately wander to my soulmate, as Denielle had put it the day I finally admitted my feelings to myself.

"You're thinking about Rhys." He doesn't ask; he has the proof in the form of multiple incriminating photographs to know that Rhys and I are more than adopted siblings.

"Yes," I mumble, heat creeping up my face, and I'm not sure why it all of a sudden embarrasses me.

"I'm sure there are exceptions."

Is he trying to reassure me?

And then he adds, "You're definitely a better fit than that Katherine girl."

My breath increases, and I scowl at Nate. "You're the reason for what went down with Katherine at school this week?" I phrase it like a question, though there is no other way for Katherine to have gotten a hold of that photo. I'm sure he hears the warning in my questions.

"Yes." The truth. No matter how awful or painful it has been, he has not lied to me once.

"How?" It comes out as a growl.

He sighs deeply before he reveals that part of the mystery to me. "After you showed up in Santa Rosa, it took me some time to figure out who was with you. If Rhys wouldn't have introduced himself to Margery, there's a chance I still wouldn't know."

"Margery?"

"The nurse who gave you the note."

"Oh—"

How did he find all that out?

"How did I find that out?"

I swear he has a mic implanted in my brain.

I nod, not trusting my voice.

"I had a program on the hospital server, monitoring your file."

"Are you some kind of hacker?" I squeak.

That makes him grin proudly. "You could say that. Before everything started, I double-majored in business management, which was non-negotiable in my family, and computer science. Computers were, you could say, my thing. And I kept up with it. It's a hobby."

"A hobby?" I scoff. "You don't use a hobby to implant a Trojan horse at a hospital or spy on people by hacking into security cameras." My arms are now crossed tightly over my chest, and Nate narrows his eyebrows.

"How do you know about the security system?"

"You sent a picture from the school's security camera to me." *Duh.*

"I did; you're right." That's all; he says nothing else to that.

We're getting sidetracked from the actual topic. "Back to Katherine and what you did..." I leave the sentence hanging, untangle my arms from my chest, and spread them in a gesture for him to continue. I'm angry, and I'm channeling all of it toward the guy across from me. He has manipulated everyone around me to separate me from Rhys. My heart aches thinking of him.

Nate lifts both hands disarmingly. "Okay, first off, all I did was send one picture to her. Something was going on before my, uh...interference. But I have no detailed knowledge about that. Whatever your *boyfriend* did was not my doing."

I wait for him to elaborate.

"After I found out your new name, I started looking into your friends and family. Heather and Tristen McGuire have done an exhaustive job in hiding you, but some of your friends, especially Katherine—"

"She is not my friend!" I bark.

Nate sighs at my outburst.

"I know she's not. What I was going to say is that some of the people around you have a very public Internet presence, especially Katherine. It was laughably easy to see what's important to her. What I didn't know was that, until recently, you were completely in the dark about your past. All I found was that Rhys was with Katherine for years until he, suddenly, wasn't. And then George sends me pictures of you and Rhys together, but officially, you are related. My *hobby* allowed me to find out that Katherine suspected something being off with her breakup and your relationship with your brother. It wasn't hard to find some evidence that she was paying close attention and also tried to manipulate her ex-boyfriend. But Rhys kept that from you, which worked in my favor. I admit I got impatient; I didn't plan on being in Virginia that long, and in the end, I decided to fast-track some of the events that probably still would've happened eventually. As callous as this Katherine chick is, she is not dumb."

While he was talking, my body started shaking, and I wouldn't be surprised if steam comes out of my ears. I glower at him until his gaze drops to my hands in my lap. I realize I've been fisting the material of my borrowed jacked to the point of ripping the seam of one of the pockets.

"You're angry."

"You think?" I can't hide my rage any longer. "YOU.

OUTED. ME. TO. THE. ENTIRE. SCHOOL! I'm an incestuous slut for everyone now!"

"Yeah, in hindsight, that was maybe a little overboard," Nate mumbles.

Gaaaahhh! I jump out of my seat and stomp away. "I'm done," I bark, walking toward the house.

"Lilly!"

"WHAT?" I whirl around and see him pointing in the opposite direction.

"Your room is in the east wing." He doesn't sound patronizing or condescending at all, but I can't help feeling like an idiot.

"Thanks," I snap and march—now with less dignity—toward the other side of the terrace.

Great.

CHAPTER SIX

NATE

I'm sitting in my office, watching Lilly cry into her pillow. It breaks my heart that I caused my little sister so much pain. The recurring doubt I've suppressed over the years reverberates in my brain since our earlier conversation. Sometimes, I believe that I should've never been discharged—whenever I realize what I've done. *Again*. But I was deemed mentally stable and thrown back into the world. Even after all this time, I see my doctors regularly, which was part of the deal for my discharge/release. They keep changing my meds around every few years to adjust better to my current lifestyle—whatever the fuck that means. If George is not with me, he checks in regularly, and if I don't answer, he shows up at my doorstep within twenty-four hours, no matter where in the world he his. Could I turn myself in? Sure. But until now, I have been too much of a pussy for that.

Having Lilly here makes me want to be a better person—the best possible version of myself. Sitting across from my sister, who has been through so much—most of it being my fault—I genuinely want to do better—*be better*. And I will be. I'll do right by her.

There is still so much I need to tell her, but I understand she needs time, especially after our most recent conversation.

I kill the feed to her room and switch to computer monitoring only. Until she can put her password on the camera, the computer will do its job.

She also hasn't made any attempt to run since she woke up, and if I'm honest, I'm a little confused by that. She did demand to call *the boyfriend*. Thinking about that, the big brother in me comes out. I want to ask her how that came to be. First, the guy dates cheerleader Barbie for years; then, he's with Lilly. I have no right, but I can't help but feel protective of her.

LILLY HAS BEEN in her room for two hours, and I've been procrastinating, looking at the most recent design update for the new Virginia hotel. Hank has sent five text messages in the last thirty minutes, so I switch the camera in her hallway to movement alert and get to work.

An hour later, my phone rings with an incoming video call, and Margot's smiling face in a beach chair greets me.

Did she tell me she was taking a trip?

"How are you, sweetheart? I was going to call you later tonight."

"Darling! I'm so glad you answered. Guess where I am?"

Is that a trick question?

"I don't know. It looks like somewhere warm."

"We're in San Tropez," she squeals.

France? What the fuck?

"Who is 'we'? And how did that happen? I thought you're in LA this week?" I'm slightly confused, which doesn't happen often. I keep tabs on everything and everyone in my life. I don't like surprises.

"I was, but Daddy called that he purchased a new yacht and

invited me to come out. And since you're busy and all with your secret project, I figured why not. I brought Celeste with me as a pre-birthday present; it'll be so much fun." She flips the camera to Julian's fiancée, who waves into the camera from a matching beach chair before I see my fiancée's face again.

"Uh, that's great, sweetheart. The two of you will cause havoc with all the French men," I tease. "How long are you gone?"

Meaning, how long do I have until I have to make excuses for not coming back to my house in LA?

"We'll be back for the party next week."

Party? Motherfucker, I forgot about the birthday party. "Uh."

"Darling? Did you forget Celeste's party?" she scolds.

Maybe? I've had other things on my mind.

"No, not at all."

We talk for a few more minutes before disconnecting. I lean back in my desk chair, pressing the heels of my hands to my eyes. FUUUCK!

My two worlds have never overlapped before. There has only been *one other* since I started seeing Margot. And that was during a low point in our relationship. I was stressed from work and seeing Doctor Stern twice a week while he switched my meds around once again. Margot was pushing for us to set a wedding date, which was the last thing on my mind, so she disappeared to South America for a month.

I need to figure something out before next week.

CHAPTER SEVEN

LILLY

I EMERGE AFTER I CAN NO LONGER DENY THE EXISTENCE OF my growling stomach. The kitchen is empty, and I rifle through the fridge. Pulling out a bunch of random containers, I inspect my haul on the marble counter. The dishes contain cooked pasta, meatballs, sauce, steamed broccoli, more muffins, and some cheese and meats. I also saw eggs and fresh herbs in the fridge. Next, I start my hunt for some cookware and utensils. My eyes briefly stop on the knife block before moving on.

Seeing all the ingredients, the craving for an omelet settles in my mouth. I'll start with that and then maybe make my way to the pasta and meatballs. I briefly wonder where they came from and if Nate made it?

At this point, I no longer fear Nate poisoning me. Plus, since I can't leave the estate, I may as well learn how to survive here, starting with the food. Flipping the omelet, I catch myself humming Linkin' Park's "Good Goodbye" and a knot forms in my throat. *Rhys.* I press my hand to my stomach and take a deep breath. The urge to hear his voice consumes me, and I stifle a sob.

"Lilly?"

I jump at the sound of my name but don't turn around. I don't want Nate to see me vulnerable. I'm still livid with him.

"Lilly, please tell me what's wrong."

Why can he read me so well?

I take a deep breath before smoothing my features and face him.

"Did your spy cameras alert you that I'm here?" I focus on my rage instead of the suffocating sense of loss overwhelming me whenever Rhys appears in front of my mind's eye.

"No. I came in for some food." He nods toward the containers that are still sitting on the counter. "I made way too much last night when I got hungry and figured I'd finish it."

So, he actually did make it himself.

The silence between us stretches, and he stares at his feet. How can a grown man who is a computer genius and runs a billion-dollar hotel empire all of a sudden look like a five-year-old who got caught stealing his sister's toy? I snort at my pun—not toy, he stole *his sister*. Nate looks up at the sound, but I don't feel like elaborating. Instead, I glare back at him.

He shuffles from one foot to the other. "Uh, I'll just come back later." He turns and walks toward the door with slumped shoulders.

Watching him retreat, my throat thickens, but I can't make myself call out. The door swings shut, and I'm alone with my omelet sizzling in the pan. The smell alerts me to something burning.

"Crap!"

I quickly pull the pan off the stove and inspect my meal. It's burned on one side, but I deem it edible. I don't feel like starting over; my stomach doesn't have the patience for it.

SITTING at the chair that has become *my* spot at the large table, I eat the omelet but don't taste anything. My mind wanders between the two men in my life. Rhys, my boyfriend, who I miss beyond words. I worry about him more than myself since he's completely in the dark as to where I am and with whom. Then, there is Nate, the only living blood relative I have as far as I know. He is a criminal. He is mentally unstable. But he is also wicked smart, kind, and...*my brother*.

I need to find a way to contact Rhys. Let him know that I'm okay. Well, as okay as one can be in my situation. And I still want to know more about Nate and...my father. Something feels off about Brooks. It's time to share my memory with Nate, and maybe I can use that as leverage to contact Rhys. Decision made.

"NATE!"

I'm pretty sure the spy mics will alert him; I don't feel like hunting down *brother dearest* in this maze. And yup, not three minutes later, he bursts through the kitchen door, looking frantically around for possible danger.

"What happened?" He is out of breath, which makes sense if he sprinted from his NASA command center to the kitchen—or wherever in this palace he was.

My heart rate increases, but I'm not backing out now. "We need to talk."

He appears to be taken aback by the force of my voice. "Uh...sure."

He slowly walks over to his usual chair and lowers himself down. Neither of us speaks. I close my eyes and take a deep breath to prepare myself.

When our gazes lock, it's comforting and unsettling how similar our eyes are. We have the same shade of hazel, a little bit of everything, blue, green, with an outer ring of brown. My eyes are more almond-shaped, but we both have the same long lashes —obviously, courtesy of Brooks.

"I want to know more about our father." Oddly enough, I can call Brooks *my father* when I still have problems referring to Heather, Tristen, or even Emily and Henry as my parents.

"Do you have anything specific in mind?" His head is slightly tilted; he's studying me. It's almost comical how I can read him now. I guess having half of the same genetic makeup helps.

"I do. I have something to tell you as well. And a request."

His eyebrows turn skyward again. "That sounds intriguing. What would you like to begin with?" His tone is businesslike, almost cold.

How does this intimidate me, but not his outbursts?

"I want to call Rhys. Today. I can't wait any longer. In return, I think my recent memory revealed something you'd want to know."

We sit in silence while he ponders my words. Finally, he asks, "A deal? What makes you think it's of interest to me?"

"Because I remembered our father."

Nate sucks in a breath. "You what?"

"Do we have a deal?" Folding my hands on top of the table, I mimic his businesslike demeanor. I count seventeen breaths before he answers.

"We have a deal. But..." *I knew this was too good to be true.* "I need some time to set up the call. It can't be traceable, and I don't have it all in place here at the moment."

Oh.

"How long?"

"Twenty-four hours. I need to finish some other things first."

Another day? I feel like all of the air has been sucked out of the room, and I push the urge to raise my hand to my chest down.

"Not one minute longer," I say with as much force as I can muster without the appropriate amount of oxygen in my lungs. Not that I could do anything if it takes two minutes longer, but I need him to see that I'm serious.

Nate gives me a tight smile and nods.

"So? Would you care to elaborate on what you meant with your last memory being about our father?"

"I think the picture in your NASA command center triggered something."

"My what?" He looks genuinely confused, and a laugh bubbles up in my throat.

"Your computer room upstairs."

The light bulb turns on, and he grins. "Oh, I guess that's a somewhat accurate description."

And just like that, everything is back at ease between us.

This is beyond disconcerting.

"I knew Brooks." I pause for a second before explaining. "I met him—at least once."

Nate goes rigid and sits up straight. "How?"

"My memories are never very long, but I'm a hundred percent sure it was Brooks. It must've been around the same time the picture upstairs was taken. I was at a park with Emily. Brooks was there. Emily introduced him as a friend. He shook my hand, and the way he looked at me...he knew who I was."

"Uh. This is...I...uh, I'm not sure what—" Nate's stammering tells me that this is as much a shock to him as it is to me.

"What does this mean?" It's a whisper because I'm as curious as I am terrified.

Nate's face has turned all shades of red, and his fists ball on top of the table.

"This means our father lied to me."

He pushes the chair back with so much force that it topples over and storms out of the kitchen.

That went well.

THE CLOCK in the kitchen tells me it's almost six in the evening. Do I go after Nate, or do I wait for him to come back to me? If I wait, will this impact my timeline to call Rhys?

I clean up everything I used for dinner and head toward the center of the house. Few lamps are on, but between the dwindling light coming through the floor-to-ceiling windows and the illumination along the hallway, I'm able to trace my way through the house. I wonder if there is a way to get to my room from the foyer; it's getting old always having to go through the kitchen.

Great, now I'm acting like this is my house.

I smack the palm of my hand against my forehead, and the sound echoes through the quiet entryway.

Climbing the stairs to the second floor, I turn right toward Nate's room. He really could be anywhere, but I'll start my search at his command center.

I need to come up with a shorter name for that room.

Slowly approaching the door, I hesitate. Do I knock? What if the door zaps me? I wouldn't put it past him to add something like that to his security measures. Oh, what the hell. I step in front of the door and knock. No zap. I wait. And wait some more. Nothing. Maybe the room is soundproof?

"Nate?" I call hesitantly.

Again nothing. What now? Still contemplating my next plan of action, Nate comes around the corner to the right of me—the west wing of the estate, if my orientation is correct.

"Lilly?" I immediately take note of his state of dishevelment. His sweater is gone, the white t-shirt rumpled, and a fine sheen of sweat covers his forehead.

"Uh, I was looking for you."

"You were?" He stops in front of me, eyebrows squished together.

Looks like his spyware didn't alert him—that's new.

The proximity stirs up polar opposite emotions. After his earlier outburst to my revelation of our father and Emily still being in touch years after their supposed affair, I have the urge to comfort him. I can relate to feeling betrayed by one's parents —more than he already was by Brooks's betrayal. To believe one thing and the truth being something different altogether. But the voice in my head tells me that I cannot feel sympathy for him. He is a criminal. He took children from their parents. He kidnapped me against my will. *But he's also your brother,* the other voice chimes in once more.

"I wanted to make sure you're okay. Are you...okay?"

Nate hangs his head. "My father swore up and down that the affair was over when he confessed everything after the funeral. I assumed he meant back when it first happened. I'm not so sure anymore."

His fists begin to ball again, and I do something that startles us both. I reach out and slide my hand in his. We both stare at our joined hands, and then our eyes lock. My brother's eyes are wide, disbelief written all over his face.

I squeeze his hand. "Do you want to talk about it? That's what helped me...I mean, uh, working through it all."

In one, lightning-fast move, he engulfs me in a bear hug and holds on tight. My body stiffens; that's the last reaction I expected from him. His chin rests on top of my head, and he whispers, "Thank you, Lilly." His voice cracks, and I'm as shocked as he is when I return his hug. His spine goes rigid at first before he relaxes again, and we stand like this for several minutes—brother and sister comforting each other.

We both loosen our hold at the same time and take a step back. Everything has changed. We both can feel it. How we move forward from here will need to be determined.

I follow Nate to the library he mentioned during our brief tour. The room is ginormous. Heather and Tristen's entire first floor could easily fit in here. Floor-to-ceiling bookshelves cover three of the walls, complete with a sliding ladder. The fourth wall is all windows. The combination of espresso-colored wooden shelves and floors, more of the same large leather couches as in the sitting room downstairs, and heavy moss-green curtains is completed with different oriental-looking rugs in the same shades of green, beige, and brown. This room has officially become my new favorite place. It's warm and inviting.

"Can I move in here?" I can't stop myself before the words come out in an awed whisper.

"Sure." Nate is completely genuine, and I stare at him, mouth agape.

"But I'm a prisoner. You can't just let me do whatever I want."

What the ever-loving——? It seems my brain-to-mouth connection is currently out of commission, and I peer at him like a deer in the headlights. So much for making progress in the brother-sister relationship department.

Nate goes completely still before he bursts into a fit of laughter. He all but howls until tears run down his cheeks, and he doubles over, holding his belly.

"Ow—tha-t hu-rt-s—"

I just stand there, watching him. Is this part of his less mentally stable side? Eventually, I get slightly annoyed and cross my arms in front of my chest, frowning.

Finally, he regains some composure and faces me straight on. "I'm sorry." Another giggle escapes him. An actual giggle from this grown-ass man. "Okay, sorry. Phew. Man, I haven't laughed like that in years."

I'm still confused about why he deemed this so funny.

"Um...why are you laughing exactly? I'm pretty sure I just insulted you."

He's totally serious now. "You didn't mean it," he deadpans. "That was clear as day written across your face when you realized what you said. Your face is very...expressive, and I think you would've looked less mortified if you'd punched me in the junk."

All the tension leaves me, and my mouth turns into a grin. "You're probably right. So, uh...what are we doing here?"

Nate walks over to one of the shelves on the farthest wall. Following him, I notice a slew of papers on the floor in front of it and between the closest couch. It immediately reminds me of my room when I started my research.

Nate squats down next to it and looks up. "I started going through my father's papers again."

That's when I realize that the bottom two rows on this wall

are filing cabinets with several of the drawers pulled out, revealing massive amounts of papers.

Nate points at the pile on the floor. "Those are the letters Emily sent. The ones I know about."

I crouch next to him. "What do you mean 'know about'?"

"After I found the first stack of letters from Emily at my parents' house—the letters that contained the pictures of you—I never looked at any of his shit again. I wanted nothing to do with him. His office at the firm was already packed up in boxes, and I shipped most of it up here. There is still a ton of paperwork at their LA house, but nothing of consequence. I started my research into Emily, and any other important documents came straight from the lawyers. I had no reason to look again—until now. I guess I just assumed that she kept sending him updates, and that's it."

I begin to understand what he means. "You think there has to be more?" This conversation gives me déjà vu. Rhys and I had the same type of exchange just a few months ago.

"I do."

Nate's gaze drops to my stomach, and I realize that my arms are wrapped around my midsection again.

"You do that every time you think of *him*." His tone is subdued, and I'm stunned by his perceptiveness. I can only nod, trying to swallow past the lump in my throat.

I squeeze my eyes shut and feel Nate placing a hand carefully on my shoulder. "Hey."

I peek at him from under my lashes, and he says, "We'll figure this out, okay?"

And with that, I lose it. I crumble to the floor and start sobbing. He has no idea that Rhys said almost the same exact words to me.

Rhys. Oh God. How can I sit here and make nice with the guy who kidnapped me?

Despite my inner turmoil, I let Nate pull me close and wrap his arms around me while I cry against his chest. He rocks me back and forth like a little child and mutters something that sounds like, "I'm sorry, I'm so sorry," over and over.

When I finally pull away from him, his eyes shine with unshed tears, and his mouth is in a flat line.

I whisper, "I want to go home."

Nate's gaze drops to his hands. "Okay."

CHAPTER EIGHT

LILLY

NATE LEADS ME BACK TO MY ROOM.

Even in my post-cry haze, I notice that we are not going through the kitchen. He walks past the double staircase that leads down to the first-floor foyer. I expect to see the same bend in the hallway as in the west wing; instead, we stop at another door. It looks like every other door we just passed, and if I hadn't learned the layout of the building by now, I would expect only to find one more room. Nate steps through, and we're standing in *my* hallway. My room is not two doors down, and I grumble, "You could've shown me this way earlier, instead of making me go through the kitchen every time."

Nate doesn't respond. He simply lets me walk past him. Everything is how I left it, and despite this not being my actual sanctuary, being in these lavender walls calms me instantly.

"I'll see you tomorrow," he says, and before I can respond, the door closes with a soft click.

Exhaustion takes over once more, and I fall face down onto the bed.

. . .

I WAKE UP WITH A START. The room is pitch black, and it takes a moment for my eyes to adjust. My dream has left me breathless. It was so vivid it almost felt like one of my memories.

RHYS and I were at Bones, eating dinner, when Brooks and Emily walked in. They sat down at a table nearby, talking animatedly, but I couldn't make out what they were saying. Emily was yelling at Brooks, who tried to calm her down. It was like they were in a soundproof bubble.

My focus went back to Rhys, who was scowling at me. "Babe, what's wrong?"

"I'm not sure. I think I know those people over there." I pointed to Brooks and Emily only to realize they were replaced with Nate and Katherine having a romantic candlelight dinner, holding hands.

What the hell?

"You should be happy that your psycho brother is finally out of your life." Rhys scoffed.

I turned to him and saw disgust written all over his face.

I was confused. "Nate is engaged to Margot. What is he doing here with Katherine?"

"Nate and Kat are married. You gave him an ultimatum—you or Kat. He chose Kat."

"He would never choose her over me. I'm his SISTER." My voice turned panicked.

"Then you and I can't be together. You made your choice." Contempt dripped off his voice.

NOW, sitting in my bed, panting, I massage my temple. That was — Shit, what was that? Leaning back into the pillow, I replay the words in my head. *I'm his sister.* I don't have to be a therapist to understand that, subconsciously, I've made my choice. I've accepted the fact that Nate is my brother. He would put me first, no matter what. I'm certain of that. Of course, there is still the issue of him being a criminal, and he has to pay for it, but first, he is my brother. Hands in front of my eyes, I exhale a shuttering breath.

All of this because I picked the wrong topic for my journalism paper. Or was it the right one?

THROWING BACK THE COMFORTER, I get up and dress in yesterday's clothes, adding a thick black hoodie due to the chilly temperature at night. There is no way I'll fall back asleep. Barefoot, I pad back to the library. Thankfully, a dim hallway illumination remains on at night, or Nate did this for my benefit. Either way, it helps to find the library. Everything is as we left it.

I settle in the middle of the pile of papers and start pulling individual pieces out. They're all handwritten letters from Emily to Brooks, dating back over several years. I briefly wonder why she would write by hand instead of emailing him but then dismiss the thought. It's not really important. I start putting them in order until I have a neat pile in front of me. Then, I begin to read.

The very first one is dated eight months before I was born. Emily tells Brooks how glad she is that she visited Heather during her conference, and she never thought she'd meet someone like him, how much she misses him, etcetera. At the mention of Heather's name, my heart rate doubles. Did she know? Emily was Heather's best friend. According to Rhys's recollection, Emily and Henry were already married at the time, which means she cheated on her husband. What kind of woman was Emily? Rage surges up inside of me, and I fight the urge to rip the piece of paper to shreds. I read each letter in detail and, based on the way Emily phrased things, it's clear they contained pictures. I wonder if seeing them would trigger more memories. Emily mentions how tall I've grown and the uncanny resemblance to "my father." She means Brooks, not Henry—*her husband*. The dates are pretty spaced out, and I'm starting to understand where Nate was coming from. They are superficial; if someone—Payton, for example—would find them, it just seems that Emily kept Brooks up to date on his illegitimate daughter. But nothing points toward the affair still being ongoing.

When I'm through all of them, I sit back and lean against the back of the couch. I've learned more about myself, but nothing of consequence about Emily and Brooks's relationship. I know that I had a teddy named Bobo that came from Brooks and that I never let it out of my sight. I have to ask Rhys if he remembers that teddy. Apparently, I also got my peach allergy from Brooks. Interesting. In one letter, Emily describes that I'm getting more and more daring, playing with Heather's son, climbing trees, balancing on the top of the swing set, and that she thinks she should enroll me in gymnastics. That makes me smile because it relates to two of my favorites—Rhys and gymnastics.

It's the type of information I've been hoping to learn about myself, but the fact that I find it here, in the house my half-brother brought me to against my will, is almost comical.

My stomach starts growling, and I look over the back of the couch. The clock on one of the shelves shows it's almost five in the morning. I decide to take a break to get some caffeine and food. At home, it's already past my usual breakfast time.

Home. Rhys. God, I hope Nate comes through with the call today.

Twenty minutes later, I'm back in my spot; next to me is a steaming mug of tea and a plate with yet another muffin. I've consumed more carbs in the last three months than in the past few years.

Pulling open the drawer to the left to see what kind of files this one hides, I start taking out stacks of yellow manila folders. The first few are annual tax returns, nothing of interest to me.

The fifth folder, however, draws my attention. The first page is a bank statement, Brooks's name on the top, and initially, I don't think anything of it. My eyes scan over it, and most transactions are your usual day-to-day expenses—gas station charges, little amounts for something that looks like a coffee house. Nothing out of the ordinary until my gaze stops at a number with way too many zeros. This can't be a regular expense. Brooks transferred fifteen thousand dollars to an account that's only listed with an account number. No merchant or accountholder name. Every other transaction is meticulously labeled with some information on what the charge is for. I flip to the next statement, and there it is—same date of the month, same amount. Brooks transfers the same amount every month for two years from what looks like his personal bank account. Every so often, there is an even more significant number coming in. I make a note to ask Nate about that later. After the two years, the amount increased to twenty-five thousand dollars.

Where does he get that kind of money as a patent attorney?

I set the bank statements aside to not mix them up with the rest of the pile and focus on the next yellow folder. I find the closing documents for a house in Los Angeles dated around the time Nate was born. Not relevant. Moving on.

I pull several financial documents and legal papers from the next folder. Audrey's name is on the top of the first stack neatly stapled at the corner, and further reading reveals that it's a trust fund Payton and Brooks set up for her. I flip to the following one, and my hands freeze. There, in black and white, is my name. Not my current name but my birth name: Lilly Ann Sumner.

What. The. Fuck?

My hands shake while I turn the pages. When I come to the page that contains the amount of the trust fund, I drop the entire stack. My hands fly to my mouth, and I'm sure my eyes are about to pop out of their sockets. This can't be real.

"Holy shit!" I whisper against my hands.

Gingerly picking the pages back up, I sit there staring at it. My brain has stopped processing information; all I can do is count the black digits over and over.

I must've stayed like this for quite some time because, all of a sudden, I hear the door open, and Nate stumbles around the couch.

"There you are." The last word is drawn out as he yawns. I can't peel my eyes away from the paper. My hands are clasped around it so tightly that it's starting to wrinkle.

"Lilly? What is it?" He squats down next to me and tries to catch my eye. But I can't look away. Ten million dollars. TEN. MILLION. DOLLARS. There must be a mistake. Where did Brooks get that kind of money?

Finally, I'm able to turn my head; my eyes remain glued to the number until I can't see it anymore, and then my gaze meets Nate's. Eyes narrowed, he's trying to figure out what's wrong with me.

Carefully, like handing him a bomb, I start extending my arms. Both hands remain wrapped around the pile until Nate pries it from my grasp. He scans the first page, and his eyebrows shoot up to his hairline. Seems he wasn't aware of it either. He flips the first page, second page, third page—bingo. His wide eyes snap to mine and ping-pong between my face and the paper several times before he ungracefully plumps on his butt.

"Ho-ly shit!"

A giggle bubbles up in my throat, and his focus is back on me, narrowing his eyes as if to assess if I've finally lost it.

"We"—more giggles—"we tru-ly are re-la-ted." My hands are covering my mouth to hide my idiotic expression.

"Yes?" His head slants to the side.

The giggles subside and I explain, "I had the exact same reaction. It's pretty funny, given the circumstances." I shrug one shoulder and smirk.

Nate's mouth tilts up in the corner. "I guess so."

"What does this mean?" I nod toward the papers in his hands. I feel like I am back in control of my thoughts.

"This"—he waves the document in front of me—"means that *you*, little sister, are rich!"

Why? How?

Nate keeps scanning the pages, and his eyes widen several times before his gaze settles back on me.

"I stand corrected. You are *more* than rich."

"WHAT!" I tear the pages from his hand and flip through it. I have no clue what I'm looking for, though. My gaze swivels back to him. "What does it say?"

"We need to find my father's will. But if this document is accurate, your trust fund has been accumulating for the last fifteen years, plus there is one passage that refers to his wealth if something would happen to him."

"But—" Words leave me. I'm back in shock mode.

Nate rubs his face. "Here is what we're going to do. First, I need to prepare your call; give me a few hours to set everything up. Then, we will *tear* this fucking library apart and find out what was really going on ten years ago." The anger in his voice sends a shiver down my spine.

"You'll still let me call Rhys?" I sound hesitant, almost timid.

"I told you I would, didn't I?" He looks genuinely offended.

"You did...but I figured..." I trail off.

Nate places his hand under my chin and makes sure I look straight at him. "Lilly, *you* are *my* sister. My *only* living relative, and when I tell you I will do something for you, I will do it, no matter what. Okay?"

The seriousness in his tone causes my pulse to increase.

CHAPTER NINE

LILLY

NATE LEAVES ME ALONE IN THE LIBRARY WITH THE PROMISE TO get the call ready as quickly as possible. I keep sifting through two more drawers before I give up and trudge back to my room to shower and change.

All clean, I want to lie down for a minute to rest my eyes, but I must've been more tired than I thought because I wake up with the sun high in the sky.

That's what you get for waking up in the middle of the night.

I MAKE my way across the second floor—not the kitchen—to Nate's spy center.

Knocking once, I don't have to wait long. I look him up and down and burst out laughing. *What the—?* He is still wearing the pajama pants he slumped into the library with, but up top, he wears a crisp white cufflink shirt with a navy-blue tie, his blond hair styled impeccably.

He scowls at me. "I had to take a call from the board of directors."

That immediately dampens my amusement. If Nate was working, he wasn't setting up my call. He picks up on the shift of my mood and opens the door wider for me to step in.

Every single monitor is lit up. The top three show a dozen different security-camera feeds from all across the estate. Looking closer, I can see the pictures change every so often to a news feed.

How many cameras are on this property?

The bottom three show different news channels, as well as something—I'm guessing, the stock exchange? But to be honest, I have no idea. Lots of numbers and graphs, totally over my head.

My gaze swings to the desk, and the remaining laptop—the one that didn't end up against the wall—has some sort of documents displayed. The two other monitors have...what is that? Command line windows? I turn to Nate, who watches me take everything in. He doesn't hide anything this time; he lets me see it all.

"I'm sorry I'm not done. Hank called with an urgent issue that couldn't wait. But I should be done soon."

"How long have you known Hank?"

"He's been with me since the day I took over. He was an intern at the time and worked his way up. His grandfather was a friend of mine. He can be a pain in the ass, but he's been a good friend. All the senior guys still see me as the..." He leaves the sentence hanging. He's referring to his stay at the mental hospital.

Maybe they're not so far off, given the fact that...

"Does Hank know?"

Nate blinks at me. "About...? Oh. No. He has no idea about you or..." *The girls.*

I take a deep breath. "Eventually, we have to talk about that."

Silence.

"Yes, we do." Nate looks at his feet. "But let's get your call done first, okay?"

If we start on the other topic now and you hear what I have to say,
I'm not sure I'll get my call.

"Okay." I try to give him something resembling an encouraging smile, but I'm not sure I succeed.

Settling back behind the desk, Nate's fingers start flying across the keyboard, and I can see him work in both command line windows simultaneously. The programming courses in school have always come easy to me, and I guess I know now from which side I inherited that trade. I'm not computer illiterate by any means, but seeing Nate at work makes me feel like Grandma Ruth when she decided to use the self-checkout line to save time. None of the produce had a bar code, and, in the end, the poor employee manning the self-scanners ended up being the object of Grandma Ruth's target practice when she whipped celery and carrots at his face, followed by her dropping several F-bombs and leaving without her groceries. To this day, she refuses to set foot into that store again. Chuckling, I shake myself out of the memory and watch Nate, fascinated. I have no clue what he's doing.

All of a sudden, a phone starts ringing, and I jump. I haven't heard that sound in so long, and I frantically look for the device. Zeroing in on the desk, I realize it's not mine, but nonetheless, my heart stops a beat. Taking a step closer, I take in the picture on the screen. A stunningly beautiful woman with an elegant hairdo and evening gown smiles back with brilliant white teeth.

Nate catches me staring and answers my unspoken question. "Margot."

"She's gorgeous."

He smiles. "She is."

"Don't you want to get that?"

He hesitates. "Uh, not right now. She probably wants to tell me about all the trouble she and Ce-Ce are causing in the south of France."

"Oh, wow. That uh...that sounds fun. *Who* is Ce-Ce?" I don't want to be nosy, but I am. He's talking openly with me about everything, and I'm soaking it in like a sponge.

"Julian's fiancée. Celeste. He calls her Ce-Ce, and every so often, I slip and use the nickname. J is the only one getting away with it, though. She hates it." Nate chuckles.

Why does the thought of him having a best friend surprise me? He does have a life despite his, uh...other side. The topic keeps creeping up, and we will cover it in the near future, if I want to or not.

The ringing stops, and Nate clears the screen and starts typing again. A few minutes later, he looks over his shoulder. "I should be done in an hour or two."

Two hours?

I get to talk to Rhys in two hours. My pulse speeds up, and the insides of my palms dampen in anticipation.

When I don't move, Nate says, "I'll come find you. You should go eat something; you haven't had anything since early this morning." And as if on cue, my stomach rumbles.

I guess I could use some nourishment.

THAT'S where Nate finds me two hours later, as promised. Although, I didn't eat. I made food, but it's still sitting untouched in front of me. Before I could take my first bite, I thought about hearing Rhys's voice, my mouth went dry, and my hands were shaking so bad that I couldn't bring the fork to my mouth without losing everything on it in the process.

What am I going to say to him? He's probably worried out of his mind.

"You didn't eat."

Looking up, Nate drops into his usual chair.

"No."

"Talk to me." Eyebrows knit together, concern is written all over his face.

"I'm scared." It's a whisper.

OUT OF THE DARK • 75

"About?"

"What am I going to tell him?"

Nate draws in a breath and exhales slowly while looking out the window. "You're going to tell him that you will explain everything to him and that you will call him again soon."

"Am I?" I'm too scared to hope.

My brother stretches across the table as if to take my hand, but with the table being the size of a one-bedroom apartment, he can't reach me and places his hands, palm down, on the table.

"Yes, you will. As for the actual explaining, keep it to a minimum for now."

I contemplate his words. I will talk to Rhys again. I have no reason to doubt Nate's words.

"Ready?" He looks at me expectantly.

Pushing back from the table, I exhale. "Ready."

I'M SITTING on the leather couch with the headset Nate handed me a minute ago.

"You'll have two minutes."

I raise my eyebrows. "Not thirty seconds?" I'm joking —mostly.

Nate snorts. "I'm better than that. I could give you ten, and they wouldn't trace the call. But you and I need to work out some things before you have a longer chat with your boyfriend." He says the last part so seriously that I feel slapped in the face.

Has my desire to have a brother clouded my judgment too much?

"Okay, here we go. Stick to what we said earlier."

I nod and put the headset on. My heart is in my throat, and I wipe my palms on my pants. The phone starts ringing in my ear, and my breath hitches. Come on, come on, come on—nothing. Rhys's voicemail picks up, but before I can even listen to his recording, Nate hangs up and dials again. This repeats two more times, and I can't hide my panic.

"He's not answering. What if something happened to him?"

"Nothing happened to him." Nate speaks with such conviction that I wonder what he's done to be so sure.

He dials again, and this time, it only rings four times before someone accepts the call. When I don't hear anything, I look up at Nate, who motions for me to talk with his hand.

"Rhys?"

Please don't have anyone else pick up his phone.

A strangled sob travels through the earpiece, and my heart breaks into a million shards of glass. What have I done, playing family while my love thinks the worst?

"Are you there?"

Please say something.

"Yes." His response is barely audible, but no matter how low, I would recognize his voice anywhere.

An instant calm settles over me. My anchor. I smile. "Hey."

"Cal, I'm so sor—" I avoid looking at Nate; I'm sure he's listening in anyway.

"It's okay. I don't have much time."

That seems to get Rhys's attention. "Where are you? Did he hurt you?"

Shit.

Out of the corner of my eye, I note Nate is making a motion to move on. He *is* listening in.

"I'm fine. That's why I'm calling. I...I just wanted to let you know that I'm safe. I'm fine." What am I saying? I sound insane.

"What do you mean? Is he threatening you? Where are you? The house was taken over by the FBI; they will find you." He's getting louder, and I look with wide eyes at Nate.

FBI?

My half-brother gives a casual shrug as if that's the most normal thing in the world. He knows, and I understand that they have nothing on him. The call is untraceable.

I wonder if they even know that I'm not a McGuire?

"No, they won't. This call can't be traced." I exhale slowly. "I...I just wanted to hear your voice. And tell you that I'm okay.

I'll explain everything to you when I see you." I avert my eyes from Nate. He had said *call him again*, not *see*.

"What are you talking about? Babe, where are you? See me when?" He is full-on shouting, and the panic laced with anger is clearly noticeable.

Nate snaps his fingers to get my attention and makes a "wrap it up" motion. No! It's not been two minutes. I send him a pleading look, but he shakes his head. "I have to go. I'll call again. Please tell them to stop looking for me. They won't find me." I rush everything out as fast as I can.

"Please don't hang up."

Tears start welling up in my eyes, hearing his desperation, and I whisper, "I have to go." Swallowing a sob, I add, "I'll see you soon."

Click.

"Rhys?" I yell into the headpiece, even though I know he's no longer there.

"I'm sorry, Lilly."

"THAT WAS LESS THAN TWO MINUTES!" I roar with tears running down my face.

"His phone is bugged," Nate says calmly.

"Bugged?" I echo, incredulous, all fury gone. "Can they trace it?"

"No." He doesn't elaborate. Simply no.

"What's the problem then?" I don't understand.

Nate leans back in his chair, crossing his arms over his chest. "The problem is that someone was listening. You just told him you're fine—that you're *safe*. They will hear that and start asking questions. How can you be fine if you are held against your will?"

Oh.

"What are we going to do now? I told him I would call him again." Panic starts building up, and my nails dig into the leather of the couch.

"You will talk to him again, but we need to get the story straight. And we need a different way to contact him."

I cover my face with my hands and let my entire upper body rest on my thighs. I'm not going to lose it; I'm not going to lose it; fuck, I am going to lose it. I jump up and start pacing with my hands interlaced behind my neck. This cannot be happening.

"We can contact him through Wes...or Den. They can get him out of the house."

Nate watches me. "Okay."

"We need to figure out what the deal with Emily and Brooks was; something is off."

"I agree." There is no emotion in his response.

I fully face him and swallow several times before I get the next words out. "And we need to talk about what you did and how you are going to make it right." I almost said *pay for it,* but the phrase feels wrong. He has done terrible things; there is no excuse for taking a girl from her home, no matter what the motivation was. But I also learned a lot of good about him in the last few days, and deep down, I believe he will listen to me.

"We will, and I will make it right."

CHAPTER TEN

HER

I DIAL GRAY'S NUMBER FOR THE THIRD TIME—NO ANSWER. *HOW dare he ignore my calls; he knows better. Especially after the news he broke to me the day before.*

THE SOUND *of the infinity pool's water is like a rushing river. I massage my temples, but it's not helping. Neither the cloudless sky nor the azure-colored water of the ocean I can see in the distance calms my nerves today.*

I adore this house, which was why I refused to move after our time in this location was up. People sooner or later ask questions, but this property reminds me of the only person I ever loved. Instead, I replaced the staff and ensured none of the old would be able to talk.

Last night still has me on edge. That irritating tremor in my right arm hasn't stopped, and my head is throbbing. When that idiot doctor is done upstairs, we're going to have a friendly little chat. He assured me this would stop after the new injections. I tip my chin with my index finger—it might be time to replace the medical staff as well.

. . .

I USE my left hand to reach over to the small square wooden table and pick up the glass with the 2002 Chateau Lafite Rothschild I had Elise pull from the wine cellar. She gave me her usual disapproving look when she brought it out but knows better than to voice her opinions. She is not being paid to think. Plus, she heard what I did to the last maid that refused my request.

It's only nine, but since I haven't slept since the alarm went off at one a.m., it might as well be afternoon. My gaze lands on the monitor sitting on the table. The screen is linked to the camera in his bedroom—he's sleeping. Good, the new sedative seems to be working. That's at least something the staff managed to do right in the last twenty-four hours. I watch our personal physician move around the room and check all the vitals. If he would've gotten to the house phone in the hallway, all hell would've broken loose.

I grab my cell phone next to the monitor and send a voice message to my head of maintenance to remove that phone. I dislike voice messages, but my right hand won't obey to type, and my left is holding the wine.

It's the first time he got that far. I may have to add the restraints back to his bed. I'm not going to risk him ruining everything. Not now. Not ever.

THE COINCIDENCE of that happening the same night I get the call about Lilly's disappearance is not lost on me. I've had my eyes on her for years, but when Gray called to tell me that he hasn't been able to locate her in several days, it was clear the only other person interested in Lilly found her again.

AND SO IT BEGINS.

CHAPTER ELEVEN

RHYS

I'M FINALLY ALONE.

In the kitchen, Dad and our *houseguests* kept going over the conversation so many times that, eventually, I tuned them out. One guy kept looking between me and his laptop as if he was comparing something. I replayed Lilly's words over and over in my head—the way she sounded, what she said. She wasn't scared. Then, the agent in charge focused on my father and made a comment that caused me to snap back to attention.

"Miss McGuire said she is safe. What do you think she meant by that?"

I sure as shit hadn't mentioned that particular phrase. Something is off. My father eyed me, assessing if I was listening. I averted my gaze and looked back down at my hands.

"I'm not sure. Let's go over the other case files again." I wonder if he tried to divert the conversation while I was in the room or if there was something in the other files that would help.

Up until then, Mom had been sitting silently next to me at the table. "Excuse me. I'm going to lie down."

She stood up and left the room without waiting for anyone's response or a backward glance. I took that as my opportunity to flee as well.

I caught up to her on the second floor. "Mom?"

She turned, her eyes red-rimmed and her usually perfect eye makeup smeared. I'd never seen her that exhausted. She loves Lilly like a daughter, and where Dad is *unusually* calm, she is the opposite. I haven't seen either of my parents like that. I can only explain it that Dad is in full-on military mode, and Mom is— well, she is the mother whose daughter disappeared.

"Yes, honey?"

We've never been super affectionate, besides with Natty. I think forcing me to keep Lilly's secret drove a wedge between us years ago. "Uh, do you need anything?"

She gave me a tight smile and took a step closer, touching her hand to the side of my face.

"No, honey. I just need to lie down for a bit. The call was a good sign; it was just...it was a lot. For both of us."

Her comment startled me.

Does she know?

I nodded, and she released my cheek, disappearing to the third floor.

CLOSING the door behind me in my room now, I immediately zero in on my phone. I want to call Wes or Denielle and tell them about Lilly, but I can't shake the feeling that something is off. The agent knew what she said without me telling them. There is only one explanation, and my father allowing this to happen makes my hackles rise.

I glance at the spot on the floor I occupied not too long ago after Lilly hung up on me. The walls start to close in, and I can't breathe. I need to get out. Pulling my boots on, I slip a hoodie over my head, not bothering with a jacket. I grab my keys and barrel down the stairs. I can hear my father call after me as I sprint to my car in the driveway. Pulling out, the silhouettes of two men appear in the doorway, but I back out of the driveway without slowing down. I'm glad Wes left the Defender in the driveway when he drove us home. If I would've had to go through the kitchen to get to my car, I wouldn't have been able to leave that easily.

SEVERAL HOURS LATER, I let myself in, unannounced, to Wes's house through the side door. It's the middle of the night, but having had a key for years, no one in the Sheats's household bats an eye anymore when I walk in at all hours. However, this time, when I round the corner to the kitchen, I find Wes and Denielle huddled at the table. Wes's parents are on the opposite side, mugs in front of them. Four exhausted sets of eyes swivel to me, and I stop in my tracks. Denielle's usually impeccably applied mascara is smudged, and even Wes's eyes show red rims.

What the fuck is going on?

Before I can say anything, Denielle launches herself out of the chair, fresh tears running down her face, and I can barely brace myself for the impact before she tackles me. Denielle is taller than Lilly, and with her wearing her usual heels—even in the middle of the night—she is almost my height. Her arms wind around my midsection and squeeze so tightly I have trouble breathing.

"We didn't know where you were," she hiccups into my neck.

I return her embrace and blink rapidly. I want to be strong for my friends who have been my support for the last few days. I mumble, "She's fine," into Denielle's hair, which makes Wes look up from his place at the table. He's been my best friend for ten years, but I've never seen him anything but joking or with a tough exterior. Wes is like me; we don't show vulnerability. But looking at him now, it sinks in how the last few days have impacted him as well. His eyes are bloodshot and have dark circles. Like me, he hasn't shaved since Tuesday morning.

I untangle one arm from Den and hold it out to Wes, who doesn't hesitate and stands up from his chair. Wrapping his arms around both of us, I feel him shudder, and my control snaps, tears streaking my cheeks and soaking Denielle's hair. At school, all three of us are *the tough ones*. We're at the top. We don't show weakness. But right now, we stand in a tangle of arms and hold onto each other. Supporting each other.

I hear footsteps leave the room and turn my head to see Mr. and Mrs. Sheats's retreating forms. My guess is they want to give us space.

Wes steps back first and rubs his eyes with the heel of his hands. "Let's go to my room. We have something for you."

Huh?

Denielle mirrors Wes's motion, but it only results in her creating more black streaks under her eyes. She has taken Lilly's disappearance just as hard and keeps holding onto my arm as we follow Wes. I'm still confused why she is at Wes's house in the middle of the night, but I figure with Charlie at school, Wes is the only other person for her to lean on. It's not like I'm very useful these days.

Once inside, I drop into my usual spot on his couch, and Denielle sits close beside me. Wes walks over to his desk, grabbing his laptop. While he walks back over to me, he types in something, and I raise my eyebrows.

"Since when do you have a password?"

"Since two hours ago," Wes deadpans. He holds the computer out to me, and I scan the screen. HOLY FUCK! I tear the device out of his hands and place it onto my thighs. Denielle leans in but doesn't say anything.

SENDER: *UNKNOWN*
Subject: Rhys McGuire
Message:
Weston,

Or should I call you Wes? I'm contacting you despite my better judgment. Lilly believes that you are trustworthy and that you can reach Rhys without the FBI or his father knowing.

Before I get to the reason for this message, let me begin with, you prefer hot cocoa over coffee but pretend with your "buddies" that you drink your coffee black. Let me ask you, do the cool kids drink their coffee black these days? When did that become a thing?

Your history shows that every night before you go to bed, you check the local and world news, followed by the stock market. You are not the dumb jock you want your peers to think you are. Which brings me to the following question: why? But this is a topic for a later, in-person discussion.

As for this message, I promised Lilly two minutes, but her phone call to Rhys was cut short due to an unfortunate bug infestation on the other end. Not that this would've made the call more traceable. So far, no one has been able to trace me. But Lilly revealed information that was solely meant for her boyfriend's ears, and I had to step in. She was not happy when I disconnected the call, and despite my assurance of her speaking with him again soon, I realize soon is not fast enough. I do not like to see her unhappy.

You will receive a delivery that needs to be handed over to Rhys. Lilly will call him tomorrow at 6:30 p.m. to finish their conversation.

Here are the rules:

1. No one besides the people currently in your room is to know about this message, or there will be no call.

2. At the time of the call, Rhys is to be in the same spot where Lilly's favorite picture of them was taken, or there will be no call.

3. If anyone—and I mean ANYONE—is in the vicinity of Rhys at the time of the call, there will be no call.

I apologize for involving you and Denielle in this exchange, but Lilly's well-being is of utmost importance, and it seems her talking to Rhys is an integral part of it.

Rhys and I will have a separate conversation as to how he believes he is good enough for her after spending two years with Cheerleader Barbie.

This email is untraceable, but for Lilly and Rhys's ability to talk, I must advise you again: DO NOT share this message with anyone besides the three people involved in this exchange.

I. WILL. KNOW.

P.S.: Please tell Denielle that she should get the bird excrement on her Audi's hood taken care of. Unless she doesn't plan to trade it in again next year. I did prefer her last model, though—much more her style.

I STARE at the words on the screen, trying to comprehend what I've just read. I mean, I do understand the words, but...how? I glance up and find both Wes and Denielle watching me. Then something clicks—*involving you and Denielle.* I zero in on the girl next to me. She must've sensed that I caught on, because she reaches behind her, pulling out a cell phone from the back pocket of her jeans.

What. The. Fuck?

"This is for you." Her tone is flat as she holds it out. I can't tell if she's upset that she got dragged into this—more than she already was—or what? My hands won't obey and take the small gadget from her. My gaze ping-pongs between the phone, Denielle, and my best friend.

"How?" is all I can muster before my voice cracks.

Wes plops down at the foot of his bed and faces the couch.

"The email came a few hours ago. Your father had just called, telling me that you took off and asked if you were here. You left your phone?" He scowls at me. "I tried to reach you."

I don't respond; I just hold his gaze, and Wes nods. The bug infestation.

"They called me, too, but I just told your dad that I hadn't seen you since I left your house. I was about to go to bed when I got this." Denielle wiggles the phone in her hand.

"How?" My entire vocabulary is reduced to one word.

Wes leans forward and rests his interlaced hands on his thighs, looking at me.

"After I read the email, I puked in my fucking trash can." Shaking his head, he nods toward the now empty and clean basket next to his desk. "How does he know these things about me?"

I would like to know the same thing.

I know about the cocoa-coffee deception, but only because we ride to school enough that he can't hide the smell from me. He's never admitted it, though, always pretending it was black coffee—extra strong. However, I didn't know about his news obsession. My stomach clenches. I don't care that he's interested in the world's affairs, but I thought I knew everything about my best friend. And the knowledge that the psycho stalker knows more than me about Wes rubs me the wrong way.

Before I can question him further, Denielle speaks up. "I got a text message to check the door around ten, and I found this on the doormat with a note to go to Wes's." She holds the flat phone in the palm of her hand. "Guess he knew you'd be turning up here at one point or another."

"Why are you so calm?" I narrow my eyes at her. Where Wes is freaked out, she is entirely composed. It's unnerving.

Denielle snorts. "Oh, I'm not calm. I dropped the thing like it was on fire and hid in my closet for a good thirty minutes, hyperventilating. How Lilly can function at all is beyond me," she says, sarcasm dripping off her voice.

"She was still in the closet when I called her," Wes chuckles.

Denielle glares at him. "Fuck you, asshat; at least I didn't hurl."

Wes flips her off, and I can't hold back. "Why did you never tell me about the news?"

"That's what you care about?" Wes stares at me incredulously.

"I thought I was your best friend?" I'm acting like a ten-year-old but can't stop myself.

"Oh, you thought I was your best friend. What about you? Why didn't you tell me that you're in love with your sister—who is not your sister? You've been hiding at my house for years, and I just took your dumbass excuses." Wes sneers at me.

"Are you fucking kidding me? I couldn't tell Lilly, but I should've told you?" He can't be serious. I rake my hands through my hair and grab a fistful, pulling on it.

"WHO. THE. FUCK. CARES!" Denielle barks. "Get it together, BOTH OF YOU! You act like fucking imbeciles." Then, she turns to me. "And stop always raking your hands through your freaking hair; it'll decrease your hairline."

What?

"Fuck." My hands let go of my hair, and I rub them over my face then focus on the only two people I can trust these days. "You're right; I'm sorry. The psycho has Lilly, who acts like she's on vacation, my phone is bugged, and that freak knows more about us than we know about each other."

"What do you mean she acts like she's on vacation?" Denielle whispers, squinting at me.

I exhale to the count of five before I recap the phone call to them, followed by what I picked up from the agent in the kitchen. My suspicion was confirmed by the email; my father allowed them to bug my phone. Or was it always bugged? Is that why they never cared where I was? They already knew. My hands curl into fists and squeeze so tight that my nails leave crescent indentations on my palms.

"Do you think the dude brainwashed Lilly somehow?" Wes asks hesitantly.

"I don't know," I sigh.

We sit in silence, all in our heads for what seems like forever, when the phone that now lies between Denielle and me lights up with an incoming text message. As in the past, it merely shows UNKNOWN.

I peer at the little square next to me and can feel two sets of eyes focused on me.

"Rhys?" Denielle prods.

I carefully pick up the phone and stare a moment longer before swiping right to open the message.

Rhys,

I see you got my message and package.

I want to remind you again to adhere to the rules if you want to talk to your girlfriend tomorrow.

She is fine and wishes all three of you a good night.

I think I'm going to be sick. I definitely can't fault Wes for puking. This. Is. Fucked. Up. Instinctively, I glance around as if to find a camera attached to a drone hovering outside the window.

"What does it say?" Wes's tone is hesitant but curious.

I hold the phone out to him, but he doesn't take it, just reads the screen. I get it; I wouldn't touch this thing either if I had a choice.

"I feel watched." Denielle shudders beside me.

"No shit." Wes rolls his eyes.

I don't like how this psycho is playing with us. I doubt there is a camera in here, but he knows we're together. This only leaves two alternatives: he is either out there right now or has someone watching us, which means there is more than one.

Logic should tell me to contact the authorities stationed at my house immediately, but the urge to hear Lilly's voice leaves no room, even remotely, to consider that.

"Can I stay here until tomorrow?" I ask Wes. Not that he has ever said no, but the circumstances have changed. I'd understand if he wants this phone and me out of his house.

"Sure, man. It's probably best if neither of us is alone." He turns to Denielle. "You need to call home?"

"No, my parents know I'm here. I called them before I came over. I had no intention of going back tonight."

"They're still gone?"

When are her parents ever home?

"Again. They were home for two days, but Mom left with Dad for his conference in San Fran. Agnes is at the house, but it's not like I need supervision anymore."

Agnes is the Kellers' live-in housekeeper slash Denielle's nanny growing up. She's worked for them for as long as we've known Den. One would think her mom would stay behind, given the fact her daughter's best friend disappeared and all, but I guess everyone handles things differently. Plus, knowing Denielle, she also puts up a strong front for her parents. This week was the first time she has allowed me to see her as anything but stone-cold and confident. She's Lilly's rock where I'm her anchor, as Lilly said to me one night when we were lying in her bed.

"Let's try to get some rest. Den, you take the bed. Rhys, you know the drill. I'll go get more blankets."

Wes leaves the room, and I head into his closet to grab my pillow and blanket that took permanent residence there years ago. I send my mom a quick text from Wes's phone, and despite the early-morning hour, she responds immediately, letting me know to be safe.

Sleep does not come that night. Instead, I'm hiding under the blanket, staring at the phone's screen. **She is fine and wishes all three of you a good night.**

I start typing several times and erase it again.

Fuck, what am I doing?

The little clock at the top of the screen shows it's 3:12 a.m., and despite my physical exhaustion, I'm unable to sleep. After one last deliberation, I cave. What's he gonna do? Stalk me some more? Or maybe he'll kidnap me and I'd be back with Lilly. My thoughts are in a state between sleep deprivation and borderline crazy.

I type: **Please tell Lilly good night. And I love her.**

I'm about to turn the device off when the bubble with the three little dots appears. Sucking in a breath, my heart beats so fast I have trouble catching my breath. The blanket is suffocating me, but I don't dare take it off and alert Den or Wes to what I'm doing. The bubble disappears, and internally I start panicking. No, no, no—

Then the message appears: **ILY2. It's late. Please get some rest. We'll talk tomorrow. ~Calla**

My eyes sting, and I blink. It's her. Sure, he could know my nickname for her—he knows everything as it seems—but somehow, there's no question in my mind.

Another one pops up: **You need to delete my texts. Wes and Den cannot know. Please trust me.**

I stare at the words for several hours before I finally delete both right before sleep overtakes me. I trust Lilly with my life.

CHAPTER TWELVE

LILLY

I'M TOO WIRED; THERE IS NO WAY I WILL SLEEP ANYTIME SOON tonight. The sound of fear and desperation in Rhys's voice plays on repeat in my head. Guilt is choking me. I'm playing family with my criminal half-brother, while the family who raised me is going out of its mind. I couldn't even tell Rhys how much I love him.

I beg Nate to let me call him back, but his answer remains a firm *no*. He's right, because me being safe either means I'm brainwashed, or I'm collaborating with a criminal—which, I guess, I am.

Oh God, what am I doing?

NATE SAYS he needs to get work done and kicks me out with the vague assurance that we will figure out the next steps tomorrow.

Not hungry and unsure what else to do, I head back to the library. I wonder if this place has a gym. I'm in desperate need of a distraction. My gaze falls onto the financial statements I put on one of the upper shelves to not lose track of them. I forgot to tell Nate about them earlier—being distracted with the whole call situation and all. Something else I have to do later. I can't shake the feeling that these transactions mean something.

I've made my way through two more drawers, which as far as I can see only contain Brooks's old case files, when Nate saunters in with an open laptop in hand. He plops down on the couch I'm sitting behind and leans over the back of it.

"Anything interesting?" He has a suspicious gleam in his eyes, which I choose to ignore.

"As a matter of fact, yes."

His eyebrows shoot up, and I stand to retrieve the bank statements, handing them over.

"Look toward the bottom of the page." I point at the amount. "He transfers that amount every month for years before it increases from fifteen to twenty-five thousand dollars. All the accounts and transactions are meticulously labeled, except this one."

Nate flips through a few pages before he looks up. "It's the same account number every time?"

I nod.

"I'll look into it. Shouldn't take too long." He grins up at me. "Good work, sis." His praise, coupled with the endearment, makes my cheeks heat.

I can no longer ignore the mischievous look he gives me. He looks like a little kid who's done something naughty.

Narrowing my eyes, I peer over to the laptop screen. I freeze, instantly recognizing the location of the photo that's taking up most of the screen. Something like an email is partially hidden behind it.

"Nate," I start cautiously, "what did you do?" I can't pry my eyes from the house and three cars displayed on the screen. I would recognize Wes's house anywhere, but the red 4Runner, Denielle's Audi, and Rhys's Defender are a dead giveaway.

"I made sure you get to talk to your boyfriend sooner rather than later," my half-brother says with a smug face.

Oh. No.

I'm scared to ask. "How exactly did you do that?"

"I had an untraceable phone delivered to your friend, Denielle, and the instructions for the call to Wes," he says as if he's simply telling me it rained earlier today.

"YOU DID WHAT?" I shriek and dive for the laptop. He relinquishes it without a fight, and I click on the email in the background. My eyes grow wider with every line I read until I feel like they're about to pop out of their sockets.

I re-read the message twice before I close my eyes and take a moment to not go ballistic on my half-brother. Opening them again, I face the man in front of me and level him with what I hope is a death glare.

"Why on earth did you have to sound like a psychopath?" I tilt my head and pause. *Wait a minute.* "And how do you know any of that information? And why do you have a picture of Wes's house? From when is that picture?"

Nate takes the computer back and sets it on the low coffee table across the couch. He motions for me to take a seat, and I make my way around the sofa.

"Any particular order you want those questions answered?" Again, he's devoid of emotion.

I look at him—like, really look at him—and he holds my gaze. He has no remorse for what he's done. Another epiphany about my brother hits me. He shows no emotion because this is equivalent to business for him. He removes any feelings and deals with the problem at hand. I wonder if this is part of his level of genius or a result of his mental instability?

I probably shouldn't ask him about that.

I blink once, twice, and peek over at the screen. Taking in a deep breath, I ask, "When was this picture taken?"

"About an hour ago."

Zeroing in on the clock on the bookshelf, I internally add three hours to it. "That was one in the morning."

"That would be correct." Nate smirks as if to amuse a small child who just said something idiotic.

"Stop being such an ass," I snap.

"Ass?" His mouth morphs into a thin line.

"Yes, ASS. Do you get off on these mind games? Why do you have to scare the only people who mean something to me shitless?"

Nate's eyebrows draw dangerously close together.

I wince as it sinks in what I said, and I mumble, "You know what I mean."

"No, little sister, I don't. Why don't you enlighten me?" It's clear I've pushed it too far. My initial reaction is to flee and hide in my room—preferably inside the clawfoot tub behind the curtain.

I have to save this somehow.

"Shit. Nate, I'm sorry." I am. Despite everything, we have formed a bond over the last few days. No matter how much I deny it or avoid thinking about it, it's as certain as the fact that Nate has committed several crimes he needs to be held accountable for. "I...uh..." After a deep breath, I go for the truth. "I feel guilty as hell. I'm playing house with my brother while my adopted family, my boyfriend, and my two best friends are going out of their minds. And then you are scaring them half to death. I mean, think about it. How would you feel if someone did that to *me?*" I'm pretty sure that's a cheap shot, but he needs to understand.

I'm rambling without making eye contact. When he doesn't respond, I chance a glance and am stunned by the change in demeanor. Nate's entire expression has softened, and he looks at me with pure affection—not creepy, but brotherly love.

"You just called me your brother," he states with awe.

"I guess I did," I reply with a small smile.

"Thank you." Just like that, all the anger and fight has left both of us. I remember the times when I got into arguments with my *adopted* siblings. You fight; you make up.

"Can we talk about this? I promise I won't attack you anymore." I nod toward the computer.

Nate glances at the screen and back at me. "I may have gone a bit psycho on them." He looks slightly guilty. "Old habits?" He shrugs, and one side of his mouth pulls up.

I only roll my eyes. "Explain. How do you know all of this?"

He settles into the corner of the couch and faces me. "I told you George is still in Westbridge."

"Your bodyguard?" I want to clarify that there are not any more players in this I don't know about.

Nate nods once. "Head of security, but yes. He delivered the phone to Denielle, and he also took the picture earlier."

I narrow my eyes at him. "And why does George think he is spying on my friends and delivering phones?"

"As I mentioned before..." He huffs, exasperated. "He's dealing with the consequences of me bringing you here. Your family thinks you've gone missing, and I want to know what's transpiring on that end. As long as I don't request him to do something illegal, he doesn't ask questions—this time."

"But you did kidnap me. Twice." I cross my arms over my chest and give him a pointed look.

"You're right; I did. But I also said you could go home, so technically, the situation doesn't apply anymore." He grins like he just negotiated his way in or out of a business deal.

"How did you know that it would be the three of them there and not just two when you sent the email?" What if someone else would've been there? Not that I could think of anyone really, but Rhys could've stayed home, or Denielle could've not gone until tomorrow.

"I've watched all of you long enough; I'd say the chances were pretty good. Plus, if one of them wouldn't have shown up, I could've always given that person a little push in the right direction."

I'm not going to ask what said push would've been.

"So, what now?" I have to pass the time until tomorrow somehow.

Nate grabs the laptop and clicks a few times. "They're all still at Wes's. Your friend really should get curtains or at least close the blinds."

My eyebrows narrow. He states that so casually that I pull the laptop over to get a better view of the screen again. Sure enough, there is a zoomed-in picture of Wes's room. Rhys and Denielle are sitting on the couch, and Wes is across from them on the bed. Wes's parents' house is a split-level with Wes's room on the first floor, which made taking the picture through the open blinds probably laughably easy. I see another picture behind this one and click on it without asking for permission. It just shows that the room is dark now, and there is a soft glow of...a phone screen under something. A blanket?

"What is this?"

Nate leans over. "The latest picture. George made sure to stay until we knew if one of them left again."

"I get that. But what is *this*?" I point at the glow.

"Probably your boyfriend staring at the text I sent him?"

"WHAT TEXT? You didn't say anything about a text." My voice immediately goes Minnie Mouse on helium.

A rueful Nate looks everywhere but at me.

"Nate." The warning is clear in my tone.

"Chill. Here." He grabs the laptop and pulls another window to the forefront that I didn't notice. He turns the computer toward me, and reading it, my blood starts boiling once more.

"This sounds completely psycho. AGAIN! *If you want to talk to your girlfriend tomorrow*," I purposefully imitate his tone.

Nate looks at me steadily before he places the laptop back on the table. "I am looking out for us. For you! We are not scheduling a lunch date with your BFF. Do you understand the severity of the situation?" I know he doesn't mean to sound condescending, but I can't help but feel talked down to.

"No shit," I snap. "But if you hadn't kidnapped me in the first place, we wouldn't be in this situation."

How ludicrous is this conversation? I'm talking about my kidnapping but refer to it as our situation. I smack my palm against my forehead, and Nate arches one eyebrow.

Shaking my head, I say, "This situation is beyond insane. Just listen to us."

Nate chuckles. "Yeah, I guess you could say that."

At that moment, a ping comes from the laptop, and both of us turn simultaneously.

"What was that?" A chill runs down my spine, and I can't help but glance over to Nate suspiciously.

He grabs the computer and smirks at me. "Loverboy says goodnight and that he loves you."

It takes a few seconds for his words to sink in. Loverboy? Who is he talking—Rhys! I rip the device from Nate's hands and stare at the words in front of me. Tears well up immediately.

"Can I reply to him?" My voice is just a whisper.

I can't avert my gaze from the screen. Rhys loves me. He sent the message, not knowing who would read it or if I would ever get it. My heart aches. I miss him so much.

I hear Nate inhale deeply, deliberating. "Yes."

The magnitude of this is not lost on me—what it means for Nate to let me respond. The logical side of my brain tells me to give Rhys my location; there can't be that many massive vineyards up here. My heart, however, swells at the knowledge of how much my brother trusts me to not expose him, and I can't abuse that—I just can't.

My hands hover over the keyboard...what should I type? I glance sideways. "Can this be traced?"

I'm met with a look that means *You did not just ask me that.*

Turning back, I look at the clock in the corner of the screen. It's so late; Rhys should be sleeping. As much as I want to tell him how sorry I am for running off or that I am not upset anymore about him keeping the Katherine stuff from me, I decide to keep it short.

ILY2. It's late. Please get some rest. We'll talk tomorrow. ~Calla

I sign the message with Rhys's name for me. I need him to know it's me. Though, I have no clue if Nate knows about the nickname.

"Remind him to delete the message." Nate's voice brings me back to the present. I quickly type the request and hand the laptop back before I'm tempted to write more. Or completely break down.

"Are you tired?" Nate looks at me with concerned eyes.

"Not really. You?" I slept too long earlier.

"Not really. I never sleep more than a couple of hours."

"Do you have a gym in this palace?"

I'm mostly joking, but I could use a good workout right about now.

"How is your shoulder?"

My shoulder? Oh wow, I totally forgot about that. I slowly rotate my shoulder, move my arm up and down. It's still a little sore, but nothing like it was just a few days ago. It feels more like a faint bruise now. I should probably take it easy, but the need to work myself to utter exhaustion is too overpowering.

"It's fine."

WITHOUT ANOTHER WORD, Nate stands up, and I trail after him. He leads me through the foyer and down the hall of the west wing. I haven't been down this way yet.

Maybe I should ask him for a map.

At the end of the corridor, Nate opens a set of double doors, and I follow him down another set of stairs. The staircase is double-wide, wider than I would have expected it to be. This was probably another one of his additions. The color scheme of espresso floors and white walls extends to the lower level as well. Stopping on the last step, Nate flips a switch and—whoa.

"What the—?"

Standing on the step next to him, I take it all in. In front of me is a gym that puts the one at school to shame. Any equipment one could ever use is set up in neat clusters.

Nate walks farther into the room and starts pointing at the different groupings. "Free weights, cardio, sandbag, weight machines." He turns to the far wall with two sets of double doors. "The showers are over there." He points at the left set, followed by the right. "And the pool is through there." Before I can say anything, he continues, "The running track is over there."

"Pool? Running track? What the fuck, Nate?" I don't know why I sound so angry; I'm more stunned than anything else. Maybe it's that he has surprised me once again? I'm tired of getting blindsided. Nate stares at me as if to assess the reason for my outburst. I rub my hands over my face. "Shit, I'm sorry. I don't know why I just went off on you."

The corner of Nate's mouth pulls up into a smirk. "You had an eventful day. And night." He leaves it at that.

"I guess," I concede.

"Well,"—he puts one hand on my shoulder—"knock yourself out. I'm heading back up; I need to go through some paperwork before the morning." And with that, he turns and walks up the stairs.

I spin in a circle and grin. The area must span most of the estate's footprint above, if not more.

CHAPTER THIRTEEN

LILLY

IT'S PAST FOUR IN THE MORNING WHEN I FINALLY GET BACK TO my room.

After I scrutinized the entire gym—everything was high-end, of course—I decided to hit the running track. In the locker room, I found shelves stocked with workout clothes—male and female. I briefly wondered if the female clothes were *mine* or Margot's. In the end, it didn't matter.

Note to self: ask Nate what to do with the dirty laundry.

Indoors, I usually stick to the treadmill for my cardio, but running "free" was just too tempting. Despite Nate letting me move around on my own, I didn't realize how caged I felt until it was treadmill versus track. I have no clue how far I ran; the distance seemed longer than the average running track, but it also could've been an illusion since it's all underground. The first few rounds, I marveled how Nate, or maybe his grandfather, had pulled that off—the construction must've been extensive. After that, I turned my brain off and just ran...and ran...until my legs gave out. I'm no long-distance runner by any means; however, when I finally stopped, the clock on the wall showed that it was an hour and a half later. Not to mention that I couldn't even see through the sweat dripping down my forehead. Looking in the mirror, I might as well have jumped into the pool with my clothes on.

Post shower, I found myself sitting by the pool on one of the lounge chairs, staring at the almost sapphire-looking water.

I replayed the phone call with Rhys in my head; he was so broken. Seeing the pictures from Wes's house didn't help ease my guilt either. My friends are worried sick. They're probably scared out of their minds, and I'm playing house in this mansion. I had just worked out for Christ's sake while my family and friends probably haven't slept in days.

What the fuck is wrong with me?

My breathing increased, and I put my head between my legs.

I'm not sure how long I tried to get it back under control before the door behind me opened. A moment later, the lounge chair next to me dipped, and I felt a hand between my shoulder blades.

"Talk to me." Nate's voice was low and hesitant.

"Were you spying on me again?" Still being bent over, the question came out muffled.

"I was worried. You're still injured. I didn't want anything happening to you."

That would be a yes.

At his admission, my throat tightened, and a whimper escaped me. I tried to keep it all in, but my body had a mind of its own. The tears started flowing. Despite my attempt to keep the sobs to myself, Nate felt the tremors going through my body. Carefully, he grabbed me by the shoulders and turned me toward him. I didn't want to look at his face; if I saw his worry and love for me, I wouldn't be able to focus on my guilt. I shouldn't feel happy about Nate's affection for me. I shouldn't enjoy spending time with a criminal. He took me against my will. He took me from Rhys.

I tried to push him away, but his hold just tightened.

"Let me go!" There was no force behind the words, and we both knew it.

I didn't even attempt to struggle. Instead, I slumped against my big brother and let him hold me. He didn't say anything; he just held me until I had no more tears left.

"You need to get some rest."

Not responding, I just nodded, stood up, and left him sitting there.

OPENING the door to my room, I get yet another surprise. There, on my nightstand, lays a phone. My heart rate increases, and I dive at the small device. As soon as I pick it up, I realize it's not *my* phone. It's a newer model. My gaze falls on a short, handwritten note on the nightstand.

LILLY,

This is your new phone. Your old one was damaged in the accident. With everything that's going on, it took me some time to download your personal data and transfer it over. This is a secure device, but until we can get all the details straight, I won't connect the phone to the network. However, I thought you might want to have your pictures. I also took the liberty of adding some new ones.

N.

SECURE DEVICE? Not connected? What does that even mean? Tapping the screen, the phone lights up, and I stare at the *Enter Passcode* screen. Is this a joke? He's giving me a locked phone. No, he isn't. Nate would find a way to reprogram this phone with *my* passcode.

Slowly, I press my thumb on the four digits, and sure enough, I'm met with my background screen—a picture of Denielle and me from last summer. Sloane took the photo when we all were at the lake together.

Hesitantly, I click on the rainbow-colored flower. At the top is an additional folder labeled "Lilly." I tap the album, and my breath hitches. The first picture is the one of Rhys and me at Bones. The one in which I had leaned into him, eyes closed, looking so...happy.

I keep scrolling and find the picture that made it to the Internet, thanks to brother dearest. As much as I would love this photo for reminding me of the moment Rhys kissed me on the steps of Denielle's house, the negative association of everyone staring at me with judgment and contempt has ruined the picture for me. My thumb briefly hovers over the little trash can icon, but I decide against it. I want—no, I *need* every picture of Rhys I can get at the moment.

Next is a picture of me at Magnolia's. It's the day I met with Denielle and told her everything. Denielle is walking away from the counter, and I'm looking at her retreating form—probably trying to figure out what my best friend is wearing. I smile to myself, remembering the moment I took in her unusual attire, when something else catches my eye. I zoom in with my thumb and middle finger. A few steps beside me is the creepy guy who talked to me that day. He is slightly blurry as the camera's focus is on me, but you can make out how he's staring at me. Leering. A shudder runs down my spine.

Following are random shots of me with Denielle. From the gymnastics meet and us walking to or from school. I don't look closer and keep scrolling.

The surprises keep coming as I stare at the photo now displayed on the small screen. We were so careful. We waited over ten minutes to even get out of the car, but there it is, clear as day—or night, for that matter. Rhys and I are sitting at the small corner table in the café several towns over the night Nate sent his first message. Rhys is holding my hand, and we are looking at each other.

I'm sure that no one entered the café after us that evening.

The last photo makes my breath hitch. It's not a photo at all; it's the still of a surveillance or security camera. In. My. Living room. Rhys and I are cuddled up on the couch under my favorite throw blanket. He's placing a kiss on my temple, both of us holding a mug in our hands. What is this? I'm going to be sick. I jump off the bed and race out of my room.

"NATE!" *Where the fuck is this piece-of-shit brother? He went too far!* I roar his name as I run past the staircase coming up from the foyer. I pound at his office slash NASA control center but don't get an answer.

"NAAAATE!" I'm shaking from rage.

My brother comes tearing out of the last room before the hallway turns; he is still trying to pull his shirt over his head when I attack. I hit him full force across the jaw, and he stumbles back—stunned.

"What the—?" He's holding his jaw, and I'm panting, trying to catch my breath.

"You sick asshole! How could you?" I clench and unclench my hands. I'm ready to strike again, but I'm sure he'll block me now that I got one hit in.

"What the fuck are you talking about?" Now Nate is fuming, but at the same time, he looks at me with wary eyes.

"This!" I shove the screen in his face. "Wasn't it enough for you to spy on me from afar? You had to break into my home?"

Nate glances at the screen then back to me. "That wasn't me."

With those three words, my rage deflates. "What do you mean?" I rasp.

All of a sudden, Nate looks...nervous? Apprehensive?

"Come with me."

As soon as Nate sits down in his desk chair, all the screens come to life. It's as creepy as it is fascinating. The wall monitors currently show the surveillance cameras of the property—some inside the house, some outside with what looks like night vision.

I stand behind him as he starts typing in a command line window on his laptop. He types something and flips everything to the monitors on his desk. Then, he opens a second window and starts typing there—then a third and a fourth. Both monitors on his desk display black windows with green lines of code. It looks like he's running some kind of program, but what do I know?

"This may take a moment. Tristen changed the passwords," he murmurs.

Tris—what?

All I can do is stare at the screens. Every so often, Nate types something in, and then lines of code start scrolling over the screen again. According to the clock on one of the wall monitors, it's 4:30 a.m., and by the time all six screens on the walls go dark, the little numbers on one of the desk monitors show 5:12. The entire time, I stand there watching, neither of us talking.

"Here we go." Nate's finger hovers across the enter key. "I want you to know that I had nothing to do with this. I didn't know about it until the week I decided to speed up the timeline. George came across it while doing recon, and I later went back through the feeds as far as I could. *That's* how I got the picture. I honestly just thought that you would like that picture of you and...your boyfriend. I'm sorry. I'm an idiot." The last few words are spoken so low they're barely audible.

Nate turns for the first time since we came in here, and our gazes lock. He scrubs a hand over his mouth.

"Okay," I rasp out.

He hits the key, and all six wall screens come back to life. This can't be. I try to draw in a breath. I can't breathe. I clutch my hands to my chest and stare. In my kitchen are several strangers. Tristen sits at the head of the table, half-hidden behind his laptop. I focus on the other pictures in front of me: the living room, the entryway, the garage, Heather and Tristen's bedroom. I squint, and sure enough, Heather is curled up in the bed. My eyes take in every small rectangle displayed on the wall right now. There must be at least two dozen cameras in the house, including—FUCK.

"This is my room..." I'm going to be sick. I force myself to look at Nate. "Did you go through the feeds?" What I'm asking is *Are there videos of Rhys and me?*

"I have." Nate's face gives me the answer without having to voice the question. My knees buckle.

THE FIRST THING I hear is the clicking of keys. My cheek sticks to the material I'm lying on—what the heck? I slowly start moving, and when I attempt to turn over, a wall stops me. Oh, I'm on the leather couch in Nate's office, a blanket draped across my legs. My face was stuck to the seat cushion, and now I am plastered against the back of the sofa.

How did I get here? What time is it?

"It's almost noon," my brother's voice informs me.

Did I ask that out loud?

I drape one arm over my eyes, debating if I should go back to sleep. If I'm asleep, there can't be any more surprises. No more lies that make my life an even bigger farce.

"I'm sorry you had to find out like this." The sorrow in his statement is palpable and makes me want to curl up in a ball.

"Why are there so many cameras in my house?"

"I don't know, little sister. I'm trying to find that out."

That gets my attention, and I sit up. "What do you mean?"

"I mean, it doesn't make sense that the house is wired like it's for an episode of *Big Brother*. That your and Rhys's phones were tracked; this all seems to be overkill. If it were just about me"—Nate pauses and looks at me with his mouth pressed in a thin line before continuing—"it would be sufficient to cover the entrances, maybe the phones." He trails off again.

"You think there is more behind it?"

"I do. Until last night, I only went in once—right after George informed me of the *'internal surveillance within Miss Lilly's residence,'* as he called it." Nate chuckles, and I cock my head.

"George can be very...formal," he explains and, after a breath, amends, "when he wants to be. He switches from cussing me out to talking like an old English lord within the blink of an eye."

"Um...is he...?" I make a swirly motion with my forefinger next to my head. It wouldn't be surprising if one crazy dude employs another, right?

Nate barks out a laugh. "No, he's as sane as they get. He is more levelheaded than anyone I've ever met."

"Sooo...?" I let the sentence hang, hoping Nate will continue without me having to probe.

"He was raised very...traditionally. His parents were part of New York's high society. He had a personal tutor and all the shit that comes with it. George rebelled, left school, and joined the military. He left his life behind and didn't look back. But after he got injured—he never told me exactly what happened—he needed to start over. That's when he came back to New York and became a P.I. He refused his family's fortune. He ran into my mother one day, and she remembered him, even though he was several years older. They used to run in the same circles. Somehow, the connection to my grandfather was made. He's been working for us since, in one way or another."

Or another.

"Couldn't you find out what happened to him?" My curiosity is piqued.

My brother looks thoughtful for a moment. "I could. I checked him out on the surface, but whatever he did in his past is well hidden. He is very good at disappearing. Unless you know where to look, you won't find anything about George Weiler. He had already worked for my grandfather for years. I've seen him around for just as long growing up. I trust the man, and it seems wrong to invade his privacy more than necessary."

I almost laugh out loud. Nate, who has no qualms about hacking into a school surveillance system or implanting a program on a hospital server, doesn't want to spy on his body-guard—or whatever the man is. However, the sincerity in Nate's voice makes me refrain from making a snarky remark. Instead, I change the topic. "So, what are we doing about the cameras in my house?"

"Nothing."

"Nothing?!" I want to demand answers as to why the hell there is so much surveillance in my home. I'm about to say so when Nate's raised hand stops me. Apparently, he recognizes the signs of an oncoming rant by now.

"It's not important at the moment. They've been there for a long time from what I've seen. For now, we have to focus on the tasks at hand."

"Which are?" I finally round the desk, looking at the moni-tors. One is covered with surveillance pictures and one with—I have no clue. It seems like some interface, but I have no idea for what.

Nate holds up one finger. "Getting your story straight. Our story." Finger number two joins the first. "Making sure you get to talk to Rhys and"—he adds a third finger—"figuring out our next steps."

I blankly stare at him for several moments before conceding. "Okay"

SUDDENLY, Nate stands up and walks out of the room. Over his shoulder, he calls, "Hold on one sec."

At first, I am shocked that he leaves me here alone, all the computers unlocked, but before I can even debate using this to my advantage, the door clicks open again. Nate rolls another desk chair through the opening and positions it next to his. "Sit."

I follow his command and wait, unsure of what's happening.

"Before we do anything else, we are changing the security in your room, and I am going to show you how to navigate the system. I want you to learn your way around."

Wait. What?

I can't believe my ears. He's giving me access? To the *whole* system? I must have misunderstood. Nate starts hitting some keys, and in addition to both monitors now showing the same interface, the wall screens are lighting up with the usual surveillance footage of the property. A few more keystrokes and I am looking at the rumpled sheets of my bed on full display on the bottom middle screen.

My stomach clenches at the thought of Nate watching me sleep like that. But before I go down the rabbit hole too far, he starts pointing at the screens on his desk and explains, "This is the interface to the security system for the property. You can also control everything via command line, but until I can properly teach you, this will be easier." He points to a drop-down field. "This lets you select the main area you want to look at: 'East Wing – Second Floor.' Then, you click here and choose which camera you want to review." He points at another drop-down. "Your room is labeled 'Bedroom: Lilly.' Most rooms have just numbers unless it's something obvious, like the library or an assigned room. See..." Nate changes the first selection to "West Wing," and in the next window, I see an option for "Bedroom: Margot."

Confused, I ask, "Why does Margot have a bedroom?"

My brother grimaces. "Umm..."

My eyebrows draw together.

He finally sighs and confesses, "Margot doesn't sleep in my bedroom."

"Huh?" They don't sleep in the same bedroom?

"I don't let anyone stay in my private bedroom on this property. It's my, uh...*space* if you want to call it that. The first place I felt safe again after I left the hospital. Margot thinks that the bedroom we share here is where I always sleep. She doesn't come here that often and usually just for a weekend, so she's never questioned it."

What do you respond to that? As excited as I feel about him sharing more information with me, I'm just as weirded out. I can't fathom not wanting to share my bedroom with Rhys. But then, Nate has a whole other set of issues.

After an awkward moment of silence, he clears his throat and begins to explain more of the interface, neither of us wanting to talk further about the topic. Nate even shows me how to navigate it via command line, though he might as well have spoken Urdu at that point. Eventually, he changes it back to my bedroom and shows me how to pull up the password console with a combination of keys. There is no menu option to change the password, just a key combination.

I should probably take notes.

"Here." Nate pushes the keyboard to me. "Change the password to whatever you like, but nothing too easy. It was laughable how quickly I got into your phone and email. I didn't even need an algorithm."

My email?

I hit him over the back of the head. He looks at me sheepishly, knowing exactly why I did it.

"No more hacking into your emails; got it." That gives him another smack, and Nate laughs. "And the phone."

I glare at him. Pulling the keyboard over, I try to think of a password. Hitting the enter key after confirming my password three times—not twice—I mumble, "This is the weirdest program I have ever seen."

"I designed it."

My head jerks around, and I search his face to see if he is messing with me. He designed it? *The entire system?*

"I knew what I wanted, and it wasn't available on the market...so I built it myself."

My brother is a freaking genius. If I had any doubt before, I am sure now.

"Can you teach me?" I'm in awe. I always knew I wanted to do something with math or computers, but seeing this...I *need* to learn how.

A broad grin spreads over Nate's face. "Of course."

CHAPTER FOURTEEN

LILLY

NATE TELLS ME TO GO SHOWER AND EAT SOMETHING. HE ATE earlier while I slept and needs to talk to George about the call. George has been keeping an eye on Rhys and my friends all morning. Nate promises to bring me up to speed when I'm back but emphasizes that I should take my time. Translation: go away; you're slowing me down.

STANDING in the shower after scarfing down yet another round of carbs, my adrenaline spikes as I think about him leaving me alone with his computers. I could've woken up at any point, used the opportunity to try and contact someone. The trust he has in me after these short few days is humbling. If I thought the line between brother and criminal-slash-kidnapper was blurred before, the boundaries of acceptance of my current situation have shifted to the point of no return. I won't be able to label him a criminal, turn him over, and move on when this is over. My stance on him paying for what he's done hasn't changed; he needs to take responsibility. But I know that I will be by his side through all of it.

I'M BACK in front of the NCC—the now official callsign for Nate's NASA command center—at precisely 2:13 p.m. One hour and seventeen minutes to go. I took as much time as my nerves allowed me, which was fifty-two minutes after Nate closed the door in my face.

I knock, and I give Nate a shoulder shrug with my best *hi-I'm-back* grin when he looks me up and down. My brother's shoulders slump when he sees I am here to stay.

He swings the door open and moves out of the way. Walking in, I come face to face with—holy shit. I stumble backward and bump into my brother's tall frame. His arms shoot out to steady me, and he whispers into my ear, "Lilly, meet George."

On one of the two monitors on Nate's desk is the face of a man—a man that could haunt nightmares. All I see is the massive scar. It runs from the left side of his forehead, down across his cheekbone, over his nose, and down to the right side of his neck. His skin is weathered, and his pronounced cheekbones and small eyes remind me of the picture of a mummy I saw in history class last year.

HIS DEMEANOR SOFTENS when he spots me, and his entire face turns...friendly? "Hello, Miss Lilly. It's nice to finally meet you." George's voice is gentle and in such a stark contrast to his...appearance.

"You just cursed me out, and 'Miss Lilly' gets a full-on smile. I didn't even know your mouth could turn that way." Nate scoffs and steps around me, walking back to his desk.

George follows Nate's movement with narrowed eyes. "That's because you either act like a spoiled, entitled brat, or I have to clean up your mess. You don't give me a reason to be friendly with you." The words are harsh, but his mouth twitches ever so slightly in one corner. He cares for my brother.

"Let's get back to the task at hand. Lilly, sit! We only have one hour until call time; let's not waste it more."

I follow his command, unsure of how to take the sudden tension. Sitting down in the chair Nate brought in earlier, George's gaze meets mine before he looks back at my brother.

"Denielle Keller left the Sheats's residence a few hours ago. She is back at her house. Weston and Rhys are still at Weston's house. I scoped out the location earlier, and everything is secure. I installed the wireless cameras you requested, so we have eyes from every angle. I also added one at the entrance for early warning."

Nate nods at George's recap. "The trackers are in place?"

My head snaps up. "What trackers?"

My brother briefly glances sideways. My gaze swivels between the two men; their silent communication makes me clench my jaw. I don't like being out of the loop.

"Nate..." I growl.

Instead of Nate, George speaks up. "I advised your brother to track everyone's movement today. Not just Rhys's. I understand that your relationship with your brother has...evolved." He gives Nate a pointed look. "We can't be too careful at this point. Even though the situation has changed on your end, there are a lot of unknown factors here. With the FBI at the McGuire residence, I am making sure that Nate and you are protected."

I'm speechless. This man just met me, and yet he acts like I'm—what?

When I don't say anything, Nate addresses George. "Thanks, man. Is everything plugged into the network yet?"

"The trackers, yes. The cameras, shortly. I just finished the placement before you called. I'll message you once it's done. Shouldn't take more than twenty minutes."

"Sounds good. Establish connection in an hour."

He disconnects the video-chat without saying goodbye.

. . .

WE SIT IN SILENCE, and I replay George's words in my head.

"Should I be worried?" My voice is timid.

My question is vague, but Nate understands what I'm asking him. "Your story needs to be ironclad. And even then, I don't think I can protect you from everything. People will ask questions; some won't believe you. You'll be under surveillance."

My heart is already beating double-time, but I catch on to Nate's words. "You have a plan." It's not a question; I know he does.

"I do, but it will require you to stay, um...a little longer."

"How long?" I peer at him carefully.

"Ten days."

"WHAT? WHY?" My entire body begins to shake. Ten days? That'll make it two weeks. *No.* "NO!" I jump up and start pacing. "You said I could go home," I cry.

"Sit down, please." Nate's gaze follows my every step.

I don't want to sit. The sensation of being trapped builds inside my core and starts spreading. I can feel it all the way to my fingertips. I need to get off the property. I have access to the system. I can find my way out.

On my eighth lap, two strong arms circle my upper body, pinning mine to my side. "Lilly! Listen to me."

I begin to struggle against his hold.

"Please, little sister." Nate is pleading with me, and I stop my fight. He immediately loosens his hold, and I turn. He points at the chairs. "Sit. Please?"

Facing me in the chair, he draws in a deep breath. "I understand you want to go home. And you will; I promise you." His tone is sincere. "But..." *Here we go.* "I need to make sure my alibi is also in place, and for that, I need more time. Plus, none of the others have ever, uh...reappeared after just a few days. All these things would raise more questions—questions I can't help you with once you leave here."

I sigh, covering my face with my hands. He's right; the others were all gone between two and three weeks. Looking back at him, I ask, dejected, "What's the plan?"

"I have to go back to LA next week. It's just three days, but I can't get out of it, which in the end, will work in our favor. I'm well-known and will be recognized in public. If there's a suspicion linking me to your case, this will solidify my alibi."

At his last sentence, my eyes snap to his. The way he says it, it would sound casual to an outsider, but I notice the slight drop in his voice. Talking about it makes him uncomfortable. *As it should*, the voice in my head chimes up for the first time in a while.

"I see," is all I come up with.

"As soon as I'm back, we'll start the process of getting you home. But since you can't just get on a plane, we have to find another way. I have some ideas but need to run them by George first."

Why does he need an alibi if he's going to pay for his actions?

The voice inside of me is on a rampage.

"Nate?"

"Mhmm?" He has started typing in one of the command line windows again.

"Why do you need an alibi if you are going to take responsibility for what you've done?" Despite focusing on my hands in my lap, I notice immediately that the typing has stopped. Sweat starts building inside my clasped palms—I'm risking my phone call by confronting him.

Suddenly, my head is tilted upward with a gentle hand, and my eyes hesitantly meet my brother's. The anger I expected is not there.

"Because I have to make sure that you are safe and settled before I go away. I don't want to be rushed and risk your life in any way."

Understanding hits, and I squash the voice that is telling me that he's just making excuses to not go to jail. Deep down, I believe him. The same way I have the urge to take care of him, he wants to take care of me before he faces the consequences. I nod and turn to the monitor. No idea what he's doing, I watch, fascinated, as his fingers start flying over the keyboard again.

Fifteen minutes later, according to the clock on the screen, a message window pops open and reads: **All set**.

"Finally," Nate grumbles to himself.

Another five agonizing minutes go by before the wall monitors flicker to life. Holding my breath, I take in the scene in front of me. Woodland Park. I haven't been there in a while, but I'd recognize it anywhere. Nate adjusts certain angles, and eventually, all cameras point to the same spot. The spot our picture was taken so many years ago. My eyes sting, and I realize that tears are running down my face.

"Thirty minutes to go. George will call in shortly." Nate squeezes my leg.

NATE IS in the process of setting up the headset as an incoming video call pops up on the screen. Without pausing what he's doing, Nate says, "Accept," and George's scarred face fills the screen.

"WHAT THE HELL?" I shriek.

Nate smirks without looking up, and George assesses my probably bulging eyes with a raised eyebrow.

"How the fuck did you do that?" I address my brother, who is still ignoring me.

"Language, Miss Lilly," I'm chastised by Nate's bodyguard—how wonderful.

"Sorry," I say like a five-year-old caught repeating a curse word she heard from her big brother. Nate snorts. He seriously snorts, and I smack him over the head. Again. This seems to have become my go-to reaction.

"What? I told you I designed the system," he responds, exasperated.

I'm amazed by how much we behave like siblings. He teases me; I retaliate in juvenile, little-sister fashion. Something else occurs to me: Rhys and I never acted like this. We bantered, we teased, but in a completely different way. For as long as I remember, I had this underlying feeling that I used to chalk up to him being my best friend. But having my real brother next to me, I realize there has always been more. Den's words come back to me. "Whatever that memory doctor did to you, he wasn't able to fully erase what you and Rhys already had..."

Before I can say anything else, George begins with his updates. "Weston has left his house and is on his way to Miss Keller's residence. Two minutes out. Agent Camden left the McGuire residence and went home; no one else has come or gone. Rhys left Weston's house about four minutes ago and should be at the location in seven."

By the time he finishes, I feel like I have a unibrow. "Uh..." I hold up a finger, and two sets of eyes first look at my finger then at my face.

"Yes, Miss Lilly?"

Since George is the one giving me his attention, I face him. "How do you know all that?"

George, in return, dips his head at my brother. "Show her."

Something is sucking all the air out of my lungs. *Show me what?*

Nate remains mute and starts typing.

Does he ever use a freaking mouse?

One of the six mounted monitors changes, and it takes me a moment to grasp what I see—a map of Westbridge. There are different colored dots—red and blue. Each dot has a small rectangle next to it, showing initials. I stand up and get as close as possible. D.K., W.S., T.Mc. I scan the map, and there he is, still moving and getting closer. R.Mc. Then I notice that there are duplicates. There are two D.K.s and two W.S.s. Focusing back on the only dot I care about at the moment, I see only one R.Mc.

"What are the dots? Why are there two for some?"

Nate finally joins the conversation. "Some are trackers; some are cell phones." His tone is conversational, as if he just informed me we'd be having two different kinds of pizza for dinner.

"You hacked into my friends' phones?" I ask him incredulously.

"No, I used their Friend Finder app. It's not my fault none of them have any sense of privacy and have their location service permanently enabled. Tristen, well...yeah, he's a bit more cautious." That's where he leaves it.

I focus back on the map; Rhys has arrived at Woodland Park. I turn to the other monitors and see the Defender parked in the small lot by the picnic area.

"What time is it?" I whisper. It feels wrong to speak at a normal volume.

"3:20 Pacific Standard Time, 6:20 Eastern Standard Time," I faintly notice George answering.

"Are you in place?" Nate's question startles me, and I swivel around to see his face.

"I am."

"In place where? Where are you?" This is the second time I directly address the man with the massive scar. The bone-jarring fear his appearance initially instilled in me is gone.

George seems to notice as well; his eyes widen for a fraction of a second before he smoothes his features. "I've parked 1.3 miles away from the call location. We have eyes on everyone; there was no need for me to be on site." He sounds like he's talking about a military mission.

In my peripheral vision, something moves on the upper right wall monitor. Rhys has gotten out of the car and is making his way across the grassy field. The instant sensation in my abdomen causes me to smile. There he is. My gorgeous boyfriend. I missed him, but I didn't realize how much I missed this feeling—my hornets on steroids. Before I ended up here, I was so furious about him hiding something from me that I withdrew myself out of self-preservation, suppressed all my emotions to not risk getting hurt.

I feel a hand on my arm, and I peer at my brother over my shoulder.

"It's time." He holds out the headset.

I want to take it, but my hands start shaking, and I can only stare at the outstretched device.

"Look at me." His soft command makes my eyes travel upward to meet his. "It'll be ok. We have all the security measures in place. Talk to him." He puts the headphone on my head, making sure it sits properly, a gesture so familiar, like he's taken care of me his whole life. My lips press together in a tight smile, and I blink rapidly.

"Let's get going." Nate directs his attention back to George and the screens on the desk.

My focus is on Rhys. He is jumping in place and keeps tapping the phone in his hand. He is as nervous as I am. It's like looking into a mirror. I zone everything else out and watch. Nate and George are running through...I have no clue and, to be honest, also don't care. All I want is to hear Rhys's voice again.

"Little sis?"

"Mhmm?" The typing and chatter have stopped.

"I asked if you're ready?"

Oh!

Nate sounds hesitant, probably confused as to why I didn't respond. Watching Rhys made everything fade into the background.

"Yes," I breathe, still staring at the screen.

"Let's do this." Two more clicks and I hear the dial tone in my ears. I focus on the beeping as if I could miss Rhys picking up.

"Lilly?"

God, how I have missed his voice.

Just hearing my name from him makes everything fall into place, and I can't stop the broad grin spreading across my face.

"It's me," is all I can think of saying. I mean, duh.

George's voice penetrates my happy haze. "Car approaching!"

"FROM WHERE?" Nate is shouting. I've never heard anything even remotely close to panic in his tone—until now.

"Main gate. CUT THE LINE!" The last three words are an order. George has taken charge.

I flip around. "WHAT? NO! NATE! YOU CAN'T!" But the line is already dead. "RHYS!" I cry, gripping the headset, spinning back to the monitor, but of course, there is no answer.

I feverishly gaze between the screen and my brother. "Nate? What is happening? Who is this?" Tears are streaming down my cheeks as I witness the scene unfold in front of me.

How is this even possible?

"NATE, DO SOMETHING!" This can't be happening. My entire body is shaking. But there is nothing anyone *can* do.

I faintly register my brother questioning how George could've missed this. He is furious with his head of security. I can't watch any longer. They are still arguing when I turn and address the men in the room and on the monitor. "FIX THIS!"

"Lilly."

"Miss Lilly."

They both start at the same time, but my adrenaline is so high that I lose all control over the little rational thinking I seemed to have left in this situation.

"I DON'T GIVE A FUCK HOW YOU DO IT. FIX IT!"

I zero in on Nate and force myself to lower my tone to a less hysterical volume. "You promised me I'd get to talk to him. Fix it. YOU. PROMISED. ME!" I jab my finger at the space between his eyes.

I need to get out of here. Before either of them can respond, I charge toward the door and tear it open.

"FIX! IT!" I scream again before I let the security door slam shut.

CHAPTER FIFTEEN

RHYS

I THOUGHT SIX-THIRTY WOULD NEVER COME. FROM THE moment I opened my eyes—which, thankfully, was mid-morning due to my late night—I felt this constant current running through my body. A perpetual need to move.

Around two, Den announced that if she saw me pace the room one more time while raking my hands through my—in her words—"*already receding hairline*," she'd kick me in the balls, followed by tying my hands behind my back and stuffing me in the closet. Those were her parting words as she stormed out of the room.

Dramatic much?

I was about to yell after her where she could stick her bitch attitude when Wes put a hand on my shoulder. One head shake was all it took to deflate the anger toward Lilly's best friend. For a brief moment, my rational thinking was back. I got it. I would drive myself fucking bat-shit crazy if I had to sit there and watch.

Wes received a text from her when she got home, but she

didn't come back for the rest of the day. We attempted to distract ourselves with video games, but that only lasted for so long. I would continually stare at the phone laying on my thigh and fuck up. Eventually, I told Wes to get out. It was almost six, and I'd be leaving anyway. I wouldn't need any more babysitting. My best friend didn't look convinced until I pulled out my phone and dialed Den's number.

"Everything okay?" Her answering tone was panicked, all the earlier annoyance gone.

"Yeah. All good." I had called her on speakerphone and looked directly at Wes when I continued. "Listen...uh, I'm about to head out. Wes is coming over to your place."

Wes narrowed his eyes at me while the other end of the phone remained quiet. My friends are no idiots; they knew what I was doing. I didn't want all of us to be separated. I needed the assurance that they were together. Safe.

"I'll be over in ten," he addressed Den while giving me a curt nod.

"'Kay. You got the code for the gate. I'll open the garage for you to pull in." Den was all business. Her guard-dog persona that always watched over Lilly had extended to Wes and me over the last few days.

I hung up before either of them could add anything else.

"You sure you're okay?" My friend's concern was laced through the question.

My hands halfway to my head, I paused mid-action and huffed out a laugh. My arms fell to my sides, and I stared at the ceiling for several heartbeats.

"No. But you read the email." That was all that needed to be said.

Grabbing his jacket from the back of his desk chair, Wes left the room without another word. I was alone for the first time since getting the email and phone. The urge to send another text message overwhelmed me, but I couldn't. For one, I had deleted the incoming texts. And two, I couldn't risk not hearing her voice tonight. Tapping the screen, I saw it was 5:53. It was a ten-minute drive at this time of day.

At one point before she left, after I had paced probably a mile and a half through Wes's room, Den asked cautiously if I even knew where I was supposed to go.

"Yes," was all I said. Neither asked for more detail—not that I would've given it. The location was a no-brainer after reading the email. Woodland Park. Lilly kept the picture on her desk for ten years. It was the first picture we took together after she moved in with us. Even after I froze her out, it remained on her desk. I used to stare at it from the hallway whenever her door was open and she wasn't home—fuck, I don't think I could've been more pathetic.

Grabbing the phone and my coat, I made my way to the Defender. The current had transformed into a raging river of adrenaline coursing through my veins.

Thirty more minutes. You gotta keep it together for thirty more minutes.

THE PARK IS EERILY DARK. I don't think I've ever been here at night. Whenever someone had suggested hanging out here, I came up with a better suggestion—a suggestion that usually got one of us in trouble. But this was a place I would never tarnish with my drunk friends or Kat. This was our place: Lilly's and mine. Even when there was no us during those two years.

I drive to the parking lot closest to the picnic area. From there, it's only a couple hundred feet to the spot where I grinned into the camera while Lilly looked up at me. The picnic area, which consists of about a dozen rectangular wooden tables with attached benches, is surrounded by trees, thicker on one side with a small stream running through. The perfect place for kids to run, climb, and play, which is exactly what Lilly and I used to do whenever we came here on the weekends. God, how I loved coming here. It was almost like before. Just the two of us playing. No pretending. No hiding. Even at eight years old, the secret was suffocating me.

The screen on the phone displays 6:20. It's time. Opening the door of the Defender, my breath immediately becomes visible in the illuminated dome light. The nights are still freezing even though we're approaching spring. I shut the door and use the flashlight of the phone to make my way over to the spot. With every step, my heartbeat quickens more and my legs become unsteady. When I think I've reached the place—I sure hope the psycho doesn't expect me to stand in my ten-year-old footprints—I turn in a circle. It's pitch black on three sides. The only illumination comes from the few streetlamps along the paved road leading to the parking lot. I wonder if the lack of light was intentional by the city to avoid people loitering here at night.

Three minutes to go. I rub my hands over my arms and jump in place on the balls of my feet—the urge to move is back. I can't stand still, no matter how hard I try. Touching the screen over and over, I will the numbers to change to six-three-zero.

I tap again and see how the six, two, and nine turn into a six, followed by a three and a zero. If someone connected me to a blood pressure cuff right now, they'd call an ambulance. My pulse feels like I just did ten 50 40s in a row. My breath is so ragged that I close my eyes and start counting backward from thirteen, hoping to slow my breathing down enough to not pass out from hyperventilating.

That would be my luck, passing out right before the phone call. I make sure not to let the display go dark again the entire time when the last digit jumps to one.

Why isn't she calling?

What if everything she said was a lie, and she is not safe at all?

The phone starts vibrating in my hand, and I almost drop it.
UNKNOWN.

I stare for a second then swipe and lift it to my ear.

"Lilly?" I can barely get her name out; my voice is just a rasped whisper.

"It's me." The pitch in her tone makes it clear that she's smiling, and calm washes over me.

Before I can say anything else, I hear a male voice in the background. "FROM WHERE?" It's evident that he is yelling, or I wouldn't have heard him. This is bad. Really. Bad.

"WHAT? NO! NA—" are Lilly's last words before the phone call disconnects.

"LILLY!" My voice is back, and a guttural scream finds its way out of my previously constricted lungs.

That's when I see them. Headlights. They're slowly coming up the paved road and stop right next to my car.

WHAT. THE. FUCK? No, no, no...

This can't be real.

The beams are on me, and I'm completely blind. I shield my eyes with the hand that is not holding the phone and can make out that the driver's side door opens.

If Wes or Den followed me here, I will kill them.

"Rhys?"

Oh, you've got to be fucking kidding me. This has to be a joke. I bend over and crouch down, head in my hands, gripping my hair. I pull as hard as I can, hoping to get the utter rage under control, which has replaced the previous *nervous* current. I probably pull several chunks out, but the red haze doesn't go away. Footsteps approach on the frozen grass, and I force myself to stand up. My fists are clenched so tightly they're shaking. It's a miracle the phone casing doesn't crack.

"Rhys?" There it is again. My name. The name she only ever used when she was not happy with my performance as the perfect boyfriend.

I face the last person I expected to see tonight.

"Kat." My tone is detached. I want to wrap my hands around her throat and squeeze. I tighten my fist even more to not follow through. She is the reason the psycho disconnected the phone call. She is the reason I don't get to talk to Lilly. If I remain here, I don't think I can control myself. I want to hurt her, and I've never wanted to harm a female in my life. Ever.

I slip the phone in the back pocket of my jeans and brush past her without a word. I need to put distance between us. She tries to reach for my arm, and I round on her, getting straight in her face. "If you touch me, I can't guarantee anything. If anything happens to Lilly because of you, I will kill—"

Fuck, what am I doing?

I spin on my heels and walk away as fast as I can without breaking into a full-on sprint.

Thankfully, I didn't lock my car. I'm in the driver's seat and have the car in reverse by the time my ex reaches my window. I can hear her muffled voice calling my name again, but I don't stop. I reverse out of the spot and speed down the narrow pathway faster than I probably should.

FUCK. FUCK. FUCK.

I hit the steering wheel several times before I let go of the feral scream that has been building up all day until my throat hurts so badly I can't even swallow. What am I supposed to do now? I can't go home. The fact that my father has been spying on me still has me reeling. He betrayed me. Without thinking, I find myself keying in the code to Denielle's parents' mansion not fifteen minutes later. As I pull up to the garages, one gate is already open, and I see Wes standing at the end of the spot against the wall. His hands are clasped on top of his head, and he stares at me with worry in his eyes. I pull in and sit there, not breaking eye contact with my best friend. I hear the gate close behind me; a glance into the rearview mirror confirms the sound.

Denielle's form joins Wes's. Scanning my face, her hands fly to her mouth, and tears immediately begin running down her cheeks. I take one more deep breath before I open the door and step out. I can't even begin to process what just happened. I had Lilly on the phone. I heard her voice, and then Kat showed up. He was there in the background. He cut her off. I have no idea if I will ever get another chance to talk to her. My legs give out, and I crumble to the floor.

I'm faintly aware that two arms are wrapped around me, preventing me from face-planting onto the way too polished cement floor while gut-wrenching sobs make my entire body shake.

They lead me into the house. Wes has my arm strapped over his shoulder to keep me from tripping over my own feet. I can't see a thing with my blurred vision, and I press my free hand over my mouth in an attempt to restrain some of the whimpers escaping my hoarse throat. I'm past caring how I look.

Somehow, we end up on the back patio. It's fucking freezing outside. What the hell are we doing out here? But realization seeps into my muddled brain, and I notice the flames crackling in the massive build-in fire pit. Sitting in one of the four chairs surrounding the blaze, one of my friends drapes a blanket around my shoulders, and I slump forward. My face in my hands, I bend forward, resting my entire upper body on my thighs. This is a nightmare. No, this is worse than a nightmare.

"What happened?" I don't know how long we've been here when Wes's wary question pulls me out of my semi-catatonic state, and I untangle myself. I must've been in this position longer than I thought. My back is stiff, and my neck hurts like a mother when I look up at him.

"Kat."

"Come again?" Den's mouth hangs open.

"Kat happened." I tell my friends everything, including how I fled so I wouldn't physically assault her in my rage. With a ragged breath, I conclude, "I don't know what to do."

"Maybe I can help with that."

The deep voice is coming from outside of the illuminated

circle around the fire. The three of us spin around at the same time, and I squint, trying to make out the speaker. When a man steps into the light, I grab onto the armrest of my chair to not fall off.

"HOLY FUCK!" Wes shouts. He does fall off.

Denielle screams.

CHAPTER SIXTEEN

RHYS

I STARE. WES MAKES A NOISE SOMEWHERE BETWEEN WHEEZING and gagging while gawking up at the intruder, and Denielle continues to scream. Every time she stops to take a breath, I relish the sudden quiet—until she starts back up. If she keeps going like this, her voice is going to sound like the time Oliver, Denielle's brother, took her and Lilly to a Bieber concert. Neither of them could get out more than a pathetic croak for days. Eventually, her cries turn into a muffled whimper.

Thank you, Jesus.

During the entire time, my eyes don't leave him, and his focus is solely on me. My first thought is he is going to kill us. We're as good as dead. I mean, what other purpose could a man looking like that have? I don't think he's much older than Dad, but whatever happened to him made him age triple-time. His skin is leathery, and in combination with the ginormous scar running over his entire face, he must've been through hell—and survived. I can't look away from that jagged white line. My second, more rational thought is: why he would offer his help if he's here to kill us?

"Where is Lilly?" Nothing else matters at the moment.

"Miss Lilly is safe."

Miss?

"Are you him?" I chalk my conversational tone up to shock. In truth, I should be shitting my pants. But weirdly enough, I'm not.

"No. *He* is with Miss Lilly."

There are two? Well, fuck me.

I glance sideways. Wes is still on the floor, staring at the intruder. Even in the darkness, I can see that he is white as a ghost, but the wheezing has stopped. I sure hope he doesn't puke again. Denielle has her hands over her mouth, trying to control her sobs. Instinct takes over; I stand up and walk over to her chair. Pulling her to her feet, I wrap my arm around her shoulder. She immediately latches on to my midsection and squeezes until I can barely take in a breath. I don't tell her to stop, though. With Denielle tucked to my side, I lean over and extend my free hand to Wes. He slowly grabs it, pulling himself up, not looking away from the guy.

Fully upright, I let go of Wes, and with Den in the middle, we face *Not Him* as a united front.

When we don't talk, he says, "I am here to rectify my mistake."

I raise my eyebrows, but Wes voices my question. "Mistake?" Some of his color has come back—potential puke crisis averted.

"We don't know how Miss Rosenfield found you. She was not on my radar during all of this. An error on my part. I apologize."

"Apologize? Who. The. Fuck. Are. You?" Denielle has recovered as well, and her resting bitch face is in place. And thank fuck, I can breathe again. I suck in the much-needed oxygen.

"I am..."—he pauses—"the head of security."

Security for what?

"You obviously suck at your job," Wes mumbles, and *Not Him*, aka the head of security, trains his narrow, rodent-like eyes on my best friend, who immediately turns chalk-white again.

I can't help but snort.

"Miss Lilly is furious. And he is not happy either. We are in the process of tracing back Miss Rosenfield's steps to figure out what happened. In the meantime, Miss Lilly demanded that I fix this. So here I am."

I raise my hand to the base of my neck. She demanded? From him? Who would have the guts to demand anything from this guy? How can she make *any* demands?

As if sensing my thoughts, he amends, looking straight at me, "You will understand soon. But you have to come with me."

"WHAT?"

"HUH?"

"NO WAY! You're not taking him anywhere." Denielle is the most articulate of us.

Scarface continues, "I am here to ensure you get your answers and talk to Miss Lilly. But only you, Mr. McGuire." His formal talking stands in complete contrast to his appearance. The scar has held my attention on his face until now. For the first time, I take in his entire person. He is decked out in full paramilitary gear of dark-gray cargo pants, tight black shirt with the matching gray cargo jacket over it, and black combat boots. I recognize the bulge on the side of his hip immediately for what it is. Growing up with my Dad, I've seen the getup many times.

"Why would I go with you anywhere? You kidnapped Lilly." I'm proud of how badass I sound.

"I did not kidnap her. Watch your mouth, *boy!*" he snaps, and all badassness leaves me. The possibility of shitting my pants crosses my mind again, and I avert my eyes.

Not Him calms his tone. "The only way I can allow you to establish a connection to Miss Lilly is in a secure location. This house"—he gestures around himself—"is not secure."

"This is a gated community. We have a second gate!" Denielle exclaims like he's personally insulted her.

"That is correct, Miss Keller. However, the guard at the front gate is fast asleep, despite the two energy drinks he consumed, and your second gate only helps if the code is not a combination of your and your brother's birthdays."

"Oh." Den has joined the club of one-word answers.

I don't care about anything that was said after "establish a connection." I'm going to talk to her. "When do we leave?"

"RHYS!"

"Dude, have you lost your fucking mind?"

I face my friends. "He's giving me another shot at talking to her. There is no way I'm passing that up."

"What if this is all a game and he's going to kill you? I mean, look at him!" Denielle whisper-shouts at me, and all three of us turn to look at the head of security who, in return, arches one eyebrow.

"If he were here to kill me, I'm sure he wouldn't have had to show his face. To any of us. And I'd probably be dead already."

"That is correct," a voice lacking any emotion comes from behind us.

Well, that's reassuring.

"I have to go." I focus on Denielle and Wes. The guy is scary as fuck, but the way he talks about Lilly, I just know that his end goal is not to slit my throat—or make use of whatever he's got strapped on under that jacket.

Neither of my friends look convinced. When a shadow appears next to us, all of us jump. I guess I'm not the only one who didn't notice him moving.

I'm back to staring at the *face divider.*

"Mr. McGuire will return here tomorrow evening. Until then, no one must know that he is not here. He will contact you to let you know that he is safe. Understood?" The underlying message is clear as hell.

Denielle's eyes flick between mine and Wes's, and Wes's shoulders slump in defeat. They know I won't change my mind.

Without another word, Scarface turns around and disappears between the bushes surrounding the fire pit.

I rub my hands on my jeans, and after one more glance at the two people who are now in as deep as I am, I track past the head of security.

IT IS PITCH BLACK. I have no clue how this dude navigates his way through the property. The sky is cloudy, and there are no lights back here. Maybe he has built-in night vision, and that's how he got his scar. Surgery gone bad. Okay, probably not. This reminds me of when Wes and I were sixteen, raided his parents' liquor cabinet, and had the grandiose idea to hit the skate park in the middle of the night. Let's just say my face got very well acquainted with the concrete. Very. Well.

I stumble for the fifth time and barely catch myself on a branch while Scarface doesn't make a sound moving through the shrubbery. A curse escapes me. Finally, he takes pity on me and directs a small flashlight to the ground. Thank you very much.

When we emerge right next to Denielle's front gate, I can't keep quiet anymore. "Dude, you just led me ten minutes through the bushes when we could've just walked out the front door?"

He stops and stares at me for a long moment. I must've said something idiotic, because my mom's favorite quote comes to mind: *He couldn't pour water out of a boot with instructions on the heel.*

"What?" I ask, exasperated.

"Mr. and Mrs. Keller have security cameras around the premises. Why do you think *Miss* Keller is allowed to remain here unsupervised all the time? The east corner of the gate is not on any camera, and for forty-two seconds, every thirteen minutes, the entire gate isn't either. Unless you want to be on tape and your parents being alerted as soon as Mr. Keller reviews the online feed before he goes to bed tonight, I suggest you trust me on this."

Wow, that's the first time he's said more than one sentence. Also, I'm not going to ask how he knows any of this.

"Sorry," I mumble, eyes trained on my boots.

We wait until something starts beeping—I assume it's his

watch—and then we simply stroll out the front gate and to a black SUV parked across the street. Approaching the vehicle, I notice that there is no license plate, just a blank—is that a screen?

Who are these people?

Opening the trunk, he looks at me expectantly.

"Oh, fuck no!" I take a step back.

"You have exactly twenty-one seconds, or I will be leaving without you." His tone is devoid of emotion.

FUCK. SHIT.

"FUCK!"

Knowing that he will leave without me, I sit down and swing my legs inside. When I think it can't get worse, he holds out a black cloth.

"Oh, come on, man!" He can't be serious. I feel like Sandra Bullock in that *Bird Box* movie—minus the whole mysterious creature stuff. Well, looking back at the man in front of me...I take that back.

"I have my orders. And my orders are to get you to a secure location so Miss Lilly can talk to you." For the first time since he stepped into the light by the fire pit, the corner of his mouth twitches ever so slightly. Lilly means something to him and not in a creepy way.

I sigh, grab the cloth, and pull it over my head. Getting comfortable on my back, I cross my arms over my chest and bend my knees. The hatch closes. And to think that a week ago, my worst fear was Lilly finding out about Kat's mind games.

The car dips as my driver climbs into the front, and off we go.

"I should probably know your name now that we are basically BFFs," I tell him like it's the most normal thing in the world to be lying in the trunk of an unmarked car with a black cloth bag over my head.

I make out a chuckle and am quite proud of myself for getting a reaction out of the guy.

"My name is George."

"It's nice to meet you, George," I say with semi-false cheeri-ness. I can't figure out why, but I'm not afraid of Scarface anymore.

He doesn't talk for what seems like hours. I must've dozed off—the trunk actually turned out to be fairly comfortable—when he announces that we are almost there.

CHAPTER SEVENTEEN

RHYS

THE CAR COMES TO A HALT, AND ALL OF A SUDDEN, THE CLOTH seems to tighten around my face. My breath becomes ragged. Any attempt to suck in air fails. Faintly aware of the trunk opening, I am pulled out by the arms. My feet land on the ground, and *Not Him*—no, wait...George pushes my upper body forward so my head is almost between my knees.

"Breathe, Rhys!"

Not Mr. McGuire—I guess we really are on the next level of our friendship.

I draw in short, shallow breaths until they become manageable again, and I'm able to inhale all the way. George pulls me upright by the back of my jacket, and I'm about to pull the cloth from my head when he stops me.

"Not yet."

Fuck.

I want this thing off my face. I no longer feel like I'm being choked out during a sparring session—yes, that happens when you train with Spence—but I want to know where we are. For a split second, I wonder if Lilly will be here.

George leads me by the arm across something that sounds like gravel, up two steps, and inside a structure. Through the fabric, I can smell the rancid air—scratch that, I no longer want to know where we are. Maybe he's going to off me after all? That would definitely explain the stench—his previous BFFs. George lets go of my arm, and I hear beeping sounds. A keypad? Something clicks, and a gust of fresh-er air pushes my new favorite accessory flush against my face.

I hope George washed this thing before he forced it on me.

He latches onto my bicep once more, and we head down two flights of stairs. More beeping, something that sounds like metal grinding against metal, and another click.

What is this? Federal prison?

Not yet finished with the thought, the cloth disappears, and I squint against the blinding light. It takes an eternity for my eyes to adjust. Finally used to the harsh glare, I realize the room is lit up by dozens of fluorescent lights hanging from the ceiling. I spin in a circle. No windows, which is not really a surprise given the fact we climbed down.

On my next turn, I focus on the rest. We're in a massive rectangular room—by my guess, about a thousand plus square feet. The walls are a bright white, and the floor is polished concrete. Two green, military-style cots are set on the wall to my left, several green trunks—the same type that occupy part of our basement at home—are stacked on top of each other between the makeshift beds. The wall opposite the door has four fireproof filing cabinets lined up—also something we have in our basement. I'm starting to think the guy has some military affiliation. The far wall to my right is one massive screen with an industrial metal table a few feet in front. A single laptop sits in the center.

"Umm..." is the only thing that comes to mind when I've completed the second scan.

"You can wait over there." George points to the cots. "It'll take me a moment before I can establish the call."

I follow his instructions and lower myself onto one of the cots. Although I am ninety-nine percent certain that he didn't bring me here to dismember my body, I don't dare to mouth off. I also won't risk my chance to talk to Lilly. So, I sit and wait.

George opens one of the filing cabinets, and even from my angle, I can see that he converted the thing to a gun safe. My eyes widen when I watch him remove a Kimber .380 from a holster under his pant leg, followed by a Glock 19, which was the bulge I noticed earlier inside his jacket. Leaning further to the side, I spot several AR-15s inside the cabinet and can't stop myself from inhaling sharply.

Yup, definitely no mouthing off happening.

His eyes flick to me, but his expression is blank. It's like the man has no mannerisms except for the one time he talked about Lilly. This is so disconcerting; the term fucked-up may also come to mind.

I follow George's every move. After unloading his small arsenal and locking the cabinet, he walks over to his desk. He puts a headset on and starts typing. Part of the monitor wall lights up with individual pictures. Squinting, I make out the black SUV on one of the rectangles and deduct that this is his security system. This whole setup reminds me of a futuristic movie—it's creepy. Distracted with the wall images, I didn't notice that he's typing again. I'm so far away that there is no chance in hell to make out what he's doing. Resigned, I settle against the wall, ankles crossed, and my arms resting over my chest. My eyelids start to droop. What time is it anyway?

"He's with me."

I jump at George's voice, and my eyes pop open.

"Yes, everything is secure." Pause. "How is she?" I hold my breath. "I guess that's understandable. Have you told her yet how Miss Rosenfield located him?"

What. The. Actual. Fuck? I sit up straight and try to peer

around him on the monitor without getting up, which results in me falling off my temporary bed with a thud.

"You might as well come over." George's casual tone makes heat shoot to my face.

Busted.

I slowly push myself off the floor and approach the desk. Before he takes his headset off, and my new *bestie* says, "Yes, we'll establish connection in a few minutes. And Miss Lilly?" Pause. Is she on the other end? A knot forms in my stomach. "I am sorry for not considering Miss Rosenfield a possible interference."

The headset lays on the tabletop when I finally step next to George, and he turns to look at me.

"Was she on the other end?" My voice is no more than a rasp.

"She was."

George stands up and motions for me to sit down. I stare at the sleek black-and-silver office chair. It looks like something you'd see in a fancy high-end office, not an underground lair. I wonder how much this thing costs.

What the hell am I thinking?

Shaking my head, I slowly lower myself down and face the laptop. The background picture of the New York City skyline distracts me for a second. I didn't take good ol' George for a city guy.

He leans over my shoulder, opens a black window, and types a few quick commands. I try to follow what he's doing, but let's face it, Lilly is the computer geek in the family, not me.

Three dots appear in the bottom line. They disappear and reappear every few seconds one after another. It reminds me of a ringing phone. I'm not sure what to expect. When my lungs start to burn, I realize I've been holding my breath.

Suddenly, the screen goes black and is quickly replaced by Lilly's face. My hand flies up, covering my mouth, and I suck in a sharp breath as I stare at her. I don't know what to do...or say. I gawk at her like an idiot. She has a healing cut on her forehead, and I feel the bile rise in my throat. Did he hurt her? I scan every inch of her face—she looks fine otherwise. Her hair is straight, and she's not wearing any makeup, but she is still the most beautiful girl I've ever seen—*my* girl.

Something wet hits the hand that's still covering my mouth. I should probably feel embarrassed, but I'm not. After nearly six days of agonizing hell, I am face to face with her.

Lilly's eyes flicker to the side and back to me. Her eyes draw together. "Rhys?" She sounds confused and...scared.

Of me?

"Is he hurt?" Lilly's question draws my attention back to the screen.

"No, Miss Lilly. I believe Rhys is trying to process," comes from behind me.

She nods, and her eyes move to something outside of the frame again. My hand finally drops from my face and joins the other on my thighs.

"Is he there?" My tone is harsh, and I did not plan for them to be the first words out of my mouth.

Lilly's eyes bulge at my outburst before her shoulder's slump. "He is." Her response is just a whisper.

"If you touched her—"

"I would never harm her," my threat gets cut off, and I am stunned to silence. He is right there. Next to her. But what did I expect? Of course he wouldn't let his captive out of sight.

I immediately notice the glare Lilly throws in the direction she's been glancing at, and I frown. It's her shut-the-fuck-up look. I was on the receiving end of it for years.

What the hell is happening?

"Lilly?"

Her eyes snap back to mine. "Yes?" She looks hopeful. This is not how I envisioned seeing her again.

"Please tell me what's going on." I sigh.

This time, she doesn't look at him but closes her eyes briefly. Her shoulders rise and fall; she's collecting her thoughts. I know this girl better than myself.

Her hazel eyes open, and she looks straight at me but speaks to him. "I have to tell him."

"Lilly..." It's a one-word warning, and I hold my breath.

She turns away from the screen and addresses the voice. "Listen, N—" She stops herself and glances over for a fraction of a second. "I need to tell him. He's been through hell for almost a week. It's cruel to leave him in the dark for another."

"Another?" I sit up straight.

"The risk is too high. If he doesn't keep his mouth shut, the entire plan goes down the drain."

"He won't say anything."

Plan? Could this exchange get any more disturbing?

"Rhys?" the voice addresses me, and despite seeing how comfortable Lilly is with him, my adrenaline spikes.

"Yes?" I try not to let my wariness bleed into my response.

"If you repeat anything back to anyone—and I mean anyone —not your little friends, and most certainly not the *people* in your house..." He leaves the sentence hanging.

"Stop going all psycho again. I told you he wouldn't say anything. He didn't tell me about anything for ten years, for fuck's sake," Lilly snaps. Turning back to me, she says, "Sorry, babe. I didn't mean to say that."

"Uh, it's ok?" My response sounds more like a question.

I'm in an alternate dimension or some shit; that's the only explanation. Lilly rarely curses; she looks confident and fierce, not like someone who's held captive.

Lilly's invisible friend is still not convinced. "I have no problem ordering George to bring him back here if I find out he talked."

Lilly seems to ponder his threat but then shoots back, "Like that'll do any good. How would we explain that to anyone?"

"We?" I didn't mean to say that out loud, and Lilly's gaze swivels back to me. I can feel George's stare on the back of my head.

She sighs. "When I told you that I'm safe, it was the truth.

Not something he"—she cocks her head to the side—"told me to say." She knows that I would assume she was forced.

My brow pulls together. "So, he is not the one that kidnapped all those girls?"

Logical conclusion, right?

"No, he is the one." Lilly presses her lips together and waits for me to process the information.

He is the one that kidnapped those girls. He is the one that kidnapped her ten years ago. He is the one that kidnapped her again. She. Is. Safe.

"WHAT THE ACTUAL FUCK, CALLA!" I can't stop my outburst. "WHAT THE FUCK IS GOING ON?" And then another thought hits me. I immediately realize how irrational it is, but my mouth speaks before my brain can interject. "Are you sleeping with him?"

"WHAT?" Lilly shrieks. "EWW, NO!"

"Watch your mouth!" *he* snaps in the background.

I believe her—both of them. Both reactions were too genuine, but the possessive asshole in me still won't let it go.

"Then why the hell are you staying there if you're not—" It's a sneer, and I wouldn't be surprised if she hangs up on me any second.

"BECAUSE HE IS MY BROTHER!" Lilly shouts, and I feel like she kicked me in the balls.

Brother?

CHAPTER EIGHTEEN

LILLY

FUCK, SHIT. I PROMISED MYSELF I WOULD EXPLAIN everything to Rhys calmly and rationally. So much for that. Why did he have to go down that road?

Tears well up in my eyes, and I blink several times. This is not how this was supposed to go.

"He is my brother, Rhys," I whisper, pleading for him to hear me out.

Rhys stares back at me, dumbfounded. He opens and closes his mouth several times, and eventually turns to George. "Brother?"

I can't see George's face as he is still standing. He must have nodded or something, because Rhys slowly turns back to me.

"How?" His anger is completely gone. Instead, I see several other emotions flitter across his face. Surprise, confusion, sadness, relief...more confusion.

I'm not sure where to begin, so I start with the most obvious. "Henry wasn't my father."

Rhys's eyes widen for a second, then he bursts out laughing like a hysterical clown. I look over to Nate, who shrugs and crosses his arms over his chest. With a smug grin on his face, his entire demeanor shouts *You wanted this; now figure out how to deal with it.*

I sit on my hands so I don't slap him over the head again.

It takes Rhys several minutes to calm down. As the laughter slowly subsides, he starts shaking his head. He looks everywhere but the screen, and I'm starting to worry. I'm not sure if I should say something, leave him be, or what?

Finally, after what feels like hours, Rhys looks back at me with a somber expression. "Of course he wasn't."

I tilt my head to the side.

He must see my confusion and elaborates. "I mean, think about it. Given the shit we had already found out before you, uh...*left*, it's not really a surprise to hear that there were more secrets."

Oh.

"Oh."

Rhys takes a deep breath. "I'm sorry, Cal. I have a hard time wrapping my head around any of this."

"Me too. This is not how I wanted to tell you about..." I trail off.

"Him?" Rhys completes my sentence, lips pursed.

"Yes," I mumble, and Nate scoffs next to me.

I narrow my eyes at him, and he makes a zip motion across his mouth, chuckling. God, this is so—I can't even think of a word to appropriately describe the absurdity of the situation. I look down at my now clasped hands in my lap. I've come to terms with my relationship with my half-brother—that there will be a relationship no matter what the outcome is after I leave here. But this is the first time my old and new lives are overlapping, and I have no idea how to handle it. I want Rhys to tell me that everything will be ok, that we will figure this out together. I want him to hold me while I tell him everything. I don't want to talk to him through a computer, almost three thousand miles between us. I most definitely don't want Nate and George to listen to every word.

My dream from a few days ago comes back to mind, and a knot the size of a soccer ball starts forming in my stomach. How can I ask Rhys to accept my relationship with Nate? Tristen and Heather work for the law. Nate has broken said law—several times over. I love Rhys more than anything, but I can't expect him to take my side. If he doesn't want to be with me because of this, I can't go home. Everything I ever knew and loved would be gone. Rhys would be gone.

My breath increases, but at the same time, it feels like all the air is being expelled from my lungs. I push the chair back so I can put my head between my legs—a motion I've been getting way too familiar with lately. In the distance, I hear Rhys call my name, but I can't be sure over the ringing in my ears. My entire focus is on drawing in slow breaths.

A hand is placed on my back and starts rubbing back and forth. All of a sudden, I'm enveloped in my brother's arms. Nate murmurs in my ear to inhale and exhale.

"YOU!" This time I'm sure it's Rhys. "GET YOUR FUCKING HANDS OFF HER!"

Why is he so angry?

"Would you shut up for a minute? Don't you see that she needs a moment," Nate snarls. Who is he talking to? Oh. My. God! The realization that Nate has just revealed himself to Rhys—to help me through my panic attack—slams into me. I sit up abruptly, and my brother jumps back before I head-butt him in the chin.

With wide eyes, I glance between my brother and Rhys, who are locked in a stare-down.

SHIT! No, no, no.

I need to do something or this will turn bad quickly. I have no idea what instructions Nate gave George regarding Rhys. Now that the airflow to my lungs is reestablished, I take a deep breath and plaster the fakest smile on my face. One could say

I'm channeling my inner Katherine Rosenfield—artificial as the blonde in her always perfectly curled hair.

"Rhys, this is Nate, my brother. Nate, say hi to Rhys."

My heart is still racing from concluding what just happened, but on the outside, I sound creepily cheery. Nothing like introducing the boy, who I *thought* to be my brother then adopted brother and is now my boyfriend, to the man who I thought was a nice guy at the gym, who turned out to have kidnapped me—twice—and revealed himself as my *real* half-brother. Nope, nothing unusual about this situation. As totally normal as seeing a sparkly pink unicorn walking down the street in a tutu, drinking a macchiato while smoking a cigar.

A high-pitched titter bursts out. My life has become a terrible reality TV show.

Both guys' eyes swivel to me, and I slap my hand in front of my mouth, trying to hold in the giggles. I can see Nate glancing back and forth between Rhys and me before he fully turns to the screen.

"Rhys, man. I'm Nate, your future brother-in-law and the guy who kidnapped your girlfriend. Twice." He even adds a slow-motion, rainbow-shaped wave.

I jerk my head toward Nate, but all he does is grin at me and shrugs. "The cat is out of the bag. Now we have to figure out a way to deal with it."

Well, shit. I did not expect that.

I peer at Rhys, whose narrowed eyes are fixed on the guy beside me. Rhys's gaze flickers to me and back several times before it settles on Nate again. "Good to meet you. To be clear, you will not stand up in our wedding. Now, how about some privacy so I can talk to Lilly?"

Brother-in-law? Wedding? Wha—

I blink several times. Rhys's face is dead serious and doesn't show any signs of fear or anger. Or disgust. He's clearly in shock; that's the only explanation.

Nate huffs out a laugh. "The boy has guts. I like it." He leans forward so his face is in the middle of the screen. "G?"

"Yes?"

"Is your place secure?" In Nate terms, can Rhys contact anyone or escape?

"It is."

"Let's give them some privacy." With that, he pushes his chair back and stands up. "If you need me, I'll be in the library."

All I can do is nod before I'm alone in the NCC. Nate left me alone with all his computers. On the other end, George murmurs something to Rhys, who dips his head and then turns back to me.

We sit in silence, and I am finally able to look at him. A lone tear escapes my eye, and I stifle a whimper. I've missed him so much.

NATE INITIATED the call from one of the laptops, so I unplug the device and make my way over to the couch. It's almost midnight, and I'm exhausted. Today's rollercoaster of events has left me completely drained, but the need to talk to Rhys is more powerful than my physical requirement for sleep.

With the computer settled on my lap, I stifle a yawn. I'm trying to figure out where to start when Rhys whispers, "I love you so much, Calla."

The affection reflected in his eyes is my undoing. A sob escapes, and the floodgates open. I cover my face with my hands.

"It's ok, babe. I'm here," Rhys's voice comes through the speaker.

This is all too much.

"Calla, please don't cry. It'll be ok..."

I pry my hands away from my face and look at the boy on the screen. "You think?" I hiccup.

"I know." Rhys's confidence is contagious, but how could he possibly know that?

"How?" I whisper.

His face gentles, and the corner of his mouth quirks up. "Because we'll get through it together."

I want to believe him. I do. But I can't shake the small doubt remaining in the back of my head. "How can you still want to be with me?"

Rhys's eyebrows furrow. "Why wouldn't I?"

I'm scared to speak the words out loud, the thoughts that have been occupying my mind for the last few days. I close my eyes, and without looking at him, I say, "Because I am related to a criminal." I draw in a deep breath. "And because I will stand by my brother's side."

When I don't get a response for several moments, I slowly open my eyes, prepared for Rhys to have disconnected or walked away from the computer. He is still there, but his face is unreadable.

"Please say something." My heart is beating in my throat.

"You're only saying this because you are still angry with Mom and Dad. And with me, for keeping the whole Kat thing from you." His voice is cold and detached.

It would be easier to deal with him being upset.

"No, I'm saying this because I know Nate—"

"IT'S BEEN A FUCKING WEEK. ONE. WEEK," Rhys bursts out.

He is angry.

"How can you possibly know this guy? He's a fucking psycho!" Rhys is trying to rein in his temper, and I'm waiting for George to show up in the background after Rhys called Nate "a fucking psycho." George remains absent.

"Please let me explain?" I rasp out.

If he'd hear me out, maybe I can make him understand? Heck, I don't even comprehend what's going on inside of my head; how can I expect him to? That realization makes a wave of panic surge through me like a tidal wave, and the thought of not being able to return home threatens to choke me again. I put the laptop next to me on the couch and bend forward to concentrate on breathing. This is the second time in one night. Ugh.

"Calla?"

When I don't react, Rhys gentles his tone. "Babe, look at me. Please."

It's still hard to breathe, but I force myself to face the boy who essentially will decide for me if I'm going home or not. Without him accepting my relationship with my half-brother, I don't have a home to go back to.

"Listen, Cal. I, uh...I'm trying. I am, but I know I will fuck this up. This past week has been a nightmare. Mom is a mess; Natty is with Olivia; Den and Wes are a shit-show. We had no idea where you were—if you were alive. I can't put into words how relieved I am that you are...safe. But how you can be ok with what this guy has done..." Rhys trails off, sadness in his eyes. Hearing him say out loud what I feared my friends and family were going through while I played family is devastating.

"I'm not ok with it. Nate will take responsibility. For everything," I tell him cautiously. Perceptive as he is, he picks up on what I'm not saying.

"But?"

"There is more. More than any of us thought. Until Nate and I can sort through that, he won't come forward." I neglect the part of Nate also wanting to make sure that my finances are sorted before he goes away. My new money situation is a conversation for another day. Somehow, I don't want Rhys to know— yet. After a pause, I add, "I won't make him. Not yet. We both need answers," I beg Rhys to understand.

The boy on the screen shakes his head, and my heart sinks. We don't speak for a long time. Rhys stares at something in the distance, and I can't look away from his distraught face. I'm hurting him with my decision, and it kills me, but I also can't turn my back on Nate.

My gaze keeps moving to the clock on the top of the screen.

We sit there for almost twenty minutes before Rhys's eyes find mine again.

"Tell me," is all he says to me, and I do.

Over the next two hours, I try to summarize everything that has happened from the moment I walked out of school on Tuesday. Apparently, no one could figure out why I crashed my Jeep and assumed I was run off the road by my captor. I confess how angry I was at Rhys for keeping Kat's games from me but that I don't care about that anymore. He wanted to protect me, and the relief in his face is palpable. For the most part, Rhys lets me talk. I explain how Nate found me after our visit to Santa Rosa, and Rhys curses under his breath. We led him straight to us. When I mention my most recent migraine, his eyes widen, but he remains mute. Though, when I get to the financial statements, Rhys starts asking questions.

"You think Emily and...uh, Brooks had an affair all those years?" Tone skeptical, Rhys still assumes this is all part of an elaborate scheme Nate came up with.

"I don't know. Between my memories and the letters, it makes sense. And then there is the money Brooks transferred every month. But some things don't add up. I have this gut feeling..." I try to put it in words as well as I can. "It's like when I started researching for my paper. The more articles I read, the more I was drawn to it. It's the same with this." Deep down, I'm convinced everything we've discovered so far is still just the tip of the iceberg.

"Since your brother is such an awesome hacker, can't he just track the money?" Sarcasm drips from Rhys's tone.

"He's working on it." I don't want to start fighting again, so I leave it at that.

We sit in silence until Rhys points out, "None of this explains why he kidnapped you in the first place—or the other girls."

Up until now, I haven't mentioned much about Nate's past, so I backtrack and tell Rhys about Payton and Audrey, what happened to Nate after their accident, and how he later found out about me.

"Well, fuck. That'd make anyone crazy."

"I don't think it was just that. At least not the only reason..." I mumble. I've kept my suspicion to myself ever since Nate told me about his mental health.

"What do you mean?" Rhys is squinting at me, probably questioning if I've also lost my mind.

I glance at the door as if Nate may barrel through it at any moment, subconsciously knowing that I'm revealing personal information about him.

"I think it's his meds..." I leave the sentence hanging.

"His meds?" Clearly, Rhys doesn't buy it.

"Nate and I talked a lot, and something he said stuck with me. I want to do more research on it, but I haven't had access to a computer until today." I pause, and Rhys lets me collect my thoughts. "He mentioned that every time he, uh...needed company..."—I can't bring myself to say *kidnapped a girl*—"it's right after his shrink switches his meds around. So...uh, remember when Heather and Tristen talked about that guy who used to be in Tristen's unit? The guy who, after his discharge, always went off the rails when his counselor put him on new antidepressants?" I'm referring to a conversation Rhys and I had eavesdropped on years ago and were not supposed to hear. We got caught lurking on the stairs while Heather and Tristen were in the living room and got a massive tongue lashing never to repeat a word about that to anyone. I see a flicker of recognition in Rhys's eyes—he remembers—so I continue, "That's what I think happens to Nate whenever he gets new meds."

Rhys purses his mouth in a slash of disbelief. "Don't you think that's a little farfetched? That you're looking for an excuse?"

I understand where he's coming from but can't suppress the anger that his statement sparks inside of me. "He's going to pay no matter what, Rhys," I snap. "But there is a difference between intentionally committing a crime and being helpless to meds fucking with the chemicals in your brain."

Rhys winces at my outburst. Up until now, I've taken the brunt of his anger and suspicion. I feel like I deserve it after hanging out with my brother while my loved ones were worried out of their minds. But I'm tired, and my patience—even for the boy that I would do almost anything for—wears thin. It's past two in the morning, which makes it after five for Rhys, and as if on cue, Rhys starts yawning.

"Can we talk about something else for a bit? I don't want to fight anymore," I murmur.

Rhys's face immediately softens, and he smiles. "Of course, babe."

With that small gesture, my chaotic world falls into place, and for this brief moment, we're just us again. We're in the little bubble we created every time Rhys snuck into my room at night. I settle deeper into the couch and lean my head against the back of it. Rhys rests his chin on his stacked fists on the tabletop and softly smiles at me. At that moment, everything else is forgotten, and my heart is full. We talk about frivolous things. Magnolia's took Wes's favorite drink off the menu—some Christmas-y hot cocoa concoction with a bunch of seasonal flavors—and he's outraged. He threatened the owner to start a petition, who just responded that it'd be back next Christmas. I laugh out loud because that's typical Wes; the poor guy does not like change. At. All. Rhys is looking forward to a new video game that's coming out in a few weeks. It's "the shit," and all the guys from school are taking bets against each other on who will get the higher score. Boys. But that's what I needed to hear—something that has absolutely nothing to do with our situation.

CHAPTER NINETEEN

LILLY

I WAKE UP WITH A START AND GRAB THE COMPUTER RIGHT before it completely slides off my lap toward the floor.

Where is my bed?

Rhys! The video-chat. We were talking and must've fallen asleep? I hit the space bar on the laptop—nothing. I press the power button—again nothing. The laptop is dead. No, no, no. I didn't say goodbye.

I jump up without thinking, and this time, the laptop does hit the ground. Shit. I pause for a second and then dismiss the device, charging out of the room.

"NATE!" I stop outside the door in the hallway. Silence. I run to the library, but there is no sign of him. The clock on the shelf shows 10:37. Oh God, I slept for-like-ever. Fuck, what if George took Rhys back already?

Racing downstairs to the kitchen, I keep calling my brother, but he is nowhere to be found. He always comes to me when I'm looking for him. Where is he? Finding the kitchen empty as well, I spin in a circle. My entire body is vibrating from the inside out.

Back in the hallway, I start flinging open doors along the way, but all I find are either empty rooms or bare-looking guest rooms.

On the second floor, I find Margot's bedroom—the room she believes is hers and Nate's. I recognize it from the brief view on the security feed. It's the only room I've found so far that looks somewhat lived in with a white, fluffy duvet draped over the four-poster bed and about a hundred throw pillows accurately positioned. Three picture frames are on the dresser across from the bed. I take a step closer; all the pictures display Nate and Margot. In the one closest to me, both are wearing formal wear. Nate wears a sleek, black tux with a crisp, white cufflink shirt, while Margot looks stunning in a strapless, floor-length, blood-red sheath dress that clings to her every curve. The second picture was taken at a—is that a racetrack? Margot is dressed to the nines in skinny jeans, knee-high stiletto boots, and a cropped leather jacket—everything black. She looks like a fashionable assassin. Nate, however, is wearing a black-and-gray racesuit, standing next to a dangerous-looking motorcycle. He races? Squinting, I can make out the letters MV and, further up, F4, but because of the angle, the rest is unreadable. Let's be honest; even if I could read it, I know as much about motorcycles as a third-grader does about the stock market. The last picture was taken at a New Year's party. A ginormous "Happy New Year" banner is in the background, and they're kissing. But something stands out to me; besides the kiss in the third photograph, they all look staged. Nate's words echo inside my head: *I don't believe in a soul mate, that there is the one. Margot and I work well together.* My mind completes the unspoken part of the statement; they don't love each other. Knowing how I feel about Rhys, that realization makes me sad for my brother.

The room has completely distracted me; I'm wasting time. Spinning around, I finish my search on the second floor. I even walk into Nate's actual bedroom—knocking first, of course—and take in the stark contrast to his fake bedroom. This one is masculine and sparse. Dark-navy sheets, no throw pillows, and no pictures.

Closing the door behind me, I'm running out of options. Fuck. What if he left the property? Then it hits me: the gym.

HE IS SWIMMING LAPS. I'm standing at the edge of the pool and watching Nate swim one lane after the other. He's in the zone, and I have never seen him not on guard. It's fascinating. Glancing around, I see his phone and tablet on one of the lounge chairs, and the small voice inside my head perks up, telling me to grab both and make a run for it. My gaze shifts between the devices and my brother a few times before I sit down on the other chair. I'm past running.

I'll give him a few more minutes before I make myself known and walk back to the edge of the pool. He is about to turn for another lap when he notices me and pauses.

"You're awake."

Attempting to stifle my giggle, I look him up and down. He looks ridiculous with only his head sticking out of the water, goggles over his eyes, and his hair dripping in his face. It's a whole new side of my brother.

"You left me," I say accusingly after my initial amusement has worn off.

Nate pulls himself out of the pool and walks over to the shelf containing a stack of towels. Dropping into the lounge chair I previously occupied, he drawls, "Little sister, you were out of it. I came in several times, even called your name. You were out like a light."

Oh.

"Is Rhys home?" I'm scared to hear his answer.

"No, but he has to leave soon. He has to be back before anyone starts asking questions—more questions, I should say."

I put my hands on my hips and tilt my head toward the ceiling, calculating how long he's been with George. Would Heather and Tristen be looking for him? They never have before.

As if guessing my train of thought, Nate says, "Rhys has been in touch with his parents through Wes. Since he left his phone at home when he ran out Saturday, Wes has been sending messages for your boyfriend from his phone."

I furrow my eyebrows.

I guess with me missing, they care *where he is?*

"Tristen had been checking up on him through Wes's parents. Now that neither of them is at Wes's house, Tristen called Denielle's father, who gave him access to the security system. I'm telling you, your adopted father has quite the cards up his sleeve. I'm no longer surprised I couldn't find you until..."

I made myself known, I finish the sentence in my head. Then, Nate's words register, and my heart rate increases. "If he has access to the security feed, wouldn't he know that Rhys is not there?"

A smug smile appears on my brother's face. "George is the best at his job. There is no trace of Rhys leaving on any of the footage, and the cameras inside the house are only in very specific locations. Wes got detailed instructions on what to communicate. As far as Tristen is concerned, Rhys has locked himself in one of the guest rooms on the top floor and will only open the door when Wes brings him food."

"But..." I pause; I'm still confused. "Heather and Tristen have never checked up on Rhys before. They just let him leave two years ago. Is it because I'm, uh...gone?"

Nate glances to the side before his eyes lock on mine. He looks almost pained. "My guess? They never had to check up on Rhys because they always tracked him through his phone."

What?

"Why? Why didn't they just make him stay home?" My voice is just slightly above a whisper.

"I wish I could answer you that. But I'm suspecting it has

something to do with the reason they wired the entire house with cameras like a high-security prison."

More secrets.

BEFORE HEADING BACK to the NCC, we take a detour through the kitchen. Nate assures me we can spare ten minutes to eat. He's been in touch with George and Rhys, and they're just hanging out. When I inquire what that means, he switches the topic and tells me about what he is planning on putting in his post-workout protein shake.

Yup, my brother is insane.

I'm leaning against the cabinets next to the fridge while Nate has his butt parked on the edge of the massive kitchen table across from me. He is sucking away on a shake that looks like something between throw-up and swamp water. I'm wolfing down another round of carbs, followed by some fruit, as Nate informs me that George procured a secure device for Rhys. I almost choke on a grape as he says the words.

"You're letting me talk to him? Any time I want?" My mouth hangs open.

"I am. But only if you and Loverboy follow my instructions. If anyone finds out about the phone, I will remote wipe it and cut the connection immediately."

I'm too stunned by Nate's show of good faith that I just mumble something resembling, "I promise," crumbs of breakfast falling out of my mouth.

My brother chuckles at my dumbfounded expression. "I can't cut you two off for another week, can I? George and I had an extensive conversation this morning while the two of you were getting your beauty rest. I already spoke with Rhys a little bit ago to get a better feel for my future brother-in-law," Nate says nonchalantly.

I gape at him for a long moment before I push off the counter and tackle-hug him around his midsection. He reached out to Rhys. He is letting me talk to him. My voice is choked up as I whisper, "Thank you."

Nate's arms wrap automatically around my shoulders as if we've always been brother and sister—ordinary siblings, without the whole kidnapping history. Hugging him starts to feel natural.

WITH THE LAPTOP STILL CHARGING, Nate establishes the connection from one of the desktops. He doesn't have to wait for the other end to pick up or anything; it connects straight to George's place.

Note to self: Ask where that is.

What I see on the screen makes me spray my tea all over Nate's keyboards, and he curses, diving for a box of tissues. He allowed me to bring my caffeine in a secure travel mug. What he didn't take into account was that there would be another way for me to ruin his tech with my tea.

"Uh, George? I thought we concluded that the boyfriend is not a threat?" Nate seems as shocked as I am.

In front of us, several feet away from the computer on George's end, are both men in a standoff. George has an AR-15 trained at Rhys—thanks to Tristen, I knew the difference between an AR and an MP5 before I turned thirteen. Instead of looking alarmed, Rhys is standing across from him with his hands on his hips and head cocked to the side.

At Nate's question, the guys turn to the monitor.

"Hey, babe." Rhys grins at me.

"Good morning, Miss Lilly." George nods in the same direction and lowers the rifle.

Nate and I look at each other and then back at the screen.

What the hell is going on?

Rhys takes quick strides toward the desk and plops down in the chair like it's the most natural thing in the world. "Babe, did you know George was a Marine back in the day? His stories make Dad look like a boy scout. And how he got the scar...holy fuck. I can't believe he survived that..." He trails off.

I open and close my mouth several times but can't come up with an adequate response. I glance over at my brother, and his confused expression confirms that he is out of the loop as well.

"How come the boy knows how you got your scar, and I don't?" Nate growls.

George slowly walks over and chuckles. That's the most emotion I have seen on his face to date. "That's because you never asked. I don't run around advertising my past."

Okay, then.

"George was just showing me the silencer he got for his AR-15. This thing is so badass; Wes would shit his pants." Rhys literally jumps in the seat. I'm not sure if that is cute or disturbing.

"What happened since I last spoke to you two hours ago? You barely looked at each other," Nate inquires with narrowed eyes.

"We bonded. Your head of security is not so scary once you get to know him." When neither Nate nor I say anything, Rhys looks straight at my brother and smirks. "What? Are you jealous he likes me better?"

"Since I fund his little operation, he doesn't have to like me," Nate snaps, and George's eyebrows lift in the background. He concluded the same as me at this point. My brother is, in fact, jealous. I press my lips together to stop myself from laughing out loud. This is just absurd.

I clear my throat. "So, uh, George. Where exactly are you right now?" I'm not sure if he'll tell me, but I need to change the topic somehow.

"We're near Morristown, New Jersey," George immediately responds.

"Really? You made me lie in that fucking trunk for over four hours?" Rhys looks up.

"You fell asleep for three and a half of that; stop complaining," he shoots back.

They are seriously bantering with each other. What the ever-loving—

"Okay, let's get back to business. My sister needs to talk to her boyfriend before he has to head back. We still have to go over some of the logistics for the next week. Let's postpone this little bonding thing you two have going on until your road trip." Nate's tone sends a cold shiver down my spine, and I wonder if he is truly mad at George or Rhys.

George nods. "I will get the car ready. We'll be leaving in thirty minutes."

Nate turns to me. "I'm going to shower and be back before that."

"Okay." Before I can say anything else, he is out of his chair and out the door.

I turn back to the monitor, and Rhys grins at me. "He is so jealous."

This time, I allow myself to laugh and shake my head.

CHAPTER TWENTY

RHYS

LILLY FELL ASLEEP AT SOME POINT, AND I WATCHED HER UNTIL I couldn't keep my eyes open anymore, which was somewhere around six a.m., I think. I wake up with a start, trying to figure out where I am.

"Good morning, Rhys," a deep voice comes from behind me, and my head whips around.

George is standing in the middle of the room with a compound bow in his hand.

"Uh...good morning?"

What the fuck is he doing with that? In here!

Without elaborating, he opens one of the fireproof cabinets and puts his archery equipment away. "I spoke to Nate while you were napping."

"O-kay?"

"We have concluded that you are not a threat to Miss Lilly."

"No shit, dude!" Great, my brain still seems to be napping as my mouth talks without considering the consequences. The guy has enough firepower for a small town during the zombie apocalypse in this room, and I have to run my stupid trap.

This time, George turns to me and chuckles.

"Whoa, man. You have actual facial expressions!"

Shut up, shut up, shut up.

But instead of choking or shooting me, he barks out a genuine laugh. "Rhys McGuire, I like you."

"You do?" I can feel my eyebrows rise.

"Yes. You have guts. Miss Lilly means more to you than your own safety, and now that you are aware of her brother, we will see a lot of each other," George deadpans.

"We will?"

A stoic nod.

And there go the facial expressions.

The man with the huge scar walks over to me and leans against the table. "Nate wants to talk to you when you're awake. Let's get that over with so the man can say his piece."

"Where is Lilly?"

"Miss Lilly is still asleep. Nate assured me that he'd wake her up before we have to leave."

"What's with the *Miss* Lilly thing?"

"It's a way to show respect; you may try it sometime," he says with a not-stoic face; unfortunately, the facial expression he does display is not a friendly one either.

Okay, officially shutting my piehole now.

George leans over me to reach the laptop and establishes the connection to Nate, aka Psycho.

His face appears on the screen, and before I can say anything, I'm greeted with, "If that's not my future brother-in-law," sarcasm dripping from his words.

He would get along perfectly with Denielle.

He seems to be sitting in a kitchen, based on the white cabinets in the background. I stay quiet. I'm not sure how smart it is to provoke the guy who holds Lilly captive—well, not captive, but you know what I mean.

Nate looks at George. "Have you filled him in yet? How his ex-girlfriend ruined the call to his *new* girlfriend?"

The mention of Kat perks my attention.

"I have not. I was leaving that up to you. He just woke up."

"Awesome." Nate rubs his hands together like a loon. I'm starting to question Lilly's assessment of his sanity—more than I already was.

I swallow over the lump in my throat and try to sound like he doesn't intimidate the shit out of me—now that his sister is not sitting next to him. I channel my school persona and drawl, "So? How did she find me?"

Nate chuckles, entertaining my charade, but I don't give him the satisfaction of showing him any other emotion besides indifference.

He looks down, and I see the top of some type of tablet at the bottom of the screen. "I've spent quite some time tracing back Barbie's steps." I snort at Nate's accurate assessment of Kat, and he looks up.

"Sorry, just a perfect description for her," I explain myself.

Nate nods, and a smirk appears at the corner of his mouth. If I didn't know better, I'd say we're bonding—a little.

"As I said, I retraced her steps. What I was able to find is that when neither Lilly nor you showed up in school, she started asking questions. As of now, there are no news reports about Lilly's, uh...disappearance, and all I could find is that your parents excused both of you from school. The same goes for your two friends. I assume your father kept everything—including the people camping out at your house—under wraps. My question for him would be why, but we're getting off topic.

"I checked Barbie's phone activity. You never disabled your Friend Finder for her. She had access to your location, as well as your friend Wes's at all times." Nate looks up and gives me a disapproving glare before he continues. "As her location service is permanently enabled as well, I was able to retrace her steps laughably easy. She regularly drove by your house and Wes's. My guess is she noticed your car was gone, but your phone was still at home, so she checked the next best option. While doing that, she kept texting half your class, asking if they had seen Lilly, but no one could give her any answers. The only responses she got were that no one had seen Lilly, your friends, or you since the incident last week. Some speculated that you were all hiding out somewhere together." His face grimaces in disgust, and I'm betting it's about the shit my so-called friend said.

"Saturday, she was staked out at the coffee shop near Wes's house all afternoon. She must've seen Wes's location changing and decided to drive by and check on you." Nate's eyes meet mine. "By the way, suggest to your friend to get some curtains." His eyes drop back to the tablet. "She followed you from Wes's house to the park. I'm not sure why she didn't drive up immediately since you were there for over ten minutes. Since then, she's been driving by Wes's and Denielle's house several times. I have advised both of your friends to turn off their location services and disable the numerous Friend Finder apps you kids all have."

Nate seems to be done with his report and faces me now straight on.

"Advised?" I can't help myself.

"I've been in touch with both of them to make sure they relay the correct information to their and your parents."

"And they're doing it?" I'm a bit stunned by Denielle and Wes cooperating so easily—mostly Den.

George chuckles, and Nate throws him a death glare. When neither of them answers my question, I turn to the man behind me. George looks down, and for the third time since waking up with my face stuck to the metal desk, I see real emotion on the man's face. Amusement. "Miss Lilly previously ensured that her brother would not sound like a '*complete psycho*' anymore."

I bark out a laugh. That's my girl.

"Well, now that this is clarified," Nate's voice pulls my attention back to the screen, "let's talk about your part in this."

Nate fills me in on the plan, as much as it already exists, and when he says that he would provide a phone for me, my eyes nearly bulge out of their sockets. Maybe he's not so bad after all

—besides the kidnapping issue, of course. He reiterates what I am to tell everyone, and after the fourth time of him explaining in detail what would happen if I don't comply, my brain goes into nap mode again.

A sleek new cell phone is placed in front of me on the desk, and Nate explains that I can reach Lilly, George, and him with it —no one else. The phone will only connect to the numbers he makes me repeat several times. I'm to memorize them before George deposits me back at Denielle's. If I don't know them by then, I have to wait until one of them contacts me. Biting my tongue, I swallow the retort I want to spout off out of fear he'll take the phone back.

After we disconnect, George has me learn the phone numbers backward and forward. When he's satisfied that I finally have them etched into my brain, he provides me with coffee and granola bars. That he doesn't bust out MREs from one of his green trunks surprises me a bit. We have several storage bins in the basement that contain *Meals Ready-to-Eat*. As Dad always says, "You never know when you can use them." So far, we haven't needed them, and I'm sure some date back to a Pre-Rhys or Lilly time.

The wait for Lilly to wake up is excruciating. I need to find something to pass the time.

"So..." I tentatively probe, "were you in the military or what?"

George, who is head deep in one of the fireproof cabinets yet again, turns to me. "I was."

"Is that where you got that, uh...scar?" I don't know if I'm brave or utterly stupid.

"Yes."

I shouldn't, but I ask anyway. "What happened?"

Staring past me, he remains quiet for several moments, and I assume that means he won't tell me shit. His eyes swivel back to me. "I haven't spoken about that in over twenty-five years."

"Why?"

"Most people are not as intrusive as you, Rhys." He might as well have said *suicidal*.

"Most people are scared shitless by you."

Fuck my stupid mouth.

"And you are not?" Eyebrows raised, he means to look intimidating, but he can't hide the smirk.

No one probably ever challenges him, looking like the child of Kylo Ren and Matt Addison before he fully turned Nemesis. As obsessed as Lilly is about all the *Blade* movies, I'm the same way with the *Star Wars* and *Resident Evil* franchises—movies, video games, you name it.

George seems to enjoy me having no control over my trap. I'm also pretty good at reading people, and he has shown, on many occasions since yesterday, that he cares about Lilly, and even her psycho brother. He won't hurt me—*much*.

"Not really. Not anymore, at least," I admit. "You care about Lilly in a way I don't fully get yet, but you do care. You protect her, and that tells me you're not all that bad." I shrug and grin at the man.

"I was on a mission—the details of what or where are not important. I was distracted, and the enemy used that to their advantage. They overpowered me—six to one." I lean forward in my seat as George keeps talking in a detached voice. "I was able to incapacitate three, but my strength was dwindling fast. I had been on recon all night. One was able to get close and sliced a knife across my stomach, stabbed my right kidney." He lifts his shirt and reveals a just as gruesome scar as on his face. Before I can exclaim how fucked up that is, he continues. "His mistake was coming close, and I returned the favor." The diabolical grin spreading across his face makes my blood run cold. Maybe I should be scared for myself. "I was losing blood fast, and the last two managed to pin me down. They told me they would use me to set an example; they planned to cut my face off, return me to my unit, and use it as a warning." Bile starts to rise in my throat, but George is oblivious. "One was sitting on my legs, the other

on the chest. He had just started cutting when a bomb somewhere nearby went off. That was my chance. They jumped from
the explosion and gave me the leverage on my body to kick them
off. Unfortunately, the knife was still close to my face." He traces
his scar almost subconsciously. "I was told that I overpowered
both and stabbed them a combined eighty-three times. The next
thing I remember is waking up in the hospital."

"HO-LY FUCK!" My mouth hangs open, and I'm not sure
what the appropriate response here is.

I squeeze as much information out of George as I can—once
you get past the scary exterior, the guy is like a wet dream for
badass war stories. Don't ask me why, but he answers every question I throw at him. We already established that I'm nosy as
fuck, so I guess he has resigned himself to my *intrusive* personality. Most of his replies are completely expressionless, though, as
if he detaches himself from recalling the memories. He's just
shown me the new scope he got for the AR-15 at this location—
he wouldn't divulge how many others he has—when we are interrupted by Nate's voice.

It probably wasn't the most genius idea to provoke Psycho
with my bonding with his head of security, but I couldn't stop
myself. It made me feel like shoving both middle fingers in his
face and doing a whole na-na, na-na, na dance. He deserves so
much more after what he has put my family and me through.

GEORGE LEAVES my favorite accessory in his secret lair. I look at
him curiously as he drops the black cloth on one of the cots on
the way out, but he ignores me. When he leads me to the backseat, he says I need to lie down until we're out of city limits. I
stare at him, and he deadpans, "Traffic cameras." The duh after-
ward was not spoken out loud but written all over his face. That
makes four facial expressions total, and I want to pat my own
back. We've totally bonded over the last twenty-four hours.

Occasionally, he quizzes me on the phone numbers; I'm

proud to say that I can rattle them off like they've been part of me for years.

I replay the conversation I had with Lilly before it was time to leave. She told me that Nate has to go to LA for the weekend, and that's one of the reasons it'll be another week before she can come home. The alarm bells in my head immediately start to shrill when she mentions the word *alibi*. Yes, her reason makes sense, but I can't shake the feeling that she's hiding something from me. Of course, my brain goes to the worst-case scenarios, like she's not coming home, or he won't take responsibility after all. What happened to these poor girls will never be rectified. Lastly, even though I know deep down it's bullshit, my mind goes down the rabbit hole of Nate not being her biological brother, and this is all a big fat lie. She is *with* him and will never come home. I keep shaking my head several times at that thought. I. Trust. Lilly.

Eventually, George asks me if I'm having some sort of seizure. I guess I'm still shaking my head, and after a deep breath, I ask flat out, "Is Nate really Lilly's brother?"

George's eyebrows knit together as he looks at me, puzzled, through the rearview mirror. I push further. "I mean, how do we know? After all, he kidnaps little girls for fun."

With squealing tires, George brings the car to a standstill on the side of the deserted road. We're in the middle of nowhere in the state of New Jersey. I curse myself once again for my stupid mouth. He may be my new BFF, but I'm pretty sure his loyalty lies with Nate first.

George turns in his seat and pins me down with a glare. "I want you to listen to me very carefully, Rhys. Nate has his faults, but he is Miss Lilly's biological brother. I made sure of that as soon as Nate informed me that he had found her. I have known of Miss Lilly for years, but neither of us was able to locate her. Once I had the DNA proof, I did most of the work. I followed Miss Lilly, not Nate. You can say what you want about him and his past, but he loves his sister. He would do anything for her. If she'd ask him to turn himself over tomorrow, he would. However, both of them need closure. There are a lot more questions to be answered. And Nate needs to make sure Miss Lilly is taken care of. I worked for Mr. Altman for years before his death. I kept in the background after that, but when Miss Payton died, I made myself available to Nate. Someone had to look after him. His mother and sister's death broke him. After everything Mr. Altman had done for me, that was the least I could do. You need to trust your girlfriend to do the right thing. This past week has not been easy for her, either. If she keeps something from you, she has her reasons."

My mouth hangs open, and I stare at George wide-eyed. This is the first time he has spoken like this about Nate, and it makes it clear that he cares about him in a way that goes beyond employer and head of security. I simply jerk my head up and down.

We're quiet for the rest of the drive, and eventually, I lie back down in the seat, not even caring to see the route.

CHAPTER TWENTY-ONE

RHYS

IT'S PAST SEVEN IN THE EVENING WHEN WE ARRIVE BACK IN Westbridge. When the car comes to a halt, I don't bother getting up. I know the drill and wait for George to bark the next order at me.

Through the gap between the front seats, I see him typing on his phone before he lifts it to his ear. "We're here." Pause. "Nine minutes. Send the message. I will text you when it's time." Another pause. "Yes, understood."

When he places the phone on the armrest in the middle, I can't contain my curiosity. "Time for what?"

George turns around for the first time since giving me the lecture about Nate and trusting Lilly. "To cut the power."

That does make me sit up. "What?"

"I have to get you back in the house unseen. Furthermore, into the guest room that everyone believes you've been in for the past twenty-four hours."

Oh.

"What's the plan?" I'm genuinely curious.

"We can't cut the security feed unnoticed; therefore, your

friend will flip the breakers from inside the house. The only cameras with night-vision capability are the ones outside and at the main entrances."

"Uh, and how do we get in if they will still see us?"

George flashes me a wide, toothy grin that makes alarm bells shrill in my ears fire-engine-siren style.

I. AM. SO. FUCKED.

YUP, fucked indeed. After, once again, stomping through the shrubbery of Denielle's parents' backyard property for God knows how long, we emerge at the southeast end of the house near the kitchen. I can see the freaking SUV on the other side of the fence from where we're sitting ducked between two massive planters. George pulls out his phone, set to the dimmest brightness; I have no idea what he is doing even though I am right next to him. He types several words and pockets the device again. I try to catch his eye, but he stares at something along the wall I can't identify.

Suddenly, the entire house goes dark, and a few seconds later, something hits me on the head from above.

Mother—

I look up and wait for my eyes to adjust to the complete darkness. The "something" is a free-climbing rope Oliver must've left behind when he went to college. I remember this was one of his hobbies growing up. It's hanging down from the third story window, and a head peeks out from above. I glance over, and George's Pennywise grin is back.

Just. Great.

He gestures at me, then at the window, and I mouth, "What?"

He points again, and I get what he expects me to do. "You're not fucking serious?" I keep my voice low, but I might as well have shouted; it's that silent.

Pennywise turns his usual self again. "Get your ass up that

rope and into the house. You have three minutes before the backup generator kicks in, and then you can kiss the phone in your pocket goodbye. Nate was very clear about what to do when you don't follow the plan. And this is the plan."

My inner five-year-old comes out, and I mumble, "Nate can kiss my ass!"

George starts reaching for the pocket I stashed the phone in, and I jump backward. "Jeez, dude. Chill out. I'm going!" He seriously would've taken the phone back. Fucker.

The grin is back on George's face. He is enjoying himself immensely, and for the first time, I have the urge to clock my new friend. Scary or not.

I wrap the rope around my calf and ankle and grasp it with both hands. One more look to the side and I'm off. Thankfully, this is something we do regularly during practice, and I reach the window's ledge in no time. Wes grabs me by the belt loop and hauls me into the room. We land ungracefully on the floor, and before I can say anything, Wes has the rest of the rope pulled into the house, the window shut, and is dragging me across the hallway into another room. The door closes behind us, and when I turn, I see Denielle leaning against it. She scans every inch of me—probably for injuries—while both her hands cover her mouth.

"You're back," she breathes out.

Without another word, she launches herself at me. My arms instinctively wrap around her. Wes's hand lands on my shoulder, and I glance over at my best friend of ten years. Standing here, the last day seems unreal.

I'M SITTING at the foot of the bed in the guest room I supposedly have occupied since arriving here last night. Denielle and Wes take the floor, sitting oddly close together—shoulders, hips, and knees touching. I cock my head and examine them closer. There is nothing romantic going on, but everyone's relationships are shifting. Denielle and Wes are growing closer while I'm drifting apart from my friends—and girlfriend. A sharp pain shoots through my jaw, and I realize I've been grinding my teeth.

"So...?" Denielle looks at me expectantly.

Guilt travels upward, coating my throat. I want to tell them that Lilly will be home soon, but I am not allowed to reveal anything but the agreed-upon story. All I can do is channel my mask—the façade I've perfected over the years. Don't show your true feelings and most importantly, lie your ass off. I pray my friends will forgive me.

"This cannot leave this room. This has to stay between the three of us." I level both with the George-face—stoic and serious. "I am telling you as much as I can—am allowed to."

Before I can continue, Wes interjects, "Allowed to? What the fuck is that supposed to mean?"

And it's already starting.

I have difficulty swallowing. I want to blurt everything out, but one, it wouldn't be fair to Lilly—it's her life, past, and future. And two, if I'm honest, Nate still scares the crap out of me, despite what I said to George earlier. He's a genius with the computer, and I'm a little worried about what he could do to me on a cyber level.

I sigh. "Please just let me get it all out."

Wes opens his mouth again, but Denielle places a hand on his knee, and some silent communication passes between them.

Fucking perfect.

I lean forward with my elbows on my thighs, hands clasped, and start talking toward the floor, making sure I stick to the script. "As I said, I am telling you everything I'm allowed to. In the end, this is Lilly's story; she needs to tell it to you, not me." I lift my head and make sure both my friends see how serious I am. "She is safe. She is not harmed in any way—besides the injuries she sustained from the car accident. She is healthy."

Denielle's eyebrows rise, and I amend, "Lilly crashed the Jeep because she was avoiding a fox that ran across the road. He did not run her off as the feds suspected. She has a cut on her forehead, and her shoulder was injured. But both are healing."

"Did she tell you who the psycho is when you talked to her?" I don't think I have ever seen Wes this angry. Unsettled. He is the goofy one, always a joke or sarcastic remark ready.

Here comes lie number one. "No." I pause to collect my thoughts. "I video-chatted with her—saw her. She is telling the truth. Her..."—I can't bring myself to use the word kidnapping anymore—"disappearance, then and now, has something to do with her past. With her...family. She is trying to get the answers she needs to be able to move on. She wants to come home, but other things have to fall into place first."

I don't think I could be more vague if I tried.

"Do you know when she's coming home?" Denielle asks fervently.

Lie number two. "No. She didn't say, and I'm not sure she knows."

"Where is she? Why can't she figure all this stuff out from here? Why would she stay with this...*person*? WHO. IS. THIS. GUY?" Denielle is starting to work herself up. She's worried about her best friend, and I can't fault her.

"I didn't get to talk to her for long." Lie number three.

"THIS IS FUCKING BULLSHIT!" Wes jumps up and storms out of the room, slamming the door so hard that the picture on the wall crashes to the floor.

My head swivels from the door to Denielle, who is slowly getting up. I have to peer up at her from my position.

Lilly's best friend inhales deeply before she opens her mouth. "Wes is... He's been fighting with his parents to cover for you, lying to your parents. That psycho has been blowing up our phones with instructions. Wes hasn't slept. He was worried sick that crazy-scar-dude was going to kill you. And you just lied to our faces like it's nothing. I hope you have some pretty good reasons for that, because I'm not sure Wes will forgive you otherwise."

With those parting words, she turns and follows my best friend.

CHAPTER TWENTY-TWO

LILLY

I DON'T KNOW IF I CAN DO THIS.

I stare at Rhys's text. Nate and I are sitting at the kitchen table, ready to eat dinner, when my phone lights up. I haven't let it out of my sight since my brother informed me that they're on their way to Westbridge. I've forced myself not to message Rhys, even though that's all I want to do. He seemed as okay as he could be when we disconnected, but I can only assume what's going on in his head. He's forced to lie to everyone. Again. The more I think about it, the less appealing the homemade pizza in front of me looks.

George dropped him off about an hour ago and has stayed in the vicinity of Den's house in case he's needed. I could tell he was worried about Rhys when he called in for the status update. Nate made a scoffing sound at George's suggestion to stick around, and I elbowed him in the ribs. As weird as it is that he and George *connected*, it's a huge relief for me. It was no surprise that Rhys has issues with my brother—who wouldn't?

"What does Loverboy have to say?" Nate mumbles while shoving almost an entire slice into his mouth.

"Has no one ever taught you to not speak with a full mouth?" It was meant as a joke but came out much harsher as I glance at the screen again. My chest tightens, and I force myself to inhale and exhale to the count of five.

Nate looks at me for an indefinable amount of time. "He can't handle it, can he?"

I flip the phone over so my brother sees the text.

"Fucking great. I knew it," he curses under his breath.

"Stop it! Let me talk to him and see what's going on before you jump to conclusions."

I pull the device back and type: **What happened?**

The little bubble with the three dots appears, and it seems like an eternity until the reply pops up. I put the phone on the tabletop and rub my palms against the cotton of my gray sweats.

D knows I'm lying my ass off. She made that uber-clear before she stormed out. Wes is pissed that I have no fucking answers for them. He's been lying to his parents and Mom and Dad for me. 4 US. And to top that, the 2 of them are now BFFs or some shit. And I'm stuck in this damn room by myself while you hang out with brother dearest.

Shit.

I glance up at Nate, who, in return, raises his eyebrows.

What do I say to that? I'm stunned by Rhys's angry reply. I don't remember him ever talking to me like this. I push the phone back over to Nate so he can read it himself.

I wait for my brother to make more snide comments, but instead, he looks back at me, forehead wrinkled and mouth in a thin line. "Do you think he can stick to the plan?"

Do I?

"I don't know," I admit with a sigh.

What's the alternative? Kidnap him as well?

"That's a problem, Lilly." Nate is calm; he doesn't have the *I-told-you-so* voice I expected.

Hands clasped next to the phone, I stare at the untouched slice of pizza on my plate.

We sit in silence when my screen lights up again: **Can we talk?**

With the device in hand, I push back from the table and tap the video icon while walking out of the kitchen. Rhys's face fills the screen immediately. He's sitting with his back to a tiled wall, water running in the background, and I assume he's in the guest bathroom. His mouth moves, but I don't understand a word over the background noise. I point to my ear and shake my head. He nods in understanding and disappears, the phone facing the ceiling. A moment later, he's back with headphones in his ears.

When he doesn't speak, I attempt a reassuring smile, which probably makes me look more constipated than anything, and say, "I'm so sorry." I blink several times as my eyes start watering.

"I'm sorry, too." Rhys looks past the screen with his lips pressed together.

I stop in the large sitting room and plop down on one of the couches close to the fireplace and pull my legs underneath me.

I stare off into the small fire when Rhys's voice brings me out of my guilty thoughts.

"How big is this place you're at?"

I glance at the small picture of myself and see why he would ask that. He can see the rest of the room and part of the foyer in the background.

"Big," is all I can come up with. I want to tell him about the estate and how beautiful it is, the vineyard and the underground gym—he'd love the gym. However, this is not the time.

Rhys nods.

"Talk to me."

He sighs. "It's just all crashing down on me. Wes is so fucking angry. I've never seen him this way. And when Den called me out on my lies..." He trails off, and my chest constricts. I want to help him, but I don't know how.

"I'm so sorry." I sound like a broken record.

"I gotta go." Before I can say anything else, Rhys disconnects.

What the—

My heart starts racing a million miles a minute as I try to make sense of what just happened. Why did he hang up like that? Was someone in his room? Is he that mad at me that he can't even bear talking to me? Am I losing him?

I'm paralyzed.

I don't know how long I sit there when my phone starts ringing. I pick up before even looking at the caller ID and am startled when George's face appears on the screen.

"Miss Lilly," he greets me.

"Is he safe?" The call has to do with Rhys, no question.

"He is."

The unspoken is hanging between us and I whisper, "What's going on?"

"I just got off the phone with him." Rhys called George. My eyes widen, and he continues, "I believe I was able to get through to him. He's going to stick to the script, but I'm not sure what this will do to his friendship with Miss Keller and Weston."

Tears are running down my face. What have I done? "This is all my fault."

"It is not, Miss Lilly. If someone is at fault, it is Nate. But even he can't be blamed for all of it."

I nod. Could Nate have handled everything differently when he first found out about me? Probably. But I don't blame him anymore either.

"Give him time. It's been only twenty-four hours. He has a lot on his shoulders for the next seven days. But I am confident that he will be able to handle it. I will remain close by until Friday morning."

"Why Friday?" But before George can answer, it clicks. "The party. You're coming here while Nate is gone?"

"Yes."

"It's not that I don't trust you. But I'll feel better if you are not all alone on the property," Nate's voice interrupts from the doorway to the kitchen hallway. He's leaning against the doorframe, and I assume he's been eavesdropping for a while.

Suddenly, I'm completely drained. I look back at the screen. "Thank you for being there for Rhys, George."

"It is my pleasure, Miss Lilly."

Is that a smile on his face?

We disconnect, and I slowly stand up.

Nate walks toward me, stopping a couple of feet away. He seems unsure of what to do.

I step forward and wrap my arms around his midsection. He's not Rhys, but the next best thing. He's family. Nate returns the embrace, seemingly knowing what I need. No words are spoken.

Eventually, I step back, my brother's arms fall to his sides, and I walk away.

I SPEND the next several hours in the library. I intended to look through more files; there are still half a dozen drawers unopened. But instead, I curl up on one of the couches, clutching my phone and just staring at the bookshelves on the opposite wall. I feel like this heavy blanket has settled over me, and it takes too much effort to move.

The antique table clock on one of the shelves shows 10:23 when my phone vibrates in my hand.

ILY.

Tears start immediately flowing. It's a miracle I am not completely dehydrated the way things are going.

I sit up and cross my legs. Holding my phone in both hands, I start typing.

I love you more than I can ever put in words. I can't imagine what you must be going through, and I am so so

sorry. I promise I will make everything right. Please forgive me.

The bubble appears immediately, then disappear. I stare at the screen, but nothing happens. Rhys is not responding. Did I make a mistake in choosing to stand by Nate? Have I lost him already?

When the little digital clock in the top right corner of my screen switches to 10:30, and there still is no reply, I press the button on the side. The screen goes dark, and something inside of me breaks into a thousand pieces.

EARLIER TODAY, Nate gave me my access code for the NCC. I'm one hundred percent in. I have access to his computers and the security system—though I don't fully understand how that works yet. But any way you look at it. I. Am. In.

Still, the thought of betraying my brother's trust doesn't cross my mind. Instead of snooping or trying to figure out how to work my way out of here, I simply sit down at the massive desk and pull one of the keyboards toward me. I need a distraction, or I'll break down.

The left monitor on the desk lights up when I hit the space bar. I pull up a search engine and start researching my suspicion of Nate's mental state. I don't know how smart I am for doing this on his computer, but I'm beyond caring. Let him get mad. He's invaded my privacy more than enough.

Around four in the morning, my eyes are burning, but I'm ninety-five percent sure that my hunch is correct. I found several studies, articles, and even personal blogs. People recount their experiences of how certain drugs impacted their ability for rational thinking, their feelings, and what they did while taking said medications. Some of it is more than scary, and to think of losing control over your mind like this makes my chest ache. Next, I plan on finding out what medications Nate is currently on and digging further into cases with the same ones.

· · ·

I'm on my way back to my room, eyes barely open, when I smack into a hard body coming up the stairs from the first floor. I yelp in surprise, and two arms shoot out to steady me.

"It's me," Nate's voice penetrates the sleepy fog.

"God, you scared the crap out of me. Turn on some lights next time," I mumble while rubbing both eyes with the heel of my palms.

The irony of me walking in the dark is not lost on me. But rather than pointing that out, he asks, "Are you still or already up?"

I'm more alert now that the adrenaline rush from the impact is subsiding. "I was researching something on the computer." I won't elaborate; he can look up the browser history anyway. "Why are you awake?" I finally get a closer look, and my brother is a sweaty mess. I raise my eyebrows and take a whiff. "Ewww... you smell."

Nate snorts. "That's what tends to happen when one exercises."

My eyes narrow. "It's not even five in the morning."

"Your point?" he drawls. "Between you and my job, I have to fit it in my schedule somehow." The response is a big, fat *duh!*

Usually, I'd enjoy the easy banter, but fatigue takes over again. I've lost track of how long I've been awake, and my brain and body are screaming for a break. In the dorkiest way possible, I bump my right fist against Nate's left shoulder as I start moving again. "Cool. See you tomorrow."

Before I make it through the door that leads to my *wing*, Nate calls, "It is tomorrow, little sister."

Instead of dignifying his statement with a response, I just hold up my middle finger. Right before the door closes, I hear him bark out a laugh.

The last thing I remember is falling face-first into my pillow.

CHAPTER TWENTY-THREE

HER

It's been eight days since Lilly was last seen. No missing person's report was filed, yet there are unmarked black SUVs parked in front of the house. It doesn't take a genius to know what Tristen is doing. He is pulling strings. Calling in favors, yet again. I'm growing very tired of this—of him.

Usually, Gray returns to me right after he has checked on Lilly. His visits have increased over the last few months now that the date gets closer. Not that he complains; it gives him an excuse to check on her. *However, when I order him to remain in Westbridge, Gray is not happy with me. He has already been there for a week, and he doesn't want to risk detection. Plus, he now has to change his usual detour.*

But until I can set everything in motion, I need to know what's happening locally. Moving up the timetable was not something I foresaw. I scheduled the plane for three weeks from now. If things progress this way, I may have to leave my "pawn" behind and return sooner.

It's late afternoon, and I'm standing at the foot of his bed. He's been in and out for the past five days. Every time he comes out of the seda-

tion, I order the nurse to administer more—until today. She thought I didn't notice the relief in her eyes when I agreed to her continuous pleas to reduce the dosage. As if I don't know what the long-term effects are—I simply don't care. He is nothing to me, but I'll need him to get to Lilly. Maybe.

It's time he hears about what happened. Again. Not that he can do anything about it, but it still brings me great pleasure to witness his torment when it comes to his little girl.

When I see movement under his closed eyelids, I know I don't have to wait much longer.

Ten minutes later, we are locked in a stare-down. I haven't visited him in two years—while he was awake. He knows something is up. Lips pressed in a thin line, he refuses to speak first.

This is going to be so much fun.

"How are you, my love?" I smile sweetly at the man lying motionless in front of me. I made sure the idiotic nurse did not reduce the paralytic drugs along with the sedative.

"What do you want?" His voice is raspy from years of barely using it.

I tilt my head. His courage is entertaining. "Now, now. If I were you, I'd watch my tone."

"What are you going to do? Drug me some more?"

Is he challenging me?

"Well, if you put it like that, we can always change the approach to keep you from running." I arch my eyebrows, pointedly glancing at his legs.

Turning chalk white, he understands my insinuation, knowing I won't hesitate to follow through with my threat. Usually, Gray does the dirty work for me, but it might be a nice change to assist in a procedure.

Realizing that my thoughts have wandered off topic, I focus back on his face. "Lilly is missing. Again."

That gets a reaction, and his head jerks, no doubt trying to push himself up, but his muscles won't obey.

"What do you mean?" he whispers, wide-eyed.

I make sure my tone is low and void of any emotion. Not that this is *a challenge, I haven't felt anything in a decade. "He found her. He took her again."*

"How?"

I would like to know the same thing, but I won't admit that. Tristen has kept Lilly under lock and key for so long; if he knew where she was, he would have collected her sooner.

"If she hasn't returned within the next forty-eight hours, I will take the necessary steps."

I turn and am halfway to the door when his voice stops me. "You know who has her?"

Without turning, I say, "I do."

But he is of no consequence to me—never has been.

I'm about to close the door to the bedroom when he whispers, "You have always known."

"Of course I have."

CHAPTER TWENTY-FOUR

LILLY

I don't get up until Nate barges into my bedroom. I've been awake on and off, but every time I tap the screen of my phone, it basically screams at me: *NO NEW MESSAGES*. So, what does a girl do? Go back to sleep. Which is not a hard task, given the fact that my body demands more rest.

"I've waited long enough. GET. UP!" Nate pulls on the comforter until it hits the floor.

I sit up. "What the fuck? I could've been naked."

"You've been wearing the same shirt for the past two days. The likelihood of you also wearing the same pants was high enough to risk it," my brother deadpans. "Now get your ass in the shower and then come to my office. It's time to start."

"Start what?" I curl into a fetal position, phone clutched in my hand.

All of a sudden, my phone is gone, and I'm pulled up by the hands. "You wanted to learn how to get information."

I want to get my phone back.

My damn brother is holding it over his head and even jumping; I can't reach it. Heat floods my veins, and I'm tempted to kick him in the junk. "Give. Me. My. Phone," I growl.

"No." He takes a step back. "Loverboy is in his room. He's fine. He will contact you when he pulls the stick out of his ass." And with that, he turns and walks out *with* my phone.

Balling my fists, I let out a blood-curdling scream and stomp my foot. Yes, I'm throwing a total temper tantrum. Rhys ignores me. Nate treats me like a little child. I'm stuck in this mansion for seven more days with nothing to do but wait. I grab the comforter from the floor and haul it onto the mattress. Staring at the rumpled sheets, my shoulders slump. Resigned, I make my way to the bathroom with *no* intention of rushing through my shower.

Take that, brother.

IT'S past three in the afternoon when I walk through the door to the office. Nate turns briefly before he starts typing again. The top three wall monitors show the usual surveillance footage of the property. The bottom three have the news, stock market, and—what the hell?

"Are you watching *The Bachelor?*" I look between my brother and the screen.

A sheepish grin appears on his face. "I missed the last two episodes and figured I'd catch up on it while I prepare your homework."

"Why on earth would you watch—wait, what? Homework?" My head is spinning.

"The current Bachelor is Julian's little brother, and I can't miss a chance to bust his balls over it this weekend. Plus, it's pretty entertaining. All the drama. Almost makes me miss the LA scene."

He has lost his mind.

I let his TV choice go. "What homework?"

"You said you want me to teach you how to hack. That's what

we're going to do for the next few days. Maybe then you will also stop moping." Nate shrugs.

"I'm not moping," I mumble while I push the spare chair closer to the desk.

Nate is typing again and doesn't turn when he says, "I'm not going to dignify that with an answer."

His condescending tone makes the blood pound in my ears. "Well, not everyone can have a surface-level relationship like you. I love Rhys, and he's going through all of this BECAUSE OF ME." My voice raises at the end.

Instead of snapping an angry retort at me, my brother turns, and his eyes gentle. "Rhys will come around. I may not be able to relate to what the two of you have, but I do know that it is special. If you could forgive him for all the secrets he kept from you, he will get over this as well. And if not, we can always have George torture him a little." Nate winks at me.

That makes me smile for the first time since yesterday, and I try to push everything else out of my mind.

I will give Rhys space to deal.

I wish I could talk to Den and Wes and tell them everything, but I can't. At least not until I am back home.

It's Friday morning. Nate is getting ready to leave for LA, George is on his way, and I've spent the last two days *studying* under my brother's watchful eyes. I still haven't heard from Rhys, and the only thing that keeps me from blowing up his phone is George's assurance that he's fine.

George relayed that he spoke to Rhys and that he moved back to Wes's house Wednesday afternoon. I tell myself that he probably isn't alone and can't contact me, but a voice inside my mind keeps whispering, *If he was not alone, how could George talk to him? What if he won't come around after all? Nate is a criminal.*

"Are you done?" Nate's question penetrates the cloud of doubt that's been overshadowing my mind.

Hands hovering over the keyboard, I glance over. "Almost."

THE FIRST DAY, we went over what I know about coding, which is what school taught me. Nothing out of the ordinary—basics. Once Nate was satisfied, he started giving me little tasks: write a program that does XYZ. Simple things. Then he started timing me. I thought he was messing with me, but he just stared at me blankly and pressed the start button on his phone's stopwatch.

Later that evening, he handed me several textbooks to go over. He'd be quizzing me in the morning. He wasn't joking about that either. I got to see a whole other side of my brother. He was in his element, and his genius was apparent. Instead of going to my room that night, I napped for a few hours on the leather couch in the NCC—books all around me. I didn't anticipate that an eight-hundred-page textbook could make such a comfortable headrest.

After I passed his pop quiz, he pulled up several scripts written in what I had to study up on, and said, "Tell me what that does." He started the timer again. Oddly enough, I scanned the lines on the screen and was able to give him the correct answer. It just made sense as soon as I read over it. There were still several commands I didn't know, but something clicked into place in my brain. I've always known that computer science comes easily to me, but by Thursday afternoon, my brother declared that I'm a natural.

After dinner, for which we had to go to the kitchen—no food in the computer room after my tea incident—he showed me how to execute the scripts he uses to get into *places*, what he needs to modify every time, and how he obtains said information. As an example, he used my high school's security feed. A shiver ran down my spine as I scanned the empty hallways of Westbridge High. I immediately recognized the frame where Rhys and Katherine's encounter had taken place a few weeks earlier.

"And they don't know that we're watching?" That was mind-boggling to me.

"No. As long as you don't forget to run the first three commands that execute the subroutines, you're invisible to the system," Nate reiterated. He'd shown me everything in detail, answered all my questions, and explained why he designed it the way he did.

"How did you learn all this?" I asked him at almost two in the morning on Friday.

A small smile appeared on his face. "I told you that anything computer-related always came easily to me." I nodded, and he continued, "My high school teacher had me do college-level course work freshman year. Eventually, he called one of his old friends at MIT, who let me attend his online lectures. I started designing my own stuff sophomore year and had a full ride to several of the best colleges in the country. But I wanted to stay close to Audrey and chose Caltech instead of going to the East Coast. While I was, uh...away, I read. A lot. Every textbook I could get my hands on since I didn't have access to an actual computer."

We talked more about how he designed the estate's security system, and I started studying the code for that until I literally passed out on the keyboard.

BEFORE NATE GOES to pack his bag mid-morning on Friday, (he doesn't need much since he has everything at his house in LA) he tasks me to write a subroutine for my security camera and mics. He wants the system to send an alert if the mic detects a specific phrase. Essentially, it's nothing useful, only good exercise. Nate leaves the details to me, and my pulse speeds up as I grin to myself and finish the final lines of code.

"So, what did you decide?" My brother tries to look over my shoulder, but I quickly minimize the window.

"You'll have to wait and see." His narrowed eyes tell me he

doesn't like that one bit, which gives me even greater satisfaction.

Nate lets the topic go. Instead, he says, "George will be here soon, and I'll head out around one. You have the plans for the weekend on your phone. I'll be back Sunday night."

I nod, trying not to roll my eyes. That he didn't plan out his potty breaks and put them on my calendar is a surprise. He even put in when he plans to go to bed, and at what time he'll be with whom. I have all of Margot's information, including the IMEI to her phone. Nate installed a GPS tracking program on his phone and modified it so it is only visible to George and me. A simple Friend Finder app wouldn't do—not secure enough. Hence, why my friends had to remove those from their phones.

Sitting next to me in his desk chair, my brother is playing with his phone. I look at him for a long moment before I voice my thought. I haven't spoken to Nate about Rhys in two days, mainly because my brother has kept me busy the entire time, but that doesn't mean I didn't think about it.

"Nate?"

"Hmmm..." He doesn't look up, typing away on what looks like an email.

"What if Rhys won't forgive me? He still hasn't texted or called," I whisper.

My brother's eyes meet mine, lips pressed in a thin line. "I don't know, little sis. He'd be a fool. His problem is with me, not you."

"Has George mentioned anything to you?" I haven't spoken to George either since his last status update on Wednesday out of fear of what he might tell me.

Nate sighs, and I don't know how to take that reaction. "George says Rhys has texted him a few times, mainly to check how you are. He's been playing a lot of video games since Wes went back to school. Denielle has been by in the evenings—she went back to school as well. Also, Heather came by earlier today to bring Rhys his phone. She stayed for about an hour."

And that's why I didn't ask.

My mind starts reeling. Den and Wes are back in school. Has anyone said anything to them? Or, more importantly, how did they explain where they were? Heather went to see Rhys. Why now? If he's been alone all this time, why hasn't he contacted me?

I bite my lip and swallow over the lump in my throat. Whenever my thoughts have gone there, I've forced myself to block everything out not to fall apart, but the mention of my adoptive mother makes a wave of emotion crash down on me that I can barely control. We haven't discussed yet what I will tell them when I'm back home. It's only five days away, but it seems like a lifetime.

"We need to talk about what I will say to everyone when I go home," I start hesitantly, not sure if this is a good time to bring that up.

Before Nate can respond, a beeping sound comes out of a speaker I didn't know existed in this room. The top right wall monitor, as well as one of the screens on the desk, switch to full-screen, showing the circular driveway in front of the main door. A blacked-out Explorer is pulling into the drive, and I glance at my brother. Nate doesn't seem alarmed at all, which can only mean that our head of security has arrived.

Our? When did his change to our head of security?

I STAND at the top of the stairs while Nate is halfway down when the front door swings open. I've seen George on the screen several times; I've spoken to him just as many. However, seeing the man in person is a whole different story. The heavy wrought-iron door slams shut, and the noise makes me jump. The flutter in my stomach is swallowed up by a pit the size of the Grand Canyon as I watch the scene below unfold.

Nate greets the other man with a handshake and one of those half *guy*-hugs.

"It's good to see you, George. Any trouble coming in?"

"Nate," he greets my brother. "No, Joel had a new co-pilot that almost shit his pants when I got on board, but otherwise, no issues." The corner of George's mouth twitches ever so slightly.

My brother takes a step back, and both men turn to look up the stairs at me.

"Miss Lilly. It's a pleasure to meet you in person."

CHAPTER TWENTY-FIVE

NATE

SPEEDING DOWN THE DRIVEWAY, I WATCH MY LITTLE SISTER IN the rearview mirror. She stands in front of the main door with her arms wrapped around her midsection. Behind her, George's gaze follows my car until I'm out of sight. I shift down and push the gas pedal of my silver Ferrari 812 to the floor. If I don't get out of here, I'll turn around and stay—consequences be damned.

I don't think Lilly is aware of how well I can read her—the small tic she has, snapping her thumb against the rest of her fingers when she's nervous or, like now, hugging herself when she thinks about her boyfriend.

Rhys McGuire, what am I going to do with you?

WHILE I LOADED my bag in the passenger seat, Lilly was admiring the other vehicles I keep here at the estate. I keep several model cars on all my properties—anything from my toys, aka fast but impractical, to big-ass SUVs, like the Escalade two spots down.

I don't think she realized it herself when she mumbled,

"Rhys would love this one." All the while, she walked the length of my matte-black Audi R8. I bought it on a whim when Julian and I decided to race on one of our boys' weekends, and neither of us had a bike available. We had driven his Viper to the place we stayed at, so what does a person with an unlimited amount of money do? They walk into the next luxury dealership and buy the fastest car on the floor. Which was a showroom model to demonstrate the custom options they offered. I've barely driven it since because, with the 5 % tint, you can't see shit—the things I did in my twenties. I shake my head at my younger self.

Lilly had stared off into the distance, hand still on the roof of the R8, as George met my eyes in understanding. She's not taking Rhys's silence well—one of the reasons I pushed her to the brink of mental exhaustion for the last two days. All so she would not think about him.

George has kept me updated on Rhys's whereabouts, which aren't a whole lot. He hasn't left Wes's house at all, and according to George, all he's been doing is playing video games and sleeping. I guess the boy also needs a distraction.

I twist my arm and glance at the Richard Mille 031 watch my fiancée gave me for Christmas last year. I made sure to put it on before I left. Going back to LA means ensuring I look the part. Joel sent a text right before I left that we're delayed for two hours due to weather along the route. I have three hours until takeoff. I pull over to the side of the road and take my laptop out of the canvas messenger bag I've had since college. One of the last few memories I made with Audrey—she picked out the patches that are sewn all over it. This bag goes everywhere with me, despite Margot's objections.

I push the driver's seat back as far as possible, which makes typing on the laptop propped up in the middle a tad bit easier. I installed all the necessary programs on this computer before I packed it up. The set-up only takes a few minutes, and I hit dial. I can't stop the smirk on my face, thinking about the name that's about to pop up on the screen on the other end.

Knowing that it may take a moment for him to answer, I try to be patient. But when I listen to it ring for the seventeenth time, I grow frustrated. Just as I'm about to stop the call program on my laptop, he picks up.

"Hello?" He sounds cautious.

"Soon-to-be brother-in-law!" I greet him with exaggerated cheer.

"Really? What if someone would've seen the screen?" he hisses. Aww, I detect annoyance, which makes me grin even more.

"It was worth it. We need to talk."

"Is that so, PSY-CHO?" Rhys repeats the ID I programmed in for this call. I know what he's been calling me behind my back, but it doesn't bother me. He's a kid in love, and even my baby sister has called me that a few times over this past week. Neither of them is that far off—sadly. But things will change soon enough.

"It is. Our girl is upset, and I don't like her upset," I explain my call.

"She's not your girl! Stay out of our business," he seethes into the phone.

"She is my sister. Everything involving her is my business." I consciously make my tone go cold.

After all, I am a psycho, right?

That shuts him up, and I continue. "I understand that you have a problem with me. That's fine. But none of this is Lilly's fault. You are making her believe her loyalty to me—her *real* brother—is something she needs to regret. I never asked her to choose me over you, and that's not what she did. You need to get your head out of your ass and try to see her side. She is my only family, and I am hers—as far as we know. But she also needs you. You ignoring her makes her question everything you promised her."

There is more silence on the other end, and I gaze at the dash to make sure I'm not running out of time. I hear Rhys inhale deeply before he says, "I need time. I'm tired of lying. I don't want to lie to her and tell her everything is fine when it's not."

"Of course nothing is fine. I fucked up. You fucked up. But she still forgave both of us. *Our* girl has more heart than you and I combined. She doesn't deserve this. Even if you need time... Talk. To. Her! Tell her that."

I don't wait for a response. I've said my peace and will know soon enough if he listens or not.

THANKS TO LA TRAFFIC, I pull up to my house as the sun starts setting. I notice several rooms on the top floor are lit up.

FUCK!

I take my time parking my Aston Martin One-77 in its usual spot next to the white G-Wagon in the motor pool. I texted Hank earlier to leave it at the company's private hanger. I had no desire to deal with a car service today, and he stopped asking questions about my random requests a long time ago—rich people's eccentrics, as you could call it. I basically turned him into my P.A. years ago.

Glancing over, my first thought is that Lilly would probably enjoy the Mercedes since she totaled her Jeep. "Maybe someday I'll be able to give it to her."

Mentally preparing myself, I slowly make my way inside. I stop in the kitchen for a glass of water before heading upstairs. Margot stands in the middle of my bedroom with several garment bags draped over the king-size bed, both armchairs that sit in front of the floor-to-ceiling window overlooking the pool, and even hanging from the doorframes leading to the master bath and closet.

You've got to be fucking kidding me.

She hasn't noticed me yet, digging through one of her three Louis Vuitton Courriers—also occupying my bedroom.

"Sweetheart?" I keep my voice low and force my hands to

unclench. I hadn't expected to see my fiancée tonight. It's almost nine, and I want to check in with Lilly. George has sent me several texts, and I know everything that's happened since I left, but I want to talk to my sister. Seeing her face, even if it's on a screen, would help release the tightness in my chest.

Margot whirls around. "DARLING!" Her face lights up with a smile, but she doesn't move away from the trunk. For the first time since we've been together, I notice how *atypical* our relationship is. Any normal couple that hasn't seen each other in weeks would at least embrace, if not rip each other's clothes off. But neither of us makes any indication to do any of that.

I try not to sound like an ass, but the urge to just kick her out is taking root and spreading through my entire body. "Why are you here, sweetheart?"

She has her own seven-bedroom house on the other side of town.

Why is she in my house?

She finally straightens and comes over to me. Placing her hand on my chest, she raises to her tiptoes and places a kiss on my cheek. "Your house is closer to the airport. We just landed from France, and I didn't want to drive all the way home if I have to be back here tomorrow for the party."

"What do you mean *here?*" I hope she is just using here as the figurative way of describing this part of the greater Los Angeles area.

"Darling, don't you remember? Celeste's party is here. Julian is renovating the pool, and their house is a disaster."

Fucking Julian.

I swallow my curse. He did that on purpose so that he doesn't have to deal with this ridiculous party.

"No, I don't remember. When exactly did we decide on that?" There is no point in arguing now. I'm sure everything is already planned, ordered, and paid for.

Margot puts her finger on her chin, looking away—a gesture

that is endearing on my sister but makes me want to rip my hair out looking at the woman in front of me.

"I think we talked about that while I was in France."

We most certainly did not.

"I want everything back in order by the time I leave Sunday afternoon." I can no longer hide my annoyance and stalk out of my bedroom before I say something I'll regret.

I should've stayed home.

Home? This is the first time I've referred to the vineyard as home. It's always been my "sanctuary," but home? Though, it's not actually the vineyard that prompted the thought.

MARGOT DOESN'T KNOW about my NCC—as Lilly has started calling my office—here in LA. It's in the basement, behind the gym, and my fiancée rarely ventures down here—sweat stench and all. It has the same security measures and the same security system I have at all my properties. I don't hide my office from my fiancée, but it has also never come up. Here. At the vineyard, it's in plain sight, and she accepted that my office is for business only. I could hide a dozen clowns on unicycles in there, and she wouldn't know—or care.

Again, what does that say about our relationship?

I start up the cameras for this property, make sure Margot remains on the second floor, and set the motion sensors for the stairs on alert before booting up the other computer to log into the feed of the vineyard.

The one room I have no cameras in, on any property, is my office. I find Lilly running on the track. Based on the appearance of her hair and clothes, she must've been at it for a while. When I don't see George on any of the cameras, I dial his phone.

"Nate," George greets me as usual. He has never wasted time with formalities, though my sister at least gets *Miss* Lilly.

"How is she?" The tightness in my chest turned into a vice when I discovered the state my little sister is in.

"He called," is all George has to say.

Glancing back at the monitor, Lilly is just starting another round of the quarter-mile track.

This is not good.

AFTER HAVING TURNED my bedroom into the showroom of *La Déesse*, one of the most overpriced boutiques I've ever had to set foot in and lose three hours of my life, Margot eventually ventured downstairs. I abandon my post watching my sister run for dear life in order to avoid my fiancée coming down to find me.

Margot wants to order in Chinese, something we used to do all the time, and I used to enjoy with her. However, right at this moment, I don't want to eat or have meaningless chitchat. I want to banter with my little sister, push her buttons to get a rise out of her. I need to know she is okay. I never expected our relationship to develop the way it did when I brought her back. I don't know what I expected at all, to be honest.

"Did you hear what I just said?" Margot's sharp tone snaps me out of my thoughts.

"I'm sorry, what?"

She huffs and pushes her chair back. Both hands on the table, she leans over. "What is going on with you? I've basically been talking to myself for the last forty-five minutes. You could at least pretend to care about Celeste's birthday."

But I don't.

At that precise moment, my phone vibrates in my pocket, and I fumble to get it out as fast as possible.

She is back in the office.

I push my chair back and walk out without a second glance.

"NATE!" Margot yells after me, exasperated.

This will most likely bite me in the ass very soon.

. . .

"CALL LILLY," I bark out as soon as the door of my office closes behind me.

The monitor on my desk comes to life, and before I can sit down, my sister fills the screen. Her face is still red from the run, and I immediately notice the puffy eyes.

I'm going to kill this boy—figuratively speaking, of course.

I have tunnel vision, and the urge to throw another monitor across the room overcomes me, but instead, I try to steady my voice. "Little sis. Talk to me."

The dam immediately breaks, and I curse under my breath. All the different ways how I can make Rhys's life hell—or worse than it already is—assault my brain at lightning speed.

"What happened?" I try to control my accelerated breathing.

Between hiccupping sobs, I understand something along the lines of, "Rhys called," "Heather," and "my fault." The rest is drowned out by her crying. While Lilly is still trying to get herself under control, I text George.

WHAT THE FUCK HAPPENED?

His response is immediate: **I don't know. She was in the gym when he called, and he won't answer my texts or calls.**

That little shit. He's lucky I'm stuck here for another thirty-six hours, or I would go to Virginia myself.

Since Lilly is in my office and we are still on the phone-slash-video call, I can't pull up the historical feed of the gym—yet.

Another message from George lights up my phone: **Do you want me to check on her?**

I see him pacing the entire length of the kitchen on one of the little rectangles.

Not yet. Still have her on the screen.

I focus back on my sister who is slowly starting to calm down.

"Baby sis?" I try again.

Her eyes find mine, and she whispers, "This is all my fault."

My eyebrows draw together. "What is?"

Lilly takes a deep breath. "Rhys called earlier." I gathered that, but I swallow my sarcastic remark and let her get it out at her own pace. "We didn't talk long. I asked why he hasn't called." The moisture wells up again, but this time she stays in control. "He said because he doesn't want to hear anything else he has to lie about."

I nod. "I see. What else did he say?" I hope he at least gave her some assurances.

"He said Mom came by earlier to bring him his phone." Mom, not Heather. She continues, "He said she's lost weight, she's not sleeping, and Natty keeps asking when she can come home. He's been avoiding Dad's attempts to talk to him. He can't face anyone, knowing what he does."

We're quiet for some time, and an idea starts forming. "What if we let them?"

Confusion clouds her features. "Huh?"

"Let them know," I clarify.

My sister's eyes widen. "How?"

I press my lips together. I don't like it, and, in the end, it will be her choice, but the option is there. "Give me a minute. I want George to be in the room with you."

I shoot a message to the man pacing a hole into my kitchen floor to get his ass to the NCC. When he sends me a question mark back, I have to chuckle. Lilly's nickname has already taken root in my brain.

The office, I reply.

Not a minute later, I see the door in the background opening, and our head of security takes the seat next to my sister. He is her bodyguard now as he is mine.

She props up her phone against one of the monitors on the desk, and two sets of eyes look back at me. One with hope, the other with wariness. George suspects that whatever I'm going to say will be a "security risk."

I lay out my plan, and Lilly immediately shouts, "I'll do it," while George barks, "Absolutely not!"

Yup, I knew that would go over well.

Lilly turns to the man next to her. "Why not? They need to know!"

"Miss Lilly. Please think about it. It will cause more questions. Especially when you return and all of a sudden have no recollection. You need to lie to everyone to protect your brother's identity." Quietly, he amends, "If that is what you still want."

My sister looks appalled, and I have to chuckle.

"Of course I do. He is my brother!"

Hearing her say that makes my heart beat faster. I'm her brother.

George tries to reason with her again. "We don't know what chain reaction this will set off. It could cause more problems than it solves. The authorities won't believe you."

"I can do it! They need to know," she says with such conviction that I almost believe her. But to be honest, I am terrified of the outcome. I won't be able to protect her, and even if I send George with her, he won't be able to interfere. All he can do is stand by in the shadows.

The man that has protected me for the past ten years turns to me. "I don't like this, Nate. You are both risking too much. If this goes sideways, you may have to take responsibility sooner than either of you wants."

I know he is right, but there is only one answer. "Lilly comes first."

"Very well. I'll make the necessary arrangements and will contact you when we're ready."

CHAPTER TWENTY-SIX

RHYS

I DIDN'T THINK MY DAY COULD GET ANY WORSE.

After Mom's visit to bring me my phone—per Dad's order—and Wes recounting the newest rumors about Lilly when he got home from school, the last thing I expected was to receive a call from *him*. Thank fuck my best friend was in the bathroom, taking a shower, when the phone in the front pocket of my hoodie started vibrating.

It was the same hoodie that hasn't fit me since freshman year. I probably looked like Wes's dad in his high school yearbook—he swore up and down that crop tops on men used to be in, but whatever. I couldn't have cared less at that point. When Mom called Wes's cell at seven a.m. to inform me she'd be coming by, I asked her to bring the sweatshirt with her. She didn't question why, and I'm beginning to suspect she knows.

Wes and Den have been back to school for the last few days, and from what they've been telling me, it's not pretty. Wes even skips practice because of the shit our teammates spewed out the first day. Wes got into a massive blowout with Jager and had to be pulled apart by Coach and several of the guys. He hasn't been back since.

Jager was lucky it was Wes and not me.

I let the phone ring until I was certain Wes wouldn't suddenly come out. Unfortunately, that involved sneaking in and making sure he was indeed in the shower. What I witnessed can never be unseen but will make for excellent blackmailing material. Humming Carrie Underwood's "Blown Away," my best friend was rubbing one out—God, I wish I had taken a video.

Door securely closed, I answered the phone and had one of the most bizarre conversations of my life. Getting patronized by Lilly's kidnapper-slash-psychotic-brother was the last thing I'd expected. But his words had hit home.

"Of course nothing is fine. I fucked up. You fucked up. But she still forgave both of us."

The words kept reverberating through my mind for several hours. Wes no longer questions my behavior. I've walked out on him multiple times to message George when I was about to lose it. He is the only person I don't have to pretend with, one way or another.

How ironic is that?

So, when I left my roommate this time, he didn't even look up. I wanted to be as far away as possible from potential listeners when I made the call. I ventured down to the family room's adjacent bathroom and turned on all the water sources at my disposal. This time, I also came prepared with headphones.

I typed the number to Lilly's cell phone several times before I could get myself to press the green button. It rang three times before I heard the one voice I'd missed and dreaded hearing so much the last few days come through the earpiece.

"Rhys?"

We were both quiet after that. She knew it was me but didn't seem to know what to say. Or she was giving me time until I was ready. I didn't know.

"Hey," I finally whispered after several minutes of silence.

"Hey." The relief in her tone was palpable.

The knots in my stomach started loosening. If I could just hold her right now...the need to feel her was consuming me.

"I'm sorry I haven't called." The words had been on my mind for days, yet I couldn't bring myself to call her until he put me in my place.

She sniffled but didn't say anything, and all I heard was her slowly inhaling and exhaling. I counted to five for each; she was trying to gain control. The loosened knot tightened back up. I'd been selfish; I'd distanced myself from everyone, including Lilly, so that I wouldn't have to lie. I didn't want to pretend I was fine, having to reassure her. But hearing her like this...

Before I could say anything to explain myself, she whispered, "Why haven't you called?"

The tightness from my stomach spread to my chest. As much as I didn't want to admit it, I told her the truth. "I didn't want to hear anything else I have to lie about."

"Oh," she breathed.

I could only imagine what admitting this did to her. I tried to lighten the mood and changed the topic. "What have you been up to the last few days?"

When she was quiet again, unease spread through me, and I probed. "Babe?"

"I, um...Nate has been teaching me some computer stuff."

What the—?

It didn't take a genius to read between the lines. Her psycho of a brother had been teaching her to hack! To become a criminal—like him.

Something inside of me snapped, and before I could stop myself, the words just flew out. "So, while I had to face my mother who, by the way, looks like she's lost twenty pounds, listen to her tell me how all Dad does is try to find you, and my little sister is not allowed to come home, your psychotic child-kidnapping brother is teaching you how to hack? You've got to be FUCKING KIDDING ME!" My tone rose with every word until I was shouting. Panting, I clutched the phone in my hand so tightly that it was a miracle that it was still fully intact.

Lilly's sobs came through the phone. "I'm so sorry, Rhys. Please, you have to believe me. I'm sorry. Please. I love you."

I love you, too. More than anything. That's why this is so hard.

But once again, instead of saying the right thing—the one thing that would help both of us and most likely save our relationship—I couldn't get the words out.

All of a sudden, a banging at the door startled me.

"Dude! What the hell are you doing in there?"

Wes! Shit!

I hung up in a panic and shoved the phone back into the hoodie.

Not only did I yell at the love of my life, but now I also hung up on her after she told me she loved me.

FUCK, FUCK, FUCK!!!

Face flushed, I swung the bathroom door open. "WHAT?"

The urge to sucker punch my best friend was so strong I tightened my grip on the door and shoved the other hand into the pocket of my sweats, hiding my balled fist.

Wes looked me up and down, and his face contorted into what probably was meant to be a knowing grin.

"Ahhh, I get it, man. You needed some 'alone time.'" He made air quotes around "alone time."

He's got to be fucking kidding me.

"Get what?" I ground out between clenched teeth, still gripping the doorframe.

His face fell a bit, and he stammered, "Uh, you know...uh."

Too far gone, I blurted out the first thing that came to mind. "Oh, you mean whacking it while singing a fucking country song? No, I didn't need alone time for *that*."

Wes's face turned a shade of burgundy. I finally stopped my attempt to permanently imprint my hand into Mr. and Mrs. Sheats's family bathroom door and pushed past my best friend.

Halfway across the room, I turned and walked backward. "And by the way, I would've chosen Taylor Swift's 'Shake it Off.'"

Wes's mouth fell open, and as I was almost out the door, I heard him burst out laughing, which put a small grin on my face as well.

Until I remembered what he interrupted.

I needed to fix this.

I DIDN'T GET to fix it. I couldn't find any alone time to contact Lilly or George. After the call, I felt the phone vibrate several times inside my hoodie, but I couldn't check who it was. Wes had been glued to my side since the moment I got back to his room, and an hour later, Denielle joined us. If I had disappeared again for more than taking a piss, he would've started asking questions, especially after blowing up in his face.

I did get to check some of the texts during my 1.5 minute bathroom break, but I hadn't even read half of George's messages when Wes hollered, "If you are not *whacking* it, what's taking so long?"

Motherfu—

The only thing that kept me semi-distracted was Denielle's odd behavior. She wasn't her usual self—no snarky remarks about my second-skin-looking crop top, as I would've expected. She plopped herself next to me on the couch while Wes and I engaged in another video game. The entire time, she didn't say a word.

Eventually, Wes coaxed it out of her in his usual sledgehammer, charming way. "Why are you acting so fucking weird, D? There were no new rumors at school today, so what's crawled up your hot ass?"

As it turned out, Denielle and Charlie got into a fight, which explains a lot; they never fight. They don't even argue; Charlie is too much of a pussy to ever stand up to his strong-willed girlfriend. Den asked him if he would visit for the weekend. With everything going on, Wes and I were always together, and she wanted him home. Her admission stunned and humbled me at the same time. Denielle never lets her guard down, and her telling us that meant she trusted us. Anyway, Charlie made some excuse about a party he had already RSVP'd to and couldn't get out of. Even to me, that sounded like utter bull, but seeing Den's face, I bit my tongue.

We played until three in the morning, and by the time Wes turned the TV off, Denielle was fast asleep on Wes's bed. Wes looked at me questioningly, and I shrugged, so he simply scooted in beside her, and I took my place on the couch.

I REREAD George's texts several times.

Rhys, what happened?

Rhys, I know you contacted Miss Lilly. What happened? She is upset.

Rhys, if you have any sense of self-preservation, you will answer me. I like you, boy, but I work for Nate. When Nate sees the state his sister is currently in, I cannot guarantee your safety.

His last text came almost two hours ago, and despite being suffocated under my covers to hide the glow of the phone, a shudder runs down my spine. I don't doubt the damage this man could do to me. His loyalty is to Nate and Lilly first.

I waited until almost four before sending a message to Lilly.

I got cut off earlier. Wes came in. I didn't mean to hang up. I love you.

I wait several minutes, and when she doesn't respond, I text George.

I texted Lilly. She's not responding. Wes caught me on the phone earlier, and I haven't been alone since. Is she ok?

The bubble pops up almost immediately, and I sigh in relief... until I read the message.

Things have been set in motion, despite my advice against it.

What the fuck does that mean?

What things???

I wait, but my BFF ghosts me. I'm as confused as I am worried. Sleep doesn't come that night.

IT'S SATURDAY—AGAIN, and we have nowhere else to be. The only way I know this is because my friends don't have school. I stopped actively keeping track of the day of the week when I found Lilly's Jeep flipped on the side of the road. Mr. and Mrs. Sheats left earlier, and who knows where in the world Denielle's parents are.

The three of us sit in the kitchen, eating a late breakfast. And by eating, I mean Wes is using his fork like a conveyor belt. He probably should've made the entire carton of eggs, instead of only six. Denielle nibbles on some plain whole-grain toast, and I'm sipping black coffee. My barely existent appetite had officially said goodbye at four a.m. last night.

As if on command, all our phones—my personal one, not the phone I got from George that is stashed in my pocket—start vibrating on the table. I ignore mine since no one besides my parents have contacted me in over a week. Wes and Denielle both pick up their phones. Denielle's eyes turn to saucers, and my best friend spits an orange mass across the table.

Neither of them says anything and just stare at their screens. I tap my phone and nearly choke on the sip of coffee that I held in my mouth. There, in all caps, is the last name I expected to see on my phone: LILLY.

When I glance back up, two sets of eyes are on me, and Wes mumbles, still with some remaining food in his mouth, "Uh, dude?"

Both hold their phones out to me and show the exact same.

I'm at a loss. What is this? Without a word, I open the message.

"It's a video," I tell my friends.

Almost synchronized, they click on their messages.

"Same."

"I got one, too."

After a moment of silence, I say, "Let's do this together."

Den and Wes move their chairs closer to look at my screen. My heart rate is out of control, and my hands shake so hard that I can barely press play. I place the device on the table since there is no way my hands can hold it steady enough to watch. Lilly fills the screen, and I hold my breath. I can't look away from her beautiful face; the cut on her forehead is almost healed. She sits cross-legged on the leather couch in Nate's office, the bare wall behind her gives no indication where she could be if I hadn't spent hours talking to her in the same spot.

"Hey, guys," her hesitant voice comes through the speaker. "God, this is weird." She chuckles to herself, wringing her hands. "Um...I know you are worried about me, and I'm so so sorry that I haven't been able to contact you sooner. I, uh... I just wanted you guys to see that I'm fine." She points at her head. "This is from the accident. A fox ran across the road when I left school after the whole Kat *thing*, and I crashed my Jeep. We all learned you're not supposed to swerve the wheel to avoid an animal, but as you can see, I did it anyway." She shrugs sheepishly, and I feel the all too familiar flutter in my belly when I look at her. "I promise it was an accident." She takes a deep breath, and her eyes flicker briefly to the side. "Which I told Rhys during my brief call with him. I can't tell you where I am or with whom, but I want you to know that I'm ok and that I'll be back soon. I will make everything right. For everyone. I promise." Lilly's eyes start glossing over, and she wipes them—it is clear what she is thinking, or more likely of whom. "All of you are receiving the same video, but I wanted to say something to each of you indi-vidually." She pauses and glances to the side as if waiting for a signal. "Wes." The boy next to me makes a choked sound while she continues. "I want to thank you for being there for Rhys and for letting him crash on your couch. Being there with you gives him a lot of, uh, comfort. Den...hey, babe. I'm pretty sure you're at Wes's right now, and that also means the world to me, knowing the three of you are together and there for each other." Den's hands are covering her mouth, and tears are running down her face. I wrap my arm around her shoulder, and she leans into me. "Rhys. None of this is your fault. I'm fine, and everything will be ok." I read between the lines; she means us and our relationship. George told her that I got cut off yesterday. "I need you to do me a favor. Please show this video to Mom and Dad, but no one else. I need them to know that I'm fine and that I'm coming home soon. You cannot tell anyone about this message, and I apologize in advance about what I have to do to make sure unwanted eyes won't see it. Den and Wes, I really hope you backed up your phones." *What the—?* While Wes dives for his phone, Lilly continues, "Rhys, once you play this video again, your phone will wipe itself. I'm sorry."

Man, Nate is good. Or is it Lilly who's doing all this?

"One last thing." She doesn't attempt to hide the tears now. "Mom, Dad, Rhys, Natty, Den, Wes, I love you. Please trust me. I'll see you soon."

The video goes blank, and I hear Wes cursing under his breath.

"What the fuck. My phone is reset to factory setting." He looks at me incredulously.

Den is not moving away from me. Instead, she turns into my embrace and faces me. "You are not surprised."

I narrow my eyes at her. "What do you mean?"

"The way she worded everything. The way you acted when you got back. You've been in touch with her since..." Den states it so matter-of-factly that I'm at a loss for words.

My eyes hold hers, and I'm pleading with her to stop asking questions.

"I don't want to lie to you," I whisper so low that only she can hear it. Still engrossed in his phone, I doubt Wes is even paying attention.

Lilly's best friend stares at me for several moments before she disentangles herself from my arm. The unspoken message is clear, though; she will get her answers sooner or later. Denielle doesn't concede that readily; however, she trusts her best friend. She reaches for her phone and is not even phased when it's reset as well.

"Thank goodness I have it set to back up every night." She shrugs and winks at Wes with a smug smile. That's the Denielle I know. She swipes a few times, types something in, and puts it back down. Glancing over, I see the small bar that indicates she's restoring her backup.

Wes is not that lucky and spends the next few hours copying over phone numbers from Den's and my phones.

It's been a week since I've last been home. The closer I get, the more my heart rate accelerates. Only one black SUV is parked in front of the house, and I pull straight into the garage into my spot. Agent Lanning and Agent Camden are in their usual places at the kitchen table.

Do they ever go home?

"Where is my father?" I address no one in particular.

Camden, the only female agent assigned to Lilly's case, looks up. "He is upstairs with your mother."

If she's surprised to see me, she doesn't let it show.

Climbing the stairs, my phone feels like it's burning a hole into the back pocket of my jeans.

I knock on the door before turning the knob and let myself into my parents' room on the third floor. Mom is sitting on the bed, legs covered with a throw blanket, book on her lap, while Dad is in one of the chairs in the small sitting area, typing on his phone.

Mom straightens. "Honey!" The surprise in her voice is audible.

I'm frozen inside the doorframe. I force myself to unclench my jaw. " Can I come in?" I don't think I've ever asked to enter my parents' bedroom, but at this moment...

"Of course." Mom pats the spot next to her. Slowly, I make my way across the room, inhaling and exhaling through my nose. Dad tracks my every move.

I lower myself down next to my mother, and she wraps her arm around me. Leaning into her, my pulse calms a little. Mom has always had that ability.

I allow myself to relish in the sensation for a few heartbeats before turning toward Dad. "I need to show you something."

Bile rises in my throat, and I swallow several times.

Mom places a hand on my forehead. "Honey, you are covered in sweat. What's wrong?"

Dad's eyes haven't left mine, and I can see the wheels turning in his head. I shift so I can pull my phone from my jeans.

"Dad, you want to come over for this."

Eyebrows raised, my father pushes himself out of the chair and makes his way over to the bed. He sits on Mom's other side.

I place my phone in my mother's hand; the video is already pulled up. She glances down and notices Lilly's frozen face immediately. "Oh, my God!" She grips the phone, glancing between my face and the screen.

Dad leans in and draws in a sharp breath. "Rhys?" His tone is almost detached, yet he is asking a million questions at once with just my name.

I press play for them, and my parents watch Lilly's video with wide eyes. Tears are streaming down Mom's cheeks, and even Dad is stunned. It's the first time since this all started that I'm seeing him with unfiltered emotion.

When the video finishes, my phone immediately goes dark.

Mom keeps pressing on the screen, but besides the little bar indicating that the phone is being reset, nothing else is happening.

Her gaze flicks between her husband and me. "What does this mean? She is ok? When is she coming home? I don't understand. Where is she? Why can't she tell us?"

I gently pry my phone from my mother's hands, and she turns to Dad as if he has the answers. "Tristen?"

My father stares at me like he knows that there is a lot more I'm not revealing—the same way he's been keeping secrets from us. I hold his gaze, waiting for him to yell or interrogate me. Instead, my father stands up and storms out of the room.

Well, that's not what I expected.

CHAPTER TWENTY-SEVEN

LILLY

I'M GLUED TO THE SCREENS. ALL SIX WALL MONITORS IN THE NCC show the security feed, and I follow Rhys's every move. When the tracker on his phone alerted us about movement fifteen minutes ago, my heart rate immediately doubled. By the time he pulls into the driveway, my hands are clammy, and I keep counting my breaths.

WITH NATE BEING COERCED to host Celeste's birthday party, we knew he wouldn't be able to help today. Instead, he walked me through the necessary steps ahead of time. Before he went offline, I probed if my brother wasn't happy to see his fiancée this weekend, but he just grumbled something about "fucking Courriers everywhere" and "no privacy."

O-kay, then.

George chuckled but remained otherwise mute. He'd been planted on the leather couch in the NCC all day, reading a weathered-looking paperback. At one point, I asked flat out if he is supposed to shadow me the entire weekend Nate is gone, to which he simply ignored me.

The feed doesn't have sound, but nonetheless, I haven't looked away since the first picture appeared on the top left wall monitor hours ago. At one point, I maximized the kitchen to get a better look at the two strangers in the house. When Nate revealed the cameras to me a few days ago, a lot more agents were sitting at the table. I wondered why the number changed but then got distracted by movement in the master bedroom. I switched to that camera and watched Tristen place a throw on Heather's legs on the bed. Heat crept up my cheeks; I was invading their privacy.

But they have invaded your privacy for years, the voice piped up inside my head.

A beeping sound brought my attention to the screen on the desk. George got up and walked around to stand beside me.

"He's on the move."

It's time.

"WHAT JUST HAPPENED?" I ask George with eyes that must resemble saucers.

Rhys sits with Heather on their bed, arm wrapped around his mother, while Tristen rushes out of the room. They watched my video, and the wipe routine activated as soon as the signal came through. I can't focus on the satisfaction that I was able to run all the commands and steps without Nate's guidance, because Tristen's reaction has completely thrown me off. I was prepared to see him be angry, question Rhys, maybe get upset like Heather, but as soon as the video finished, he jumped up and left.

George looks just as confused as I am. "I don't know."

I focus on the other cameras in the house and find Tristen in his office, typing away on his laptop.

What the—?

An hour later, Heather looks like she is taking a nap, and Rhys makes his way to his room. The urge to talk to him is all-consuming. I want to know if Heather is okay, if he has any idea why Tristen has locked himself in his office, but I can't risk it. Rhys needs to initiate contact when it's safe.

My stomach rumbles, and George scowls. "When was the last time you've eaten?"

"Umm..." I rack my brain but come up blank.

"Let's go," the man next to me commands and leaves the room without a second glance.

I look at the wall monitors one more time and decide to leave the feed up—no one is going to come in here.

I SPEND the rest of the afternoon between watching the camera feed of my house and working on a small project to keep myself busy. I'm not sure if Nate will be proud or upset if I manage to pull off what I set my mind to.

I'm updating another line of code when a video call pops up on the second screen on the desk. I glance over, expecting it to be my brother, but instead, I see Rhys's name on the caller ID. Welcoming the familiar hornets in my belly, I answer the call, and Rhys's face fills the screen.

A smile tugs on his mouth. "Hey, babe."

God, I've missed him looking at me like that.

"Hi," I sigh. Warmth is radiating through my body, our last conversation forgotten. I do a double-take. "Where are you?" It's dark around him, and his face is illuminated only by the phone's screen.

"In the car. Dad wants me home from now on, and the only way to call was telling him that I'm going to get my stuff from Wes's."

"Oh." I'm biting my lip. "What happened? I don't have any sound on this end."

Rhys snorts out a laugh. "Of course you were watching. Why

am I not surprised?"

I grin sheepishly. "I was worried."

"Riiiight." He winks at me. "So, what did you see?"

That's a good question.

"I saw you showing Heather and Tristen the video, Tristen running out and locking himself in his office, you in your room, and, uh, Heather taking a nap..." I trail off.

"You didn't see Dad giving me the third degree?" Rhys asks surprised.

"No. When was that?"

He shrugs one shoulder. "As soon as I went to my room."

Crap.

"That must've been while I was in the kitchen."

A quizzical expression flits over Rhys's face, but he doesn't say anything.

"How is Heather? Please tell me I didn't make it worse. I was just trying to help." I wrap my arms around myself, wishing it could be Rhys holding me.

He exhales slowly. "Mom was upset. She doesn't understand. She kept asking how I got the video, when you would be home. But I think seeing you, seeing that you are not injured and stuff, helped her."

Still hugging myself, my hands fist into the fabric of my shirt. "What did you tell her?"

Rhys stares off into the distance for several moments before he speaks. "I avoided answering her for the most part. I said, 'Lilly wouldn't send us this message unless it was the truth. No one would be able to manipulate her to lie to the people she loves. We have to believe that she is okay and will be able to give us answers when she is back.'"

My mouth hangs open, and I'm not sure what to reply. Pride and dread equally build inside of me. Rhys found a way to give Heather what I intended with the video, but at the same time, he also had to bend the truth again.

"Thank you," I whisper.

Rhys's eyes are gentle. "You did the right thing. Though, I never would've expected you to send us a video," he chuckles. "You should've seen Wes's face when his phone reset. I thought he was gonna cry like the time he ran over Riddell."

I bark out a laugh. Riddell was the football Wes got for his seventh birthday. It became the fourth member of the Sheats's family, and we used to make fun of Wes whenever he brought it along—which was all. The. Time. He treated Riddell like a little brother—until the day Wes got his license. The second he got home with his license in hand, Wes wanted to take his brand-new 4Runner for a ride. He backed out of the driveway, running over poor Riddell in the process. The whole scene was like a bad horror movie. You'd have thought someone had chopped off Wes's arms for how he was wailing.

"You need to tell me how you did that. It was sick." Rhys shakes me out of the memory, and the proud undertone in his voice makes my cheeks heat.

"I will, but first, I want to know what Tristen said to you. Was he pissed?"

He leans his head against the headrest and stares at the roof of the car. "Confused would be a better description." Rhys looks back at the phone in his hand.

"Confused?" My brows draw together.

"The first thing he asked was what phone that is. When I told him it's mine, he wanted to see it. He inspected it as if you were gonna climb out of the screen like the creepy girl from *The Ring*. I wouldn't have been surprised if he'd busted out a screwdriver to take it apart."

Something clicks, and I smack my hand against my forehead. "He checked because the bug didn't alert him or record anything."

"WHAT?" Rhys's voice goes an octave higher.

"You know your phone was bugged." Rhys nods. "It was a pretty sophisticated program, according to Nate. He wrote a subroutine that executed when you opened the text and deactivated the tracker," I explain proudly. Mainly because Nate made me write the execution part, and it actually worked.

Surprise, surprise.

"That's fucking insane. This sounds like a bad sci-fi movie." Rhys rubs his free hand across his face.

"What else did Tristen say?" That cannot have been all.

"He asked if this is the first time you contacted me. I told him yes. He kept staring at me forever and then walked out with my phone. I yelled after him, asking what he intended to do with it, but he didn't answer. You know how he gets." Rhys huffs a non-comical laugh. "He brought it back an hour later, saying I'm staying home from now on. I told him, 'Fuck that. I'm going back to Wes's.' That's when it got interesting..."

I inhale sharply. Rhys's expression speaks volumes. "What happened?"

"He went big bad Marine on my poor door. Slammed his palm against it, yelling I will remain at home, and that it is not up for discussion. All he has ever done was to keep us safe. Not you; he said *us*. He was dead serious. It was the first time he's showed some type of reaction since you...uh, left."

Tristen is a professional. He doesn't let emotions get the best of him. Ever. We're missing something here.

"He is hiding something."

Rhys nods in agreement. "There is more than just him getting surprised by the video."

We sit in silence for several minutes before Rhys asks, "Now tell me, how did you pull that off?"

I open and close my mouth. My pulse accelerates. The last time I told him Nate had been teaching me, Rhys flipped his lid. "Do you really want to know?" My voice is low.

He picks up on my hesitation. "I'm not gonna go apeshit on you again, Cal. I promise."

I press my lips together, still not convinced.

"You surprised me last time," Rhys adds.

I take a deep breath. Here goes nothing. "It wasn't that difficult. Nate is a genius; he can type out the most complex code in a matter of minutes. And he's a good teacher. He says I'm a natural." I pause, assessing Rhys's face. He seems relaxed and listening, so I continue. "Den's and Wes's videos had a subroutine with a counter and a timer. As soon as they opened their texts, the timer activated. The video is less than three minutes, so I implemented it for the wipe to execute five minutes after the message was opened. If they had played it, the counter would've started the wipe as soon as it switched to 'played once'."

"You?" Rhys interrupts.

"Um, yes. Nate helped with the main part, though." My cheeks heat.

"What about my video?" Rhys's tone is now emotionless, and I don't want to continue.

"Calla?" he pushes.

"Are you mad?" I can't help but ask.

"Uh, not mad. I don't know. I guess it's a bit weird that you are so into it." He sucks in his lower lip and looks off to the side. When I think he won't say anything else, he adds with a wink, "But I also think it's pretty hot that you can do this."

"Hot?"

I must've heard him wrong.

Rhys grins sheepishly and shrugs. "My girlfriend, the badass hacker. We need to give you one of those hacker names."

There is a flutter in my belly; I don't know what to say.

"So, explain my video. Obviously, you couldn't put a timer on that one since it had to play twice, and you didn't know when I'd be home." Rhys seems genuinely curious, and my adrenaline level spikes. I didn't realize how much this new skill excites me until I tell him about it.

"Yours had a timer as well, but I set it to twelve hours—I was guessing there. The counter on yours was set to execute the wipe once it hits two or if the time ran out."

"Why not leave it just with the counters?" His eyebrows draw together.

"Well, uh..." I feel a little bad saying it out loud. "There was always a chance one of you wouldn't watch it since you guys were most likely together, and George didn't want to leave it to chance that the video could end up in the wrong hands. Even though Den or Wes would never do that intentionally." I add the last part quickly because I do trust my friends completely. "We were sure that they would at least open the text."

Rhys seems to think that over. "I guess that makes sense."

I let out a huge breath.

We sit in comfortable silence for a while, and I glance at the clock. "When do you have to be back home?"

"Soon. But grabbing my stuff doesn't take long. I'd rather talk to you as long as possible." The affection in his eyes makes tears prick in mine.

My paranoia takes over. "What if Tristen checks your tracker? He'll think you're hiding something from him."

"It's fine. I'm parked on the street in front of Wes's house. If Dad wants to get into it, I'll just tell him I left my phone in the car, which I had planned anyway. He can start following me in person for all I care." Contempt is dripping from every syllable.

"I miss you so much." I sniff.

Rhys sits up straighter. "Babe, why are you crying?"

The tears flow faster, and all the suppressed emotions from the last few days seem to rise to the surface.

"I...this...I...a-all...s-s-so...m-much..." is all I get out between sobs.

"Calla, look at me." Rhys's gentle voice penetrates my violent cries.

When my full attention is on him, he continues, "Babe, this is a clusterfuck of epic proportions. You feel guilty for spending time with your brother while we've all been worried out of our minds. Mom still is. There are more secrets than answers. And I can't even begin to comprehend how confusing this all is for you. You will be home soon. We will figure this out." He pauses for a second. "And when all of this is behind us, we will go on a proper date."

How does this boy always know what I need to hear to feel better?

The moisture on my face has dried. Remembering something he said to me not too long ago, I try to make light of this messed-up situation. "You just want to take me on a date so you can finally get into my pants."

Rhys snorts out a laugh. "You caught me, babe. Though I've already been in your pants, just not that...deep." He winks, and heat fills my body, remembering the night in my room he is referring to.

"Remember when I had to press my hand over your mouth because you were about to wake Natty up?" he teases, and every cell of my body is officially on fire.

It's at that moment that the door behind me clicks, and George walks in. I turn, and he pauses, his gaze swiveling between Rhys and me.

"Uh, Miss Lilly. Rhys."

Oh my God, he so knows what he just interrupted.

I fight the urge to cover my face.

"GEORGE, MY FRIEND!" Rhys's shout redirects my attention back to the screen.

It is my turn to chuckle. Both men's faces show genuine happiness to see each other. Who would've thought?

"Did you need something?" I ask him.

Still standing, he looks down at me. "No, Miss Lilly. Nate just asked me to check on you since you didn't answer his message."

Sure enough, I didn't notice Nate's text come in on my cell.

"I was distracted," I admit.

"I gathered that."

Is that a smirk on George's face?

"I probably should get going anyway," Rhys interjects. I'm not sure if he needs to go or if he wants to ease the embarrassment factor the three of us are experiencing.

I don't want to hang up, but I understand that he has to get home. "Okay. Will you text me if you can?" I know that calling will be out of the question from now on.

"I promise, babe." His smile tells me everything I want to hear but he doesn't want to say in front of the man next to me. And with that, he is gone. Instantly, a part of me is missing.

I must've been staring at the dark screen for quite some time when a hand gently touches my shoulder. "Why don't you respond to Nate and then take a break? You've been in this room all day."

My gaze meets George's, and I marvel how this man scared the bejesus out of me just a few days ago.

CHAPTER TWENTY-EIGHT

NATE

MY PHONE KEEPS BUZZING IN THE POCKET OF MY FADED JEANS. Whereas Margot is dressed like we're attending a dinner at the White House, I could blend in with the crowd at skid row—except for my watch. My jeans are most likely ten plus years old, have several holes, and I've paired them with a faded black T. This is my way of expressing my displeasure for being ambushed with this party.

Buzz, buzz, buzz.

What. The. Fuck?

Except for my sister and George, everyone who'd contact me is right in front of me. George knows to only call me if there's a real emergency.

I glance around. My backyard is decked out with two dozen cocktail tables. Each is draped in white and gold chiffon with an ostentatious bow on the table's leg and topped with flower bouquets the size of a hot air balloon. Fairy lights hang from every tree on the property, and candles float on little white plastic swans in the pool. I turn to head inside and—what the fuck is that? Oh, for Christ's sake, she didn't. Next to the pool house, two swans waddle between the guests—actual fucking birds. There is no way in hell this shit will be cleaned up by the time I leave tomorrow.

Margot is in deep conversation with Celeste and one of their friends. Despite having grown up in these circles, attending galas and fancy events regularly, I am like a fish out of water. This. Is. My. Home. Pulse pounding in my ears, I'm completely on edge. I don't want any of these people here. My nostrils flare, and I try to rein in the urge to physically kick every single one of these pretentious assholes out—including the swans. Margot and I will have a serious conversation when this is over.

Buzz, buzz, buzz.

Oh, for fuck's sake.

I tear my gaze off my fiancée, turn, and stalk into the house. I pass Julian without sparing him a second glance and ignore him calling out my name. Taking two steps at a time, I aim for my bedroom. Disappearing downstairs would be too suspicious at the moment.

I'm almost at the double doors when I pull out my phone and halt—fifteen text messages from UNKNOWN.

What the—?

I enter my room and close the doors behind me, locking them for good measure.

Clicking on the texts, I begin reading.

Margot looks pretty tonight.

The red dress suits her.

Is the dude with the pink shirt Julian? I saw you talking to him when he first arrived.

Which one is the birthday girl?

Is this the only pool you have? How do you swim your laps in that tiny thing?

Are those actual swans in your yard? Holy shit!

Oh...I finally get your Courrier comment, what's in those things?

I stop reading and turn to the corner above the door, staring straight at the spot on the ceiling.

Buzz, buzz, buzz.

I look down and scan the newest text message.

Hi. :)

A flush of adrenaline hits me. I don't believe this.

Pulling up the number pad, I key in the digits I never saved to my contacts. She picks up on the first ring but doesn't say anything.

"Little sister, did you hack into my security feed?" I inquire with a purposefully icy tone. I turn away from the camera.

"Maybe?" she answers meekly.

Holy fucking shit. She's probably smarter than me.

A broad grin spreads across my face, but I keep my back to her.

"And you thought that was a good idea, why?"

Do. Not. Laugh.

"Um..." Lilly seems worried, and I can no longer pretend.

I turn and look up at the camera. She inhales sharply when she sees my expression.

"You're not angry with me?" she inquires, still hesitantly.

I laugh. "Fuck no. That's genius! How did you get past the second firewall?"

The excitement in her voice is contagious when she explains to me how she altered the script I showed her when I walked her through getting into the feed at her house in Westbridge. I'm floored.

"That is some serious coding, sis. I don't know if I should leave you unattended with a computer anymore."

She laughs, but I'm serious. Not that I don't trust her, but hell.

We talk a moment longer, and I confirm that the guy in the pink shirt is, in fact, Julian. She tells me he looks nice, and she's happy I have my best friend there. Such a simple statement. Her sentiment makes warmth spread in my chest. When was the last time I felt anything like that? The last time someone was genuinely happy for me and it had nothing to do with business or my fortune?

AFTER I HANG up the phone, I remain in the bedroom for a few more minutes, collecting my thoughts. With a little more training and proper education, my sister will surpass my abilities without much effort. I make a mental note to look into the best schooling for her—if she wants to go down that road. She said as much, but I would never force her.

Julian meets me at the bottom of the stairs. "Dude, where did you disappear to?"

"Had to take a call." I'm still pissed at him for allowing this party to happen at my house.

He raises an eyebrow with the unspoken question.

"None of your business," I tell him flat out. Let him come to his own conclusions.

He blocks my attempt to walk around him. "I'm sorry, man. I know how you hate people in your space."

"I do." I cross my arms over my chest.

"I figured it'd be fine. Margot will soften you up. You always end up giving her what she wants." He must've seen the ghost of something on my face. "Nate? What's going on?"

I want to tell my best friend about Lilly. He knows what Audrey's death did to me. He was there. Instead, I say, "I'm not so sure Margot is right for me anymore."

Julian's eyes nearly bulge out. "Where is that coming from?"

He's known me most of my life and thought Margot filled the void Audrey and Mom's death left behind. For a while, I thought the same. However, spending time with my sister, seeing the effect she has on George—a man who I've seen smile more in the last week than in the previous decade—and seeing her relationship with Rhys and her friends...it's made me realize everything I've been missing and want to have—one day.

"I can't talk about it yet. But I will. Soon."

Looking at me sideways and then glancing through the French doors out at the patio where both our fiancées are standing and laughing with the other guests, he nods.

"Okay. But you call me as soon as you are ready." Worry is laced in his tone.

"I will." I give him a stern nod then plaster a broad grin on my face. "Now, let's go give your brother shit for his latest episode. What the fuck was he thinking, giving that hot blonde the boot off the show?"

Julian snorts. "Man, you don't know the half of it. That chick was nuts. She snuck into his hotel room after they wrapped the day before and laid on his bed covered in whipped cream with cherries on her tits and pussy."

I squint at my friend. "And that's bad how?"

"Her fucktard boyfriend was there as well—in the same getup."

I stare, unblinking, as a mental image forms in my head, and I can no longer stop myself from cracking up.

I slap Julian on the shoulder and smirk. "Dude, you just made my night. Let's go find baby bro."

CHAPTER TWENTY-NINE

LILLY

I SPIED ON THE PARTY A LITTLE LONGER. I FELT LIKE I WAS watching one of those *The Real Whoever of Wherever* shows—just, you know...*real*. It was equally addicting and disturbing; I swear I saw several people snort white powder off the pretty cocktail tables. I wondered if I should send Nate another text, but George assured me that Nate was aware of what was going on at his property and would intervene if he deemed it necessary.

HAVING SPENT my entire Saturday sedentary, I start the next day off at the gym. Well, technically, it's already noon when I emerge from my room, but it's still Sunday—just not that early on Sunday.

Rhys had messaged me after Heather and Tristen went to bed, and we continued texting until the early morning hours. He refused to get off the phone until someone started to move around in the house. We had already exchanged "Good Nights" when a video call popped up on my screen. However, my initial panic immediately subsided when I saw Rhys's smirking face. I grinned like a loon as he held his finger against his lips, mouthed "I love you," and hung back up.

Seventy-two more hours.

I DON'T EXPECT to hear from Rhys for a while, and Nate messaged last night that he is going to meet up with Julian before heading back to the vineyard. I find George in the sitting room with another book. This guy reads faster than Natty. He looks content, and I smile to myself. It's probably the least he's done in months—stalking me and all. I'm about to walk toward the door leading to the gym when I stop in my tracks.

I must've stood there for a while, because all of a sudden, I hear George's voice. "Miss Lilly? Is everything okay?"

Glancing around the sitting room and foyer, I take it all in before settling back on him and smile. "Yes, everything is good."

I turn on my heel and head to the gym. For once, I'm not driven by anger, fear, or guilt. Something has shifted, but instead of trying to analyze it, I've decided to leave it be. Just for a few hours, I want to feel okay.

I GOT three hours before everything came crumbling down. Three. Hours.

Emerging from the bathroom, I find a message from Nate on my screen: **NCC. NOW!**

Shit.

I glance at the clock in the top corner. It's four p.m. I spent over an hour in the bath, indulging in all the fancy toiletries my little spa contains—a decision I regret now. Nate wasn't supposed to be back until late tonight. Something happened. Unease immediately builds in my core.

I dress quickly, not bothering to blow-dry my hair, and speed-walk across the second floor to the office. As soon as the door opens, I am bombarded with a cacophony. Every monitor has a different news channel running.

I didn't even realize the monitors had sound.

George and Nate hover over the desk; my brother is ferociously typing. Neither man has noticed me over all the noise.

"What's going on?" I try to take it all in, but I don't know where to begin.

Two sets of eyes jerk in my direction, and I stumble back like being pushed. George is trained to keep his cool—at all times. Taking in the man in front of me, a pit opens up in my stomach. His forehead is scrunched, and his mouth is pressed so tightly that almost the entire pink is invisible. The only thing missing is a flashing neon sign with the words "WE'RE FUCKED" above his head. One of those that illuminate one letter at a time, then all the letters start blinking, followed by a border of multicolored lightbulbs. My brother, however, radiates white-hot rage. His nostrils are flared, and the only thing missing is steam coming out of his ears.

I swallow a few times. My attention snaps to the wall monitors when two words jump out from the multitude of voices.

"Lilly McGuire."

I try to figure out which monitor spit out my name when everything goes quiet.

"Someone released to the media that you are victim number one and have gone missing again." Nate's voice is like a bucket of ice.

NO!

I can't turn my head away from the bottom left screen. My face just popped up, a picture from our last gymnastics meet with a caption that reads: "Lilly McGuire, the alleged first victim of The Babysitter has gone missing again."

"The Babysitter?" I croak.

What is going on?

A hand settles on my shoulder and slowly forces me to turn away from my picture. Angling my head up, hazel eyes meet mine, and the anger is replaced with fear. My brother's mouth is in a thin line, and I glance over to our head of security.

Our. Because that's what George is. He protects both of us.

"How?" I whisper.

Nate doesn't look away from me, but George answers, "We don't know. The news broke shortly after you went to the gym."

"I had already seen the first report when George called. I was on my way to the airport. If your name pops up anywhere on the Internet, I'll know about it." My brother's tone is fierce.

"What about Rhys?"

Does he know?

"I haven't been able to reach him," George answers.

I turn back to the six wall screens. "Can we see if he's okay?" Meaning, I want to see the security feed. At this point, I could do it myself, but Nate is still faster.

I see him sit down out of the corner of my eye, and not long after, the feed in front of me switches.

I inhale sharply. Heather and Rhys are sitting in the living room in front of the TV. His arm is wrapped around his mother, and she is wiping her eyes with a tissue. Tristen is pacing his office, talking—no, yelling into a phone. The two agents that previously occupied the kitchen table have multiplied as well and are talking animatedly.

"We need to get ahold of Rhys. We need to know what happened on that end," Nate announces with an icy tone. He can't possibly think Rhys or someone there leaked the info?

"They don't seem to know what's going on either. Look at them." I gesture at the monitor displaying the kitchen. The authorities don't look very authoritarian. The scene is almost too painful to watch. They seem as lost—no, confused as I was after my first migraine.

"Rhys is not going to answer his phone for a while," George interjects, watching the living room feed closely.

An idea starts forming, and I turn to my brother. "My phone is untraceable, correct?"

He squints at me. "Yes, what do you—" He's unable to finish his question.

I've already hit dial and pressed the speaker button. Three sets of eyes are glued to the device in my hand.

Come on, come on, come on.

"Hello?" a hesitant voice comes through the phone.

"WES!"

Oh, thank God.

"Lilly?" Rhys's best friend squeaks.

Nate slaps his forehead and gives me a what-the-fuck look, and I avert my eyes, focusing on the conversation.

"Hey, um...I need you to do something for me."

"Wha—?" Poor Wes has never handled surprises well, and I don't have time to explain either.

"Listen, I'm sorry I'm calling like this. I need you to go to my house and get Rhys to answer his phone. Don't call him. You need to go over in person."

"Bu—?"

Oh, for Christ's sake.

"WES!"

"Lilly?"

"Yes," I sigh. "Tell Rhys I called you. But only when you two are alone. My parents can't know."

When he doesn't say anything, I add, "Please, Wes!"

"Okay." His response is only a whisper.

I hang up.

"WHAT THE FUCK WERE YOU THINKING?" Nate roars at me.

"Miss Lilly, that was not wise," George adds, calmer, but his anger with my rash decision is clear.

"We need to figure out what happened, and we can't just call the house phone and ask for Rhys," I defend myself.

My brother throws his arms up. I brace myself for more shouting, but instead, he storms out of the room.

I chance a glance at George, who remains mute. He must see

238 • DANAH LOGAN

something on my face, because his expression gentles. "Give your brother time to calm down. He is worried about you. This took us all by surprise."

I'm not sure if by "this" he means the news or my call, so I stay quiet. I hope I didn't make a mistake. Sitting down, I watch the security feed on the wall monitors. I should probably Google myself to find out what is being reported, but I'm not ready yet.

TEN MINUTES LATER, Nate walks back in and plants himself in the chair next to mine. George has moved to the couch and is looking at something on his phone.

None of us talk until George announces, "Weston is on the move, heading toward the McGuire residence."

So that's what he's been doing.

Sure enough, not long after, Wes's red 4Runner pulls up and parks behind the black SUVs in the driveway. I hold my breath as I watch Rhys's best friend make his way into the house—walking straight in. All eyes are on him, and Rhys and Heather jump up from the couch, Heather's hand on Rhys's forearm as they face the newcomer.

Wes says something. I can't see Rhys's expression, but I notice Heather nod at him. Both boys make their way upstairs.

Nate enlarges the camera in Rhys's room to full screen, but when neither of them shows up, I frantically search the remaining feed. Rhys and Wes are in my bedroom, and a blush creeps up my cheeks.

What are they doing?

Not that I have anything to hide in there, but seeing the two boys in my private space...my face, neck, and ears feel like I just opened the door to an oven.

We switch to that frame, and I recognize my name on Wes's lips. Rhys darts into my closet and emerges with—what the hell? He has my purple satin grip bag in one hand, and he latches onto Wes's arm in passing, dragging him into my bathroom.

"Uh, little sister, why is your boyfriend and his best friend going into your bathroom with sex toys?"

My head whips to my brother. "WHAT?" I shriek, then it clicks, and I smack him across the head. "That's my grip bag." When he just raises an eyebrow, I slap him again. "For gymnastics, you moron."

"Ohhh." He grins. "Not my fault that it looks like the, uh... gift I gave Margot for our second anniversary."

I cover my face. "Oh my God, just shut up. Rhys probably used it to hide the phone." I keep the *duh* to myself.

I hear a snort from the couch, and even George can't keep it together. Thankfully, that's the moment my phone starts vibrating on the desk.

Before I can answer, Nate snatches it and swipes, pressing the device to his ear. "This better not have been you or your little friends!" His tone is calculated, and I recognize how my brother is running through several scenarios in his head. He listens and nods to himself. "How do you know?" Pause. Another nod. "Okay, keep me posted. Here." Nate hands me the phone, and I give him the evil eye.

"Rhys?"

"Hey, babe! Sounds like he is not too happy right now." Rhys's tone is subdued, and I hear water running in the background.

"This, yeah...this was quite a shock."

"No, shit!" I hear Wes's muffled voice.

"Am I on speakerphone?" My heart rate picks up.

"No! Do you think I'm an idiot?" Rhys huffs. "Wes has one of my headphones."

Wes heard Nate talking. Oh my gosh, this is getting worse by the minute.

"Did he hear..." I trail off.

Instead of Rhys, Wes answers coolly, "I did. You have a helluva lot to explain."

SHIT!

"I will," I mumble. Glancing over at Nate, he's glaring, and I shrink in my seat. "Rhys?"

"Yeah, babe?"

"Tell Wes."

There is silence on the other end.

"Maybe Den as well, while you're at it. But only if there is no chance of anyone overhearing you."

George jumps up from the couch, staring at me. He shows no expression whatsoever, which is worse than the way Nate glowers at me. He is close to blowing a gasket. Holding George's gaze, a cold shiver runs down my spine.

"Uh, are you sure?" Rhys also seems to think I've lost my mind.

"Wes?" I address him directly.

"Here."

"Can we trust you?"

"You kidding me?"

Why is everyone so angry with me? I'm the one who got freaking kidnapped.

A red haze starts forming in front of my eyes. "No, I am not kidding. This. Is. *My.* Life."

"Of course you can trust me, Lil." Wes is himself again.

"Thank you." I exhale slowly. "Then yes, Rhys, I am sure."

"Okay."

"He's going to catch you up. You guys need to get out of my bathroom before someone comes looking."

Rhys chuckles, but Wes's reaction is less amusing.

"How does she—?"

"Don't ask, man." Then Rhys addresses me one more time. "I'll be in touch later. Love you."

"Love you more."

Wes and Nate simultaneously make a gagging sound, and I hang up.

. . .

FOR THE NEXT COUPLE HOURS, we try to make sense of what happened. Rhys told Nate that they were just as surprised as we were. One of the agents got a call, followed by several more suits showing up at the house with screeching tires. Tristen had been on the phone with the different news channels for hours, dodging questions and, at the same time, trying to figure out how they got their information. I'm not surprised that he won't let the FBI handle it. One fact that no one has caught on to yet: I am not a McGuire. And I wonder how long that will take, given the fact that the whole incest thing is all over social media.

Nate can identify the first report, and almost all the news channels followed suit, reporting mostly the same. Some used my most recent yearbook photo, others one from a gymnastics meet that is posted on Butler's website. The news started calling Nate "The Babysitter," as he treated all the girls like he was just *watching* them for a while. The nickname seems to be what gets to him the most. At one point, he excuses himself without an explanation and leaves. We're in the middle of another news video, and I pause it, watching the door close behind my brother.

Unsure what to do, I look at George, who nods at me. I push myself out of the chair and go after my brother. I find him two floors down, swimming laps. Looking at the pile of clothes on the floor, I squint at my brother, butterflying his way through the pool with violent strokes. He didn't even take his jeans off.

This could take a while.

EVENTUALLY, Nate changes to freestyle but doesn't slow down for a good twenty minutes. When he pulls himself out of the water, his chest is heaving, and he leaves a trail of water on the floor, walking to the lounger next to mine. He lowers himself down, facing my chair, and I mimic his position, our knees almost touching. Head in his hands, he's leaning on his thighs, and neither of us speaks.

"I'm sorry."

Nate's pained voice startles me. We've sat in silence for so long that his whisper sounds like yelled words inside an echo chamber.

I reach over and pry one of his hands away from his head, trying to catch his eyes.

"What for?" I ask carefully.

My brother looks up, holding my gaze. "If I weren't so fucked up in the head, none of this would've ever happened."

I think that over and choose to give him the truth. "That's true. But we can't change the past. All we can do is deal with it and move forward. As a family."

CHAPTER THIRTY

HER

FOR THE LAST FORTY-EIGHT HOURS, GRAY HAS BEEN FOLLOWING *every lead I've thrown at him. Especially when I stumbled across the social media accounts for one Kat Rosenfield. The rest of the McGuires have never been of interest to me, as long as they kept Lilly alive and away from him. What I didn't take into account was the possibility that they would allow their children to enter into a relationship. It seems to be a relatively recent development, so I consider the possibility of them not being aware of it yet. Though, knowing Tristen, there is no way the kids could've kept this from him. There is nothing the man doesn't find out. All they had to do was keep Lilly in the dark until the date. What set all these events in motion?*

I'M SITTING *in my office, staring at the white walls. There are no pictures—anywhere. I like my house clean. Art is distracting; it evokes feelings—a characteristic I no longer value having.*

My hand swipes over the top of my glass desk and stops at the keyboard to my silver laptop. Silver, gray, and white—the only shades I tolerate in my space.

Gray's room is full of color, blues and greens with mismatched furniture. I refuse to set foot in it. He can come to me whenever he desires, but I will not engage in any physical contact in that dreadful bedevilment. It's appalling.

I open my untraceable email account, the one I use to contact my source of information that has kept me up to date on him. It's pathetic how easy one can get people to talk if you throw enough money at them. If it's not cash, it's something else. Everyone can be bought.

Gray doesn't know about my informant or him. He is useful on different levels, my tool for many tasks—sex, murder, he makes the most delicious Russian cheesecake—but confiding in him? No. No one is worth my trust. I lost that ability years ago.

IT'S *time to change the story.*

MY DEAREST FRIEND,

We have a problem, and I am incredibly disappointed. You know what happens when I am not satisfied with your performance.

You are being compensated very generously in the currency of your choosing. May I remind you that I can change this instantly by sending an anonymous message to our mutual acquaintance?

It is in your best interest to execute this next task precisely as I will outline in the attached file. I want the information to be broadcasted by every news station by the end of the day tomorrow.

Failure to complete the request will end our very lucrative arrangement, effective immediately, and I will have my associate pay you a visit to collect.

CHAPTER THIRTY-ONE

LILLY

DAD ISSUED A PRESS RELEASE.

The chime of the incoming text wakes me, and I squint at the clock in the corner of the screen, trying to clear the fog in my brain. 5:37. Rubbing my eyes, I read the words over and over. Press release. Press...release. I drop the device onto the comforter and sit up in a jerked motion. Tristen issued a press release. I throw the covers back and dash out of my bedroom and across the second floor.

Placing my index and middle finger on the small glass panel, I immediately raise myself on my tiptoes to reach the retina scanner—this was not designed for short people.

Come on, come on, come on.

I rattle off my string of words as soon as the mic is exposed and push the door open. The NCC is empty, and I stand in the middle of the room, unsure of what to do. Goosebumps appear on my bare legs and arms. Looking down, realization sets in that I'm just wearing a pair of sleep shorts and a tank top.

Finding more clothes or my brother? Another full-on body shiver decides for me—clothes first. I race back to my room and grab a pair of gray sweats and a white hoodie from the dresser. Pants on, I start speed-walking out of my room, sweatshirt halfway over my head, and slam into something solid. Owww.

Pushing my head through the opening, I look around, disoriented. I ran straight into the door frame. Rubbing the bump on my forehead, I wince and look at my hand; red stains my fingertips. Beautiful. I managed to aim perfectly at my almost healed cut.

It's too early for any of this.

DRESSED and with a wad of paper towel pressed against my forehead, I set off to find my brother. After checking the gym, library, and even the kitchen, I make my way back to the office—nothing. He is usually long awake at this time. The possibility of him sleeping didn't even occur to me until I stare at the empty desk chair.

Knocking gently, I push the door to Nate's bedroom open. A gap between the curtains lets enough moonlight in for me to identify his sprawled-out form in the king-size bed. I watch him from the door. One arm is draped over his head; the other rests on top of the navy comforter over his chest. His features are relaxed for the first time in days, and I don't have the heart to wake him.

We didn't leave the pool area until George came for us, and then we finished going over the news reports for the rest of the night. The entire time, Nate was withdrawn, no snarky remarks —very unlike the big brother I've gotten to know.

Closing the door, I make my way back to the computer room.

WE RECEIVED an exclusive statement from the agent in charge assigned to Lilly McGuire's second disappearance. Miss McGuire has been missing for the past ten days after her totaled Jeep Wrangler was discovered on the side of the road between Westbridge, Virginia and the neighboring town of Fallsbrook. It is confirmed that Lilly McGuire was indeed the first victim of The Babysitter, a perpetrator who has kidnapped five girls between the ages of five and seven in the last ten years. Miss McGuire was abducted at age six, during a field trip to the San Diego Zoo, and reappeared at a hospital in Santa Rosa, California several days later. Miss McGuire had no recollection of the time she had been held captive and was released into the custody of Col. Tristen McGuire, USMC, and his wife, corporate attorney at Webb, Sinclair, and Sinclair, Heather McGuire, who later adopted the girl. The statement did not reveal why there was never a missing person's report filed for either kidnapping or where Miss McGuire's birth parents are. We will keep you updated on the case as the authorities release more information.

OR YOU START DIGGING *into my personal life.*

I pause the video and sit back, exhaling slowly. It's just a matter of time before someone figures out my birth name and who my biological parents are—well, mother, since I doubt they'd be able to track down Brooks.

I pull out my phone and send Rhys a text.

Why did T issue the statement now? They already reported yesterday that I was the first.

As expected, there is no reply. The door behind me opens, and George walks in with a travel mug. Handing it over, he sits down in Nate's chair.

"He's still sleeping?"

I nod and raise my eyebrow, glancing at the mug in my hand.

"I assumed you wanted your morning tea."

I smirk. "How did you know I didn't already have it?"

He looks at me in true George-fashion and deadpans, "I know everything."

I must've resembled a telescope eye, because he winks. "You've been using the same thermos every day, and it was still sitting in the kitchen."

Oh.

Instead of continuing this trivial conversation, I move on to the more pressing topic at hand. "Did you see the news?"

"I have."

"Why now?" I whisper.

George thinks that over before responding. "If it were me, I would want to get ahead of the press—before they start digging into your personal life."

I bark out a laugh. "They'll still dig. I mean, the statement basically told them that something happened to or with my birth parents. They never reported me missing."

"That is true. However, I believe the press release was not meant to deal with that part of your past. If your brother couldn't find that information, the press definitely won't." He pauses for a breath. "I've been following Miss Rosenfield's online activities since last week. She's been busy. She's asked around if anyone has heard from Rhys, putting out speculations as to why neither you nor your boyfriend have been to school. And my favorite, why Weston is, all of a sudden, acting as if his dick is permanently shoved down Miss Keller's STD-infested mouth."

Offended on my friends' behalf, my nose scrunches. "That. Is. Disgusting." Tilting my head to the side, I add, "And it doesn't even make sense!"

"Miss Rosenfield's words, not mine." George's disdain is as visible as the white line across his face. Not making eye contact, he continues, "The social media posts with the photograph have increased as well."

That damn picture.

"Do I want to know what's being said about me?" I have a pretty good guess. Having gone to school with Katherine for the past three years, I've witnessed how she operates. It never ends well for the target of her obsession.

"You have to face the consequences of Miss Rosenfield's virtual rampage eventually, but while you are here, I would advise concentrating on the task at hand. There is nothing any of us can do about the girl at the moment."

Or to the girl.

My fists ball, and I visualize using Rhys's ex as a Sparring Bob. Executing every single offensive move Spence has taught me over the years on her in my head, a diabolical grin spreads across my face.

"Miss Lilly?"

Hearing my name, the red haze clears, and I blink a few times. "Uh, yes?"

"Dare I ask what just went on in that head of yours?"

No doubt I looked like a rabid animal poised to strike. "Um, probably not."

Suddenly, a thought hits me as if George has slapped me across the face. "Do you think Katherine leaked the information about me to the press? I mean, she saw Rhys in the park."

"No."

"How can you be so sure?"

"Miss Rosenfield is fixated on the relationship with Rhys. I would know if she had anything leading toward Nate or what actually is happening." His response is matter-of-fact.

"Nate did something to her phone," I state, not ask.

"I underestimated the girl once. I will not make the same mistake again." His sneer makes the scar around his mouth contort, and he looks downright terrifying. Thank goodness his contempt is not directed toward me, or I'd pee my pants.

Trying to make light of the situation and distract both of us, I quip, "Why George, that's, like, the fifth time this morning you've shown some emotion."

The man in front of me lifts a hand to his chest and grins—a full-on toothy grin from ear to ear.

"Don't tell your brother. You have that effect on people." He winks.

Feeling all warm and fuzzy, it sinks in. I was so focused on the secrets that are piling up higher than Natty's collection of classic novels and my guilt of putting my adoptive family and Rhys in the middle of me figuring out the relationship with my criminal brother that I ignored what I did find. Amid this pandemonium, I have gained a new family. A slightly—scratch that, a dysfunctional family, but both men, Nate and George, care deeply about me. And I'm pretty sure George's affection extends to Rhys as well.

Taking a sip of my tea, I voice the question. "So, who?"

"Leave that up to me," Nate's voice interrupts from the door, and I take in his disheveled appearance of a rumpled gray t-shirt and low-hanging blue-and-green plaid pajama pants. I was so concentrated on George that I didn't hear the usual buzzing sound of the door opening. He slouches in, and when George makes a move to get out of the second chair, my brother waves him off and, instead, makes his way to the leather couch, grabbing the laptop off the desk in passing.

George focuses back on me and amends our previous conversation. "I believe the statement was to clarify your blood relations with the McGuires."

Oh.

"Oh!"

Settling into the couch, Nate opens the computer and starts typing. Not stopping at all, he informs us casually, "Lilly, we will have to start medicating you, effective immediately."

Wait, what?

"Excuse me?" Oh, goody. Minnie Mouse is back. I must've heard him wrong.

Nate completely ignores me and addresses George. "I need you to call your guy and get everything we need. Come Wednesday, her bloodstream needs to match the story."

Oh, hell no!

My body tenses.

George nods and is about to get up when I latch onto his wrist. The guy who could haunt the nightmares of grown men raises an eyebrow, but I don't care if no one ever touches him.

"You're not leaving until one of you explains to me What. The. Hell. Is. Going. On." They can't just dump this shit on me and move on, like, "Oh, let's go grab some donuts for Lilly before we send her off."

What. The. F?

George lowers himself back down while I intensify my grasp on his wrist.

I steady my tone and turn to my brother. "Explain!"

Nate closes the laptop and pinches the bridge of his nose. "This is the only way I can protect you."

"By drugging me?" I shriek. *So much for keeping it together.*

Nate's voice is eerily calm, almost detached. Over the last week, I've suppressed this side of my brother—the scary, calculated part of his genius personality. "We have two separate situations to deal with. I told you sending the video would have consequences. Your friends and parents know that you are not a typical kidnapping victim. Even if you manage to keep the truth from Heather and Tristen for a while longer, the media will tear you apart. You are not a scared child anymore; you should remember what happened to you, especially if nothing *traumatizing* happened to you." He makes air quotes around traumatizing. "You don't have a mark on you. I didn't beat or rape you." I flinch, but Nate continues with brutal honesty. "The other issue is the fucking press release and all the shit Barbie has put online the last few days. Your relationship with your brother will be another focus. How long have you been together? Have your parents known and condoned the relationship?"

My heart beats so fast I have trouble catching my breath.

For the first time since starting his speech, my brother looks me straight in the eye. "The only way we can take some of the pressure off of you is by letting the public believe that you don't remember a thing from the last two weeks. I can't help you with the other problem. I can try to block and take down some of the posts, but I won't be able to get them all. Someone will question who is doing it." With a sigh, he finishes, "I'm sorry, little sis."

Nodding, I shove my shaking hands in the pocket of my white hoodie.

I'M SITTING in the kitchen when George returns with a large black duffel bag slung over his shoulder. I nearly choke on a cracker when he drops it on the table with a thud. How many drugs do they need? My entire body would fit in that thing.

I still haven't been able to reach Rhys; all I know is that he's at home and that Wes and Den are there as well. Nate wouldn't let me hack into the feed; he said it would only make it harder for me to see them. There was some yelling and throwing of a wireless mouse involved—he never used that damn thing anyway—and in the end, he kicked me out.

George settles across from me. "Talk to me, Miss Lilly."

"Can you drop the Miss? I think we're way past that." I try to sound annoyed but can't stop the smile forming on my lips.

"As you wish, my lady."

I roll my eyes.

At that moment, my phone starts ringing, and my breath hitches. My hands start shaking so violently that the device slips though my hands twice.

"Shit!" I hiss.

George reaches over and picks it up, pressing the speakerphone button. "Rhys." His tone is stoic, but he winks at me.

"Uh."

"How can I help you, Rhys?" George sounds murderous but cracks a smile.

Good Lord, he's enjoying this.

"Um."

"Oh, for fuck's sake, George. Give the kid a break," Nate snaps, coming from the hallway, and I jump. I snatch my phone, turn the speaker off, and press it to my ear.

"I'm here. Sorry."

Nate saunters over to the fridge, George still grins to himself, and I turn around to leave the room when my brother calls after me, "Tell the boyfriend that you will be out of touch the next two days."

Wha—?

I face Nate again and raise my eyebrows.

"Lilly?" Rhys's voice echoes in my ear, but I can't form a reply.

He points his head toward the duffel on the table, and it clicks. I won't be able to contact him. Oh God, my memory. My brother is going to mess with my mind. My chest tightens and everything starts to spin. I race up the stairs. I need to be alone.

Somehow, I make it to my room. Leaning against the back of the door, my legs give out, and I slide down in slow motion. Every breath feels like it stops in the back of my throat, the oxygen not making it to my lungs.

Between the blackspots, the face of a man flashes in front of my eyes. The memory is accompanied by the sharp pain I almost forgot about—*almost*. A moan escapes me, and I press the heel of my free hand against my forehead. He has thinning brown hair, beady eyes, and an oval face, but the lower half is covered with one of those surgical masks. The memory doctor.

Bile rises in my throat. The stabbing sensation won't go away.

Why won't it go away?

"Babe, are you there? What's going on?"

Why does his voice sound so far away?

Leaning forward, I put my head between my legs and mumble something along the lines of, "I'm here. Need...a...moment."

"Lilly, what is going on? Put George back on. You're freaking me—"

That's the last I hear before the phone slips out of my hand.

"—DEHYDRATED—"

"—fucking panic attack—"

"What the fuck are—"

"Calm the fuck—"

"Stop saying fuck!" I rasp out, and everyone goes quiet.

"Babe?" Rhys's voice is close to my ear. He's here? No, he can't be.

I blink my eyes open, and my brother's face slowly comes into focus, hovering above me.

"What happened?" My words are slurred.

"Rhys called me when you didn't answer. We came to check on you." I turn my head and see George squatting beside me, phone in hand and lit up with a call.

I pat next to my body.

Where is my phone?

"Are you looking for this?" Nate holds something out. "You dropped it when you passed out."

I push myself into a sitting position and take my phone, cradling it to my chest like it's my actual boyfriend. He's not even on that line.

"I felt dizzy. I couldn't breathe..." I trail off, neglecting to mention the migraine.

"I had to push the door open because you were blocking it. Never knew your tiny body could be that heavy." My brother winks.

"You had another panic attack. Not surprising, considering what's about to happen," George says matter-of-factly.

"Dude, what is he talking about?"

Wes?

"Oh great, the whole *Scooby gang* is on the phone," Nate snarls.

"Rhys, Lilly will call you back in a few minutes." Before anyone on the other end can respond, George ends the call.

. . .

ABOUT TEN MINUTES LATER, I'm alone in my room. Two glasses of water downed and propped against a mountain of pillows— not sure where they all came from—I dial Rhys's number.

"Oh, thank fuck!" are the first words through the earpiece.

"Hey." I still sound raspy.

"Babe, what the hell happened? Why did you have a panic attack? George wouldn't tell me shit. I was about to drive to the fucking airport." He speaks so fast it takes me a moment to comprehend it all. I don't want to talk about it.

"I'm sorry. It's been a...long day." I exhale slowly. "Is Wes with you?"

"No, I am," my best friend's voice startles me, and my pulse accelerates instantly.

"Oh."

"Yeah. Oh. What the fuck, babe?" Denielle whisper-shouts.

"Where is Wes?" I mumble.

"He's on watch duty—not that it is any less suspicious that Den and I are in the bathroom together," Rhys huffs out with a laugh.

"D?" I ask meekly.

"Yes." Her tone is clipped.

"I'm so sorry." Moisture building in my eyes, I sniff loudly.

"Babe. All I care about is that you are okay. The rest is fucked up, and I'm sure there is a shit-ton Rhys hasn't told us yet, but seriously? Your brother? And what's up with the scary scar dude? I'm just glad he's not going to kill us; Wes can finally stop pissing himself."

A sound between a sniffle, a hiccup, and a laugh comes out of my throat. "I swear I will tell you guys everything soon."

"I'm going to hold you to it." Den sounds more like herself again.

"Can I talk to Rhys for a moment?" I feel bad asking her to leave, but it's bad enough having to tell him about the upcoming days.

After a prolonged pause, she says, "Sure, babe. I'll see you soon?"

"See you soon." I force some enthusiasm into the three words.

A minute or two go by without anyone speaking; then, I hear the voice my body has been craving all day.

"Okay, I'm alone. Now tell me what's really going on, Cal!"

He knows me well. A sob bubbles up. "I love you!"

"I love you, too. What. Is. Going. On? Why are you freaking out, babe?"

I inhale and exhale several times before I lay out Nate's plan.

"ARE YOU FUCKING SHITTING ME? NO! NOT HAPPENING!" Rhys didn't take the medication part well.

"It's our only option." No matter how much it scares me that someone will mess with my memory again, it's necessary.

"There has to be another way!" He sounds desperate.

"Nate would never harm me." Am I reassuring Rhys or myself?

"FUCK! Babe, I don't like this." In front of my mind's eye, I see Rhys pacing the small bathroom, tugging on his hair. "I want George to keep me updated if you can't. But if you can, you have to call or text. Give me some type of sign. I need to know you're okay." I'm pretty sure I can hear Rhys choke up.

"I promise." Not that I can enforce the promise, but I believe that my brother and George will follow through.

We talk for a few more minutes, about nothing in particular; I'm simply not ready to get off the phone.

After we hang up, I swing my legs off the bed and make my way to the NCC. Both George and Nate sit in front of the desk. Newsfeeds are still playing on half the wall monitors; the other half is our local security feed.

They turn, and I ask, "Anything new I need to know?"

Nate shakes his head. "No, same stuff."

I inhale deeply then look at the bag that's now sitting next to George's chair. "Okay, how are we going to do this?"

CHAPTER THIRTY-TWO

RHYS

I'VE BARELY SLEPT IN OVER 48 HOURS, AND EVEN CAFFEINE doesn't help anymore. I feel like I'm in a constant state of being buzzed with a side of jitters. In short, I'm a mess. George followed through and sent regular texts. I even got two messages from Lilly, but all they said were, "I'm fine. Don't worry. See you soon." Nate could've sent those for all I know. The only reason I believed Lilly herself sent the texts was that "worry" was spelled with three Rs and "soon" with four Ns. What the fuck were they pumping into her bloodstream?

I've successfully dodged spending more than five minutes with either of my parents. Avoiding Mom makes me feel like a piece of shit. The only reprieve is that she's barely left the third floor, which has reduced the likelihood of me randomly blurting out that her daughter would be coming home in a few days. Also, the increased testosterone presence in the kitchen was making my dick itch. But it served as the perfect excuse when Dad cornered me yesterday as to why I'm holed up in my room. Wes and Denielle are an additional buffer toward my father, taking turns babysitting me since he's ordered me home.

By day two, I've caught my friends up on everything I know, including the constant surveillance by my own family. That tidbit freaked Den out more than Lilly being kidnapped by her biological brother or said brother's mental issues. We talked in the confinement of my bathroom—shower and faucet running—which would raise questions in itself if my father checked his feed. He's not stupid; he could put two and two together. Why he hasn't confronted me yet is a mystery.

One would think that a tragedy like this would bring a family together—not mine. Everyone is on their own, hiding more secrets than Area 51.

Lilly has been officially missing for fifteen days, and George filled me in on the plan last night. Nate already left for LA and is meeting with his business partner to solidify his alibi—part of me still believes that this is all just a ruse not to have to get locked up. Before reaching the drop-off point, Lilly would get another dose of God-knows-what. George refused to reveal their destination, probably assuming I'd be on my way immediately.

He knows me well.

A BUZZING UNDER MY PILLOW, which is where I keep my second phone at night, made me jerk to a sitting position around five this morning. I couldn't have slept more than an hour and a half, because the last time I rolled over to stare at the alarm clock on my nightstand was 3:32. I stumbled out of bed and beelined for the bathroom, having to get away from the prying eyes of our home surveillance. Denielle and Wes both slept over, but in my groggy haze, I forgot about Wes's sprawled-out form in front of my bed. Denielle took the recliner while Wes ended up on the floor. Neither wanted to co-sleep—more space for me. Fumbling my way across the floor, eyes mostly closed, I stepped on Wes in the process, who, in return, started bitching like a little girl. Ignoring the whining, I locked myself in the bathroom—the only room where I'm not being watched these days.

. . .

Now, several hours later, I'm again sitting on the closed toilet seat, re-reading the text messages for the hundredth time. They were the first coherent messages from Lilly since Monday.

We're about to leave. I'm scared.

Letting her words sink in, nausea made me swallow several times before I was able to respond.

I know, babe. I will be there as soon as I can. We'll get through this. ILY.

I didn't expect her to reply again, so when I saw the bubble pop up immediately, I held my breath. Her next words calmed my churning stomach but caused an entirely different reaction in another body part.

I love u so much. I can't wait to be able to touch u again. You have no idea how badly I want to kiss u.

No matter how many times I read the message, my brain is unable to tell my groin area how inappropriate its reaction in the current situation is. My dick will never be mine again when it comes to Lilly.

I just put the phone back in its current hiding spot and am about done readjusting my jeans once more when my father's shouts fill the house.

"RHYS! HEATHER! COME DOWN HERE!"

Showtime.

We arrive in Podunk, Nebraska a little after nine p.m. local time. I don't bother remembering the town's actual name. Nate chose this place for two reasons: the security is minimal, and George would be able to get in and out undetected. Nate can monitor everything through the hospital's security system which hasn't been updated in over a decade.

The hospital entrance is a madhouse. I count seven news vans. As soon as we pull up, we're swarmed from all sides. It

reminds me of the day the cheerleaders noticed a cafeteria atten-
dant add fat-free yogurt to the lunch line. The poor woman
couldn't get out of the way fast enough.

Dad leads Mom and me through without acknowledging the
press, and even Mom looks like she's on her way to court. Both
my parents have their professional fronts up. I channel the quar-
terback and follow their lead, ignoring the microphones that are
shoved in my face.

A local FBI agent greets us and the two suits that accompanied us from Virginia as we pass the double doors.

"Where is she?" My mom drops her calm facade as soon as
we're in the privacy of the elevator and reaches for my hand, eyes
glistening over.

I squeeze her fingers in return, needing the physical contact
just as much. Dad, standing behind us, places both hands on
Mom's shoulders, and all of us wait for the local dude to
answer.

"She's in a private room on the third floor. We have security
staff posted in front of her door because a member of the press
was able to sneak in about an hour ago and tried to corner Miss
McGuire."

Mom's other hand flies to her mouth, and I swallow a curse.
We knew this could happen, but I assured George that I would
be with her to face the media. I hope Lilly has been able to stick
to the plan. I have no clue how out of it she is.

We exit the elevator, and I immediately spot the two
wannabe cops down the hallway. Without thinking, I take off.
Dad shouts after me, but I don't stop. The two guards close
ranks when I reach the door, but before I can say anything,
someone behind me calls, "Let him through."

I shoulder past them and burst through the door. As soon as
I'm past the threshold, every muscle in my body locks. I skid to
a halt in the middle of the room, unable to move. Heart beating
in my throat—if from the sprint or nervousness, I don't know—
my eyes zero in on Lilly. I suddenly have a hard time compre-

hending that she's here, in front of me. It's like I'm watching the scene from the outside. It doesn't feel real.

Lilly sits cross-legged on top of the covers in the bed. She's wearing a green hospital gown up top and blue scrubs at the bottom. Her head snaps up at the sound of my entrance, and her eyes widen. Her lips part, and she blinks a couple of times as if to ensure that I'm really here.

Our eyes lock, and everything snaps into place. It's been *only* two weeks, but it feels like I haven't seen her in years. My need to touch her, to feel her, propels me forward. I'm at her side in two strides, yet not fast enough. Moving up to a kneeling position, Lilly wraps her arms around my neck and buries her face in the crook right underneath my ear. Her shuddered exhale sends goosebumps down my spine, and my arms encircle her midsection. I hold on as tight as I can without causing her physical pain —I hope. My fingers want to dig into her skin, make contact in every way possible. I can't get close enough. The whole thing is somewhat awkward as she has multiple drips going into both arms, but my girl doesn't seem to care. She clings to me as if her life depends on it—in a way, it does.

"I missed you so much," I whisper, letting my lips graze the top of her ear.

Knowing Mom and Dad will walk through the door any second, it's the only slip I allow myself from the script the four of us agreed upon.

I pull back to get a better look at Lilly's face, and my heart skips a beat. The corners of my mouth turn down as I study her. The cut on her forehead looks like it reopened recently. What happened? Apart from the head wound and being paler than her already fair complexion, she looks fine. Her eyes, however, convey her actual state of mind. She's as scared as I am. Lilly is torn between two worlds and has to navigate them alone, for the most part. I will do my damndest to protect her, but even I know a time will come when I can't be there.

By their own volition, my hands move to either side of her

face. My thumb moves along her cheekbone, and she turns into the caress. Finally close to her again, being able to touch her, instinct takes over. I lean in and press my mouth to hers. Lilly immediately opens up for me like I'm the oxygen she needs to survive. God, how I have missed these lips, not to mention the feel of her tongue tangling with mine. It's like I've touched a live wire; every nerve ending in my body buzzes with the need to feel her.

The clearing of a throat makes us break apart. I reluctantly pull away, but instead of letting go, I interlace my left hand with her right.

So much for the script.

My parents and three agents stand in the doorway with various expressions. The agents look stunned, Dad's face is expressionless, and Mom has a smug smile on her face. At that moment, I'm sure she's been aware of us the entire time; I'm just not sure how she figured it out—home security feed or, well, our inability to hide our feelings.

A tear slowly runs down Lilly's cheek, and she reaches her other hand out. "Mom?"

With that one word, Mom bursts into violent sobs and launches herself at her daughter. Lilly lets go of my hand and wraps herself around our mother.

I glance at Dad, trying to gauge his level of anger about our show of affection, but instead of the expected disapproval, I see my father tear up. Not once, in eighteen years, have I seen the man cry, and it shocks me to the core.

His gaze meets mine, and he gives me a small nod. I have no clue what it means—for us, or Lilly and me.

Time will tell.

THE ATTENDING physician comes in and gives my parents a thorough rundown of Lilly's bloodwork and physical well-being. The agents moved toward the corner of the room but keep taking notes on their tablets and phones. It's a lot of medical blah blah, but my parents both keep nodding in understanding. Mom hasn't left Lilly's side, her right hand in her daughter's left and the other permanently attached to a spot right under her throat, while she listens intently. Lilly's free hand finds mine again, and I squeeze it. We don't make eye contact.

When the doctor concludes his report, everyone turns to Lilly as if they expect her to say something. Her eyes widen, and her hand becomes a vice around mine.

Fuuuck, that hurts.

One of the agents is about to say something, but Dad holds up a hand.

"When can we take her home?" My father wants to know. His entire person emanates *I'm in charge*, and the other man snaps his mouth closed.

The local agent, however, has no clue who my father is. "We need to finish questioning Miss McGuire before, uh..." He trails off when he looks up from his tablet and meets Dad's glare. There is a reason my father is one of the best in his profession. No one tells him what to do, and I hide a snicker by coughing into my fist. Mom gives me a disapproving look, and I mouth, "Sorry."

For the first time since Lilly's attending physician entered the room, our eyes meet, and I can see the slight tuck at the corner of her mouth. This ghost of a smile results in a flutter within my chest equal to a level seven earthquake. Still standing next to her bed, I smirk down at her before letting go of her hand and lowering myself to sit on the edge of the bed. I drape my arm around her shoulder, and she stiffens for a fraction of a second but then melts into my side. Neither Mom nor Dad give any indication that our behavior is unusual.

Our family is damn good at pretending.

"As I was saying," my father begins again, "when can we take her home?" Turning to the authorities, who hold zero authority, he adds, "You can ask all your questions when my daughter is back in her regular environment."

The doctor clears his throat. "The repeat tox screen shows that her body is responding to the treatment, and the drugs she had in her system will have cleared in about twenty-four to forty-eight hours. I want to repeat the test in twelve hours. If Miss McGuire keeps improving at the same rate she has since she was brought in, I am willing to release her into your custody by the end of the day tomorrow." He pauses. "However, I will advise you to keep her under observation by your family doctor to make sure there are no permanent side effects of the sedative."

Permanent side effects? What the fuck—

George didn't say anything about this shit causing long-term damage. As if she is reading my mind, Lilly places her palm on my thigh—her way of reassuring me that she's okay. I need to get her alone—and soon. I have way too many questions I want answers to.

A NURSE BRINGS in a second recliner and two more chairs, though the agents excuse themselves to the hallway once they realize they won't be questioning Lilly—not here. Mom keeps fussing over her, constantly asking if she needs something, fluffing her pillows, and patting her hair—reassuring herself that her daughter is really in front of her. Reading Lilly like an open book, I see how exhausted she is, but she takes it in stride. She won't tell Mom to stop.

After the agents leave, Dad makes his way over. I slide off the bed and take a step back, giving him space. His eyes briefly flick to mine then down to our once again joined hands before he places his hand on Lilly's leg.

"How are you, sweetheart?" It's the first time he's addressed her directly. His tone is gentle.

Lilly smiles weakly. "I'm fine, Dad. Just really tired."

My father's throat bobs. She hasn't called him "Dad" in

forever. He peers down at his phone and nods. "It's late. Why don't we all get some rest?"

When he's seated in one of the chairs, his legs propped up on another, he tries to get Mom's attention, but she doesn't look away from Lilly. "Heather? Why don't you take the recliner?" He nods to the one positioned next to his.

Mom glances back and forth between her husband and her daughter until Lilly touches her arm and smiles. "I'm okay." Mom nods hesitantly before she slowly makes her way to the other side of the room.

I pull the second recliner closer, so it's lined up with Lilly's bed, and make myself comfortable. There is no fucking way I am leaving her side. Suddenly, *the phone* vibrates in the inside pocket of my jacket, and my body involuntarily stiffens. Lilly's head snaps up, sensing the change in my posture. I watch her for several heartbeats before she dips her chin ever so slightly, and I make my way to the private bath attached to her room.

So much for not leaving her side.

Both my parents turn, and I stammer, "Uh... gotta take a piss."

"Language, sweetheart," Mom admonishes, and I hear a chuckle behind me.

With the door securely closed, I pull out the phone.

How is she?

Nate. I want to ask why Lilly, according to the attending physician, could have permanent side effects, but if I start this now, I have no clue how long I will be in this bathroom. One can only pee for so long—even if I'd say I took a dump.

Ok. Tired. Doc said she'll prob be released tmrw.

Good. Thanks, FBIL. G is close by if you need him.

FBIL? Oh, future brother-in-law.

Ha, this is the *friendliest* message I've gotten from him, and I can't keep from replying.

NP, PBIL. I'll take over from here.

Btw you have a stain on the right sleeve of your fancy leather jacket.

Fuck, this guy really is everywhere. Heat creeps up my face, and my eyes dart around in the bathroom before shaking my head. There are no cameras inside the rooms; he saw us walking in earlier.

A knock on the door makes me shove the phone back into my jacket pocket, and I crack the door open. Outside, Mom has an arm wrapped around Lilly while Lilly holds onto the IV pole.

"Lilly needs to use the bathroom as well. Are you done?" Mom asks with raised eyebrows.

"Uh, yeah, sure."

I'm about to squeeze past them when Dad's voice comes from across the room. "Flush?"

Shit!

I backtrack, flush, and then head back to my recliner without making eye contact with anyone. In my peripheral vision, I see my father staring at me, but I eagerly inspect the stain on my leather jacket.

Thank you, Nate, for giving me a distraction.

CHAPTER THIRTY-THREE

LILLY

I'M SLOWLY EMERGING FROM THE BLACK VOID THAT PULLED ME under as soon as Heather turned off the overhead light last night. The blinds are lowered, and the room is dark except for the faint glow coming in through the glass window in the door.

I lie still, trying to figure out why I'm awake, when the soft murmurs of Heather and Tristen register in my mind. Heather sounds upset. Quickly closing my eyes again, I don't dare move and alert them to me eavesdropping.

"I'm sorry, honey. I didn't want you to worry about anything else right now."

"Are you sure?" Heather whisper-shouts, confusion and agitation equally present in her tone.

Tristen draws in a deep breath. "There are some things I haven't told you. And right now is not the right time to talk about this."

"Since when have you known?" The question sounds more like an accusation.

"A while." I don't think I've ever heard Tristen sound so...uncomfortable?

"What is that supposed to mean? How. Long?" Heather's voice rises, and her husband shushes her.

I hear rustling, followed by footsteps and the door softly opening and closing.

What the—?

Rhys's hand is still securely in mine. Turning my head, I blink slowly. Instead of his sleeping body, I find green eyes staring back at me.

"You heard that, too, huh?" he whispers with raised eyebrows.

"Yeah, what was that about?" My throat feels like sandpaper, and I add, "Water."

Rhys turns in the recliner, reaching behind him and grabbing a plastic straw cup with water from the nightstand. I take gentle sips. The nurse told me that the stuff they're pumping into me could make me nauseous. As if on cue, my stomach revolts, and I swallow multiple times.

Too much saliva. I cover my mouth with my free hand, closing my eyes again.

I hate you, Nate. No, I don't, but you will pay for this—somehow.

"Babe? What's wrong?" Rhys sounds panicked, and his grip intensifies. I hold up my pointer finger without removing the other hand from my mouth.

Inhale. Three, two, one. Exhale. Three, two, one. Repeat.

When I'm sure I don't have to make a beeline to the bathroom, I face him. "Sorry...I'm fine. Just got nauseated. They told me that could happen."

"They?" Rhys narrows his eyes at me.

I smile weakly. "The nurse."

He blows out a long breath. I know when he's trying to rein in his temper. My thumb moves back and forth over his hand, a gesture I know soothes him. "I'm okay," I assure.

Rhys glances toward the door and lowers his tone even more. "What the fuck did George give you?" His nostrils flare. "Why would the doctor assume there could be permanent damage?"

I shrug, trying to play it down. "Any drug could cause long-term effects."

Just take my brother, for example.

Not satisfied with my explanation, his mouth is in a thin line.

I add, "They think I've been getting it for the past two weeks, so that's what they treated me for. I. Am. Fine. Nate's plan worked, and that's all that counts."

"I'm going to have a nice chat with my BFF when we get outta here," Rhys growls, and I have to chuckle. Their relationship is so bizarre, even to me who shouldn't say anything given my *family* situation.

"What time is it?" Subject change.

Rhys glances over to the small alarm clock situated behind us. "Almost six."

I scoot over as far as my IVs allow it. "Come here."

There is no point in keeping up the pretense. Heather and Tristen obviously know about us and, so far, haven't commented one way or another. And I want to be close to Rhys. No, *I need* to be close to him. Is that appropriate for our current situation or location? Probably not. Okay, *definitely not.* But from the moment he burst into this room, a low current has been buzzing through my body like an itch I'm unable to scratch. *I want him.*

His eyebrows almost touch his hairline, and he looks back and forth between me and the door. "I don't know if that's a good idea. We're in a—" Rhys's eyes widen, and he trails off when I lift the covers.

All I'm wearing is the hospital gown; I rid myself of the scrubs at some point last night when I got too hot—apparently, another side effect from detoxing.

"Fuuuuuck," he groans and rubs both hands over his face. Glancing at me between his fingers, he mumbles, "Why are you doing this to me?" His chest is rising faster than just a few seconds ago, and I can't deny that I take great pleasure in the effect I have on him.

Inhibition and fear of getting caught have officially exited.

"Because I want to feel you. That's all I could think about for the last two weeks. I need you to hold me."

Rhys blows out a sharp breath and *readjusts* in his seat. I chuckle, raising my eyebrows.

Clearing his throat, he pushes off the recliner and climbs onto the bed next to me. I drape the covers over his lap, and he motions for me to lift my head so he can place his arm around me. He gently untangles my IVs, making sure he's not cutting off any tubes going into my arms. I curl myself into his side, one leg over his, and nuzzle my face in the crook of his neck.

Home.

A gentle hand tilts my head up, the sensation of his touch sending tingles through my body, and I gaze into the eyes that will always be my undoing.

"I love you so much, Cal. Don't ever do this to me again." His tone is soft, but I can read him like an open book. The concern for my safety and the rage over what Nate has put us through is as visible as his love for me. A vulnerable boy replaces the always strong and confident guy everyone else gets to see. This side of him is usually as sealed as a vault, but I know the combination.

Instead of answering, I reach up and trace the contour of Rhys's strong, angular jaw, zeroing in on his mouth. My heart rate picks up, and I move my finger over his upper lip, lingering ever so slightly. A sly grin spreads across his face, and he softly bites down on the pad of my thumb. I suck in air between my teeth and let my lids flutter closed. Oh, my God. Heat pools in my core, and in an attempt to press my thighs together—still having his leg between both of mine—I create more friction. My eyes spring open, and a whimper escapes my throat. My hazels find his greens—gone is the little boy. Nostrils flared, it only takes the shortest of moments before he crashes his mouth to mine. There is nothing gentle about this kiss. Rhys invades my mouth with expert movement, forcing me to open up. His tongue frantically stroking against mine, I nip at his bottom lip.

I need more.

With a groan, his free hand tangles in my hair, tugging on it as he angles my face to gain better access. My entire body is on fire, and I grasp for the hem of his sweater. Slipping my hand under the fabric, I trace the contours of his taut abs. Rhys tenses under my touch, and his thigh pushes against my most sensitive spot. *More.* His reaction and the feel of his skin under my fingertips ignites something feral inside of me. The IV in my arm constricts my movement; I've stretched the tubing to its max, but I can't bring myself to care. The room fades into the background as I give in to the desperate need to mold myself to him. Hiking up my leg, the thin hospital gown shifts and exposes my light-gray boy shorts and lower abdomen. With a moan, I grind against Rhys's body, and he utters a string of incoherent words that resemble something like, "Oh God" and "Feels so fucking good."

Mimicking my movements, I feel his hard length straining against his jeans. The room is suddenly way too hot, and I fight the urge to rip the constricting material off my body. I shift to move on top of him. Need. To. Get. Closer. A loud crash and stinging pain in my arm brings everything to a halt. We spring apart and stare at each other, panting. Rhys's cheeks are flushed, eyes hooded, and we both look down at my arm. The IV pole didn't withstand my urge to climb the boy in my bed. It toppled to the floor and, in the process, dislodged the IV in my arm. Wide eyes, we face each other, and I can't stop the giggle that bubbles up in my throat. Rhys places his forehead to mine and chuckles, "Only you can make me dry hump you in a hospital bed with my parents and FBI outside."

"Sorry?" I grin.

"You. Are. Not. And neither am I. I needed this." He gives me a peck on the nose before pulling back and glancing down at my arm. Following his line of sight, I scrunch my nose. It doesn't hurt anymore, but there is a little blood where the IV should be.

"I should probably call a nurse to fix this mess I made." I smirk.

Shaking his head, Rhys gets up. "I'll go get one."

When he's gone, I sink into the pillow and pull the covers back over my legs. This is the first time I've been alone since my family arrived last night. Even when I went to the bathroom, Heather was with me. A shiver runs down my spine. I wrap my arms around myself and glance at the door out of the corner of my eye. I know there is at least one security guard outside, but nonetheless, I wait for another reporter to ambush me. I was still slightly out of it when a guy, disguised as a male nurse, cornered me yesterday. I just stared, wide-eyed, while he threw question after question at me, shoving his phone in my face. Thank goodness my real nurse walked in and started screaming for security. Who knows what would've come out of my mouth in the state of mind I was in? It's a miracle I didn't reveal anything at all in the hours between George pulling up around the corner of the emergency entrance and Rhys walking in.

Looking over to the recliner next to my bed, I notice a phone laying there. *The phone.* Shit! It must've slipped out of Rhys's pocket. I quickly stretch over to grab it when the door opens, and I almost topple out, catching myself on the rail before making a head dive. My adrenaline level skyrockets, and the voice in my head screams, *they're back!* They as in the press. I clutch the rail, pushing myself upright, and hold my breath.

When I hear Heather's voice, my body relaxes. "Sweetie, why is Rhys looking for a—oh my gosh, what happened?" She rushes over and starts inspecting my arm.

My face heats. "It's fine. I tried to reach something and didn't pay attention."

I wanted to reach something alright.

My adopted mother's expression calls *bullshit.* We stare at each other, neither of us saying what we want to say.

I'm the first one to look away. Biting my lip, I inspect my nails like I just got the most gorgeous manicure.

Hands unexpectedly cover mine. "Sweetie?"

I don't want to look up, but in the end, I force myself to face the woman who has raised me most of my life. She is about to say something when I blurt out, "I know!"

Heather's mouth snaps shut, and she eyes me for one, two, three, four, five, six, seven—

"I know you do."

Her tone is so gentle, so understanding that floodgates open up again.

I blink several times, but it's no use. "Mo-om?" I sniff, and she places a hand on my cheek.

"My sweet Lilly, no matter what you know or *think* you know, you *are* my little girl." There is a pause before she lowers her voice even more. "We will talk about everything when we're at home. Not here."

My eyes widen.

Should I be relieved or worried?

It's that moment when Rhys returns with a nurse following close behind. He halts abruptly when he spots me crying, and the short woman plows straight into his broad back. Narrowing his eyes, his gaze flicks between his mother and me before he peers over his shoulder. The nurse seems to take that as a cue to walk around him and get to work.

"Oh my, how did that happen?" I cringe. She must be the new day nurse as I haven't had *the pleasure* yet. She sounds like the weird-ass clown Heather and Tristen hired for Natty's fourth birthday after he sucked in helium from a balloon. He scared the crap out of all the toddlers, and Tristen had to make him leave.

While the woman works on my arm, I hold Rhys's gaze. His lips are pressed in a thin line, questions written all over his face.

As soon as Heather engages the nurse in a conversation about my repeat tox screen, when it's scheduled, and when she can expect for me to be released, Rhys makes his way over. I incline my head toward the chair, and his eyes turn to saucers as he catches on and basically throws himself at the recliner. He lands with a thud on the dark-red vinyl, and I have to smother a laugh.

Smooth, babe.

Heather turns to her son with raised brows, and he grins innocently.

Five minutes later, the nurse is gone, my IV is back in place, and we know my tests are scheduled for ten. We have two hours. Suddenly drained, I unsuccessfully stifle a yawn.

Heather places a hand on my thigh. "Why don't you rest some more, and we'll be back in a bit." Rhys makes no move to get up, and Mom rounds my bed, leaning down to whisper something in his ear. He stiffens, and Heather straightens, winks at me, and leaves the room.

"Uh, what was that?"

Rhys clears his throat. "She, um...she said to make sure your IV stays in this time."

"Oh, God." I cover my face, and the boy next to me cracks up in hysterical laughter. "This is not funny," I mumble through my hands.

"It is a little," he cackles.

I level him with what is meant to be a death glare, but he shrugs. "Hey, at least we know one of them is on our side."

I guess he's right on that account. But we still don't know what measures Tristen will take, even if the fact that I'm adopted is out.

Rhys takes my hand and squeezes. "Let's rest. I'm beat."

I start scooting over, but he stops my movement by tugging me back to the middle. "Babe, if I climb into that bed again, there is no way we will get any rest."

Rhys's tone is low, and my entire body heats at his insinuation. I would love nothing more than to pick up where we left off; I crave this boy more than finding the truth at this point, which feels *so* right and *so* wrong at the same time.

Exaggeratedly, I let myself fall back into the pillow. "Fine."

He places a lingering kiss on my knuckles and winks. "Soon, babe."

I MUST'VE DRIFTED off to sleep because, the next thing I know, the nurse is back and taking my vitals. She draws more blood for the next round of tests, and when I sweep the room, Heather and Tristen are both back in their seats. Tristen is murmuring intently into his phone, but I can't understand a word. Heather looks stiff while she stares at her husband. Turning, I see Rhys softly snoring in the recliner. His hand is still in mine, headphones in place. He hasn't noticed the commotion in the room.

A few hours later, the test results come back as expected, and I am being released into my parents' care by eight p.m. Rhys excused himself to the bathroom at one point and gave me an imperceptible nod when he returned to his place by my side. He was able to give my other family an update.

Tristen or the agents—though my money is on my adopted father—somehow arranged for us to leave the hospital through a side door. We avoid the media vans that are still camped out front and drive straight to a small airport. When I spot the private plane we are aiming toward, I pull on Rhys's arm. His hand has not left mine since we entered the car, and neither Heather nor Tristen seem to care anymore. Though, I've noticed the female agent that came with my family from Virginia sneaking glances when she thinks no one sees.

Rhys's focus is on me, and I nod toward the plane's direction, mouthing, "What the hell?"

He leans over and murmurs, "No clue who scored that little toy, but that's how we came here."

What. The. Heck!

CHAPTER THIRTY-FOUR

LILLY

Umpf.

Turning toward the door just in time, Denielle tackles me, and I catch us at the last moment before we would've gone down in a tangle of arms and legs. My best friend is sobbing into my hair, her arms around my neck like a chokehold. I cling to her midsection and squeeze just as hard. It feels like a lifetime since I've seen her. In a way, it has been. My life, more accurately. *I* am not the same girl I was a little over two weeks ago.

A sniffle makes me glance over Den's shoulder. Wes is standing in the doorway, hands shoved into the pockets of his dark-gray hoodie. His favorite blue beanie is covering most of his shaggy, sandy-blond hair and matches his school-issued sweat-pants the boys always wear before and after wrestling matches. Scruff on his jaw, he looks exhausted, and my chest tightens at the sight of Rhys's best friend. His eyes glisten as he watches us, and I smile. The corners of his mouth tilt upward, but it doesn't reach his eyes. Behind him, I can make out the form of Rhys, who had gone downstairs to open the door for them. It's almost one in the morning, but my friends refused to wait to come over.

Rhys texted them updates throughout our travel, and they arrived not fifteen minutes after we got home.

Home.

Walking into the house, I felt like an intruder—a stranger that doesn't belong. Since waking up in the hospital, the doubt about how we would look for answers when I'd be in Westbridge and Nate in California has steadily grown. Lord knows where George is. Probably somewhere close by, but I mean, he wouldn't be able to do anything without revealing himself. Before leaving California, I was convinced I could do this. I was not prepared for the increasing havoc inside my mind as the hours tick by and I face my old life.

I promised Rhys that Nate would take responsibility, but the condition is that we learn the truth first. I may not be in the dark anymore, but I'm also not out of it. I'm rooted to a spot between light and dark. Rhys had years of perfecting his façade; he convinced everyone that he couldn't stand me. I, on the other hand... I can't act for shit. No matter how many times I told people I didn't care about Rhys's actions, everyone knew that I did. As Nate put it one night, *Your face is very expressive.*

Now, facing my two closest friends, a sheen of sweat starts building on my skin, and my mouth feels like it's full of cotton. I swallow several times—it's no use. All the air is getting sucked out of my lungs, and I can't get any oxygen in.

Rhys must see what is about to happen, because he's at my side in milliseconds. He pries me out of Denielle's hug, and his strong arms envelop me.

"Breathe, babe," his voice filters through the cotton that has also taken root in my ears.

As he counts for me, I draw in slow breaths, and the nausea subsides. Tears streaming down my face, I cling to the front of his shirt, pressing my forehead against his chest.

"I'm so sorry," I mumble, avoiding eye contact with the other two people in the room.

A hand carefully touches my shoulder, and I turn slightly.

"You have nothing to be sorry for, Lil." Wes's tone is gentle, understanding.

The guilt that has been festering for so long finally destroys the fragile dam that has kept my emotions in check, and I crumble to the floor. Rocking back and forth with my arms around my bent legs, I can't keep it together. Somewhere in the distance, I hear a buzzing, and instead of Rhys, I am suddenly sandwiched between Denielle and Wes. I'm half in Wes's lap, and Denielle has her arms around me, stroking my hair.

Neither of them speaks. However, I hear Rhys's muffled voice from my bathroom. Water is running, and I know who he's talking to. I jump up like from a four-point start, knocking my two friends backward in the process, and burst into my bathroom. Startled by my entrance, Rhys jumps back and hits the shower door, which slams into the tiled wall.

"Hold on," he interrupts the person on the other end.

I stare at him, and he nods, holding the phone out.

Similar to when you watch someone in a movie having an out-of-body experience, I watch my hand reach out in slow motion and take the device.

Holding it to my ear, I whisper, "Nate?"

"Yes."

I never anticipated these two men, who couldn't be more opposite, would end up having the same calming effect on me. They dislodged the life I had become content with in the most unexpected ways, making me question who I am over and over, evoking different emotions I didn't know I was capable of and pushing me to my limits at the same time. I need them to make it through this. Both have become my home in their own ways: my family and my love.

"How are you?" I don't know if he has ever spoken to me with such uncertainty.

I confess, "I can't do this."

Rhys has made his way over and wraps his arms around me. Leaning my back into his front, I listen to my brother.

"Yes, you can. We knew this wouldn't be easy, but you're a fighter."

He sounds so convinced that I blurt out my biggest fear. "What if I slip and give you up before we find all the answers?"

"Then you will find the truth on your own," he replies without hesitation. "You are smart—probably smarter than me." My brother chuckles. "And George will be at your side." There is no trace of anger in his tone; he truly means it. He would go away without a second thought if it meant keeping me safe.

The words slip out of their own volition. "I love you, big brother."

I stiffen. I never thought about it before, but even in these short few weeks, Nate has become family. I hold my breath, knowing Rhys heard my surprising admission, but he doesn't give any indication one way or another.

Through the phone, I hear Nate choke up before he replies, "I love you, too, little sis."

"Are you watching?" I assume that's why he called.

"I was, but I'm going to exit out now. I had to make sure you got back okay." He doesn't use the word *home*. Does he know that I'm no longer sure where my home is? That it's no longer tied to a place.

"Will you call again?" I press my hand against my chest—a similar gesture to what I used to do when I thought of Rhys while being separated from him.

"No. George is going to check in with you. I'm still working on the other...thing." After a pause, Nate adds, "The one tied to your birthday."

Oh!

Rhys goes rigid, and I know for sure that he's been listening to both sides of this conversation. I still haven't divulged the extent of my inheritance to him.

My brother continues, "Stick to the story, and we'll figure out the rest soon enough." He blows out a long breath. "After that, I will do what's right...like I promised."

I nod, more to myself than anyone else. A lump forms in my throat.

"Okay."

"We'll talk soon." Before I can reply, my brother hangs up.

Rhys and I stand in the bathroom, back to front.

"I'm going to take a shower." The sudden urge to scrub the last few days off of my body is overpowering me.

"Do you want me to wait?"

I turn in his arms and raise my eyebrows.

Rhys smirks. "I won't peek."

I try to smile at him but fail miserably. So instead, I raise on my tiptoes, planting a brief kiss on his lips, and tell him the truth. "I want to be alone for a little while."

"Whatever you need." He kisses me on the forehead. "I'll be outside."

I DON'T KNOW how long I stand under the hot spray. I go through my *ritual* of letting the scorching water wash away the turmoil inside of me.

I'm back in Westbridge. My brother is across the country. We are no closer to finding answers. I have to lie about what happened to me—about who I am—and I still have to face my adopted parents. Thanks to Rhys not leaving my side, I haven't had to deal with them alone—yet. I have no clue how much to reveal to them or what they will think of me.

When exhaustion overcomes me, I turn off the water and wrap myself in the towel that hangs on the hook outside the glass door. I search for the monogram I've gotten so used to, but of course, it's not there. My throat thickens. Swiping over the mirror above my sink, I take in the features of the girl staring back at me.

Who are you?

Arms around my midsection, I close my eyes. Before I can go down the rabbit hole of conflicting emotions any further, I grab

Rhys's old hoodie and a pair of gray-and-pink plaid pajama pants from the hook behind the door. He must've snuck them in while I was in the shower.

Stepping out, I blink. My bedroom is almost dark; the only light comes from the small lamp on the nightstand.

Rhys's large frame is sprawled across my comforter, one arm draped across his eyes, the other resting on his belly. There's a gap between his hem and waistband, and I instantly zero in on his smooth skin. My feet start moving of their own volition. He changed out of his travel clothes as well and is wearing his own school hoodie and gray sweatpants. Despite the loungewear being loose, the outfit emphasizes his physique, and my tongue sweeps over my bottom lip. I glance around, but Den and Wes are nowhere in sight.

Almost to the bed, I peek into the hallway. I have a direct line of sight to Rhys's room and can make out the shape of a body in his bed—that's where the others are.

Climbing on the mattress, I pull on the covers. Rhys startles awake, his eyes frantically searching the room for a potential threat. I place my hand on his arm, and as soon as he finds me beside him, all the tension leaves his body.

"You were in there for a while." He yawns and sits up so his head is leaned against my headboard. Holding out an arm for me to come closer, my heart skips a beat, and I glance at the door before looking back at him.

Reading my mind, Rhys says, "It's okay. The 'rents gave their approval. Den and Wes took my room."

I choke on my saliva and start coughing. It takes several moments to regain control and to be able to voice my question. "You asked their permission to sleep in my bed?"

He chuckles. "No, I simply declared I'd be in your room if they needed me. We already knew they—"

I interrupt him in typical Minnie Mouse fashion. "And they were fine with that? Tristen okay'ed it? Just like that?" Something isn't right here.

Sighing, he pulls me across the bed and tucks me under his arm, like I weigh nothing. Wrapped in his embrace, Rhys continues, "They agreed to let us *sleep* together, under the condition the door stays open. Mom added that we would all have a long conversation tomorrow."

"And Tristen?"

He hugs me closer and, with his arm around my shoulders, starts tracing small circles. "He was his usual unreadable self. Didn't say a word."

His caress causes shivers to run down my spine.

"I don't know if that is comforting or not," I admit, mimicking Rhys's movement with my fingers on the blue material that clings to his chest.

The circles stop, and I'm about to protest, when he tightens his hold. His other hand lifts and pushes a strand of hair from my forehead. His fingers linger near the cut, before moving down and resting on my neck.

He needs the physical contact as much as me, and I'm sure he's fully aware of my rapid pulse under his palm.

"Let's deal with that tomorrow. All I care about is that you're here, and we'll get some rest."

"Rest?" I tilt my head upward and meet Rhys's gaze, my hand flattened against his pecs, heat igniting in my core, and I move my hand slowly down his abs.

With hooded lids, he smirks at me. "Rest. As much as I want a repeat of the hospital—sans the blood and gore you caused—I need to get some sleep. We both do."

Face ablaze, I swat his arm.

"You act like I had blood spewing out of several open wounds."

"Well, not spewing, but..." He trails off, and a devilish grin crosses his face. "I wouldn't mind a little tongue action, though."

He did not just say that.

I pull back, and Rhys bursts out laughing. "Shit, babe. I'm sorry. I couldn't resist."

"That's something I would've expected to come out of Wes's mouth." I huff.

"Forgive me?" Rhys pulls me back into his arms and places a tender kiss on my forehead. "I'm sorry. I was just trying to distract you from whatever was going on inside that head of yours."

Snuggling closer, I smile. "Mission accomplished."

Reaching over me, Rhys switches off the bedside lamp, and I wrap my arms around him as soon as he is back in place.

"I'm glad you're back, babe," he murmurs into my hair.

"Me, too," I reply automatically.

AT SOME POINT, I managed to shift both of us under the covers. Rhys is snoring softly, but I can't calm my mind. The last two days are a blur, and being at the vineyard seems like a lifetime ago. Instead, I keep rewinding our trip home in my head. Tristen's behavior is getting weirder by the day, and I wonder if he knows more about my past than he is letting on.

Getting discharged took forever. I'm still baffled by our mode of transportation—a freaking private jet. How did Tristen organize that thing? The two agents ushered us on board, and I curled up in one of the oversized, buttery-soft leather seats. Rhys settled in next to me, and Heather across from us. After takeoff, Tristen brought all of us blankets and took the seat next to his wife. It was the first time he had addressed me in hours.

"Are you comfortable, sweetheart?"

I forced a smile on my face. "I'm fine, Dad."

Rhys automatically reached over and grabbed my hand, knowing that I was far from fine. Physically, I was, but mentally, I was slowly losing the battle against blocking out the ginormous elephants in the room: my kidnapping and the social media incest posts about Rhys and me. I'd have to address both sooner or later.

I shook myself out of the thoughts and faced my adopted

father, who was eyeing my hand in Rhys's. My insides constricted, and I instinctively pulled away. Rhys glared at his father, who, in return, watched me more closely. I've known this man my entire life, and he's been the only father I remember, but that was the first time I was afraid. Not for my safety, but if he would take Rhys away from me again.

Tristen looked away first and pulled out his phone—something he has always done to shut everyone out. I flicked my gaze to Heather, who was in a stare-down with her son. She gave him the briefest of nods, and my hand was back in his. I curiously turned to Rhys, but he avoided making eye contact by pulling his phone out as well. Resigned, I leaned my head back against the seat.

What has happened to all of us?

I WAKE UP WITH A START, my heart hammering in my chest. I'm alone in bed, and there's honking and shouting outside. What the—then it clicks. The reporters have arrived. I have no clue how we've managed to avoid them this long, but I'm sure it—again—has something to do with Tristen's connections.

I listen to the muffled yelling, unable to make out what's being said. Swallowing several times, I try to calm my breathing. Thank goodness my room is facing the back of the house. The urge to know that George is close by overcomes me, and I jump out of bed. Unsure where the phone is, I stop in the middle of my room, arms hanging at my sides. I don't remember what happened to it after the call. Rhys must've hidden it somewhere.

Shit.

Still rooted to the spot, a soft knock comes from the open door. Spinning around, I am face to face with my best friend. She looks disheveled—so unlike the Denielle I'm used to. Even when she just wakes up, she usually looks all put together and presentable—not like me, who sports a bird's nest of epic proportions every morning.

"Hey." My tone is subdued.

"Hey, yourself." Den attempts a smile. Aside from her not being a morning person, there is a lot of damage repair to be done to our friendship.

A hollow feeling settles in my stomach. We stare at each other for a long time before she crosses to my bed and plops down at the foot. "Where are the guys?"

I follow her movement and sit down next to her. "Not sure, I just woke up."

She wrings her hands in her lap. "So, uh...how are you doing?" She won't look at me.

"I have no clue." Heart pounding in my throat, I whisper, "I'm scared everyone will find out the truth and he has to leave before we get answers."

Denielle remains quiet for several breaths. My palms start sweating profusely, and I swipe them on my pajama pants. Den's fingers close on mine, and she finally faces me. "Babe, I have no idea what you're dealing with. Rhys has told us some, but I'm sure there is a lot more. I have no clue what to think or how to deal with this. I don't think anyone would, given the circumstances. I mean, babe...he's a..." She trails off, and my heart sinks. "But..." she adds after an indefinable amount of time, "I know you. There is no one out there that's more levelheaded. You would never allow anything to happen to your family or friends."

"Of course not!" I squeeze her hand. "D, I swear to you, there is so much I never expected to find when I woke up after the accident."

I'm about to confess how smart and funny Nate is, how peaceful the vineyard is, and the way George looks out for my brother, when we get interrupted. The yelling outside gets louder, and I cock my head, still unable to make out actual words. My fingers tighten around my friend's, and I slowly stand up, pulling her with me. Walking across the hall to Rhys's room, my steps falter for a second before I reach the window. It has a direct line of sight to the driveway and street. Denielle follows close behind, and I step up to the wooden blinds but remain far enough in the shadows that my silhouette is hidden from view. I see three news vans and four unmarked cars—not counting the black SUV and Wes's red 4Runner. Some of our neighbors are lingering on their front lawns, and I rub my upper arms with my hands. This was expected, but at the same time, I'm unprepared. A middle-aged man in jeans and a gray bomber jacket argues with a dark-haired woman dressed in a cream pantsuit. I do a double take and recognition hits. I've seen him in several videos. It's Lancaster, the reporter who's obsessed with the missing girls' cases. I don't recognize the woman and assume she's from another media outlet. Suddenly, a muffled, "Upper left window," makes every single head snap up, and three cameras focus instantly on the house. Denielle pulls on my arm, and we both drop to the floor.

"This is fucking nuts!" my friend hisses as I try to figure out why my lungs start burning.

Oh God, I can't do this.

Arms wrap around my stomach from behind and force me out of the crouched position, dragging me into the hallway. Fingers still clasped around my best friend's hand, she follows close behind.

"Breathe, babe." Rhys's voice reaches my ears, but it's like I'm underwater. "Cal. I. Need. You. To. Inhale."

I can't. Why can't I breathe?

I open my mouth to do as he ordered, but the air doesn't reach my lungs. It's like someone has me in a choke hold, and my vision turns blurry.

"Calla, look at me!"

I want to, but everything is out of focus. A wheezing sound reaches my ears, and I realize it's coming from me.

"What's wrong with her?"

"Sweetheart?"

So many voices. I can't do this.

My legs leave the ground. I'm tucked against a chest. The

faint scent of a familiar shower gel mixed with laundry detergent and coffee penetrates my nose—Rhys. I want to tell him that I'm okay, but I can't make the words come out. I'm not okay.

Back on my feet, I sway when something cold and wet hits me in the face. A scream rips from my throat. Stumbling, I try to get away. Arms wrap back around me.

"I told you to breathe, babe. You should've listened," he growls, but there is no anger behind his words.

"Oh, thank fuck." Wes.

"Wes!" Another male voice barks. Tristen.

"Sorry, sir."

My breathing is regulating itself again, and I blink against the water, drops clinging to my lashes.

"EVERYONE OUT!" This time Rhys does sound murderous.

"Rhys," a calm and collected Tristen addresses his son.

"Not now, Dad! We'll be downstairs in a few. She needs a fucking minute; not everyone is a robot like you." I've never heard him talk to his father like this. No one challenges Tristen —except maybe Heather.

After a pause, there is shuffling, murmurs, and a door is closing.

A towel wraps around my shoulders, and Rhys's forehead touches mine. "Babe, you need to stop scaring the shit out of me. I've aged ten years in the last two weeks. I'm not ready to turn thirty," he softly chuckles.

CHAPTER THIRTY-FIVE

RHYS

I DON'T KNOW HOW LONG I CAN KEEP THIS UP.

With a clenched jaw, I help Lilly change out of her drenched clothes, and for once, my dick has zero reaction to seeing her naked. Pulling the soaked hoodie off her body, I wrap a fresh towel around her shoulders. I'm not even tempted to take a peek. Lilly shimmies out of her PJ pants while I return to her room to find something dry to wear.

Her panic attacks are becoming more frequent, and it's starting to freak me out. I mean, sure, who wouldn't lose their shit in her situation? It's a miracle that she still functions the way she is, but how long is this supposed to go on? The press just arrived; she hasn't even faced the vultures yet. Not to mention everything that's been going on at school. She has to go back eventually, and from what Wes and Den have been reporting, Kat has basically resurrected the Salem witch hunt with Lilly as the main target. I fight the urge to embed an imprint of my fist in the drywall of her closet.

Fuck, I'm exhausted.

"Rhys?" Lilly's tentative voice drifts to where I still stand, staring at her neatly hung shirts. I grab the first thing off a hanger and make my way back to the bathroom.

Sitting on the closed toilet, she peers up at me. "Do you hate me?"

I kneel in front of her, and she scans my face, tears pooling in her beautiful eyes. My chest constricts, seeing her like this.

I gently place my hand on the side of her face and wipe away a tear with my thumb. "Why on earth would you think that?"

Lilly leans into my touch, closing her eyes. "Because all I've done is make a mess out of your life."

Unable to respond right away, I mull that over for a moment. "Babe, I'm not going to lie to you that all of this doesn't affect me. The last few weeks have been hell. I'm so fucking tired, and not knowing what the future will bring freaks me out, but what's worse is seeing you like this. I don't agree on much—or really anything—with your brother, but Nate was right on one account. You are a fighter." I place a kiss on her nose.

She smiles sadly. "I don't feel like one right now."

I stand up, pulling her with me, and wrap my arms around her shoulders. Lilly clings to my midsection, burying her nose in my damp sweater. I should probably change as well. Inhaling her signature coconut shampoo, I silently swear to myself that I will find a way to help her through this, even if I have to involve her brother and George.

LILLY'S HAND securely in mine, we make our way downstairs. The first thing I notice is that all the blinds are closed, and the curtains in the living room are drawn. Agent Lanning and Agent Camden are in their usual spots in the kitchen, and both glance up from their laptops as I lead Lilly through the kitchen to the living room. The other suits haven't returned since we got back with Lilly.

Mom and Dad are quietly talking to each other. Wes and Den are opposite my parents on the U-shaped couch. Wes is scrolling with his thumb over something on his phone; Den has her arms crossed, head leaned back, and eyes closed. This is the first time since last night I take in Den's appearance; she's a mess. She's wearing an oversized green hoodie that I'm pretty sure is Wes's, black leggings, and her hair is up in a loose bun.

I purposefully ignore Dad as he tracks our movements. We sit down on the middle section of the couch, and I wrap my arm around Lilly's shoulders.

Out of the corner of my eye, I see two figures hovering in the doorway. Lanning and Camden have abandoned their chairs at the kitchen table.

"Not yet." Dad's barked command makes everyone jolt to attention, and the two agents retreat without a word.

"How are you, sweetheart?" Mom addresses Lilly with a genuine smile.

Lilly leans closer to me and stares at her hands in her lap. "I'm fine, Mom."

Her go-to response to that question.

"Uh, do you guys want us to leave?" Wes hesitantly asks no one in particular.

Lilly's eyes snap to his. "No! Stay. Please." The last word is almost spoken like a plea.

Dad clears his throat. "Lilly, we need to talk about what happened."

I peer down and find her already looking at me. I have no clue how my parents will react; my mouth has gone dry, and I force myself to put on a façade. I don't like pretending in front of Lilly, but it's as much for her as it is for me. I give her a nod, relaying everything I can't put into words in front of the people in the room or the listening agents in the kitchen in this one movement.

Lilly presses her lips into a thin line and inhales deeply through her nose before letting the air back out. She talks to the room but doesn't avert her eyes from mine.

"I was working on a journalism assignment when I came

across an article about a missing girl. After reading the first one, I knew there was something...I had to find out more. The longer I looked into the case..." She pauses, a slight quiver in her voice. "I got this feeling. Then I started seeing these flashes. Memories that were not mine—or at least I didn't think they were at first."

"Oh God." Mom's hands fly to her mouth. I take in my father's face, and even he looks surprised. Not much can rattle Tristen McGuire.

Lilly doesn't go into details about her migraines; she leaves out the ones about Nate and, instead, recaps her memories about Emily and Henry. She tells them how I confronted her and how she talked me into going to California. My dry mouth has extended down my throat, and I would kill for some water right about now. My insides are one giant knot.

"I am sorry I lied to you." She finally turns toward Mom and Dad. Mom is so shocked that all she does is stare at her daughter, wide-eyed.

It's Dad that surprises all of us. "I knew where you were."

My eyes snap to him. *Motherfucker!* I had my suspicions when I found out that he tracked our phones, but I wasn't positive until now.

"You did?" Lilly squeaks.

My father scans the room. Both Wes and Den shrink into the couch under his scrutiny, aware they got caught as accomplices to our deception, but when he lands on his wife, he says, "I'm sorry, honey."

She didn't know.

Mom straightens, slowly removes her hands from her mouth, and places them folded in her lap. "You knew, and you didn't tell me?"

When she is not in the courtroom, my mother is the kindest and most nurturing woman I've ever known. Looking at her right now, though, she scares the shit out of me—she's seething.

Dad opens his mouth, but she holds up a palm. "We've kept Lilly safe for ten years. She is my daughter, even if not by blood.

I stood by your decision when you forced Rhys out of the house because he fell in love with her—something we knew would happen—but I trusted your judgment on the situation."

My cheeks are burning. Can we please move on from my relationship?

Mom continues, oblivious that the four of us are staring at her like she's grown a second head. "I've given you free rein on how to protect us, but you promised me you would never keep anything from me anymore after Hannah. It's not bad enough that you kept *the other thing* from me, but now I have to find out that you knew Lilly was putting herself back onto his radar. What else is there?"

The other thing? And who the fuck is Hannah?

My leg won't stop bouncing. As fascinated as I am by this exchange, I'm fighting the urge to bolt from the room. Lilly's hand lands on my leg, and the contact calms me instantly.

Mom turns away from her husband, and Dad's face reminds me of the time they caught me driving the Defender down the street at age fourteen. I thought Mom would never forgive me. No one puts Tristen McGuire in his place.

Back in control and eerily calm, she says, "I'm sorry you had to witness this. Your father and I will talk about that later." She meets Lilly's gaze, and her hand clenches down on my leg.

Fuuuck, that hurts.

I try not to wince or make a sound, but her hand is like a claw digging into my muscle.

"Sweetheart, what happened after California?"

All eyes are back on Lilly. I pry her hand from my thigh, interlacing our fingers and squeezing them gently.

"I started getting text messages, with pictures of myself. Later, some of me with Den and Rhys."

"Why didn't you tell us?" Mom's tone is quiet. Careful.

Lilly turns to me, and I dip my head, urging her to tell them.

She whispers, "You betrayed me."

Dad rubs his hands over his face, and Mom swipes a tear

away that has escaped her glistening eyes.

Suddenly, Lilly's head snaps up, and I pull my hand away, startled by the sudden movement. She glances at me sideways, and I take her hand back, shrugging a shoulder. We're all jumpy.

She pins Dad down with a glare that would make George proud. "So, if you bugged our phones, how didn't you know about the texts?"

Dad's eyebrows shoot up. "I didn't bug your phone."

My vision instantly clouds, and I'm interjecting myself into the conversation. "Yes, you did. Or how did that suit know what Lilly said when she called the first time?"

I mean, we know he did because of Nate, the genius hacker, but I can't say that.

Dad clears his throat and won't look in Mom's direction. "I only tracked your phones. I didn't install the listeners until Lilly went missing."

Wes eyes his phone, and Denielle snorts, "Not yours, dumbass." Then she peers to my father. "Uh, right?"

"Correct," Dad deadpans, and Lilly stifles a laugh next to me.

Mom collects herself and moves the conversation back on track. "Okay, so you got text messages. What then?"

Lilly swallows hard. The closer we get to Nate, the more she struggles.

I decide to take over and give her a break. "Lilly wanted to know what he wanted before she told anyone else. Kat tried to blackmail me into getting back with her. She figured out that something was going on but couldn't put her finger on it until she got a hold of the picture." I don't have to tell them which picture; everyone has seen it by now. "She posted it on her social media and cornered Lilly in front of the entire school. Lilly didn't take her bullshit and left."

"What happened after you left the school grounds?" The voice behind us startles everyone, and Agent Camden steps forward.

Lilly's eyes widen, and she quietly seeks my encouragement. I squeeze her hand and nod.

"I wanted to be alone. I was going to drive home but needed a moment. I was on the back road when I noticed another car behind me. It didn't come close, so I couldn't make out who was in it. A fox ran across the street, and I jerked the steering wheel to avoid hitting it. I missed the fox but lost control of the Jeep instead." She takes a long pause, and my heart is hammering in my throat while I wait.

Here it comes. Let the acting begin.

"I don't remember anything else until I woke up in the hospital three days ago."

No one speaks for several minutes.

Agent Lanning breaks the silence. "Tristen, can we speak in private?"

Dad gets up without a word and leads the agent to his office, Agent Camden following on their heels. I glance around the room, and everyone seems unsure what to do next.

Are we done with the interrogation?

Mom pushes off the couch. "Let's all get some breakfast. We'll continue when your father is back."

And with that, it's like the last weeks haven't happened. What the fuck? I exchange a confused look with Lilly and our friends. That's it? That can't be it.

Mom gets busy in the kitchen, and Denielle helps her make pancakes while Wes sets to the task of brewing enough coffee to keep us all awake for a week. Narrowing my eyes at the scene in front of me, I take a seat next to Lilly on the barstools. Pressing my thigh against hers, I get her attention and mouth, "Are you okay?"

She gives me a jerked nod, and my stomach sinks. No.

WHEN DAD DOESN'T COME out of his office even after our house guests take their seats at the kitchen table again, the four of us go upstairs to my room. Inside, I flip the lock, and we pile into my bathroom. At this point, I don't give a flying fuck what Dad thinks if he checks the security feed. Looks like his pile of secrets grows by the day, and Mom doesn't know the half of it.

I sit with my back against the bathtub, Lilly between my legs, Den on the closed toilet seat to the left, and Wes across, leaning against the door. Six months ago, I would've laughed my ass off if someone would've told me I'd be *hanging out* in my bathroom with my best friend, *sister*, and Denielle 'The Bulldog' Keller—in Wes's hoodie, nonetheless.

"How are you doing, babe?" Denielle looks at Lilly with her head cocked to the side.

Lilly is nestled against my chest sideways with her legs pulled up and her head tucked under my chin. She turns to get a better look at her friend and shrugs a shoulder. "I feel like a prisoner."

Not surprising with the media camped out on the front lawn.

Mom informed us earlier that she's going to pick Natty up from Olivia's tomorrow but is worried what this chaos outside the house will do to her. We've tried to keep her routine as normal as possible under the circumstances, and so far, it has worked. Mom would spend time with her at Olivia's house, but we've kept her away from the FBI in our home. With the press now trying to track down information on Lilly, Dad wants everyone under the same roof. He doesn't want to risk someone cornering my little sister at her ballet lesson or school.

"Were you not held prisoner by your brother?" Wes voices the question that I had bounced around in my head for a while in his usual sledgehammer way. The few times we FaceTime'd, I got a small glimpse of the place. I know it was not a one-bedroom apartment, but Lilly had been mum about more details.

She doesn't answer right away, and I lean forward to assess her face better. She chews on her lower lip, flicking her thumb against her fingers.

Why is she nervous?

I exchange a look with the other two in the room, and both

mirror my confused expression. When I think she won't answer at all, she whispers, "I wasn't. I couldn't leave the estate, but I never felt like a prisoner."

Estate?

"Estate?" Denielle hesitantly asks.

Lilly inhales and holds her breath for several beats. "I haven't told any of you where I was for several reasons. For one, no one can know about the location. Not because I...*we* have to hide anything there, but because it's Nate's home. The only place he feels at peace, and I would never take that from him."

She is protecting her brother.

"Two, I didn't know how you would react or look at me if you knew the truth. But there is no point in keeping this fact from you now since you know everything else."

Lilly turns to me and places a hand on the side of my face. "I didn't want you to feel differently about me."

Alarm bells instantly start to shrill in my head. What the hell is she talking about? I narrow my eyes. "Why would I do that?"

As she continues, Denielle and Wes hang on her every word. The longer she talks, the lower their jaws drop.

"I was at the family vineyard. It belonged to Payton's father, and Nate restored most of it over the years. He grows grapes there but doesn't allow the processing on the property. He has a ten-foot wall around the whole place and a huge wrought-iron gate, which is the only way in or out. An electric current secures everything, and the only way on or off the property is with a code. If you try to get in, or out, you get shocked—not terribly, but enough to knock you on your ass and fry any electronic you may carry with you. There's no cell service unless you're hooked into the network. I have no clue how he did all this, but he designed his security system, so it wasn't a surprise. The house is a massive Mediterranean-style building with two separate wings. It has an outdoor pool in the back, and the indoor pool is underground next to the gym. He built an indoor track under the house and a motor pool that can hold twelve plus cars. He has an

R8 there that you guys would lose your shit over." She stops and presses her lips together, realizing how she got carried away. It's obvious now that she loves the place.

The three of us must have similar expressions: gaping at Lilly.

"Uh...why would you leave there?" Wes attempts to break the tension, and Denielle whacks him over the head. But the goal is accomplished. Lilly smiles.

"Babe, did you think I'd be upset about where he took you? That you liked it there?" I'm still confused as to why she was so scared to tell me. She must've been worried about what I would think of her, knowing that she was content where she was. It sounds like she was living the dream—minus the kidnapping and secrets.

She looks everywhere but my face. "The estate is one thing. There is something else I haven't told you yet."

What now?

My pulse picks up, and everything from Nate not taking responsibility to her choosing to leave me and stay with her real family crosses my mind.

"Brooks left me money."

Okay, so she got a small inheritance. What's the big deal?

"That's, uh...great. I mean, that means he cared about you, right? You can buy yourself something and know it's from your biological father." I try to make sense of why she looks like she's about to throw up the half pancake she forced herself to eat earlier.

"It's ten million dollars." Her voice is so low I'm sure I misheard.

"Come again?" Denielle's shrill voice echoes like a bullhorn through my small bathroom.

Wes chokes and goes into a coughing fit.

I guess I did hear her right.

"Plus interest for fifteen years."

Fuck. Me.

CHAPTER THIRTY-SIX

LILLY

I TOLD THEM. IN TWELVE DAYS, ON MY EIGHTEENTH BIRTHDAY, I will have more money than every single person I know combined—not counting brother dearest. Before I left the vineyard, Nate spent several hours dissecting the trust Brooks set up. It took us hours and emptying every single file cabinet drawer in the library, but we found a copy of my biological father's testament. Just weeks before his death, he revised his will. Besides half of his fortune, my trust, I was to inherit every last penny that was meant for Audrey. Nate is set through Payton and the Altman Empire; I got the rest. It's been accumulating interest over the last ten plus years since Nate never considered there being additional funds to what his mother's attorneys handed him. When Nate gave me his final estimate, I crushed the plastic water bottle in my hand. Unfortunately, said bottle was open, and the water splashed all over the desk. Again.

After that, my brother was close to frisking me whenever I entered the NCC. He even sent George out with his covered mug because there was a chance I could spill it. I had a few choice words for him on that.

I still haven't admitted the full extent of my future fortune to Rhys or my friends; the amount of the trust alone was enough to put them into a state of shock. The tension finally left my body when neither of them made any comments one way or another or looked differently at me once the surprise wore off. I scolded myself for not confiding in them sooner.

WE'RE in Rhys's room when Heather knocks. The boys are playing a video game, sitting at the foot of the bed, and Denielle and I are lounging against the headboard. Up until that moment, I was as content as one in my situation could be. For a few hours, I pretended to be a normal girl—no secret past, no unknown future. I blocked out everything as I listened to my boyfriend and his best friend bicker over who has the better aim shooting the zombies in their various body parts. Facing my adopted mother, my stomach drops like I'm sitting in the first car of a rollercoaster and we're pushing over the edge.

"Lilly, can you come down for a few minutes?" Her face is her usual, gentle self whenever she talks to one of her kids, but deep down, I sense that something is about to happen—again. I want to say no, hide behind my friends, maybe even call George to come to pick me up...but none of that is an option. Whatever they're going to tell me, I have to face it.

Rhys pauses the game and is about to stand up when his mother holds up her hand. "Just Lilly."

"Not happening!" Rhys is on his feet in the blink of an eye and puts himself in front of me.

I place my palm between his shoulder blades. "It's okay."

Pulse rushing through my body double time, I want him with me, but Heather and Tristen would never *harm* me.

"Are you sure?" Rhys turns, and his eyes switch back and forth between mine.

"Yes." I try to smile reassuringly at him as I follow Heather out of the room.

In the hallway, she laces her arm through mine and leads me down the stairs into Tristen's office. "Sweetheart, Dad and I want to talk with you about a few things."

The reassurance I plastered on my face falls off like the sheet mask during Denielle's beauty salon sleepover party freshman year. That darn thing would not stay on—at all.

As we enter, Tristen rises from behind his desk to meet us. My heart stutters a beat as I take him in. I've never been able to read him; the man invented the poker face. However, looking at him now...I want to turn and run back upstairs.

He gestures toward the sitting area in the corner of the room —a gray twill loveseat and matching armchair with a round end table in between.

My mouth has gone dry, and I tuck my thumbs inside my fists so I don't start flicking my fingers. I take the seat next to Heather while Tristen lowers his large frame into the armchair.

Hands folded, he leans forward with his arms on his thighs. "I wanted to speak to you without Rhys in the room. He is very... protective of you, and I want to make sure you get the answers you need—without interruptions. There are many unanswered questions, and I will answer them to the best of my ability. What you want to share with him is up to you."

"Okay?" I reply warily. I barely get the word out over the sandpapery feeling in my throat. Where is this going?

Heather places her palm on my thigh, and I jump, jerking my head in her direction. "Dad and I had a long conversation, and though I'm still very upset with him for keeping certain facts from me, I understand his reasoning. We're sure there is a lot you want to know, and I wish you would've come to us before driving to California."

I furrow my brow and study her for a long moment. "Would you have told me the truth?" I challenge her.

She exchanges a look with her husband, and it's Tristen that answers. "Not if I would have seen another way."

I appreciate his honesty, yet it's like a slap in the face. I can feel the invisible handprint on my cheek.

"We cannot change the current situation. You are young, and you felt we did wrong by you. I'm trying to put myself in your shoes. As an adult, it is hard for me to relate to your decisions, but people make mistakes when they're young." Heather leaves the last sentence hanging.

I simply nod and glance between them. Waiting.

My adopted father's next sentence makes the pulse in my veins go into overdrive. "Your video was a surprise."

Do. Not. React.

"Wh-what video?" I attempt to keep my voice steady. With my eyes locked on Tristen, I clench my balled hands even harder, making my hidden thumbs crack. The compulsion to flick the rest of my fingers is like a mosquito bite you're trying not to scratch.

I told them I don't remember anything from the past two weeks, which would include the video, but if he keeps pushing...

Neither of them speaks. Tristen peers at his wife and, after another beat of silence, clears his throat. "First, I want to tell you how very sorry I am for the way you had to find out about all of this. I never expected this to happen. I was assured it wouldn't."

My breath hitches. He's letting the video go. Why? Then his words register. "Assured by whom?"

The face from my migraine appears in front of my mind's eye: *The memory doctor.*

Heather lets go of my thigh and takes my hand between hers, forcing me to open my palm to hers. "You have to understand that when you were in the hospital in California, you were in a very fragile state. We were not there yet and only knew what Emily had relayed to us. She wouldn't let me talk to Henry or a nurse to get a better picture. You have always been like a daughter to me. You and Rhys have been inseparable from the day you were born." She smiles to herself. "When you cried, I would put him in your crib, and you instantly calmed down. There were many times you would be at our house for a whole day or two. Emily was my best friend since childhood, but..." She trails off, and the hair at the nape of my neck stands. What the hell is she trying to say? Or rather, not say?

"We flew out to California as soon as we could after getting the news." Tristen directs my attention to himself. "As Mom said, you have always been like a daughter to us, and this hit us as hard as it did Henry."

Henry? Not Emily.

My heart beats so fast against my ribcage it physically hurts. But I can't voice my question before Tristen continues, "When we arrived, everything happened very fast. Henry showed us the messages Emily had received and caught us up on the medical diagnoses. You immediately asked for Rhys." The corners of his mouth tilt up. It's the first time he shows an actual reaction to *Rhys and me*, which in return makes my face heat. "Your primary nurse, uh..."

"Madeline Cross," I finish for him. No point in pretending I don't know about her.

"Yes, Madeline. She spoke to all of us at length and recommended for you to get therapy to deal with the trauma. We had already discussed this during the flight and suggested to your parents for you to stay with us for the time being. They knew I had access to the best specialists in their field. It was never meant to be forever."

Specialists? That's one way to sugarcoat it. I'm torn between fear of what else they have to say, rage for what happened to me, and curiosity. The number of questions assaulting my brain make my head hurt. "Why didn't they just go to the authorities?"

Heather looks upset. "To this day, we have asked ourselves that many times. Henry wanted to report you missing, but Emily wouldn't let him. He attempted it without her knowing, and when she found out, she threatened to take you away from him —when you came back."

I'm so confused. I knew Emily didn't want to report me missing because Nate threatened my safety, but threatening to take me away? Something isn't adding up. Pulling my hand away from Heather's, I place it in my lap and decide to change the direction of this conversation. "So, they just handed me over, and then what?"

Tristen blows out a long breath. "They did not just hand you over. We discussed this for hours. Henry refused at first; he wanted to run with you."

Alone?

Heather takes my hand back, and I have to force myself to not rip it out of her grasp. I didn't notice that I'd been flicking my thumb against my fingers until she constricts the movement. "Sweetheart, you have to believe us when we say that all we wanted was to keep you safe."

"What did you do to my mind? Why can I remember certain things and not others?"

Heather sucks in a sharp breath, and Tristen closes his eyes briefly before leveling me with a gaze devoid of emotion. The only other person I have ever seen with this expression—or lack thereof—is George. A cold shiver runs down my spine.

"I called in a favor with an associate of mine. We had worked together before, and I recently had consulted with him on another issue. He was—is—specialized in certain techniques." My adopted father seems to be struggling for the right words.

"What. Techniques?" My mouth feels like it's full of cotton.

"It's called coercive persuasion. Though he also uses a unique type of hypnosis. It's a rather delicate subject. Very controversial."

Excuse me, what? A shrill voice screams at me in my head, and I flinch to myself. I must've misheard him. This cannot be happening. How is this happening to me over and over. Why me?

Oblivious to the havoc his admission has stirred up inside of me, Tristen continues with his gaze trained at the floor. "He has the ability to arrange memories in an individual's mind. While under hypnosis, the individual is made to believe that certain events happened or didn't happen. With the help of persuasion, new memories are created. Those get connected by moving the memories around until they make sense again. There are several different techniques of persuasion, a lot of them not...*pleasant*. We consult him during operations when our regular tactics don't work; he deals with the special cases. However, he never used those types on you." He amends the last sentence so quickly that it takes me a moment to process it.

Well, if that isn't reassuring, the same voice now snarls. But the sarcasm of the internal speaker has no effect on the overwhelming panic gripping every fiber of my body. The term coercive speaks for itself—it's forced. There is nothing voluntary about altering someone's mind, and the first picture in my mind's eye is my kid-self being tied to a chair while someone messes with my head. I close my eyes and draw in slow breaths, exhaling at the same count. I need to calm down.

A hand gently touches my knee. "Lilly, please look at me."

Instinctively, my knee jerks away from the contact. I force myself to open my eyes and look at the man in front of me.

"He was able to help you forget by moving your memories around while under hypnosis. He made you believe things to be the truth, while other memories got locked away."

He tries to reassure me, but I can no longer listen to this. They violated my mind. I can barely contain the urge to jump up and run. George has to be somewhere close by; he would find me if I made it out of the house. But so would Lancaster, who is still camping out on the front lawn. I'm trapped.

I stare past Tristen, not looking at anything specific, while I attempt to calm my thrashing pulse.

"Where are my parents?" I need to change the topic. I can feel the bile rising in my throat and a fine sheen of sweat coating my skin. If he keeps talking about what happened to me, there is a good chance of me having a panic attack, and I can't let that happen. Not in front of them. I can't.

Tristen peers at Heather, and an entire, yet silent, conversation takes place in front of me. Without looking at me, he says, "We don't know."

Something is off. *Something else.*

A new kind of agitation rises to the surface. "And you never attempted to contact them? I don't believe that they would just abandon me—their only child."

My adopted mother starts tearing up. I'm so freaking tired of these riddles, never getting the full truth. I clench my jaw in an attempt not to say something I may regret. Or give something away that I shouldn't. I fail miserably on both accounts.

"So, you decided to brainwash me instead of finding real help? My mother handed me over without a second thought and took off? You make it sound like I was nothing to her. You say that Henry was upset. Henry wanted to call the cops. Not Emily. The man who wasn't even my father seemed to be the only one who actually cared. You guys tell me that you wanted to protect me. Well, fuck that. You manipulated me, lied to me, AND TOOK MY BEST FRIEND AWAY." My tone gets louder with every word until I'm full-on screaming. Heather mirrors my distraught expression, and Tristen's mouth hangs open.

Instantly, Rhys bursts into the room, eyes wild. "What the fuck is going on?" I'm not surprised he was camped out right in front of the office. He's at my side in three strides, and his arms circle me protectively. My fists clench the front of his sweater, and I bury my face in his chest. I can't face my adopted parents; I completely lost it.

Tristen is the first to collect himself. His tone is a low growl. "What do you mean by 'Henry was not your father'?"

Shit! Fuck! Shit!

Instead of waiting for me to answer, Rhys moves one arm around my waist and leads me out of the room.

"This conversation is over." He doesn't leave room for discussion.

"WHERE IS THE PHONE?" My heart still beats out of control, and my eyes are pleading for Rhys to hand it over.

"Why? What's going on?" His hands grasp my upper arms.

Rhys led me to my room. Den and Wes were about to get up from his bed across the hall to follow us when he shook his head and closed the door.

I don't want to tell him what his parents allowed to be done to me; the relationship with his father is already damaged. If he finds out the truth about my memory loss, there is no way to repair it. Hell, I don't know if I can forgive them—again. Not anytime soon. But the need to protect Rhys from the knowledge is as prominent as the fact that I will never be able to get my old life back.

"Please just give me the phone. I have to talk to him," I whisper. I need to tell someone what happened to me.

Rhys scans my face, his internal conflict playing across his features like a movie on a theater screen. Eventually, he nods and points for me to sit down on the bed. I follow suit, and he walks back out. I don't look up and only assume he goes to his room. I stare at the floor beneath my feet, focusing on my breath.

The phone appears in my vision, and I glance up at the somber face of my boyfriend—my *home*. Right now, though, I need the other home—my family. Two halves that make a whole.

"Do you want me to leave?"

I don't answer, and Rhys's face falls ever so slightly before he smoothes his features. He turns on his heel and leaves me alone in what used to be my sanctuary. The door closes a little too forcefully, and my shoulders scrunch up at the sound.

Almost robotic, I make my way to the bathroom, turn on the faucet and shower, plug in the headphones I grabbed from my desk in passing, and slide down the tiled wall. As opposed to the other times I had found out about a new lie in my life, I don't cry. Ever since entering my room, I'm numb. I don't know if that's good or bad. Dialing Nate's number, I wait.

"Lilly? What happened?" The panicked voice of my brother fills my ears after the fourth ring. We had agreed not to contact each other. If I need something, I'm supposed to call George.

I try to tell him what I just found out, but I can't get the right words to form. So, I simply say, "They used persuasion." My voice sounds detached to my own ears, like listening to someone else.

"Lilly, you're not making sense. Where is Rhys?"

"You can't tell him."

"Tell him what?" My brother's worry morphs into anger. "What did he do this time?"

"Not him." I draw in several breaths and force the words out through my clenched teeth. "Heather and Tristen wanted to talk to me alone. Tristen told me how they made me forget. They let someone brainwash me with hypnosis and coercive persuasion."

"THEY DID WHAT?" The roar forces me to pull the phone away from my ear. I hear a door slamming in the background and a faint clicking of keys.

"They said they wanted to help me. But I don't understand why they couldn't just send me to a therapist."

"There is more. It makes no sense. They were not just protecting you from me."

It's disconcerting how casual we can talk about my kidnapping these days. After everything that has come to light, it almost feels like the most trivial event of my life.

How disturbing is that?

"I know," I admit.

"I'm going to put George on it. Tell me word for word what they said."

Over the next twenty minutes, I do exactly that. I hear Nate type in the background, not sure if he's taking notes, but also not caring.

After he ensures that our head of security will be in touch, we hang up. I turn all the water sources off and make my way back to my room. Logic tells me that I should feel something—the emotional onslaught of betrayal, rage, and disappointment. However, standing at the foot of the bed, my gaze wanders over to my desk and laptop on top. All I want is to tune out the world. Forget. Everything here reminds me of my life being built on lies. I left my new phone, the replica of my old one, including my music, at the vineyard. There was no way to explain the device to anyone once I returned. With the headphones still in hand, I grab my computer. It's connected to my *Spotify* account, and I scroll through the songs until one jumps out at me, and I press play. Closing my eyes, I listen to "Castle of Glass" by Linkin Park blare into my ears.

CHAPTER THIRTY-SEVEN

LILLY

I wake up to "Master of the Pendulum" by Avantasia. It's my go-to song to get into running mode, and for a brief moment, I smile, thinking of the underground track at the vineyard. Then, the tidal wave of reality comes crashing back in. I blink my eyes open; my room is dark. Turning, I notice the curtains are not drawn. All I wanted was to block everything out for a few minutes, but I must've fallen asleep.

I shut off the music and pull the headphones out.

"Hey."

Rhys's voice comes from across the room, and I sit up with a start. Holy shit. Pressing my palm against my chest, I glance into the darkness. He's sitting with his back against the door to the hallway.

"Jesus. You almost gave me a heart attack." My tone is harsher than I mean it to sound, and I wince.

His legs are bent with his arms resting on his knees, hands dangling down. He doesn't look at me. "Sorry."

I scoot to the edge of the bed. "How long have you been sitting there?"

The silence between us stretches, and I narrow my eyes at him.

"A couple of hours?" He won't meet my gaze.

"Rhys?" I push. What's wrong with him?

He finally lifts his head, and I suck in a breath. His eyes are puffy; even in this light, I can see it clear as day.

My chest constricts as if someone has sent me to the ground with a push kick to the sternum, and I have the urge to rub the spot in the middle of my chest. "Come here." I hold out my hand.

He stares at it for a whole minute before slowly pushing himself up and walking over to the bed. I clasp his hand and pull him down next to me. We sit side by side, my fingers around his, our legs pressed together, yet there are miles between us.

"I feel like I'm losing you," Rhys confides with a raspy voice.

Another kick. My eyes sting. "I'm so sorry."

His next question shocks me. "Is it because of what they did to you? Because I'm related to them?"

My heart breaks at the sound of disdain when mentioning his parents. I allow myself time to collect my thoughts, risking him taking my hesitation as a confirmation. But I don't want to lie to him.

"I would never hold their actions against you. You've proven time and time again that I can trust you. From the day you told me the truth, you've put me first, and I know that it wasn't easy."

"What did they do to you?" Rhys speaks the words so low, so careful. He won't look at me. I should reach up and make him face me—make him see that I mean my words—but at the same time, I can't do it.

I inhale slowly and hold the air to the count of three before letting it back out. "They told me why I couldn't remember. How it happened." I can't bring myself to go into more detail. I can't bear to burden Rhys with the knowledge. "Please don't ask for more. I...I don't want to lie to you."

Finally, he turns to me, searching my eyes. "Why would you lie to me?"

"Please trust me?" I whisper. Maybe I'll tell him one day when his relationship with Tristen is not on cracked ice anymore.

His gaze moves back and forth between my eyes before he nods. He accepts my reply. Thoughts of *I don't deserve him*, and *he's too good for me* reverberate through my mind.

"Did they say anything to you?" I swallow over the lump in my throat.

"I talked to Mom for a while," Rhys answers quietly.

"About?" I know it wasn't the brainwashing, or he wouldn't be sitting here like this.

"Us."

"Us?" My voice is three octaves higher.

His eyes crinkle, and the shift in his expression makes my stomach summersault. "She asked me if we were serious."

"Oh God. And what did you say?" The mortification is clearly written all over my features.

"The truth. That there is nothing I'm more serious about. If Dad has a problem with it, it's his deal. You're eighteen in a week."

My pulse quickens, and I know what he's insinuating. Would Tristen do anything about it? The only thing he could do, at this point, is make one of us leave. But let's face it, I have the financial means to support both of us easily. I don't know how Rhys would feel about that, but money for food and a place to live is at least something I don't have to worry about. My nerves calm a little at the realization that I am not dependent on anyone—unless I want to be.

"Did she give you the sex talk?" I smirk, changing course inside my head.

He huffs out a laugh. "It's a little late for that. Thankfully, she knows I'm not a walking hard-on. When it comes down to it, I am responsible. Mom's cool; she's not oblivious to what's going on." He rakes his hand through his hair and looks at the ceiling. "Did I really just say that about my mother and sex?"

I giggle. "Yes, you did."

Rhys's face turns somber again. "She did say, though, to not make any more rash decisions. We can come to her for anything." He shrugs one shoulder. "Essentially, Mom said she is happy for us. She's known it would happen since we were little; we never had a typical sibling relationship. They would've told you the truth eventually—or part of it."

"Meaning that I'm not their daughter, but not the rest." I grind my teeth.

"Yes." He doesn't sugarcoat it.

Rhys touches his hand to the side of my face, his callused fingers caressing my cheek. The feel of his rough skin against my smooth skin makes shivers rock through my body in waves. His eyes roam my face, and he murmurs, "We can be together."

The words echo in my mind, and everything else fades into the background. We can be together. The press release announced that I'm not a McGuire. Heather said she's okay with it—us. I don't give a flying fuck what Tristen thinks, adopted father or not. I can't even look at the man after what he revealed earlier.

Leaning into his touch, I block out everything that came to light just mere hours ago—everything that has come out of the dark.

Butterflies erupt in my belly, and my body vibrates with excitement. Licking my bottom lip, his eyes track the movement, reminding me of an animal tracking its prey. It's in that moment that I decide I want this, no matter how screwed up my life is or how many secrets are still being uncovered.

Right now, I am a normal girl in a normal relationship, doing what a boy and girl in love probably would've done weeks ago.

Before reality can take this away from me, I rub my trembling palms against my thighs and stand. Stepping between Rhys's legs, I remain far enough away to take in his expression as my thumbs hook into the waistband of my black leggings. Despite the darkness in my bedroom, I can see how his breath hitches as I slowly push my pants down. I bite the inside of my cheek, not averting my gaze from the boy in front of me as he follows my movement with wide eyes.

"Calla?" His tone is full of awe.

Leggings kicked off to the side, I clasp the bottom of my shirt and pull it over my head. I am so far out of my element and am solely acting on instinct. I never put on a new bra after this morning's shower incident, and I am in front of him in nothing but a pair of white lace shorts.

Chest heaving visibly, Rhys takes in my body. He has seen pretty much all of me before, but suddenly, I fight the urge to cover myself. It felt like a good idea a minute ago, but now I wonder if I've made a mistake. What if he doesn't think I'm pretty? He's been with Katherine, and she is in a league of her own. Her body is perfect, and mine... I start to cross my arms when he stops me.

"Don't."

Rhys's hands hover at the sides of my hips before he touches them to my skin, tracing my hip bones with his thumbs. Oh, God. I'm on fire, and my breath becomes labored as his eyes slowly travel up my torso. He stops at my breasts, *inspecting* them in meticulous detail before lifting his greens to my hazels. His hands have not moved an inch, and yet, every cell in my body has come to life by him merely looking at me. My nipples harden under his lingering gaze, and Rhys's nostrils flare when he sees my body's reaction. I can feel the wetness in my shorts and press my thighs together.

"What are you doing to me, babe?" His tone is laced with the same desire that's building inside of me.

I bite my bottom lip and reach for the hem of Rhys's sweater. I want him naked, to see his mouthwatering body. He lifts his arms compliantly, and I slowly pull the fabric upward. My hands graze his ribcage, goosebumps appearing where my fingertips make contact. His physical response makes my last bit of hesitation—my insecurity over my inexperience—disappear. I throw it on the pile with my clothes and push with both hands at Rhys's shoulders, forcing him to lie back.

"Cal, you don't have to do—" He cuts off as soon as my fingers curl into the elastic of his sweatpants.

"Fuuuuuck." He rubs his hands over his face before pushing himself up on his elbows, watching me through hooded lids. He lifts his butt far enough off of the mattress, and his pants land next to my leggings. My mouth waters at the sight of him.

Only separated by my panties and his boxer briefs, I straddle his lap, leaning forward until our bodies are flush together. We've made out before, but this is different—maybe because we both know what's about to happen. The heat of his defined torso against the flesh of my sensitive breasts causes my entire body to tingle, and a soft moan escapes my mouth. This is almost too much, and we haven't even started yet.

I'm ready for the next step. *So ready.* But this whole time, my inexperienced side avoided looking directly at Rhys's lower half as I undressed him. Now, having only two very thin pieces of fabric between us, I have no doubt that he wants me. His erection is pressing against my core, and I automatically rock against him. Groaning, his hands glide down my back until he reaches my ass, squeezing it hard and forcing my already throbbing clit further against him. My eyes roll back inside my head at the sensation, and I stifle a curse.

"You are so fucking beautiful." His voice is hoarse, as if he's been screaming all day.

Holding myself up far enough, I place chaste kisses along his jaw until my lips line up with his ear, and I whisper, "Make me forget."

I yelp when Rhys flips us over with lightning speed and hovers above me. "Are you sure?"

Searching my gaze, he waits. I read him like an open book—*my* open book. He doesn't mask his worry of me changing my mind or *not* changing my mind. This gorgeous boy in my bed, who has way more experience than me, is as nervous as I am.

I reach up and trace his cheekbone with the tip of my index finger. "There is nothing I want more," I reassure him.

That's all he needs. Rhys's lips descend on mine in a heated kiss, his tongue immediately seeking entrance. He invades my mouth, and I match every stroke with one of my own. Feels. So. Good. Suddenly, his mouth leaves mine. Nooo, a voice shouts inside my head. I want to protest, but then his lips are back on me. Good Lord. I whimper, fisting my hands into the duvet underneath me, and I feel him chuckle against my skin. He trails kisses down my neck, and as he nips at my flesh, I turn my head to give him better access. I'm about to combust, and we aren't fully naked yet.

His tongue explores every inch of my body until he reaches the top of my panties. I let go of the comforter and stretch my arms over my head, holding my breath as he slowly pulls the lacey material down to my ankles. Rhys's body is completely off of mine, and I don't dare look at him. Squeezing my eyes shut, I concentrate on breathing, which has become more strained the lower his mouth travels. When I feel his warm exhale against my opening, I can no longer suppress the moan I've been holding in.

A soft growl reaches my ears, and I involuntarily open my eyes, inhaling sharply. While I tried to calm my body, Rhys rid himself of his boxer briefs and is now standing fully naked in front of my bed. *Everything* is standing. I stare at him. It. His dick. Whatever you call it. My brain has officially short-circuited.

"Last chance, babe." He smirks at me.

I lick my lips, my eyes meeting his. "Nightstand," is all I say, and his cocky smile vanishes.

I give him a devilish grin of my own.

Way too slowly, Rhys walks around the bed. I clamp my mouth shut to not order him to hurry the fuck up. It's like my body has been taken over by a stranger. Pushing myself up until my head is on my pillows, I readjust the comforter until I can slip in between the duvet and the mattress.

Reaching inside the top drawer, he pulls out a condom. I follow his every move as Rhys rips open the foil packet and rolls it down his length. Heat pools in my core, and my mouth goes dry. He is huge, and I'm starting to worry about how he'll fit inside of me.

Sliding between the sheets next to me, Rhys remains propped up on his elbow. As he lifts the covers, the motion lets much needed cool air hit my overheated body. His free arm moves up the side of my body until he reaches my face. He tenderly forces me to look at him. He's all serious. "I'll be as gentle as possible."

I nod, my whole body shaking in nervous anticipation. His hand leaves my cheek and glides down my side to my center. When he reaches his destination, Rhys circles my clit with his thumb twice before slipping a finger inside of me.

Oh God.

"So wet," he groans against the skin under my ear, and I moan loudly, quickly pressing my lips together to not make the entire house aware of what's going on in my room. I grip his shoulder with my hand, digging my nails into the muscle as he moves in and out. "Rhys, I...this..." What was I going to say?

I hike my thigh up his side to give him better access. He inserts another finger, and my hips buck.

"Ahh," I'm going to wake up the entire neighborhood if he keeps that up. I'm losing control over my body's reactions, but at the same time, I don't care.

"Fuck, you are so sexy writhing underneath me with my fingers buried deep inside of you," Rhys pants, and I haven't touched him at all.

Den and I had talked in vivid detail about her first time with Charlie, and I know it'll hurt, but she also assured me that I would know when I am ready.

My gaze roams the face of the boy hovering half above me

while his talented fingers drive me to the brink of madness. I love him with all my heart, and after everything we've been through and still have ahead of us, I need this. I need him.

I signal him that I want more than just his fingers by pulling him over my body. He removes his hand and settles between my legs. Taking charge, I reach down to position him at my entrance. As I wrap my hand around his dick, a guttural sound escapes Rhys, and he touches his forehead to mine.

"Babe, I'm about to blow if you don't take your hand away right now."

A giggle erupts in my throat. After one more torturing stroke and him making a sound between a groan and a growl, I move both my palms to his shoulders. His body trembles as he slowly pushes forward, and I don't take my eyes from his. Just feeling his tip at my opening could send me over the edge, but I force myself to take a steadying breath.

"Tell me to stop if it gets to be too much."

I nod, and he enters me. The slickness makes him sink in easily, and I try to relax. I fail. Every muscle in my body tenses. I didn't think it would be that bad, that everyone always just exaggerates, but nothing, not all the girl-talks with my best friend, prepared me for this. A sharp sting makes me squeeze my eyes shut, and I dig my nails into Rhys's shoulder blades. He instantly stops moving. "Look at me, Cal."

I can't, not right away. I breathe through my nose before I follow his command, locking eyes with Rhys.

"You're doing great. I'm sorry, babe." After a pause, he adds, "Fuck. You feel so good I got carried away. Just keep breathing; I promise I'll go slow."

But instead of letting him remain in the lead, I place my hands on his butt to urge him forward. Something tells me that slow will not make the pain go away faster. At first, I regret my rash decision; maybe I should've let him ease in. But then my body adjusts to his size, and the uncomfortable feeling morphs into something...*holy shit*. I did not anticipate that. Every nerve ending is buzzing with pleasure, and pure ecstasy takes over my body. Rhys and I are connected in a way—not just physical—that can never be undone. He's my endgame.

I start matching his every move, and soon we're both covered in a sheen of sweat. I'm pretty sure I left marks on his back.

"Babe, I...I don't think I can last much longer."

I grasp his head and pull him down to me. The ache is building deep in my core, and I begin to kiss him frantically. In my eagerness, I accidentally bite his lower lip, but instead of stopping, it only turns Rhys on more. His movement speeds up as he literally pounds into me. I never thought I would enjoy it like *that*, but I do. *Holy shit, I do.* The contact and friction on my sensitive spot whenever he buries himself to the hilt is too much. Stars explode behind my closed eyelids. I moan loudly, and Rhys muffles my sounds by tangling his tongue with mine. This is not helping; all it does is send another wave of pleasure through me. His entire body goes tense as he thrusts forward one last time and then uses my mouth to swallow the growl leaving him as he releases himself inside of me.

Rhys collapses over me but holds himself up enough to not crush me under his weight.

"What. The. Fuck?"

I raise my eyebrows, and he huffs out a laugh.

"Babe, this was...holy fuck. I...fuck, I don't have words." His expression sobers. "Did I hurt you?"

I don't have to think about my answer. "No."

Rhys was the right guy, and as much as the discomfort was part of it, I don't consider the experience *painful*.

He rolls off of me and heads to the bathroom to discard the condom. When he's back, he holds a washcloth in one hand and moves the covers out of the way with the other. As he cleans me up, our eyes meet, and the entire gesture is just as intimate as what happened minutes before. My heart skips a beat as I watch him care for me.

Back in my bed, he lies on his back and holds out his arm in an invitation to come closer. I snuggle into his side, my cheek against the side of his neck and my palm flat on his pecs.

For the first time in forever, my mind is filled with nothing but bliss. I know it can't last, but I'll take it for as long as I can.

Right before I drift off to sleep, Rhys's low voice makes its way through the fog rising in my brain. "Please don't shut me out again."

CHAPTER THIRTY-EIGHT

NATE

I STARE AT THE REMNANTS OF YET ANOTHER LAPTOP ON THE floor.

Fuck, I need to stop doing that.

When the number of Lilly and Rhys's burner flashed across my screen, I instantly knew something was *very* wrong. We agreed to communicate through George, *and only* in an emergency.

It made my skin crawl as Lilly recalled what she learned from her adopted parents. I typed as fast as I could to not miss anything she was saying.

Coercive persuasion? You've got to be kidding me. Having spent a year in a fucking mental hospital, I'm well aware of what that is. Thanks to my attorneys, I ended up in one of those places the rich and famous check themselves into for all their first-world problems. The only difference was, I wasn't allowed to check myself out until a new court order was issued.

They practiced all kinds of shit in that fancy-ass place—anything to make the client function in society again. So yes, we had specialists for all of it. One of the guys got hypno-treatments for his coke addiction. Regular detox was too simple; it would've taken effort on his part. So why not pay ten grand a day for someone to do the work for you?

But someone who can perform all of these methods is news to me. My left hand is still clenched in a tight fist as I dial George's number with my right.

"Nate?" His voice is tired.

He had been setting up perimeter surveillance around Lilly's neighborhood to keep track of all the comings and goings. Thank fuck the McGuires bought their house on a street ending in a cul-de-sac; that makes it a little easier. For the first time, I wonder if that was on purpose; Tristen McGuire doesn't leave anything to chance.

"Lilly called." My words instantly put George on edge.

"What happened?" I hear rustling on the other end, and knowing the man, he is getting ready to strike down anyone that's wronged my little sister. In the short time he's been around Lilly, he's gotten as attached as I have. Her kind heart and witty personality suck you in until you cannot *not* love her.

When I'm done repeating everything Lilly told me, my adrenaline level is once again through the roof. My fingers itch to throw something else to join the laptop.

"Motherfucker!" George shouts, and a loud crash on the other end comes through the line.

I'm not the only one losing his temper over this.

I don't think, in all the years I've known him, he has ever cursed. He doesn't even say "shit." Not until recently. Hearing him use the F-bomb in any type of combination with another word instantly triggers an alarm in my head.

"What is it?" Given his reaction, he knows something.

"Hector Lakatos." It's more a growl than words.

"Who?" I ask, confused.

"Goddamn it. I didn't know he was even on U.S. soil. Last I heard, he was still somewhere in the Middle East." More commotion on the other end.

"George! Who. The. Fuck. Is. Hector. Lakatos?"

After several beats of silence, he answers my question, and every hair on my body stands.

"Hector Lakatos is Lilly's memory doctor."

Fuck!

"You know him?"

"I know *of* him. He's an independent contractor. His services are for hire to whoever pays the price."

"Illegal?"

George scoffs. "What's not illegal when you mess around in someone's brain?"

True.

"What are we going to do about it?"

I'm leaning on him for advice because my rational thinking exited as soon as Lilly told me what happened.

"I will contact an associate who most likely would know where to find someone who can contact Hector."

As George speaks, I've already typed the name into one of my search programs. I will find out what size underwear the fucker wears, and then I will set them on fire—with him in them. Okay, most likely not, but I will make his digital presence a living hell. He won't be able to take a piss in a public bathroom without my knowledge.

I take several calming breaths, before saying, "you do that. I'll see what I can find on my end. I want to know everything he remembers about Lilly. And if he can reverse what he did to my sister. I don't believe that her memory was only fucked with because of me." My fists ball again, and I force myself not to throw more technology across the room.

"I'll be in touch," George replies before hanging up.

CHAPTER THIRTY-NINE

LILLY

I HIDE IN MY BEDROOM FOR THE REMAINDER OF THE WEEKEND.

Den and Wes left Saturday morning to give Rhys and me alone time—as my best friend informed me with a wink.

Oh God, did they hear us?

She'd be staying at Wes's until school on Monday. When I asked her about Charlie, she ignored my question, kissed me on the cheek, and dragged Rhys's best friend out of the room. Seeing the two this...close is still weird, but I guess I shouldn't say anything, having formed a connection with a former Marine who serves as personal security to my criminal brother. When we FaceTime'd that evening, Den finally confessed the suspicion of Charlie cheating on her. We spent two hours dissecting his actions and words while Rhys and Wes threw in random comments from the background, giving a *male* perspective on the situation.

Heather came in to check on us a few times, but she remained standing in the doorway, and I didn't invite her in. I'm back to not wanting to be around either of my adoptive parents, but this time, I don't have to put on a show. My contempt is as visible as the sorrow on Heather's face. Rhys only left my side when he ventured down to get us something to eat. The few times Tristen tried to talk to me, Rhys slammed the door in his face. Rhys doesn't know the truth—yet, but he knows me, and that's good enough for him.

Sunday afternoon, the door to my room bursts open, and a small, dark-haired figure launches herself at me. Natty is sobbing in my arms, and my throat thickens.

God, I missed her.

"Shhh." I hold her close with one arm, stroking her hair with my other hand as tears are running down my face. "I'm here, baby girl. Everything is okay. Shhh."

I catch Rhys's eyes over the top of Natty's head, and he blinks rapidly, trying to make the moisture disappear.

It feels like hours before the little girl in my arms starts calming down. We're still in the middle of my bed, while Rhys moved to lean against the headboard some time ago, watching us.

He mouths, "I love you," and I smile at him in return, a swarm of butterflies instantly causing havoc in my stomach.

Eventually, Natty moves away from me and scans my face, settling on the scar from my car accident. "Did he hurt you?"

My pulse increases, and I take a deep breath. "No, he didn't hurt me." I touch my forehead. "Please don't worry about that. I hit my head when I crashed the Jeep. It was an accident."

She stares at me for a moment longer. Knowing her, she's trying to figure out if I'm keeping something from her. I pull her back into a hug and whisper in her ear, "I'm fine. He didn't hurt me, I promise. You will understand very soon."

One day, the entire truth will come out. I wonder if Natty will forgive me, if she'll end up having some type of relationship with Nate. He would love having another little sister, even if they're not related by blood. I smile to myself at the thought when Natty pulls back and studies my face once again with her head cocked to the side. Her gaze flicks to her brother and back to me. "You both look happy."

It's an odd statement from an almost eleven-year-old girl, but Natty has always been mature and more intuitive than most of *my* friends. "Well, I am happy. I'm home with you." I smile at her.

Her eyes narrow, and she glances at Rhys, who straightens his shoulders under the scrutiny of this little human in front of us. "So, you and Rhys can be together now?"

"Wha—?" Rhys's eyes bulge out, and a choking sound comes from the doorway. Being so wrapped up in Natty, I didn't notice Heather and Tristen standing there. My mouth hangs open; all the words have left me. We all stare at the girl in front of us.

Heather makes the first move, stepping farther into the room. "What do you mean by that, love?"

Natty turns to her mother. "Well, Rhys loves Lilly, and the news said that Lilly is adopted. I heard Olivia's mom talk about it on the phone. You don't have to keep it a secret anymore." She turns back to me. "You love him, too, right? That's why you were always so sad when he wasn't home."

"I, uh..." I have no clue how to respond, and, in my confusion, I even make eye contact with Tristen, who's slack-jawed.

Rhys clears his throat. "Nat, um, how do you know all this?"

She looks innocently at all of us one after another. "I heard Mom and Dad talk about it."

Heather turns pale, and Tristen rubs his hands over his face before addressing his youngest. "Nat, when exactly did you hear us?"

She shrugs, eyeing her father. "I don't know—last year or so. I heard Mom crying in the living room when I came down to get more water after bedtime. She was upset that Rhys hadn't been home in a few days. You had another fight with Rhys about how he looked at Lilly. You told Mom that it was the only way to keep the secret." Natty looks between her parents before continuing, "Mom asked why you couldn't tell Lilly that she's adopted, that she is old enough to understand, and then Rhys could come home because he wouldn't have to lie about his feelings anymore. You told her it wasn't safe."

"Oh God," Heather whispers, covering her mouth with one hand.

My lungs start burning, and I realize I'd held my breath as she was talking.

Safe for us?

Rhys gently touches Natty's arm to get her attention to him. "Why haven't you said anything?"

"Because it was a secret, duh. And I wasn't supposed to be out of bed."

I can't help but snort a laugh at that. Of course my ten-year-old sister knew about my adoption before I did.

LATER, Tristen calls Rhys downstairs. I'm still digesting that Natty had picked up on all of it. We thought we were so good at pretending. But what has me more on edge is that she hasn't asked anything else about my time with Nate—I refuse to call it kidnapping anymore. Was my reassurance that she would soon understand enough? Does she know more than she told us?

I sit on the edge of my bed, flicking my thumb against the rest of my fingers. It's been twenty-one minutes since Rhys left to talk to his father. I have a sinking feeling in my stomach. Another ten or so minutes later, my bedroom door opens, and Rhys halts at the sight of me. Our eyes lock, and I know: something is wrong. He fails to put the mask in place in time.

"Tell me." My tone is flat.

Rhys sighs, crossing the distance between us, and squats down in front of me. Taking my hands in his, his thumb moves across my knuckles several times before he looks up at me through his lashes.

"I'm going back to school tomorrow."

My heart rate accelerates. "What about me?"

I forced myself earlier to look up the social media posts Katherine and her minions have been spreading on several different platforms. I don't know if I have the energy to deal with *Psycho Barbie* yet.

"He said you could take as long as you want, but..." Rhys averts his eyes again.

"What?" I can barely hear his words over my pulse rushing in my ears.

"Camden—the FBI chick—wants to give an official statement. With you. The press is getting restless."

"NO!" The word comes out as a croak.

Rhys stands up and positions himself against the pillows, pulling me with him. I end up sideways between his legs, my shoulder against his chest, while my legs are draped over one of his. His arms wrap around my waist, and I nuzzle my head in the crook of his neck.

"Babe, the longer you hide, the more shit the idiots camping out on our front lawn pull out of their asses. The articles are getting more fucked up by the day—and I mean more-than-the-truth fucked up."

His hand has started moving up and down my spine in an attempt to calm my erratic breathing.

It's not working.

I know he's right, but at the same time, I'm terrified I'm going to let something slip like with Heather and Tristen. It's a miracle they haven't followed up on what I meant by Henry not being my birth father.

Did they already know?

I press myself closer to Rhys and inhale deeply. His familiar scent in combination with the soothing movements on my back slowly calm my nerves.

"When?" I whisper as I fist his white t-shirt with my hand.

"Tomorrow morning. Before I leave for school." The worry in his tone is audible.

"Okay."

. . .

I DON'T GET any rest that night. Rhys fell asleep sometime after two in the morning.

We never had the long conversation with Heather about our relationship, and neither Rhys, nor I care. Especially not after they revealed how I lost my memory. Rhys has been sharing my bed since I got home, and I don't even bother keeping the door open.

Once I'm sure that he's out, I sneak into the bathroom and open the cabinet under the sink. I don't turn on the light to avoid alerting the boy in my bed. The faint glow coming through the narrow window that's set high into the wall by the shower is all I need. Staring at the box of tampons for a minute, I contemplate what to do. I shouldn't.

Screw it.

I reach into the carton and pull out the burner phone that's hidden under several layers of feminine products.

The phone lights up, and I navigate until I have a new text message pulled up on the screen.

They're going to give a press conference tomorrow.

Adding the number on the top of the screen, I hit send.

The response comes almost immediately: **We knew that this would happen. You know what to do.**

I inhale deeply.

I know. But what if they don't believe me?

They can't prove otherwise. Addressing the media is the appropriate step.

Ugh, he's right.

Will you come?

The three dots appear and disappear several times, and I brace myself for a rejection. It's too dangerous.

Then the reply pops up: **I will be there.**

All the tension leaves me, and my body suddenly feels like rubber. I sit in the dark bathroom for another fifteen minutes before I tuck the phone back into its hiding spot and slide back into bed next to Rhys.

He rolls over, wraps his arm around my waist, and pulls my back to his front.

"You talk to George?" he murmurs, his voice raspy from sleep.

"I did." I move his hand from my stomach and place a kiss on the inside of his palm.

THE KNOCK STARTLES me so much that I shriek. The door to my bedroom flies open, revealing a wide-eyed Heather, searching for the potential threat, while Rhys bursts into the bedroom from my bathroom—only wrapped in a towel.

Understanding settles in her eyes, probably assuming I'm on edge because of what's about to happen.

"I'm so sorry, sweetheart. I didn't mean to scare you." Heather remains inside the doorframe.

"It's okay. I didn't expect anyone." I look everywhere but at her.

Rhys and I lock gazes; he silently checks if I want him to stay. I shake my head, and he turns, disappearing back into a cloud of steam.

The little clock in the top corner of my laptop screen shows that it's six a.m. I'm showered and fully dressed since I gave up on sleep around 4:30. A long, hot, and numbing shower later, my hair is blow-dried, and I've applied a little makeup—just some foundation and mascara to make me feel presentable. I won't be able to relax until I face the vultures—as Rhys calls them.

"Did you need something?" My tone is harsher than I mean it to be.

My adoptive mother flinches. "No, I just wanted to let you know that Agent Camden notified the media that we would give the statement at seven-thirty, and she wants to talk to you ahead of time."

"I'll be down in a few." I force myself to gentle my tone. I'm still angry with both of them, but it's Tristen that makes my blood pressure rise.

Heather doesn't say anything else and just nods before closing the door again.

Turning back to the screen, I focus on what had me so distracted when the knock came.

KAT ROSENFIELD:

Our little quarterback-stealing skank has "reappeared." Wonder if the kidnapping was even real. It prob took the thirsty bitch this long to learn what to do with her mouth.

COMMENTS:

Meghan LG: Haha! She's never had a bf, 2 weeks are not enough for that.

Nora Ross: LMAO. If she even figured out how to open his pants.

Kellan J: Meow! Kitty Kat has her claws out.

Kat Rosenfield: Fuck off, Jager.

Kat Rosenfield: Meghan:: Right? She couldn't learn how to give a BJ if she had a whole YouTube library of tutorials giving her step-by-step instructions.

Lisa Bennett: Unicorn?

Nora Ross: LOL. Duh!

Owen J: Nora—articulate as always. You should give L a tutorial since I know you def know what to do with ur mouth.

Kellan J: ROFLMAO

Meghan LG: Don't be such a fucking asshole, O!

Nora Ross: You haven't complained yet, Owen. ;)

Lisa Bennett: Kellan, why don't you call Rhys and ask what his whore of a little sister still needs pointers on?

Owen J: I volunteer as tribute!

Nora Ross: OWEN!

Kat Rosenfield: You don't know what diseases you'll get touching that slut!

Owen J: I'll take my chances. Have you seen that tight ass?
Kellan J: I second that. I'd tap that.
Meghan LG: GAG!

CLOSING MY LAPTOP, I squeeze my eyes shut. I wonder if Rhys has seen how his *friends* talk about me. The bathroom door opens, and he emerges dressed in faded, light-blue jeans, a gray-and-white plaid button-down with a white t-shirt underneath, and the football team's baseball cap on backward.

My mouth waters at the sight, and I shake my head.

Not appropriate right now.

"See something you like?" Rhys smirks at me, and I forget all about the shit I just read.

I stand up and cross the distance to him. Wrapping my arms around his midsection, I lean my head on his chest. The steady thump of his heart increases, and I squeeze. "Always."

We pull apart, and Rhys's smile drops. "Ready?"

I answer honestly. "No."

DOWNSTAIRS, we find Agent Camden and Lanning in their usual spots. Heather is standing at the island with a cup of coffee in her hand, and Tristen sits on the other side on one of the barstools, typing on his laptop.

"Where is Natty?" I scan the room and look over into the living room as well.

"She is still upstairs; I told her she could play until it's time," Heather answers my question.

"You mean read," Rhys's voice comes from behind me.

"True," his mother smiles, but it doesn't reach her eyes.

Rhys and I are not touching, but he stands close enough for me to feel his body heat radiating off of him.

"Lilly?" Agent Camden brings my attention to her. "Why don't you take a seat? We need to go over what we will tell the media."

My body goes rigid. "Do I have to talk to them?"

The two FBI agents exchange a look before they both make eye contact with Tristen. Tristen gets off his seat and walks over. "Let's sit, and we'll discuss what options we have."

I glance behind me at Rhys, who, in return, gently touches my lower back, signaling for me to sit down. We take the bench seat on the opposite side of Tristen and Agent Lanning, with Camden at the head of the table. Rhys folds his hands on top of the table, leaning forward. His entire posture screams *Let's hear it*. Under the table, his thigh is tightly pressed against mine in support.

I cross my arms in front of my chest. I'm sure whoever looks at me will assume it's to shield myself from what's about to come. They're probably not too far off.

Thirty minutes later, I'm aware of everything that's about to happen, and we have another twenty to go. My stomach feels like it's about to expel the tea I sipped on while Camden filled me in. Her male counterpart only spoke up when she specifically asked him to clarify something. After handing me my mug with tea and Rhys his coffee, Heather stood behind her husband, hands on the back of his chair, while Tristen's focus jumped between the talking agents and me.

Camden looks between Rhys and me. "I am aware that this is a rather unique situation, and given the fact that we want this to focus on Lilly and her kidnapping, I would advise that you two do not touch while we are outside."

Rhys snorts, and my cheeks flush.

Could this get any more embarrassing?

"Rhys," Tristen warns.

"Jeez. Chill, Dad. I'm not gonna stick my tongue down *Lilly's* throat while we're facing the cameras."

I suck in a breath at Rhys's tone. He's been showing less and less respect toward his father.

"Rhys, that's enough," Heather says calmly but with authority behind it.

He pushes up, hands flat on the tabletop. "Sure, Mom. He can treat all of us as puppets in his little military games and do God knows what to Lilly—which by the way, she won't tell me out of fear I'll blow a gasket. That alone tells me that it has to be pretty fucked up, and for some unknown reason, she's still protecting him."

How did this situation escalate so quickly? I place my hand on Rhys's, whose knuckles have turned white from the pressure by now. "Rhys?"

His eyes flick to me, and he pulls his hand out. "I'll be back in fifteen." With that, he stalks out and up the stairs, leaving all of us stunned in the kitchen.

CHAPTER FORTY

RHYS

I PACE THE LENGTH OF MY ROOM.

"Fuck! Fuck! Fuck!"

Stopping near the window, I glance through the half-open blinds. Three news vans are parked on the curb, and the vultures are already waiting. I pull on my hair and crouch down. I need to calm my nerves before we go out there.

I had no intention to go off on Dad, but the longer I avoided him, the more wound up I got. Camden's comment was just the final straw. I need to know What. The. Fuck happened for Lilly not to be able to look at my parents anymore—again. They finally had gotten back to a point where everything seemed normal. Why can she confide in her brother but not me? I bet even George knows, and I'm the only one left in the dark.

I'm her freaking boyfriend! I chuck the first thing I can reach across the room—the controller for my video console. It shatters into pieces against the wall, and I take in the scene of black plastic shards everywhere.

Fucking great.

Then there's the minor issue of my psychotic ex. Lilly thinks

I didn't see what was pulled up on her screen earlier—well, I did. I've made it my mission to be up to date on Kat's malicious games. What pisses me off more are the comments of my so-called friends and teammates. Wes already got into it with some of them, but it seems I have to rearrange some faces today to put them back in their place. The day will probably end with my suspension.

At least then I can stay home with Lilly.

I go into the bathroom and stare at the guy in the mirror. I barely recognize myself anymore. My hands grip the edge of the sink until my knuckles turn white. Closing my eyes, I focus on breathing. Eventually, I'm calm enough to put on my poker face to make it through the freak-show of a press conference. Let's hope Lilly will be able to lie her ass off, or I'll have other things to worry about than pounding Jager's face as soon as he crosses my path.

LILLY IS STANDING in the foyer next to Natty. Her arm is around our little sister's shoulder. Blood relation or not, Natty will always be her sister.

I scan Lilly up and down; she is wearing black skinny jeans that look looser than I remember. Despite the chilly temperature this morning, she put on her white Adidas Superstars—no socks—paired with a white V-neck t-shirt and her dark-blue denim jacket over it. The warmest item is the oversized brown Burberry scarf Den gave her two Christmases ago. I love the outfit; it makes her look *I-don't-give-a-fuck* casual, but at the same time, she's put together and, to me, sexy as hell.

Mine, my inner caveman growls.

I grab my varsity jacket from the hook next to the stairs and make my way over, draping my arm around Lilly's waist. I pull her into me and bury my nose in her hair. Inhaling the scent of her shampoo, my nerves calm some more.

I can do this.

Lilly, who still has Natty in her embrace, pulls back and searches my eyes.

"You okay?" Her tone is so low that only our little sister can hear us.

I force a reassuring smile on my face. "I'm fine. I just needed a moment."

Lilly's eyes narrow; she knows there is more to it, but she doesn't push the issue with Natty next to us.

Natty looks up, "Are you still angry with Dad?"

Why does she have to be so smart?

I pull her into a hug with my other arm and decide to give her the half-truth. "I am, but I mostly don't want to leave Lilly alone today."

Truth.

Omission: I am going to rearrange my friends' faces, give Kat a piece of my mind, and hopefully not lose my shit in front of the media in a few minutes. Who knows what the fuck they'll throw at us?

"It's time," Agent Camden announces, and Lilly's arm around my waist tenses. I tighten my grip on her and lean down to her ear. "Everything will be okay. I'm right here. I don't give a fuck about her no-touching rule."

Lilly chuckles and kisses me on the cheek.

"Eww. Gross!" Natty screeches and darts over to Mom, whose eyes crinkle in response to her youngest's outburst.

The FBI agents position themselves at the door, followed by Mom and Natty. Lilly and I are next with Dad in the rear.

As soon as the door is open, the flashes start, and people haul questions at our group. Lilly takes a step back and bumps into me. My hands automatically clasp around her upper arms to steady her, but I let go quickly and move sideways. Dad steps past me to her other side, and her five-foot-four figure is now framed between two six-foot-plus walls.

We're on the patio, with ten or more people on the lawn. I see several neighbors peek out their windows, if not even

OUT OF THE DARK • 337

openly gawking from their properties' yards. The two agents close ranks in front, Mom has Natty wrapped in her arms to the left behind Lanning, and the three of us are to the right behind Camden. The female agent takes charge and holds up one hand. It's fascinating how the quiet woman all of a sudden commands the group in front of us. While she waits for them to settle down, I scan our surroundings. Lancaster, the dude who's been obsessed with the case for a decade now, is front and center. There are several unmarked cars in addition to the news vans which, I assume, belong to the reporters or whoever the people shoving their recording phones at us are. My gaze settles on a tall figure leaning against the rear end of the farthest van, and my eyes widen. He's dressed casually in dark jeans with a black hoodie under a black leather jacket. The hoodie is pulled up, and the brim of a baseball cap covers most of his face, including *the scar*. Arms crossed over his broad chest, I can see a phone sticking out in one of his hands, camera pointed toward us.

They're both here for her.

I make eye contact with my BFF, but George's expression doesn't change a millimeter. Since we're partially hidden behind the two agents, I touch Lilly's arm to get her attention. She looks up, and I lean down to her ear, whispering as low as possible. "He's here. They're *both* watching." I don't dare say more. So far, no one has paid us any attention.

Lilly's eyes close briefly, understanding the meaning of my words. Then she turns back forward and faces the vultures, not looking around at all.

The knowledge of their presence is enough to calm her nerves, and something clicks into place for me. She's told me many times how I'm her home. We've talked about it a lot, especially during the first few weeks when we analyzed why she had always felt a certain way for me, despite not knowing. Things had shifted once Nate came into the picture, and I thought I was losing her. I was dead wrong. Nate—and with extension,

George—have become an equally important part of her life. She needs all of us in different ways to make it through this.

"Ladies and gentlemen, thank you for coming." Camden's voice snaps me out of my revelation. "I am Agent Vivienne Camden and the lead agent in Miss McGuire's case. We have asked you here to give you the exclusive statement to this investigation. Miss McGuire and her family are in attendance; however, we ask you not to address them directly. Agent Lanning and I will answer your questions to the best of our ability and what we are able to disclose at this point."

Murmurs go around the group, and—surprise, surprise—Lancaster asks the first question.

"Miss McGuire was the first victim of The Babysitter. Since then, he abducted four other girls before he captured Miss McGuire again. What's his motive?"

"That is still open to investigation. Due to the perpetrator never harming any of the victims, we suspect that he has an underlying mental condition that drives him to take the girls."

"He drugs them. How can you say that he doesn't harm the little girls?" a woman holding her phone toward us snaps.

"That is correct. Let me rephrase my statement. Since Miss McGuire's first disappearance, the perpetrator has used a mild sedative to calm his victims. The girls are not being drugged to render them unconscious; he keeps them alert but calm. They receive food, have access to a bathroom, and are being entertained. He has not physically harmed any of them."

I can feel Lilly getting more agitated, and I involuntarily make eye contact with my father over her head. He's noticed as well. My heartrate picks up, and I fight the urge to grab her hand and drag her back inside.

"Agent Camden." A woman from a local news station steps forward, her cameraman right behind. "What does Miss McGuire have to say about her kidnappings? We understand that, the first time, she was severely sedated and, according to previous reports, traumatized. Why was there never a report filed or an active search for the kidnapper? If this would've been handled appropriately, the following kidnappings could've possibly been prevented."

"This is part of the investigation we cannot disclose at this point."

Yeah, because you have no clue.

I'm pretty sure my father has kept ninety percent of the facts from the suits.

"Lilly, what does The Babysitter want from you? You're the one he wants. The parents of these little girls deserve to know why their kids were taken." Lancaster steps in front of the other chick. Dad squares his shoulders, which puts me on high alert. My fingers begin to twitch, and I curl them into a fist to avoid drawing attention.

"Mister Lancaster, please take a step back," Lanning warns, looking straight at the guy.

Lancaster doesn't comply right away. Instead, he stares at Lilly, who—holy shit, she holds his gaze without so much as blinking. Finally, Lancaster mumbles something under his breath and moves back in line.

Camden takes over again. "Miss McGuire has no recollection of what happened during either kidnapping."

Shouts erupt all around us.

"How is this possible?"

"That's bullshit."

"She's lying."

"She is not a child anymore; she has to know something."

"What are you keeping from the public?" Lancaster again.

Fuck, this dude is gonna be a problem.

Out of the corner of my eye, I notice George straightening up. He's zeroed in on Lancaster. This guy better shut up, or George might snap his neck in front of everyone.

This time, Lanning holds up a hand. It takes several minutes until everyone stops yelling, and he speaks up.

"Miss McGuire was severely sedated when she was admitted

to Hill Crest Medical Center. She was found on a bench outside the facility by a staff member. Miss McGuire remained under close observation for twenty-four hours while the necessary medication to counteract the drugs were administered. The combination found in her bloodstream has the known side effect of short-term memory loss. She will continue regular visits to local specialists to ensure that there is no permanent damage to her well-being."

What the—? I fight the urge to storm over to George. He left Lilly on a fucking park bench? No one cared to tell me that tidbit—probably because I would've flipped a lid.

"Why would The Babysitter drug Miss McGuire that way if she's the one he wants?" a new voice asks, and I take in the reporter that has stepped forward. Beside me, Lilly goes rigid, and I look down. She's gone pale.

What the—?

I glance back. The dude is tall and well-built; he's got me beat by an inch or two. He has black curly hair that's thinning at the hairline, a goatee, and his nose looks like it was broken one too many times. But his most prominent facial feature is his ice-blue eyes; they're so light they appear almost white. The hairs at the nape of my neck stand in all directions. Even when George had stepped out of the dark in Denielle's backyard, I didn't have that reaction. And my BFF is scary as fuck.

Reporter guy wears a tan trench coat over a light-blue button-down and brown khakis—the outfit screams *costume* to me.

I avert my eyes and focus on Lilly. Her thumb is flicking against the rest of her fingers. She's about to bolt.

Fuck it.

I wrap my arm around her lower waist, and she immediately leans into the touch. I don't pay attention if anyone notices, mainly because I couldn't care less.

As if from a distance, Camden's voice drifts into my brain. "What's your name, sir?"

"Francis Turner," Trench Coat Guy replies without hesitation.

"Mr. Turner, at this point, we believe Miss McGuire was drugged so she couldn't fight back. As you stated, she is older, and the perpetrator could not have foreseen how she would react to him."

"So, essentially, you have no fucking clue what happened to any of the girls or who The Babysitter is!"

Ah, Lancaster is back in play.

"Mr. Lancaster, this is an ongoing investigation. We are unable to release all the information at this point, not to compromise the case."

As he said, you have no fucking clue.

THE PRESS CONFERENCE, aka joke of the year, goes on for another ten minutes, but no real information is being released. Oddly enough, none of the vultures brought up our relationship, despite it being splashed over several social media sites.

Lilly is as white as a ghost and shaking like a leaf by the time we get back inside. As soon as the front door closes, she charges upstairs, taking two steps at a time.

Mom calls after her, but Lilly doesn't respond. Dad gives me a look that I would interpret as worry if I didn't know that the man has no feelings. Okay, maybe he does, but it's easier to be pissed at him if I pretend he's the robot he always acts like.

Following Lilly to her room, I find it empty. Knowing where she is, I flip the lock and make my way to the bathroom. Water is already running, and when I step inside, I'm met by a cloud of steam. Lilly sits in front of the running shower, arms wrapped around her bent legs and forehead resting on her knees. In her one hand, she's clutching the phone, and I notice the box we stashed it in on the floor, contents spilled everywhere.

The little alarm clock she keeps above her sink shows that it's well after eight, and I should be on my way to school. I sink down next to Lilly and place my hand between her shoulder blades.

"Talk to me, babe." I lean over and place a kiss on her hair right above her temple.

"Something isn't right," she mumbles into her legs.

I squint at her, moving my hand up and down her spine. "What do you mean?"

"He was there. What was he doing here?"

I'm not sure I understand her correctly. "He, who?"

Lilly finally lifts her head, and my chest constricts. I haven't seen that expression since the text messages.

"The guy from Magnolia's," she whispers.

I'm lost.

"Babe, what are you talking about?"

As she recalls the day she met Den at Magnolia's and, later, when she saw him again right before Nate got to her, I try to make sense of it. Nothing that has happened in the last five months has been by chance—apart from Lilly stumbling over the article that started it all. My heart feels like it's about to explode out of my chest.

"Does Nate know?" I force myself to steady my tone and not follow my instinct of ripping the phone out of her hand to call her brother myself.

"No. I forgot about him. Until today." Her gaze jumps between my eyes. "Do you think it's a coincidence?"

Truth?

"No."

EPILOGUE

HER

SHE HAS GROWN UP. I'VE SEEN THE OCCASIONAL PICTURES GRAY has taken over the years, but looking at the young woman in front of me, I'm reminded more than ever who her father is. She looks so much like him—and her brother.

I'm partially hidden behind a fence, two houses down. I sent Gray to stand between the reporters and told him to make himself known. I want to see her reaction. She's smart; she'll put two and two together.

Gray revealing himself to her back in January was not part of the plan—but neither was her disappearance. I didn't account for Nate to be in the picture before I could get to her. Something happened while she was gone; otherwise, his bloodhound wouldn't be standing a hundred yards from me, watching Lilly like a hawk.

Why couldn't she have just let it go for a few more months?

Now, I have to improvise.

Thank you so much for reading *Out of the Dark*!
Were you prepared for *her*? I wasn't!

Are you ready for ***Of Light and Dark***, the **conclusion** to the
first two books in The Dark Series?

Book Three also has a special surprise at the end.
The Dark doesn't end with Lilly & Rhys.

ACKNOWLEDGEMENTS

Well...this was not how I had the second book in The Dark Series plotted.

Lilly's story with *Him*, who you now also know as Nate, was fully outlined, including how it was going to end in Of Light and Dark. But then I started writing, and Nate didn't turn out how I originally envisioned him. I tried very hard to make him the bad guy of the series, but in the end, he wasn't *it*. Yes, he is still a criminal, but he showed a lot of redeeming qualities—especially when it comes to his relationship with Lilly. What I also didn't account for was the internal struggle Lilly would experience from forming a bond with her brother. There was a chance Rhys wouldn't accept her decision—maybe there still is. As this book has taught me...things change. So, I can't promise anything as to what will happen to Lilly, Rhys, Nate, or any of the other characters in the future.

The list of people I have to thank for making this journey possible is growing, and if I forget to mention one of you, please know it's not on purpose—I simply have the same memory-span as our fifteen-year-old dog. (;

Abbi, who, for the past eighteen plus months, has let me run ideas by her and discuss scenarios for hours on end just for me to scratch them the next day because one of my characters did something we didn't take into account.

My husband and daughters, who patiently dealt with my *crab-biness* when I didn't get to write for weeks on end, or when I did and lacked time to cook dinner, do laundry or have a conversation that consisted of more than one-word answers.

Sammi (S.J. Sylvis), who took time out of her busy writing schedule to read the first draft.

My betas, Linzy, Mary, and Becca: your feedback has been invaluable to this book; my editor, Jenn Lockwood; the real Den, who has been with me on this rollercoaster since the day I announced to her I would write a book; Lyndsey, who I somewhat coerced into reading my first book and then turned her into another beta for the remaining series; and of course, the bloggers, readers, and reviewers who have helped me spread the word about Lilly and Rhys.

I'll see you all at the end of book three.

xoxo
Danah Logan

STAY CONNECTED

Born and raised in Germany, Danah moved to the US, where she met her husband, eventually trading downtown Chicago's city life for the northern Rockies.

She can be seen hanging with her twin girls and exploring the outdoors when she's not arguing plot points with the characters in her head.

But it's that exact passion that has produced *The Dark Series* and continues to keep her glued to her laptop, following her dreams.

Scan the below QR code to sign up for my newsletter and be the first to know about upcoming releases, sales, and new arrivals.

Add me on Facebook
www.facebook.com/authordanahlogan/

Follow me on Instagram
www.instagram.com/authordanahlogan/

Visit my Website for more content
and other places to stalk me
www.authordanahlogan.com

Or scan this second QR code for all the links:

ALSO BY DANAH LOGAN

The Ghost
The Beginning.
A Dark Series and Davis Order Novella
(George & Lou)

The Dark Series

In the Dark, Book 1
Out of the Dark, Book 2
Of Light and Dark, Book 3
(Lilly and Rhys)
A Dark, New-Adult, Romantic-Suspense Trilogy

Because of the Dark, Book 4
(Wes and King)
A Dark, Hidden-Identity, Romantic-Suspense Novel

Followed by the Dark, Book 5
(Denielle and Marcus)
A Dark, Enemies-to-Lovers, Age-Gap,
Romantic-Suspense Novel

I Am the Dark, Book 6
(HIM)
A Dark, Age-Gap, Romantic-Suspense Novel

The Davis Order

Rezoned, Prequel
(Ethan)
A Dark, Hate-to-Love, Second-Chance,
Romantic-Suspense Novel

Made in the USA
Middletown, DE
11 May 2023

30415214R00215